FALSE WITNESS

Lelia Kelly

PINNACLE BOOKS

KENSINGTON PUBLISHING CORP

www.pinnaclebooks.com

Kimono
Doll.

GUILTY

The photocopies of James Stanley's travel records on the night of the murder hadn't seemed very significant to her when Craig Fannin had distributed them in their meeting. She had taken for granted that Stanley had been where he said he was—the two phone calls that showed up on the hotel bill had been especially convincing. She had no more than glanced at the papers since. But now, in the light of Kenny's contempt of "paper alibis," there were a couple of things that struck her as odd.

Why had James Stanley booked a flight with a stopover in Greenville, South Carolina? There was no ecomonic reason for him to have traveled through Greenville. Could he have had a meeting there? He certainly hadn't mentioned it. Laura checked the flight times. If Stanley had scheduled a meeting in Greenville, it had to have been a fast one: there was less than a half hour between the arrival of the flight from Atlanta and its departure for Charlotte.

Laura felt distinctly satisfied with what she had found, despite the fact that it was after one A.M. when she switched off her computer and headed for bed. She knew, or thought she knew, how James Stanley had been in two places at once: he hadn't. He had gotten off that plane in Greenville and returned to Atlanta, where he killed his wife. There was, of course, the hotel record from Charlotte, and the phone calls from there to Atlanta—but these were only details. Laura knew she had her man.

Books by Lelia Kelly

PRESUMPTION OF GUILT
FALSE WITNESS

Published by Pinnacle Books

This book is dedicated to Michael, Ellen, and William

ACKNOWLEDGMENTS

Thanks are due, as always, to the team of Kay Kidde and Laura Langlie, whose advice both editorial and practical I value most highly. John Scognamiglio proved once again to be a patient as well as a creative editor.

To my Atlanta readers, I would like to say that yes, I do know that the garage at the Hyatt downtown is underground. I took a few liberties with other locales as well, though none as glaring as that one.

I would like to give special thanks to my Book Club for help and encouragement on all fronts for the past five years—every author should have such a cheering section. A shout-out also goes to all the folks at Duke University Medical Center Bone Marrow Transplant Clinic—thanks for making the unbearable bearable. As usual, Dr. Martin York is the man and his staff are the women.

I also owe a very large debt to my family, especially to my mother, who served as photocopier and proofreader, and who allowed me to play Lyle Lovett and the Mavericks as loud as I wanted to in her house while I was getting inspired. And to my Aunt Lillian, big kisses and thanks for the taxi service, the lunches, and all the bandaging. My sister-in-law deserves credit for her tireless promotion of this and my first book: Thanks, Karen! And to Cameron, Elizabeth, and Grantland: Aunt Eeyah says thank you very much, and I'm sorry there are no pictures.

PART ONE

MAY

PART ONE

CHAPTER 1

On the first day of the rest of her life, Laura Chastain stood blithering before a judge of the Superior Court of Fulton County.

Her first courtroom assignment as an assistant district attorney was simple: get a plea bargain entered in the Fulton County Superior Court. "It should take about five minutes," her boss, Meredith Gaffney, had admonished. "Keep everything moving along; the judge doesn't want to reinvent the wheel." Unfortunately, Judge Jones Talbot seemed to want to do just that. He had already spent half an hour probing the slender, innocuous record of Juwon Taylor, the defendant in the case, and he showed no sign of tiring of the subject.

"I see from the record that this . . . young man"—how carefully he avoided the word *boy*—"has graduated from truancy and vandalism to accessory in an auto theft. I don't call that very promising. If I sentence him to probation, what's to say he won't be back in here next year for some more serious crime—maybe a violent felony!'' Talbot glared down at Laura from the bench and shook his head. "I'd like to see a recommendation from the district attorney for some jail time.''

Juwon Taylor, a nineteen-year-old high school senior, jerked his head up and looked around in alarm. Laura shifted her weight from one foot to the other and glanced at him. Her eyes met those of Julia Walton, the public defender representing Juwon. The two attorneys, who had spent quite a bit of time working out the now-doubtful plea bargain, began some subtle nonverbal communication.

Julia's eyebrows lifted quizzically, which Laura understood to mean, *"What's he trying to do?"*

Laura shook her head and compressed her lips in reply. *"This is my first time before Talbot,"* she telegraphed back. *"How should I know?"*

"Well, say something *anyway,"* Julia indicated with a jerk of her head.

Say something. Sure, but what? Talk about what a great kid the defendant was? That's what she sensed the judge wanted—for the district attorney's office to look soft on criminals. A wave of irritation rose up in her. *I won't sing this kid's praises,* she thought. *I'm the prosecuting attorney— why should I act as an advocate for Juwon Taylor? That's Julia's job.* They called the justice system *adversarial* for a reason. She almost made a sarcastic reply to Judge Talbot, but her better nature held her back. She took a breath and collected herself instead. *"What would Tom do?"* she asked herself. Yes, what would Tom Bailey have done? She cleared her head, and in the silence she could almost hear his voice.

"This guy is a sadist—he's playing with you like a cat with

a chipmunk. Do not accept this behavior. Come on, Laura, what do you know about him? Think."

According to Tom, everyone had a weakness—some blind spot of vanity, some bad habit, some carefully hidden secret—and it was the duty of a good trial lawyer to know that weakness and exploit it if necessary. Okay, so what did she know about the Honorable Judge Talbot? She'd done her homework; there must be something . . . She felt herself straighten up as a notion occurred to her. *"That's the ticket!"* she thought triumphantly. She started to speak, but she seemed to hear Tom's voice again, cautioning her.

"Hold on—remember you're in open court. Don't say anything that's going to embarrass him or make him angry. You're going to spend a lot of time in his courtroom."

True. Laura cleared her throat. "Your Honor, may we approach the bench?"

He assented, and as Laura approached, she suppressed a chuckle. What would these people think if they knew she was standing here channeling the spirit of her dead mentor and lover? Not that she cared; after seven years of seeing him every day, she wasn't about to let a little thing like death interfere in her relationship with Tom Bailey. She and Julia reached the judge simultaneously.

"Your Honor," Laura began, "the district attorney's office stands by this plea recommendation."

"You can't tell me you believe this boy is a good risk!" Talbot sneered.

"As a matter of fact, I do. But even if I didn't, I would still recommend this plea."

"Why would you do a damn fool thing like that?" he asked. Even Julia looked puzzled.

"As Your Honor knows, the district attorney has been undertaking a detailed study of sentencing patterns in the county. Some, umm, significant differences have popped up, especially between sentences handed down to defendants from North Fulton"—*to white defendants,* she added silently—"versus sentences handed down in South Fulton"—*to black defendants.*

"And?" the judge inquired sarcastically.

"Now go easy, Laura," she seemed to hear Tom say. *"Don't rile him up, and whatever you do, don't say the magic letters!" No need to remind me of that,* she thought—saying "ACLU" to Judge Talbot would truly be waving a flag at a bull. His Honor had the dubious distinction of having had more decisions overturned on appeal than any other Superior Court judge in the state of Georgia, and the civil liberties group had backed a good number of those appeals.

"We wanted to avoid invidious comparisons," Laura said simply. *Like comparisons to those five preppies who got off scot-free last month after being charged with gang rape,* she added to herself. That case had caused quite a bit of consternation in the press. Talbot had taken it upon himself to nullify the jury's "guilty" verdict, reduce the charges to simple battery, and sentence each defendant to six months' probation. "Boys will be boys!" he had said, with a few wise admonishments to teenage girls not to wear "provocative clothes." Lord knows Laura was no knee-jerk feminist— she'd defended an accused rapist, once, and caught heat for it—but Talbot's actions went way beyond the pale. The district attorney's appeal on that one was still pending. Laura met Talbot's eyes steadily; he knew exactly what she meant.

The judge's face flushed, as if he could read Laura's mind. "What are you saying—that I can't judge in my own courtroom without looking at a bunch of statistics? Why don't we have a computer sitting up here instead of me, then?" He was blustering, but Laura sensed capitulation;

next year he was facing reelection, and he didn't need any more bad press. She treated his question as rhetorical, and remained silent. Judge Talbot snorted, and threw up his beefy hands. "Well, there's a kick in the pants—or the robe, I should say." Laura and Julia smiled politely at this witticism. "All right, Miss Chastain, you've made your point." As the lawyers returned to their respective tables, Judge Talbot gaveled the courtroom to order and passed the agreed-upon sentence on a relieved Juwon. Laura and Julia gathered up their papers, and walked out of the emptying room together.

"Sorry about that," Laura said to her erstwhile opponent. "I had no idea he'd be playing to the gallery."

Julia shrugged. "He hates plea bargains—unless he's the one making them, of course."

"But he's got no qualms about putting a nineteen-year-old kid in jail to make a point."

"He's trying to win over the law-and-order crowd, and they want everybody to do jail time. They're doing away with parole—next it'll be probation and plea bargains."

"Great. I hope they're ready to add about a thousand new assistant DAs and public defenders. Not to mention the new jail cells we'll be needing."

"You're preaching to the choir," Julia said with the weary shrug of a career public defender. "Want to get some lunch?"

"Maybe next time. They're expecting me back at the office. Thanks for the help in there," she added, as she turned toward the exit.

The district attorney's offices were located directly across the street from the courthouse in a steel-and-glass building that reflected the colonnaded beaux-arts front of the courthouse, appropriating some of the older building's grandeur. There was certainly no innate grandeur in the offices of the district attorney, which were a warren of cubicles, jangling with phone calls and raised voices. Over-stuffed filing cabinets banked every available wall, even in the hallways. When the building had been constructed, the designers had allowed for such amenities as conference rooms; they had lasted a year or two before being appropriated as office space. The conditions were in stark contrast to Laura's plush former quarters at the midtown law firm of Prendergrast and Crawley, but she didn't often notice the difference.

Back in her cubicle—situated in a windowless room that she suspected had been intended as storage space—Laura checked her voice mail, her e-mail, her in-box, and her calendar. She returned a few phone calls, made a few of her own, and pulled a sheaf of papers from her briefcase. She settled in to work on a brief her boss needed for an appeal of a pretrial ruling, the kind of thing Laura could do in her sleep after seven years of training at P&C.

Laura knew that some of her fellow assistant DAs were watching her closely, waiting for the grind to get to her. They thought she was soft. Little did they know how many eager young associates—all Law Review at top-ranked schools—had burned out at Prendergrast and Crawley. Although the district attorney's office ran at top speed all the time, the pace was nothing in comparison to her first three years at the old firm. And there was one great, and welcome, difference between the old life and the new: no *billable hours*. During an ordinary week at P&C she had spent about an hour each day filling out time sheets, dealing with the accounting department, and tending to other administrative details. She had gladly given up the thick carpets and china coffee cups in return for the certainty of never filling in another time sheet.

Laura was happily researching away when her boss,

the redoubtable Meredith Gaffney, popped her head in. "Back? How did the hearing go?"

"Great—I think." She told Meredith what had taken place.

"Well done," her boss said. "I should have thought to warn you about Jones. He likes to take the new prosecutors out for a spin. But I knew you could handle him. Listen. I came in here to ask you if you're up for something."

"Anything," was Laura's automatic reply.

"Don't be hasty; let me run it by you. I've been called to a crime scene. I'd like you to come with me."

"What . . . I mean, what kind of crime?" Laura asked unnecessarily. She knew that if the police had requested the presence of a representative of the district attorney's office, it had to be a "major crime"—a murder, sexual assault, or hate crime. Or maybe a prominent Atlantan was involved.

"It's a murder. A bad one—as if there's a good one. Laura, I want you there, but if you're not ready . . ."

"I'm ready. I mean, I'm not exactly eager, but I won't fall apart on you."

"Of course you won't. But I'm warning you, Laura, these things are pretty bad. I still get nightmares myself, and after what you went through . . . but if you want to come along, get your things together and meet me at my office."

Meredith turned and sped away, calling for her administrative assistant as she retreated. Laura gathered her things and found the boss a few minutes later in her cluttered office, simultaneously concluding a telephone conversation, issuing directives to the assistant, and searching for her keys. "I need you to make these changes and have this motion ready when I get back," she told her assistant. To the telephone, she said, "Call Judge Shivers's clerk and arrange a meeting on the pretrial hearing on the Tucker case. I want to set some rules about the press coverage." As she finished her conversations, she produced her keys from the bottom of her huge purse. Shouldering a bulging briefcase, she swept Laura out of the office with her, spewing directives into cubicles as she passed them.

Laura followed, bemused. She had a great admiration for Meredith, but she couldn't fathom how someone who seemed so disorganized did as much as Meredith. Nevertheless, Meredith had the best conviction record in the office, served as the deputy to the overburdened district attorney, and still managed to have an enviable marriage and two great kids. And Laura, single and without her own caseload, crawled home at night exhausted.

"So, where are we heading?" Laura asked as they waited for the elevator.

"Brookhaven," Meredith said, carefully watching for Laura's reaction. Laura remained impassive; she knew what Meredith was thinking. *Laura's old neighborhood . . . how will she feel about going back?* Meredith continued. "Lakehaven Drive. Looks like a botched burglary. The victim was a woman named Christine Stanley. She had two kids, both in the house when it happened—they weren't hurt, thank God. Here's the elevator."

The elevator pinged its arrival in the lobby, and they walked briefly into the warm spring air before entering the parking garage. They clopped across the concrete floor and climbed aboard Meredith's urban assault vehicle. Laura almost sat on a Gummi bear, which she placed pointedly in the ashtray.

"Sorry," Meredith said, as she pulled out. "I've got to get this thing washed, but when? Anyway, I thought this would be a good case for you. Not that there's anything good about it, of course, but it seems straightforward, at least. It's a chance for you to get familiar with crime-scene procedure, and Randy Travers is running it—he's one of the most experienced homicide detectives they've got. It'll be good for you to see him work."

"Do you know when it happened? Or how she was killed?"

"She was shot, late last night or early this morning. I don't have a lot of details. I do know that no one heard the shots—she wasn't discovered for several hours. Her son found her this morning."

"My God!" Laura gasped. "What about her husband? Were they divorced?"

"No, he was out of town. That's probably why the burglar chose their house. But I shouldn't speculate until we hear what the cops have to say. Our role today is just to observe, get an impression we can carry with us as the case develops. Look, Laura, I've been walking on eggshells around the subject, but it's only been four months since Tom was killed . . ."

"And since I killed Jeff Williams. You don't need to say anything, Meredith—I know it's what everyone thinks of when they see me: *'That's the girl who killed that guy!'* But believe me, nothing I see today is going to be worse than the pictures I see in my head every day."

Meredith shook her head. "I know this won't be the first violent death you've seen, but it will be the first you'll have to see *objectively*. Not *unemotionally*, just objectively. We're only invited as a courtesy, you know. Some of the police officers resent our being there. I've cultivated a relationship with Homicide, though, because it's important for me to know what happened. Maybe I lack imagination, but I feel that I can make a better case if I was really there. You see, when I go to a crime scene, I try to learn something personal about the victim, so I can be a better advocate for him or her in court, so I can bring up something about the victims that will make them real to a jury. I call them Valentines.''

"Why Valentines?"

"There was one case, when I first started out—the victim was just an average guy. He worked in computers or something. He was shot to death in a mall parking lot one day in February. When I got there, I saw that there was a little bag lying beside him. It had two Valentine cards in it—one for his mother, and one for his girlfriend. Those cards humanized him for me, gave him a life. I entered the cards in evidence—we even passed them around the jury. We got a felony murder conviction, although everyone said we should let the defendant plead to voluntary manslaughter.''

Laura nodded. "I want to do this," she reassured Meredith.

Meredith signaled a lane change and exited onto Georgia 400, which would take them directly to Brookhaven. "Tell me the best way to get there," she said to Laura as they approached their exit.

"Take Peachtree Dunwoody to Stovall, and turn right." She paused for a few seconds, contemplating her old neighborhood. "I guess there hasn't been a murder in Brookhaven—well, since . . . I mean . . .''

Meredith knew what she meant—*not since that night four months earlier.* But she didn't say that; she covered Laura's confusion. "No, not that I can recall. Burglaries, a few armed robberies in the MARTA station, but nothing really violent. That's probably why the police think we're up against a botched robbery, not a premeditated crime.''

They exited from the expressway, and began traveling through one of the most beautiful neighborhoods in Atlanta. Brookhaven was an old district of charming homes set on large wooded lots. Some of the houses there were as large and impressive as anything in the more celebrated Buckhead area. The center of Brookhaven was the Capital City Country Club, its slate-roofed clubhouse set on an emerald island of a golf course. The even more prestigious Peachtree Country Club was located on its northern fringes, its clubhouse one of the few antebellum houses remaining in the whole city. The most impressive mansions, built in the first decades of the century, overlooked the Capital City golf course, but the prosperous atmosphere extended to the streets, which extended like spokes from the roads ringing it.

Lakehaven Drive, where Laura directed Meredith, didn't have a view of the club, but it was heavily wooded and hilly, the houses barely visible behind the spring foliage. Most of the houses on the street had been built in the fifties and sixties, generously proportioned ranches and Colonials on spacious lots. Lately, with values of scarce in-town property soaring, many of these comfortable homes had been purchased by ambitious builders, who tore down the old houses, subdivided the lots, and built two or three "trophy houses." It was in front of one of these that Meredith stopped the car.

"Wow. Big house," Meredith commented.

Laura nodded. *Ugly house,* she thought. Too large for the lot it was built on, its facade was a jumble of gables and dormers—mixmaster traditional. It was finished with faux stucco in a sickly beige. Fake river stone adorned the front steps, foundation, and windows. Because the subdivided lot the house sat on was narrow, a garage jutted from the front of the house like a growth. Two large arched windows illuminated it. Laura reflected that if it weren't used to store the sport utility vehicles, it would probably be the nicest room in the house. She kept all these uncharitable thoughts to herself, however, and merely commented, "It looks new. I wonder how long she lived here."

"Let's find out," Meredith said. "You ready?"

"As ready as I'm going to be." She shouldered her purse, and set off purposefully toward her first crime scene.

CHAPTER 2

There were a number of police vehicles parked in the driveway and on the street, and yellow crime-scene tape festooned the perimeter of the lot. The crackle of two-way radios competed with birdsong from the woods nearby. Laura noticed a pale face at the window of a neighboring house, barely ten feet from the wall of the victim's house. But none of the neighbors had ventured out to stand in the street and speculate the way folks might have in another neighborhood. They thought that gawking at a crime scene would be in poor taste, Laura supposed. In fairness, this truly was not a neighborhood where crime was commonplace. In fact, Laura would be willing to bet that this was the first time a police cruiser had ever been parked on the pavement of Lakehaven Drive.

Meredith showed her ID to a patrolman standing guard on the front steps, and Laura, fumbling for her own laminated badge, followed her into the house. They entered a high-ceilinged hallway, with a black and white marble floor that, Laura registered automatically, was curiously at odds with the rustic exterior of the house. A formal, banistered stairway on the right rose to a large landing that apparently doubled as a sitting area: a couple of Art Deco-style leather club chairs were placed in front of a large and architecturally incongruous Palladian window. *What is the matter with you, Laura Chastain?* She scolded herself. *A woman is dead and you're getting snotty about her taste in interior design!* She knew, however, that it was only a protective reaction, an effort to distance herself from what she was about to see.

She glanced in the living room, which opened off the hallway to the left; it looked professionally decorated, with coordinated fabrics on the furniture and windows. It was so neat that the pattern left by a vacuum cleaner was clearly visible, marked only by a few shoe prints. The room seemed cold, not homelike at all. *It must be off-limits to the kids,* she reflected. Everything was new; Laura's keen eye spotted no idiosyncratic battered, beloved family pieces. It felt more like a hotel lobby than a home. As they passed along the hall, Laura noticed a security alarm mounted on the wall just inside the front door. *Was it armed last night?* She assumed that it had not been, or the crime would have been discovered before morning. The hall ended in an arched entryway that led into what appeared to be the family room. Laura knew without seeing any further that this was where the crime had taken place.

The room was a scene of organized chaos: a uniformed officer was keeping out everyone who didn't absolutely need to be in it, while technicians wearing "clean suits" combed the area for evidence. A photographer stood by idly, waiting for directions. The fingerprint team had evidently been through the room already—every surface likely to show prints had been dusted with a greasy black powder. *Who will clean this up?* Laura wondered, and then she remembered that there were private contractors who did nothing but clean up crime scenes. They had returned her own living room to something like its normal state after that night last December.

At the center of the activity stood Randy Travers—at least Laura assumed he was the detective in charge. He looked as if he had been cast for the part of Homicide Detective, wearing a rumpled blazer over gray polyester slacks and a wrinkled white shirt accented with a tie of indescribable ugliness. He was giving orders to the technicians, and didn't notice Meredith until she spoke.

"Oh. You're here," he said without enthusiasm when he did notice their arrival. "Come on in; they're just about done here."

Laura cast her eyes around, bracing herself for her first sight of the victim. As if reading her mind, Travers said, "Body's already gone. That's where she was." He indicated an area of the carpet that was soaked with blood. There was also blood on the sofa, and the wall, even the ceiling. Laura felt her stomach lurch. Travers seemed oblivious to her discomfort. He flipped open a notebook and began reading in a monotone: "Christine Stanley, age thirty-six. Married to James Alan Stanley, also thirty-six—he's out of town, but he's been informed. Two children: Matthew, age eleven, and Sara, age seven. She must have been sitting on the sofa, there"—Travers indicated the location by pointing—"and the TV was on. She left a magazine there, and that container of ice cream."

Laura took in the blood-spattered fashion magazine left open on the sofa, and the pint container of melted ice cream, spoon still in it, on the coffee table. The scene would be poignantly familiar to any woman who had spent an evening alone after a long day: brain candy on the television, gorgeous, unwearable clothes in the magazine, and ice cream with a heart-stopping butterfat content. *She was just like me,* she thought involuntarily. *This is the Valentine card Meredith was talking about.* Without ever having met the dead woman or even seeing a photograph of her, Laura felt that she knew her, felt a kinship with her.

Travers directed them across the room, to the kitchen, which was divided from the family room by a stylish breakfast bar. Everything in the kitchen was first-rate—slate countertops, cherry cabinets, glossy wooden floor. The refrigerator was festooned with children's artwork, birthday party invitations, and photos, all held in place by a diverse collection of magnets. It was the first sign of normal family life Laura had seen in the house. She peered closely at the pictures, scanning them for an image of Christine Stanley. One woman appeared over and over again in the photos of birthday parties, vacations, and school events. *That must be her.* In virtually every picture she was hugging one or both of her children. Her husband—if that dark-haired man with them was her husband—seemed physically distant in the family snapshots, rarely touching either his wife or his children.

"Looks like he came in here," Travers was saying, indicating French doors that led onto a deck. "He wouldn't have been seen back here, even though she had the security light on. There's a wooden fence that runs alongside the driveway on this side, and woods block the view from the other side."

"What about the burglar alarm?" Laura asked, recalling the monitor she had seen in the hall.

Travers eyed her suspiciously. "Who's she?" he asked Meredith.

"My assistant, Laura Chastain. So, what about the burglar alarm?"

"Disarmed—either she didn't have it on, or he turned it off, which I doubt. There are keypads here and in the front hall. Probably she didn't bother turning it on. We checked with their security company. The Stanleys had been having some problems with the system in the past couple of months. They got charged for a few false alarms, so I bet they'd gotten out of the habit of using it. Happens, sometimes. We'll know more after we talk to the husband."

"Where is he?" Meredith asked.

"On his way home from Charlotte. The Charlotte police sent an officer to his hotel this morning."

"Where are the children?" Laura interjected, a little frustrated by Travers's taciturnity.

"With their aunt—victim's sister. She lives in Marietta. The older kid called her right after he called 911. Kept his head pretty well, poor little guy. The little sister was in bad shape; the paramedics had to sedate her. Glad they had a close relative who could take care of them. Gonna be tough for them."

"So, what else do you have?" Meredith asked.

"Not much, yet. Two shots were fired. One missed—lodged in the wall behind her. Looks like a nine millimeter. Other slug is probably still in the body. I figure this is how it happened: She hears the guy break in the doors here, and gets up, starts into the kitchen to investigate. He probably thought no one was at home—her car was in the garage, where he couldn't have seen it, and there weren't many lights on. He comes through the kitchen as she's getting up to investigate the noise, and reaches the family room as she's standing there." Travers had led them back to the bloodstain on the carpet. "He sees her, panics, and fires. One shot goes wide—you can see the hole, over there—

the other one catches her in the chest. She falls, he flees, and she bleeds out. She mighta lived if someone had called 911 right away." He shook his head sadly.

"Why didn't someone call? Those shots made some noise. Surely the kids would have heard them." Meredith was frowning as she looked around. "Or even the neighbors."

"Maybe not. It's a big house. Might have sounded like a backfire. I'm getting a ballistics guy over here to test-fire a gun in here, see if the sound carries."

"Could he have used a silencer?" Laura didn't know much about guns, but she couldn't believe that no one would have heard two shots, no matter how large the house.

Travers looked at her contemptuously. "Silencer? I doubt it. This guy's just a punk burglar. He wouldn't have access to anything that fancy."

"Well, was anything stolen?"

Travers eyed her as if she were some fungal growth. "He ran after he shot the lady, okay? He didn't have time to shop."

Laura was spared further comment by the entry of another plainclothes detective, identifiable by the badge hanging from his belt. He was a young black man, as well-groomed as Travers was sloppy. He addressed Travers respectfully. "Excuse me, Randy—the photographer wants to know if you need him anymore."

"I guess not. Tell him I want the prints when I get back downtown. You know Meredith Gaffney?" Travers jerked his head in Meredith's direction by way of introduction.

"No, we've never met. I'm Carlton Hemingway," he said, extending his hand to Meredith.

"I'm Meredith Gaffney, from the district attorney's office, and this is my assistant, Laura Chastain."

Hemingway shook Laura's hand, too. "Pleased to meet

you. You'll have to excuse me; this is my first homicide case. I just made detective a couple weeks ago."

"It's my first, too," Laura replied, disarmed by the warmth of his smile. "I've only been with the district attorney for a few weeks."

Travers broke up the introductions. "Hemingway, why don't you tell the ladies what the crime-scene team found?"

"Sure. It's not much, really. They've recovered a slug from the wall, probably nine millimeter. The fingerprint team got some clear prints, but they haven't analyzed them yet. They might turn out to belong to the family—they need to fingerprint the husband when he gets back; they've already started collecting elimination prints from other regular vistors, like the cleaning lady. There were a couple of good footprints left in the carpet; the cleaning lady was in yesterday, and the carpet was freshly vacuumed, so it held a print. Looks like a man's dress shoe, smooth-soled, possibly size ten. Not enough prints to extrapolate height or weight, unfortunately. And there were a few fibers caught in the wood on the French door where he broke in. They're going to the GBI crime lab."

"Have all the neighbors been interviewed?"

"Yes. The couple on the right-hand side were in bed asleep; their bedroom is on the far side of the house, which is a good hundred yards away from this room. The folks in the left-hand house were watching TV—he's a little deaf, so they might easily have missed a noise. No one saw anybody or heard a car."

Travers seemed pleased with the young detective's work. "Great. Did you get the reports on those break-ins?"

"Right here," Hemingway said, producing a sheaf of fax paper. "There have been five incidents, starting last October. The first three took place during the day, when no one was home. He's gotten more reckless lately—

there's been someone at home during the last two break-ins, so we have a description of the perpetrator. African-American male, over six feet, slim build. Carries a nine-millimeter semiautomatic; we know that because he used it to force his last victim to drive to an ATM.''

"Seems like they could have caught this guy before last night," Meredith remarked dryly.

Laura decided to brave Travers's scorn again. "Why did he shoot this time? He'd been discovered by homeowners before, and he never lost his head. Why kill this woman and not the others?"

Neither detective answered her question. "One more thing," Hemingway continued. "The detective covering the break-ins says that there was another incident he thinks is related—a dog was shot a couple of months ago, also with a nine millie. They recovered the slug, so ballistics will be able to match it against what we got from this scene."

"Good work," Travers said. "Now let's get this bastard. The Dekalb County line runs right over there," he said, waving a hand northward. "Get them involved; maybe they've had some similar incidents. Could be they're looking for the guy, too. Meredith, I think that's all we've got for you. Care to join a press conference at City Hall East? It's scheduled for five, to catch the evening news. The big guy is gonna be there. Might want you to say a piece."

"Sure, we'll be there. Come on, Laura—let's get back to the office. Keep us posted, Randy," she said as they left.

They returned to Meredith's car in silence. They had driven half a block before either of them spoke. "You can . . ." Laura began.

"Are you . . ." Meredith said at the same time. "Sorry. What did you want to say?"

"You can get back to Peachtree this way," Laura said.

"Okay. Are you okay?"

"I'm glad the body was gone," Laura said.

"But otherwise?" Meredith prompted.

"But otherwise it was horrible. My God, Meredith—the children! How will they ever get over a thing like this?"

"They might not. If they have a loving family—grandparents, aunts, and uncles—that will help. And they still have their father. Poor man."

They both contemplated the magnitude of James Stanley's loss as Meredith steered the car. "Turn here," Laura said. "Club Drive goes straight to Peachtree." She remembered too late that this route would take them past the townhouse where she had lived, and which she had not seen for three months. She hoped Meredith would not remember, but she wasn't so lucky.

"Isn't that . . . ?" Meredith began to say as they passed.

"Yes, that's the place."

"Laura, I don't want to seem to pry—just tell me to shut up if you don't want me to talk about your private life, but I have to ask you if you're seeing someone."

Seeing someone? Good Lord, it had only been four months since Tom died. No one fully understood her relationship with Tom Bailey—they might have been officially "involved" only for a short time, but she and Tom had worked side by side for so long that they had been as much intertwined as any longtime couple. She gaped and tried to formulate a polite answer to Meredith's question. "It's . . . too soon," she managed to stammer.

"Too soon? I would have thought the sooner the better. It wouldn't have to be a shrink, you know—there are a lot of good grief support groups, and victim's groups . . . what's so funny?"

"Oh, Meredith, when you said 'seeing someone,' I thought you meant *dating*. But I don't see anyone in the other sense either, not officially. My family and my church have been very supportive, and there's always Amos.''

"Good old Amos Kowalski. I guess he's as good a therapist to see as any. Or *to see* in the other sense, if you know what I mean.''

"Will you just drive? I have work to do back at the office,'' Laura said sternly. Meredith laughed, and drove, the grim atmosphere of the crime scene dissipated.

CHAPTER 3

Laura was running late. She had promised to meet Amos Kowalski at her new house in Buckhead at six-thirty, but it was already later than that when she scrambled into the grocery store to assemble a takeout dinner of roasted chicken and pasta salad. The press conference had run longer than expected—*apparently, the murder of a young mother pulls ratings on the evening news, even on a Friday,* she concluded. Laura had attended, but she had not spoken. Meredith herself had said very little, fielding only one question: What charges would be filed against the burglar if and when he was apprehended? "Felony murder," Meredith had said, explaining that under Georgia law a killing committed in the course of a felony—even if the assailant did not plan to kill anyone—was legally equivalent to a premeditated murder. And, yes, felony murder was a capital crime—and they would pursue the maximum penalty.

After the press conference ended, Laura asked Meredith if she would really ask for the death penalty, assuming that the burglar was caught and the circumstances fit Travers's scenario. "Yes. We don't have a choice," was the terse reply.

"Of course we do!"

"Oh, sure, on paper—but Marshall is up for reelection next year, and he has to carry North Fulton to win." Marshall Oliver was the Fulton County district attorney, who had won his office by a slender margin three years earlier. His tenure had been marked by controversy, especially a series of civil suits filed on behalf of inmates of the overcrowded jail. Laura liked Marshall, as far as she knew him, but she wasn't sure Meredith and he always saw eye-to-eye—or that she and Marshall would. But there was no room for death-penalty dissenters in the district attorney's office; they were all sworn to uphold the law, and in Georgia that meant they swore to send the deserving to the electric chair. Laura's private doubts about the justice of the death penalty remained that way, even in friendly discussions with Meredith.

Shopping done, Laura hurried home through the snarled Buckhead traffic—or tried to hurry anyway. Just making the left turn out of the grocery store parking lot took almost ten minutes, and she got caught at every red light between the store and her turnoff at East Paces Ferry Road. From there, she was home free; East Paces had been designated for "local traffic only" on the east side of Piedmont Road. Laura had paid dearly to live in Peachtree Park, one of the oldest and most charming of Buckhead's residential areas—but she would have paid any price to remain in town. There was no way she could have moved out beyond the Perimeter Highway, into those desolate car-packed suburbs. She glanced at the dashboard clock; it read almost seven o'clock. If Amos did beat her to her house, it was no big deal; he had a key. Just the same, she wanted to get dinner out of the way so they could tackle the latest home-improvement project Amos had cooked up.

Laura had bought her new house, a two-bedroom 1920's cottage, only six weeks earlier. She had picked the house because it hadn't needed a great deal of work—the previous owner had "updated" the kitchen, reroofed, and put in new heating and air-conditioning. Laura had planned to leave the rest as she found it, but Amos was an inveterate remodeler of houses, and he had convinced her that she should refinish the wooden floors and paint the interior walls. He had been right, of course; Laura couldn't have lived with the generic beige carpet and white walls for long. After she closed on the house, Laura and Amos had spent almost every evening for three weeks sanding, sealing, and painting. While the house was a construction zone, Laura had camped in Amos's guestroom, a familiar refuge. His house had been a haven for her in the weeks after that terrible December night, when her rented townhouse in Brookhaven was inhabited by too many memories, good and bad, for her to feel at home there again. Her parents had tried mightily to persuade her to return to Nashville, where all her family lived, but Laura had stubbornly insisted on remaining in Atlanta. It wasn't that she liked the place all that much—in fact, the city was sometimes just plain annoying, with its schizoid mix of boosterism and self-loathing. But everywhere she went in her adopted city she was reminded of Tom, and those reminders comforted her in a way that no amount of sympathy from her well-meaning parents could.

Amos understood. He had eased her agony as much as anyone could have in the past four months, giving up his own social life to be available for her. She had made it through, thanks to his tireless concern and apparently inexhaustible appetite for long-winded games of Scrabble in front of his fireplace. But much as Laura appreciated his kindness, she was glad to be under her own roof, and glad that he could reclaim his own life, as well. Even so, Laura suspected that Kowalski was going to come up with an endless stream of home-improvement projects, just so he could keep an eye on her.

His latest notion had been to turn a back hallway into a study. It had been wasted space, lined with a couple of shallow closets fronted with cheap sliding doors. With the help of a builder, those had been torn out, and a window punched through the back wall in their place. Laura had designed built-in bookshelves and a desk to surround the new window. When the construction was complete, the carpenter had packed up and left the finishing details to Laura. Tonight, she and Amos were going to paint the walls a pumpkin color to match a worn Oriental rug. The bookshelves, desk, and moldings were to be white. It was going to make a nice little room.

Laura dumped the grocery bags on the kitchen table and headed back to her bedroom to change. The light on the answering machine was blinking steadily; Amos had called to say he was running late. She smiled; no need to confess to him that *she* had been behind schedule, too. Amos was chronically well-organized and maniacally punctual. Laura often wondered how he tolerated the chaos of his chosen profession. "You should have been a CPA, Kowalski," she teased him. "You have none of the personality traits of a cop." Of course, that was precisely why Amos made such a good police officer; he had a rare combination of moral authority and empathy. And he needed both as head of the sex-crimes squad, where he saw some unimaginably sordid things.

There was no sense in dressing up to get splattered with paint, so Laura pulled out some old and ratty clothes. She slipped an ancient T-shirt over her dark, wavy hair, which she had cut short a few weeks earlier so that she wouldn't have to bother with blow-drying it. As she buttoned an old pair of khakis that hadn't been worn in a while, she noticed that they were awfully loose in the waist and the seat. Eating was not something she had been interested in during the past few months; other people noticed and bothered her about it. She thought she looked just fine; she had always carried a few more pounds than she liked anyway.

Laura had set the table and was spinning lettuce for a salad when she heard the tires of Kowalski's meticulously preserved Jeep Wagoneer in the driveway. He came in the back door, dressed in an ancient pair of paint-splattered khakis, a bedraggled T-shirt, and a stained workshirt. "Oooh, you didn't have to dress up for me, Amos!" Laura said.

"For dinner with you, baby? 'Course I did." He kissed her on her forehead. "What's cooking?"

"Technically, what's reheating is chicken à la Publix. I'm making a green salad, and there's pasta salad in that container. I got some of those brownies you like for dessert, too. Would you care to select a bottle from the cellars?"

"Of course," he said, heading for the narrow pantry. "Got some of that Australian stuff?"

"The Shiraz? Sure."

"Think the wine police will cite for drinking red with poultry?"

"No, they're too busy busting the folks who store their bottles upright."

Amos opened the wine while Laura hustled the chicken and salads to the table, and they sat down. "So, how was your day?'' she asked. Amos's job could be harrowing; she had learned that it was better sometimes not to ask him about it. He seemed in a fairly benign mood this evening.

He shrugged. ''More of the usual stuff. Paperwork, mostly. How about you?''

''Mom let me take the car out today,'' she said. ''All by myself!''

''Really? What did you do?''

Laura described her appearance at Juwon Taylor's plea hearing. ''It came up in front of Judge Talbot—you know all about him, I suppose?''

''Yes. He nullified the jury in that gang rape case. Nearly drove Mike Yowell around the bend.'' Yowell was the head of the Fulton County Sheriff's department's sex-crimes unit, and a close friend of Amos's. Yowell had made the case against the 'preppy rapists.' ''Did he give you a hard time?'' Amos asked.

''He tried. But I triumphed, of course.''

''Of course.'' They clinked their wineglasses, and moved on to other topics. Laura deliberately omitted telling Amos about her visit to the murder scene; something told her that he wouldn't approve. He was overly protective of her; he hadn't wanted her to take a job in the district attorney's office. He had been especially opposed to her joining Meredith's team, which handled some of the worst crimes. Laura thought his attitude was disingenuous—if he had been in her position, he would have plunged himself right back into work, the toughest assignments he could find. But he thought Laura should handle nothing more grisly than wills and trusts.

After hurrying through dinner and cleaning up the dishes, they proceeded to the office. The previous weekend they had done the prep work: sanding, masking, and priming. Amos was a meticulous workman. Masking the moldings and trim alone had taken the better part of Saturday afternoon. Laura would have been just as happy to cut a few corners; she ragged Amos for his attention to detail. "You'll thank me for it," he had admonished. "There's nothing worse than a sloppy paint job. It'll drive you crazy for years." Laura had laughed and refrained from making a joke about "painting foreplay." She stayed off sex and romance in general with Amos; there was an unexplored zone between them that Laura was not eager to violate. He had asked her out once, but she had been so wildly in love with Tom at the time that she had declined. He had never made even the slightest move in her direction since, not during all the time they had spent together, not even when they slept under the same roof. That was another reason that Laura was glad to be finally set up in her own place—it didn't seem fair for Amos to invest all his free time in his relationship with her when there wasn't a chance of his making a return, so to speak, on his investment.

Laura's job was to paint the walls; Amos was doing the detail work. Laura pried open the can of paint and stirred it doubtfully. "Gosh, this is really very . . . orange. It didn't look quite so bright on the paint chip." Amos came and looked over her shoulder. "I'm afraid it's going to look like a sweet potato exploded in here."

"It's intense," he agreed, "but you're putting on a relatively small area. I don't think it'll be too much. What kind of music do you want to listen to while we work?"

Painting wasn't the only thing Amos was particular about; he also had very strong opinions about music. He liked "the standards," a canonical collection of songs written by talents like Johnny Mercer, Harold Arlen, Rodgers and Hart, Cole Porter, and the Gershwins, performed by great voices like Ella Fitzgerald, Frank Sinatra, and Sarah

Vaughn. He adored Duke Ellington and Harry James, and despised almost anything recorded after 1960—the Beatles excepted, of course. Laura, who was used to men whose musical development had halted at "Clapton is God," was happy to let Amos choose the tunes. He had introduced her to a lot of great music.

Tonight he had brought along the Nat King Cole Trio, and as they began painting, he delivered a short lecture on Cole's career. "One of the best piano men in jazz until they found out he could sing," he said. "Then he almost never played again—just sang."

"I like his songs. 'Mona Lisa' is great," Laura ventured.

Amos shrugged. "It's okay—but nothing like what he did in the thirties and forties. For my money, his cover of 'Laura' is the best ever recorded. It's on this CD." They listened and worked in silence for a few minutes until Amos spoke again. "I saw your press conference tonight on the news."

Laura was a little taken aback; now it looked as if she'd been hiding something—which, of course, she had been. "Oh. I meant to tell you about that. Meredith thought it would be a good case for me to get involved with—you know, to follow all the way through the system."

"And what do you think?"

She shrugged. "I handled it all right. Don't worry so much, Amos; I'm tougher than you think. It was horrible, but I didn't break down."

"I'm sure you didn't, but I can't see why Meredith chose this case."

"What is it about this case that you object to?" Laura asked a bit testily.

"Just the stupid pointless violence of it, that's all. The shooter is some penny-ante thug who thought his gun made him a big man; he'll plead out and go to jail for life before he'll face trial.''

"There's where you may be wrong," Laura said, laying down her paint roller. "There were a lot of things at that house that didn't make sense to me. Like why wasn't the alarm turned on, and why didn't anyone hear the shot? Randy Travers said himself that this guy wouldn't be likely to have a silencer. And nothing was stolen, or even disturbed—it didn't look like a burglary to me.''

"All that may be true, but Travers has good instincts. He'll find a good explanation for all the anomalies.''

"No, I don't think he will. There was just something *wrong* at that house; I could sense it.''

Amos raised his eyebrows. "Like what—other than a body on the floor?''

"Don't be sarcastic. It just wasn't a happy house; it didn't feel lived in. It was like . . . a facade. Like . . .'' Laura looked around the small room where they stood. "See that window?''

"The one I'm painting? Yes, I see it. What about it?''

"What do you call those wooden things between the panes?''

"Mullions.''

"Okay, the windows in this huge, brand-new house didn't have wooden mullions. They had these plastic things instead, like a plastic grid that just attaches to one side of the window.''

"What—that makes you suspect something more than a break-in? Come on, Laura, lots of new houses have snap-in mullions. Just look at how much this one wood-frame window cost you—imagine putting these babies in a big new house. It would cost a fortune. Plus, they're easier to clean than these divided lights.''

"But the whole house was designed to give the impression that there was tons of money, yet there were all kinds of cut corners. And there were no toys lying around, no signs of family life, really. It was nothing like where I grew up anyway. It was not a happy house, I'm telling you."

Amos chuckled and picked up his brush. "Okay, sport. Whatever you say."

Laura took up her roller again, but she watched for a few moments as Amos spread white paint on the wooden mullions of her new window. She thought about what she had been trying to articulate—without much success—to Amos. What exactly was she saying—that this had been a premeditated murder? Or maybe that the "burglar" was really some kind of psychopath? Or maybe somebody had something against the Stanley family. Whatever the truth was, Laura didn't think it was going to turn out to be a straightforward botched burglary. She dipped her roller in the yam-colored paint and began coating the wall as Nat King Cole crooned "Laura" in the background.

CHAPTER 4

Laura was in the ladies' room Monday morning scrubbing at an overlooked orange paint spot on her elbow when Cheryl, the office receptionist, found her. Cheryl, who had a somewhat fearsome reputation as a prima donna in the office, folded her arms across her chest and looked annoyed. "There you are. There's a woman out here who's *demanding* to see Meredith."

"Did you tell her that Meredith is in court today?"

Cheryl gave Laura a what-kind-of-fool-do-you-think-I-am look, and did not deign to answer. "I told her that you would talk to her."

"Me? I don't know anything about Meredith's cases. Did she say what it's about?"

"No," Cheryl sniffed. "She's just about worked my last nerve, and I can't deal with her anymore. You'll have to see her. All she'll say is that she's Christine Stanley's sister, like Christine Stanley is all that and a bag of chips."

"Christine Stanley?" Laura hastily dried her hands. "Lead me to her."

In the lobby, Cheryl jabbed a well-manicured finger in the direction of the most beautiful woman Laura had ever seen off a movie screen. She had pale skin and dark, wavy hair, at the moment swooped up into a careless ponytail, and dark, dark eyes, a little puffy and red from tears, but arresting. She was tall—an inch or two taller than Laura, who was no shrimp—and casually dressed in faded jeans and a T-shirt. Christine Stanley, judging from the photos Laura had seen on her refrigerator, had been short and blonde, nothing like this girl.

Laura approached the vision of loveliness and introduced herself. "I work with Meredith Gaffney. You need to see her about something?"

"Yes. About my sister's murder. The police won't listen to me, so I came here. Where is Ms. Gaffney?"

"In court all day, I'm afraid. I know your sister's case—maybe I can help. I can at least get a message to Meredith for you."

The woman looked at Laura appraisingly for a minute. She must have liked what she saw, because she nodded her head. "Yes. Where can we go to get some privacy?"

Not many places, Laura thought, hoping that the small conference room would be available. Cheryl checked the log, and told her it was. "I'll be in there for a half hour or so, I guess," Laura told her. "And if Meredith calls, tell her that Christine Stanley's sister is here, and that I'm with her." Cheryl, seeming more intrigued than irritated now, nodded assent, and Laura led the woman to the conference room.

"Can I get you something, Ms. . . . ?"

"Sorry. My name is Lynette Connell, and I'd love a cup of coffee. Black."

Laura got a cup for herself as well. The trip to the break room gave her a chance to gather her thoughts. *Poor woman,* she thought. Laura had only brothers, so she couldn't imagine what losing a sister would be like—but she did have a heartfelt natural empathy for any victim of a violent crime. But what she was doing here was anyone's guess; crime victims rarely dealt with the district attorney's office until a trial date had been set.

Back in the conference room Laura put the coffee down in front of Lynette Connell and took a seat. "This is about your sister, obviously. I know the case; I went to the house with Meredith."

"Then you know that the person who did this wasn't after the silver and the VCR. The police seem to believe it was a break-in that went wrong." Lynette had a soft voice, and a Southern accent smooth as butter, but Laura heard the iron in it.

"You disagree?"

"Strongly. To put it bluntly, my sister was killed by her husband."

"But he has an alibi—he was away on business, I thought."

Lynette waved her hand. "It's a fake. Or he hired someone to do the dirty work for him. Either way, that s.o.b. is guilty."

"You've spoken to Detective Travers about this?" Laura was unwilling to intrude on police turf, but if Travers had given Lynette short shrift, the least she could do was listen.

Lynette snorted contemptuously. "Oh, yes, he's got it all boxed up. It fits his little 'pattern,' so it has to be the neighborhood burglar. I *told* Christine to leave—I told her he would get violent, but she didn't believe me."

"Can I ask you to back up and give me some details? I'd like to know more about your family, and about your sister's marriage—and her husband. How long had they been married?''

"Almost fifteen years—they met in college, the University of North Carolina. She was smart. If she hadn't married The Asshole—sorry, that's my name for him; I have trouble even *thinking* of him as anything else—if she hadn't married *him*, she would have gone to law school, or gotten an MBA and run the family business. She was the smart one.''

And you were the pretty one, Laura thought—not that Lynette seemed to be lacking in the brains department. "How many brothers and sisters do you have?''

"There were just the two of us. She was older, six years older. But we were always best friends.'' She began to cry softly, producing a much-used tissue. Laura delved into her pocket for a fresh one, and offered it without comment. "I never liked James. He was 'sorry,' as we say down here. . . . Are you from the South?''

"Nashville—and I've met my share of 'sorry' men. Go on.''

"Everything was fine for a long time. I never liked James, and my daddy wasn't real fond of him, either, but there was no reason for us to suspect that they weren't happy. Not at first, at least. After they married, Christine worked for a couple of years in Daddy's company. Then, when she had Matthew, she quit and became a full-time mama.''

"Was she unhappy doing that?''

Lynette shook her head vigorously. "Oh, no—she was the best mother in the world. She just loved those children! We all lived close together—I'm not married—out near Marietta. We saw each other all the time, and after our mother died, we got even closer. Then, about five years ago, James left his job. He had been a broker at Barker Brown, but he decided that he wasn't getting ahead fast enough there. I suppose they just failed to appreciate his brilliant financial mind," she said sarcastically. "He wanted to set up his own money-management firm. Daddy helped him out by letting him manage some of his money—not all of it, thank God—and he seemed to settle down. But his business didn't exactly take off—I mean, who's going to put money with a Bozo like that when there are *competent* financial managers out there? Anyway, he told Christine that if they wanted to 'run with the big boys' they had to move into town. Fine, she said, and they did. They built that house over there in Brookhaven. I didn't care for it, and I never thought it was Chrissie's style, but she seemed pleased, so I kept my mouth shut. Then, once they got over there, he decided that he needed to join one of the clubs so he could rub shoulders with the big boys. You know what a membership at one of those museums costs?"

"I have an idea," Laura said. "How did he get the money?"

"Daddy. He's too soft. He paid the club's initiation fee, but he told James he'd have to handle the dues. From there, it was more status bullshit. They had to put the kids in private school, had to get a Lexus. Daddy turned off the spigot, but I think James had no trouble borrowing from other sources."

"He's in debt?"

"Massively, I would think. He entertained on what you might call 'a lavish scale'—golfing trips, fishing trips, hunting trips with 'potential clients.' He was always talking about landing this or that big account, but I never saw his name in the papers, if you know what I mean. Anyway, Chrissie was getting more and more unhappy all this time. She wasn't brought up to live like that—we're simple folks. Richer than hell, but simple. Daddy lives in the same old ranch house he bought when he and Mama got married.

He never had to join in all this Atlanta bullshit. Chrissie wanted to sell that house and move back to Cobb County, put the kids in public school, drop the club membership, and live the way she used to. James said no way. He had to have all this stuff for his business. If you want to know what I think, he is so damn deep in hock that selling every last asset he has won't even begin to pay the piper. Chrissie was more and more miserable. She would call me up all the time, crying and saying she couldn't stand it. I wanted her to leave him."

"Was she prepared to do that?"

Lynette shifted her eyes away from Laura's. "I think so. I mean, she never said so, not in so many words . . ."

"But you were encouraging her to?"

"Yes! And she was listening to me, these last few months. I think she wanted out any way she could. And I think he found out that she was planning to leave and take the children."

"Did he have insurance on your sister's life?"

Lynette shrugged. "Wouldn't surprise me a bit. But the real money was in the trusts."

"The trusts?"

"Yes. Like I said, we've got money. Lots of it. Sorry if that sounds tacky, but it's just the truth. Daddy grew up on a dairy farm in Cobb County. After he graduated from the University of Georgia, about 1953, he came back home and helped my granddaddy. They bought dairies all over the northern part of the state. You know what a dairy farm is?"

"Well, yes," Laura said, baffled as to why she was being patronized by this whirlwind of a woman.

"It ain't cows, shugah—it's *real estate*. And Daddy and Granddaddy owned a pantload of it, right in the path of Atlanta's growth. Cobb, North Fulton, Gwinett—even out in Cherokee, Jackson, and Forsyth counties—they bought every pasture they could lay their hands on. Then about twenty years ago they started to sell. And I am here to tell you that my daddy is no dummy—he held on until he could get absolute top dollar. He never wanted to be a developer; he just took their money and said, 'Thank you,' and invested in more property, stocks, bonds—you name it. Most folks have never heard of Lester Connell, but he's as rich as any of these sons of bitches who sit around at the Capital City Club. Probably more so. And Daddy *hates* debt—he's strictly a cash man. So you can imagine how pleased he would have been if he knew about James."

"He didn't know Christine and James were in debt?"

"No. And he didn't know how unhappy she was, either. He doesn't know that I came down to tell all this to the police, either."

"Let me back up for a minute. You say that your sister was planning to leave her husband, who was in debt, and that's why you believe he had a motive to kill her—to collect insurance?"

"No, not exactly. See, Daddy hates to pay taxes even more than he hates to owe money. He set up trusts for Chrissie and for me when we were kids. I still let him manage my money, but Chrissie took control of hers after she married. At that time her trust might have had two or three million in it, enough to produce a nice income. But I think James did some pretty stupid things with the money. And he spent so much, too—that house alone, with all the furniture and all, must have set him back about a million and a half. But the children each have trusts that are worth maybe twenty million all told, and James and Chrissie have—or had—control of the income from them until the kids turn twenty-five. Daddy and I are trustees along with Chrissie and James and our family lawyer. *But,* like I said, if Chrissie divorces The Asshole—no soup for him! If you follow my meaning."

"You all would have removed him as a trustee, I'm guessing."

"Bingo. And James would come tumbling down."

"I see." Laura thought for a moment. "Lynette—may I call you Lynette?—James might have had a motive to kill your sister, but the best motive in the world is not proof of a crime. It's not an 'element' of the crime, as we say— because there needn't be a motive for a murder to take place. A psycho can kill for no reason at all. So, providing a motive is important in understanding the crime, but proving a murder is far more complex. And your brother- in-law has a rock-solid alibi as far as I can tell. What did Detective Travers say?"

"Just what you did, but a helluva lot less tactfully."

"I'm sorry he wasn't more sympathetic, but he's right. And wouldn't it be best for all concerned if this *did* turn out to be just a random, senseless act of violence? Think of the children. They've been traumatized enough without being told that it was their father who killed their mother."

"So, you think I'm full of crap, too."

"I didn't say that. As a matter of fact, there were certain . . . anomalies at the crime scene that aren't explained by Detective Travers's theory. But he's the best, I'm told, and I think we should just let him work."

"So, you're not going to do anything?" Lynette said, standing up and preparing to leave.

"I didn't say that, either. I'll tell Meredith everything you told me, and I'll talk to the detectives. May I have your phone number so I can stay in touch with you?"

"Sure," Lynette replied, reciting a number. "Just leave a message if you don't get through. And thanks for listening to me." She turned and was gone.

Laura walked back to her cubicle with furrowed brow. What Lynette had just told her chimed very well with her own impressions of the house and the Stanley marriage. It also answered some of the nagging questions about why the alarm had not sounded, why nothing was taken—and why the heretofore cool-headed burglar had panicked and shot this time. *I wonder if James Stanley knew about those other break-ins in the neighborhood,* she mused. At her desk, she reached for the phone and started to dial the police department's homicide squad. She stopped in midnumber, hesitated, then continued. When the operator answered, she asked not for Detective Travers, but for the more user-friendly Detective Hemingway.

"Hemingway," he said in a rich baritone.

"Detective Hemingway, this is Laura Chastain. We met Friday at the Stanley crime scene."

"Sure, I remember. What can I do for you?"

"I've just seen the victim's sister, Lynette Connell. Did you speak with her?"

"Yes, I was with Randy when she came in this morning. She's very upset."

"But what did you think of what she had to say?"

There was a pause on the other end of the line; then he said, carefully, "Randy thinks she's in shock, and that she wants someone to blame. There's nothing that suggests to him that this was a premeditated crime."

"No? I know I don't have much experience, but there were several things that didn't seem right to me. Why did the burglar have to shoot? If he stuck with his pattern, wouldn't he have held her at gunpoint and robbed her?"

Hemingway sighed. "Maybe, maybe not. Who can say? The guy could be on meth, crack—his behavior may not be rational. He might have been a murder waiting to happen all this time."

"What about the alarm, and the gunshots that nobody heard?"

"Ah, *that* we can explain—Randy had the ballistics guys set up a test this morning. They fired several shots in the Stanley living room while officers were stationed upstairs and in the neighboring houses. They heard something, but not anything readily identifiable as a gunshot—and the kids could have slept right through it. Big house. And remember, one neighbor was asleep and the other had the television on. And another thing—the ballistics on the slugs we recovered at the Stanley scene matched the bullets that killed the dog a few weeks ago. We think our guy shot the dog to stop him from barking when he was casing a house."

That was more or less conclusive, Laura supposed. "Have you interviewed James Stanley?"

"Of course."

"How did he seem to you?"

Hemingway sighed. "Like a bereaved husband."

"What did he say about the alarm being turned off?"

"Just what we thought—that Mrs. Stanley sometimes left it off because she didn't want to rack up any more false alarms."

"I see. So, you're still looking for the burglar?"

"Yes. And we'll continue to until we get him, or until somebody gives us a more substantial reason not to."

"I see. Well, thanks for the time, Detective. I'm sure we'll be speaking again."

"I hope so. 'Bye now."

Laura twiddled the phone cord after she hung up, staring into the middle distance. Lynette Connell was a whole lot more convincing than Detective Hemingway, but she had no standing to push the investigation in another direction. Things would have to run their course; Laura resigned herself to waiting for the next development.

She didn't have to wait more than a couple of days, as it turned out. Late Thursday afternoon, Meredith buzzed Laura's cubicle. "Something's happened in the Stanley case. You better come along to my office now," she said tersely.

Laura hurried down the hall, forgetting everything else in her eagerness to hear the news. Christine Stanley's murder had never been far from her mind in the past week, and something major must have happened, judging from Meredith's tone of voice. "What is it?" she asked anxiously as she entered Meredith's office. To her surprise, Randy Travers and Carlton Hemingway were there.

"They got the burglar," Meredith said.

"Oh," Laura replied, a little disappointed. "Did he have the gun?"

"No," Travers said. "In fact, he has an alibi."

"You're gonna love this, Laura," Meredith said with a grin.

Travers glowered at her and continued. "Our suspect in the burglaries is Marcus Griffin, twenty-eight. He was located inside the Dekalb County Jail, where he has been for two weeks."

"Alibis just don't get any better than that, do they?" Meredith seemed amused, but Laura was impatient.

"So, does this mean you're considering alternate theories of the crime?" she asked, unable to eliminate the sarcastic tone from her voice.

"Yes," Travers said. "And we are looking first at the husband."

"But he has a pretty good alibi, too," Laura reminded the detective.

"We're looking at a killer-for-hire theory. I understand you talked to the sister."

"Yes, I did. She made a lot of sense." Laura ran down Lynette Connell's story, and ended by saying, "She is sure, absolutely, that James Stanley was involved in the killing."

"She may be right, but there's a long way to go. Chief is going to want to talk to you, Meredith, before the press gets hold of this news. And if the press comes after you, it's 'no comment,' okay?"

"Gotcha," Meredith said.

Travers and Hemingway left after exchanging a few pleasantries, leaving Laura and Meredith alone.

"So?" Laura asked. "What did I say all along?"

Meredith held up a hand. "Now, don't get on a high horse. Travers saw everything you did, but the rules of detection say always follow the simplest theory first. The burglar was the most obvious suspect, you have to admit. Okay, now he's been eliminated—on to suspect number two."

"But a whole week's been wasted!"

"Not wasted. Randy had both eyes open all along, believe me. But there was no point in getting everybody het up if the burglar killed her. You'll understand as you spend more time in this job—a whole lot of district attorneys and cops have said too much too soon. Look at that mess in LA—if they'd played that right from the start, they might have had a different outcome."

"I guess you're right. Will Travers be angry if I call Lynette Connell?"

"I doubt it. But don't run him down to her—he's still in charge, and he's going to need the family's cooperation."

"I'll be good," Laura promised. But she couldn't help feeling vindicated as she walked the narrow hallway back to her desk. She hesitated only a moment before she fished

Lynette Connell's phone number from her address file and dialed it. "Lynette?"

"Yes?"

"This is Laura Chastain, from the district attorney's office."

"Oh, hi—what's happened?"

"I wondered if Detective Travers had been in touch with you."

"No, why?"

"Because they found the guy who had been committing those burglaries in Brookhaven."

Lynette paused on her end of the line. "And has he been charged?"

"No. And he won't be." She told Lynette where the man had been on the night her sister was killed. "So, they'll be looking at other scenarios now."

"Like what?" Lynette asked.

"Well, Travers was curious about what you had told me, so I assume they'll be checking out your brother-in-law pretty thoroughly."

Lynette sighed, as if relieved. "God . . . you don't know what this week has been like. James took the kids back home—to that house—yesterday. Can you believe it? I wanted to keep them here for a while longer."

"He is their father. But I guess I would have waited until the trauma was a little more distant before I went back to the house where it happened." *What am I saying?* she thought. *I moved away as soon as I could.* "Anyway, I expect the police are going to want to talk to you and your father right away."

"Thanks for the heads-up. And, Laura . . ."

"Yes?"

"Was anything said about where James might have gotten a gun?"

"No. Why do you ask?"

"It's nothing, but I think I might know."

"Tell Detective Travers—I'm already out of line just calling you."

"Okay, I understand. And I really appreciate your doing this, Laura."

"No problem. I'm sure we'll be seeing each other again as this thing goes on."

After she hung up, Laura felt a little guilty. She should have let Travers get Lynette's reaction firsthand—but how could it hurt?

CHAPTER 5

The death of Christine Stanley drew reporters as surely as a two-for-one happy hour special. The story made the front page of the *Constitution* for two days running, then moved to the front page of the local section for a few more. Virtually every nightly newscast led with the story for the best part of a week. There was a lot of interest in the bereaved husband, and the children. The police department had to park a cruiser in front of the Stanleys' house around the clock to keep photographers from trying to shoot the family through the windows.

When a police spokesman announced at a routine press conference that the primary suspect in the Stanley case had been exonerated, the story returned to the top of the news heap. The reporters had to give up the "deadly home invasion" theme they had been working, but they were able to switch seamlessly to suspicion of the husband. Little bits of gossip about his business and the state of his marriage began to surface, unattributed, in the press. Laura suspected that she knew the source, but she kept her own counsel on that. Randy Travers cussed the reporters privately, but said only "no comment" when they swarmed around him, to no avail. James Stanley had been convicted on the Northside cocktail party circuit by the end of the weekend.

The district attorney's office had no role in the case technically until the police were prepared to make an arrest. Informally, though, Travers kept Meredith up to date. Laura stuck her head into the boss's office on Monday morning, knowing that Meredith would share whatever she knew. "Anything new?" she asked, not expecting an affirmative reply.

"On the police investigation, no. Randy has talked to your pal, Lynette Connell. . . ."

"She's not my 'pal,'" Laura corrected.

"Okay, your *informant,* Lynette Connell. She gave him all the details of that trust the grandfather set up for the Stanley children. He also met the grandfather."

"And what's his take on the thing?"

"He's an old man, and he's basically in shock, but he reluctantly conceded that he knew that Christine and James Stanley didn't have the happiest of marriages. He firmly denies that there was any talk of divorce."

"Maybe his daughter wasn't as open with him as she was with her sister."

"Could be. Anyway, Randy got a warrant to look at Stanley's business and personal financial records. He should be exercising it right about now."

"Keep me posted," Laura said. "You know, Stanley's records are probably going to be pretty complex. I know a little about the money-management business. And the police may need a lawyer to help sort out the terms of the trust, and Christine's will."

"I've told him to call on us. But the department has a forensic accountant on staff now. I think they'll be able to get answers to most of their questions from him."

Laura knew when she was being dismissed, no matter how gently Meredith did it. She grinned and shrugged. "I can't help butting in. Tom always said I had two speeds: Overdrive and turbo. It's hard for me to be patient when there's a good case on hand."

Meredith chuckled. "I'll remember that when we're ass-deep in Stanley's records. There's nothing that drives me crazier than looking at a bunch of financial documents. If there's an accountant out there willing to do it for me, I say God bless him. And if my new assistant wants to put on a green eyeshade, I say God bless *her*. You'll be fully involved as soon as Randy puts a case together. I promise."

As it turned out, Laura got "fully involved" even sooner than she hoped. She had been back at her desk only about an hour when Meredith buzzed her. "Laura? Get in overdrive and get into my office."

Laura grabbed a pad and pen and hustled down the corridor, trying to control her grin. "What's up? Is it Stanley?" she asked.

"As if you don't know. Yes, it seems that the bereaved husband objects to the jack-booted thuggery of the Atlanta Police Department. In short, he's got himself a lawyer. They've moved to suppress the warrant."

"Grounds?" Laura asked, pen at the ready.

"Privilege. Stanley says he can't show us all his records because he has confidentiality agreements with all his clients."

"Bullshit. Lynette Connell says he has hardly any clients at all."

"Bullshit or not, the judge wants us in his chambers to argue our side at four o'clock. I'm sure that the brief you're about to prepare will ensure us total victory. By the way, guess who's representing Stanley."

Laura shook her head. "I don't know the courthouse types yet. Is it someone from Prendergrast and Crawley?" She knew that it was less than likely that anyone from her old firm would take a case like Stanley's.

"Nope. It's Craig Fannin. You know him, don't you?"

"Well, I know *of* him, of course, but I've never seen him in person."

"Then this is your lucky day. Now, write me a brief that will blow him out of the water."

Laura hurried back to her desk and dumped the file she had been working on back into its jacket. She narrowed her eyes and stared at the computer screen, focusing on her task. She jotted down a couple of ideas and clicked into the legal database program to begin her research. She started to type in the number of the Code section that she thought was applicable, to search for Supreme and Appellate Court decisions, but she cleared the form before hitting 'Search'. Instead, she typed in the name Craig Fannin and clicked the button.

Craig Fannin was a busy man, judging from the number of times his name came up in connection with court cases in the state of Georgia. Laura scrolled down the list of case names in which he was listed as an attorney. There were a few that rang a bell, and one that rang a whole bell tower. Craig Fannin had represented the four infamous high-school students accused of gang rape—the kids who got a "Get Out of Jail Free" card from Laura's pal, Judge Jones Talbot. Laura wondered how she had managed not to remember Fannin's name in association with that case—the papers had certainly been full of it. Scrolling on through the list of references to Fannin, Laura noted a disproportionate number of narcotics cases, many of which had been dismissed on procedural grounds. It was an impressive record. Fannin was the kind of guy you wanted on your team when Big Trouble came to call. So, what was he doing on James Stanley's team?

Laura wasn't stupid or naïve enough to believe that hiring a lawyer was a sign of guilt. Anyone—innocent or not—who got caught up in a murder case *needed* legal advice, period. All the same, hiring a gun like Fannin, as opposed to just calling the old family retainer, indicated a certain state of mind on the part of James Stanley. You don't hire Christian Barnard to treat a cold.

Before she returned to the Search page, Laura's eye fell on a Georgia Supreme Court lawyer-discipline action, several years old. She read a summary of the decision with raised eyebrows. Any lawyer might get in trouble from time to time, for sloppy work, or just for displeasing a client. Craig Fannin, however, had been disciplined for improper contact with a witness. The impropriety seemed to have been sexual. *Oh, you bad boy!* Laura thought. She'd have to remember to ask Meredith what she knew about the incident.

By three-thirty, Laura was ready to go. Her brief—which really was brief, considering the length of time she had to prepare it—covered every eventuality. She didn't think that Fannin had a chance of suppressing the warrant based on case law, and judges usually weren't interested in making new law in motion hearings.

Judges other than Jones Talbot, that is. An hour later, a frustrated Laura sat in his chambers, listening to Fannin's argument. Stanley had confidentiality agreements with his clients, which, according to Fannin, made them privileged within the statutory meaning. He argued that the judge should invalidate the part of the search that involved Stanley's corporate records.

Craig Fannin looked just as Laura had pictured him—sleek, well-fed, middle-aged. He was a fastidious, if flashy, dresser, from the blazing shine on his shoes up to the crisp square of linen protruding from his pocket. His client, James Stanley, was equally well-groomed, wearing a silk tweed blazer with a black polo sweater beneath it—no tie. Stanley hadn't spoken a word; he merely sat and looked stricken and confused. He didn't look like a murderer, but murdering wasn't his regular line of country. What did a murderer look like anyway? Laura didn't pay much heed to Stanley, at any rate. Most of her attention was focused on Craig Fannin as he delivered his argument for the suppression of the evidence collected from Stanley's business in graceful, flowing periods.

Laura was itching to counter those silken arguments. Practically squirming in her chair, she looked at Meredith, pleading silently for permission to speak. Meredith nodded, and Laura spoke. "Your Honor, with all due respect, I find Mr. Fannin's argument flawed on two levels. First, the statute specifically addresses privilege only as it applies to attorney-client relationships. Mr. Fannin is trying to extend that privilege to Mr. Stanley, who is *not* an attorney. Second, regardless of confidentiality agreements, personal financial information is quite often released to third parties—banks and other creditors—and to the government. Mr. Stanley could not claim privilege if, say, the IRS requested information on one of his clients—in fact, he is obligated to provide information to the IRS every year. Finally, even if privilege could be extended to an individual in Mr. Stanley's position, evidence of criminal activity is *never* privileged."

"That's correct, Jones," Fannin said agreeably, addressing the judge instead of Laura, and addressing him by his first name at that. The technique would have irritated her if she hadn't just used it herself. Fannin continued. "But there's the matter of probable cause. There's no possible connection between my client's dealings with *his* clients, and the murder of his wife."

"That's incorrect," Laura countered. "The police have witness testimony indicating that the condition of Mr. Stanley's business was a material issue in his relations with the late Mrs. Stanley."

"The general condition of the business may have been at issue, but not the records of individual clients." Fannin flicked a phantom piece of lint from his trousers.

"How are the police supposed to determine the 'general condition of the business' without access to all its records?" Laura demanded.

"I have a suggestion," Meredith said.

"I'd be relieved to hear it," Judge Talbot answered.

"The statute allows for the appointment of a special master in cases like this. Why can't we do that?"

The judge's face brightened at this Solomonic suggestion. "A good idea. Yes, we'll have a special master examine the records seized by the police, and prepare a report to me which will tell us whether the evidence is relevant to the police investigation. Let's see—who would be qualified?" Judge Talbot pressed his fingertips together and stared at the ceiling, as if he expected a name to appear on the acoustic tiles.

"I have a suggestion," Laura ventured. "William Borden is an attorney and a retired partner in an accounting firm. My old firm used him many times. He'd be uniquely qualified."

Fannin cocked an eyebrow. "I don't think I like the idea of the district attorney nominating the special master."

Judge Talbot came unexpectedly to the rescue. "Oh, there's no problem there—Will's integrity is undoubted. He runs an arbitration service now. Yes, I agree with Miss Chastain. If Mr. Borden is available, he will be appointed special master. Until he assumes the post, however, the Atlanta Police Department will turn the disputed evidence collected under the warrant over to the Court."

"I assume that the personal financial records of Mr. and Mrs. Stanley can remain in police custody," Meredith said.

"Yes, of course. Well, if that's all, we can get back to work." Judge Talbot was clearly relieved to have had the matter settled for him. He seemed uncomfortable, Laura thought; maybe it was the residue of their earlier encounter. But she noticed that Talbot nodded his head curtly at Stanley as they all rose to leave. *He knows Stanley,* she thought. *Probably another country club connection—he should have recused himself, even from a pretrial matter.* It was something else to ask Meredith about.

Meredith, however, was more interested in talking to Fannin than to Laura. "So, Craig . . ." she was saying as Laura followed them into the hallway. "Got a new client, I see."

"Yep. Doing my best to keep the police state at bay," he replied.

"Oh, is that why you're not allowing him to talk to the police?"

"He has talked to the police."

"Last week, when they thought they were looking at a break-in. Now, they're more interested in the victim's personal life."

"I'm not going to have my client convicted by innuendo, Meredith."

"I wouldn't want that, either. Don't you think you could

put a lot of the innuendo to rest by sitting down with the detectives? Your client has an alibi, I think.''

Fannin drew a fat cigar from an inner pocket and sniffed at it appreciatively. "I might consider a parley—with ground rules.''

"Naturally. Just let us know what you need, Craig. Let's get this cleared up as soon as we can, okay?" Fannin shook Meredith's hand. "Pleasure meeting you," he said to Laura, clasping her hand firmly for a moment. "I knew Tom Bailey. I'm sorry about all that.''

Laura stiffened, as she always did when Tom's name came up. She murmured something inarticulate, resentful that Fannin had upset her before they even stepped into a courtroom.

Fannin led his still-silent client away. "So, what do you think of the great Craig Fannin?" Meredith asked Laura.

"Eh," Laura answered with a noncommittal shrug. "I'm not blown away. I know he's cozy with Judge Talbot, but did you get the impression that the judge knew James Stanley, as well?"

"No, but it wouldn't surprise me. They're all three prosperous Northside males. They probably know each other through an alumni group or some other club.''

"Then shouldn't Talbot have recused himself?''

"Simple acquaintance with a defendant isn't automatically prejudicial. After all, I see Jones Talbot socially from time to time, and that doesn't seem to influence his decisions. I might worry if the trial landed on his calendar, but I think we got a fair hearing today. You did a good job in there.''

"But you never let me cite the case law," Laura said mournfully. "I had a darn good little brief all ready.''

"I'm sorry. Maybe you'll get another chance to use the research. It just occurred to me that a special master might be a good idea, since neither we nor the cops have the staff to digest all that stuff.''

"I agree. I just wanted to win the point outright, I guess.''

"And I admire you for it. I believe you would have, too. Craig isn't really into research.''

"Speaking of which, I looked *him* up. There was a disciplinary action against him.''

"Oh, that's famous—he tampered with a witness. Or he *slept* with a witness; they never really nailed him for tampering, and it made no difference in the outcome of the trial. I have a friend who was on the Bar discipline committee at the time. He says Craig was hilarious; he admitted to everything. In his testimony, he said he *tampered* with her as often as possible, and sometimes *coached* her three or four times a night. They suspended him for six months—a slap on the wrist. He went to the Caribbean and came back married to the girl. I think she was wife number two. He's on number three or four now.''

Laura shook her head. "Don't tell me you like the guy.''

Meredith laughed. "What's not to like? He plays a good game; I'm glad to be up against him again. You'll see— it's always better to go against the best.''

"As long as we win,'' Laura said, dryly.

CHAPTER 6

Ilona Crawford, whom Laura thought of as "The PR Weenie," was skulking in the precincts of Meredith's office when she and Laura returned from the judge's chambers. Forcing a brief grimace that would never pass for a smile, Ilona launched into her request. "Marshall wants a statement on the Stanley murder. He wants me to prepare it, but you have to deliver it tomorrow afternoon for the TV people."

Marshall Oliver, the district attorney, held a regular weekly press conference. Lately, he hadn't had many good things to share with the news hounds, preoccupied as he was with fighting lawsuits and managing scarce resources. A prominent murder case was really a blessing in disguise for him—so long as it resulted in a conviction. Laura knew that there was much riding on the outcome of the Stanley case, and so did Meredith. That's why Meredith's reply to Ilona was so baffling.

"Laura can take it—she's up to speed."

"I can't speak at a press conference!" Laura proclaimed.

"Why not? You dealt with the press when you were at Prendergrast and Crawley. They're no worse now than they were then."

"Says you! What would I say anyway?"

"Ilona will handle that," Meredith said. "Just put on a little lipstick and read the statement she gives you."

"And if they have questions?"

"Answer them—have you never seen a baseball player get interviewed after a game? Just tell 'em that we're working as a team with the police department, that we expect the cops to make a case in the near future—you know how it goes. Say something without actually *saying* anything."

Ilona pressed her lips together. "I'm not sure this is a good idea. She hasn't had media training."

"Oh, for God's sake, Ilona—where were you last winter? She was on the news every night, and she did just fine. I can't do it anyway; I've got a conference with the clerk on the calendar for next month. It's Laura or no one."

"I'll check with Marshall," Ilona said. "Which one of you is going to brief me so I can write the release?"

"Laura will," Meredith said cheerfully. "She's free right now."

Ilona trailed after Laura back to her desk. "Where is the investigation now?" she asked, settling into a chair.

"With the police," Laura replied. "We really don't have a whole lot to add to their statement—if they're making one."

"So you're cooperating with the police department." Ilona scribbled on her pad. "Is an arrest expected soon?"

"That's a question for the police to answer."

"Well, what can we say?"

"Nothing. Just that we're cooperating with the police."

"And we have every confidence in their investigation?"

"I certainly do," Laura said. "Look, why don't you tell Marshall to wait until next week?"

"I can't. He wants to be on top of this case right from the start."

"Well, you'll just have to pad out what you have."

Ilona sighed and rose. "I'll send you a draft tomorrow morning. Let me know if anything else happens."

"Of course. I'll see you tomorrow." Laura shook her head after Ilona left. Would they never learn? More than one trial had been sunk by premature press coverage. More than one district attorney had come to grief by trying to ride a case to glory.

After five o'clock, the office got quieter. Most of the attorneys continued to work, but the phones rang less frequently and the hall traffic dropped off. It was the office's most productive time of the day, Laura had quickly realized, with no interruptions from defense lawyers, clerical staff, and colleagues. She routinely worked until seven or later, but she always tried to get home in time for a decent dinner. She'd eaten enough pizza and Chinese as an associate at P&C to last a long while. But what she really wanted tonight was a really good dinner in a restaurant—no dishes to wash. She was thinking about calling Amos and asking if he had dinner plans when her own phone rang. *I bet that's him—great minds think alike,* she thought as she picked up the receiver. It was Meredith.

"Laura? Good—you're still there. Really, you shouldn't be, but I'm glad you are. Listen, I got a call from Craig Fannin. He wants to 'parley,' as he calls it—what are we, the UN? Anyway, he's faxing some conditions to us. I'm at Chuck E. Cheese, so I told him to send them to the office. They should be coming over the machine right now. Go get them and call me back on my cell phone."

Laura hustled to the fax room, where one machine was quietly whirring as it expectorated paper. The message came from the law office of Craig Fannin, Esq. Laura allowed herself a moment to be irritated by his use of "Esq.," a meaningless title that some lawyers just insisted on using. The cover sheet was followed by two more pages, a letter that Laura could see contained a list of "bullet points," presumably Fannin's conditions for the parley. She began reading them as the fax continued to process.

Dear Meredith:

You have expressed a desire to meet with and interview my client, James A. Stanley. Mr. Stanley maintains that he has no involvement in the recent tragic death of his wife, Christine Connell Stanley. The Atlanta Police Department, however, is currently conducting an investigation of my client, which would seem to imply that he is a suspect in the murder of Mrs. Stanley.

In order to put any such speculation to rest, we agree to meet with you, accompanied by such members of your staff as you deem necessary, and the investigating officers handling the case for the Atlanta Police Department. Mr. Stanley is eager to schedule this meeting at the earliest opportunity, provided that you are willing to comply with certain conditions. I list these conditions in detail below.

- *Mr. Stanley's remarks will be 'off the record,' and may not be used against him in any court proceeding arising from the investigation of his wife's death.*

- *Your office and the Atlanta Police Department will submit*

*in writing lists of questions to be asked at the meeting;
Mr. Stanley will not respond to questions that do not
appear on the list.*

- *Mr. Stanley reserves the right to refuse to answer any
question submitted by your office or by the Atlanta Police
Department.*

- *The meeting will be recorded by a qualified court reporter, who
will prepare a transcript of the meeting and make it available
to all participants in the meeting within twenty-four hours
after the meeting's conclusion. Copies will be numbered, and
a record will be maintained of the persons to whom each copy
is distributed. The transcript may not be photocopied, nor may
parts of it be transcribed in any other form.*

- *After review of the transcript, Mr. Stanley reserves the right
to amend any of his responses in writing.*

- *Neither your office nor the Atlanta Police Department will
make details of the meeting, including the transcript, available to any member of the press. Mr. Stanley reserves the
right to make any information he chooses available to the
press.*

- *At the request of Mr. Stanley, all transcripts will be
returned to him.*

- *Mr. Stanley reserves the right to review all notes made
during the course of the meeting by any person attending
the meeting.*

- *No voice recordings will be made during the meeting.*

- *If you consent to these terms, we will be happy to schedule a meeting at the earliest mutually convenient time. We look forward to hearing from you.*

Golly, Laura thought as she finished reading. *He forgot to deal with procedures for excusing the participants for bathroom breaks. And how does Stanley take his coffee?* She dashed back to her desk and dialed Meredith's mobile phone. The sounds of Chuck E. Cheese were audible in the background. Laura cringed. "My God, what are they doing to those kids?"

"Preparing them to assume their roles as consumers. Did you get the fax?"

"Oh, yeah. You're going to love this." She read the letter to Meredith verbatim, pausing only when Meredith snorted in disbelief or screeched with outrage.

"Number the copies of the transcript? What does Craig think this is, a corporate takeover? I never heard of anything so ridiculous! And Stanley will be happy to manage the press—I guess we should thank him for that."

"Are we going to meet them?"

Meredith thought for a moment. "Yes. Craig is going to have to give up a point or two. I'm not going to give Stanley the right to recall all the transcripts, for instance. But we'll have a meeting. Can you fax that to my home office? I'll call Craig tonight and negotiate with him."

"Sure, but will he negotiate?"

"Now he has to. Otherwise, we can make this letter public. It makes Stanley look like a weasel. I'm surprised Craig didn't think of that."

"I think he's counting on having us *really* want this meeting."

"Well, I for one do—but if Craig wants to play games, I'm up to it. Now, go home—after you fax that out to me—and have a decent dinner."

"Thanks. Do they have alcohol at Chuck E. Cheese?"

"I'm consuming as we speak."

"Have one for me." She hung up and returned to the fax room, where she put the letter on the fax and punched in Meredith's home fax number. She made a photocopy, placed the original in a folder on Meredith's desk, and started to pack up her desk. The phone rang again. This time it was Amos.

"Chastain? I was hoping you'd be working late. You had dinner?"

"No. You?"

"Nope. How does Italian sound to you? I was thinking about Pulcinella."

"Make it Veni Vidi Vici and you've got a deal," she countered.

"Okay, I'm leaving now. I'll see you there in about twenty minutes. Last one there picks up the tab."

That was all the inspiration Laura needed to hurry herself along. The streets of downtown were eerily deserted at this hour, and she never liked the lonely walk to her car, even though the police department maintained surveillance of the courthouse and the surrounding buildings at all times. There were people desperate enough to try something even in the heart of the Justice Center. She hurried to her disreputable old Toyota, hastily locking the doors, and headed north.

The restaurant Laura had suggested was in midtown, about halfway home for Laura, and closer for Amos. It was a little bit fancier than their usual hangouts, but Laura was in the mood for some obsequious service and some really good wine. Her work clothes were good enough to pass muster with the pretentious staff, and she never had to worry about Amos; she knew that he would be dressed with perfect propriety for any restaurant in town.

He was waiting for her at the bar when she walked in. "What took you so long?" he asked innocently.

"Kowalski, did you call me from your car?"

"You'll never prove it."

"And you call yourself an officer of the law! I should report this."

"Don't be a sore loser—and remember, I wanted to go cheap. You're the one who suggested this palace."

"That's okay—I'll get you next time. Boy, do I have a story for you!"

When they were seated she told Amos about her day, and Craig Fannin's letter. "For a man who says he's innocent, James Stanley's acting like he has something to hide."

Amos shook his head. "If you ask me, Craig Fannin is just overlawyering. Stanley probably has no clue what was in that letter."

"Maybe not. But he's got to know he's suspect numero uno. You know, if I had been in Randy Travers's position, I would have started investigating Stanley right away. We've wasted almost two weeks!"

"I wouldn't say it was wasted—the investigation has eliminated one suspect, the burglar."

"But meanwhile the husband has had time to cover his tracks."

"If there are any. Look, Laura, you may be right, and you may have been right all along, but a police investigation has to be handled a certain way. Every possibility has to be looked at in turn. We're too short-handed to do everything simultaneously, so we take it one step at a time. The most obvious possibility was the burglar. Travers eliminated that. So, now he moves on to the family members."

"That's another thing—he's investigating Christine Stanley's sister! It's just silly."

"You think so? Maybe she's as innocent as I am, but

Travers has to eliminate her. You've got to be a little patient."

"Are you lecturing me, Amos?"

"No, just trying to curb your rookie enthusiasm. Now, what are you having?"

Laura turned her attention to the menu, and the subject changed. She didn't think about the letter again until she was brushing her teeth, pleasantly drowsy from a good dinner and half a bottle of Italian wine. *I'd have given a whole dollar to hear Meredith "negotiate" with Fannin,* she thought as she closed her eyes. Lawyers just love that kind of stuff.

CHAPTER 7

The interrogation room at the Atlanta Police Department's homicide division was not an inviting place. There was nothing in the room that could be used as, or converted to, a weapon: the chairs were the kind of one-piece molded plastic butt-busters that were favored by high school cafeterias and mental institutions; the table was bolted to the floor; the light fixtures were caged. The walls and floor were a dull institutional gray. The whole room could have been hosed down without harming its furnishings, which was precisely the point.

The choice of venue for the "parley" was a concession Meredith had won in the negotiations, so the meeting was being held here, instead of in a well-upholstered conference room at Craig Fannin's office, or even among the dubious comforts of the district attorney's quarters. "It'll put Mr. Stanley in the proper frame of mind," Meredith said.

Meredith had won a couple of other points, too. For one thing, the whole ridiculous notion of having transcripts of the meeting numbered had been discarded, as had Fannin's demands that copies of all notes taken during the meeting be turned over to him. In return, Meredith had promised Fannin that the district attorney's press release would state that James Stanley was not a suspect.

"How can you say that?" Laura wailed to Meredith when she found out. "Of course he's a suspect!"

Meredith waggled her eyebrows. "Oh, I have my reasons. Here's the release Ilona and I drafted—tell me what you think."

Laura took the piece of paper and read:

> *Good afternoon. My name is Laura Chastain, C-H-A-S-T-A-I-N. I am an assistant district attorney in the Fulton County district attorney's office. The district attorney's office is cooperating with the Atlanta Police Department in the investigation of the murder of Christine Stanley. No suspects have been named at this time, although a number of individuals are assisting in the investigation. The victim's husband, James Stanley, has agreed to meet with police investigators and representatives of the district attorney's office. The police investigators and the district attorney hope that Mr. Stanley can provide information that will be helpful in the investigation. Thank you.*

"And Fannin was satisfied with this?" she asked. Saying that "no suspects have been named at this time" was a far cry from saying that James Stanley was not a suspect.

"I didn't give him approval of the wording. I just told him that we would say that Stanley wasn't named as a suspect."

Laura snorted. "Specious reasoning, Meredith!"

Meredith shrugged, unconcerned. "It got us the meeting. Anyway, Randy likes the sister for this as much as he likes Stanley now."

"That's ridiculous. She's got no motive. But Stanley has motive coming out his ears."

"That remains to be seen. Now, let me look at you. Very nice. Just look at one of the reporters and deliver the statement to him, and step away from the microphone as soon as you've said, 'Thank you.'"

"I wish you'd reconsider this," Laura said. "You'd do much better than I will . . ."

But in the end she had delivered the release to an eager press, accompanied by Marshall Oliver. After she stepped away from the mic, he had fielded the questions, and had done as admirable a job of parsing the statement that "no suspects have been named" as any White House aide could have done. Fannin had evidently been satisfied with the tone of the press coverage the previous evening, because they were expecting him and his client at any minute. In the meantime, Laura shifted in her plastic chair and tried to get comfortable.

"Sure you won't take some coffee?" Carlton Hemingway asked. Travers had barely acknowledged Laura's arrival.

"No, thanks. I have a bottle of water." Laura had tasted police station coffee before, and in her opinion Amnesty International ought to look into it.

"Y'all got your questions ready?" Meredith asked the detectives.

Travers made a contemptuous noise in his throat that sounded like *"Bullshit."* "What if we get on to a topic that I want to explore, but I haven't written down the questions I want to ask?"

"Don't sweat it," Meredith said. "Once we get going,

Fannin knows he can't start drawing lines. I just wish that we had the special master's report."

William Borden had accepted the appointment as special master; he and a staff of two had been burrowing into Stanley's papers, at Stanley's office, for two days. His report was due by the end of the week, which was three days away. Fannin had probably engineered this meeting to take place before the report was ready.

"Well . . ." Travers said, grinning. "It just so happens that our accounting guy got a peek at those records before the judge ordered them turned over to the special master. He didn't want to say anything for attribution, but he thinks there's been some hanky-panky." Travers produced a small notebook and read from it. "Some comingling of client funds with ordinary business accounts, a few transactions he couldn't find client authorization for. He thinks they're the sort of things that could get him disciplined by the regulators, but not prima facie evidence of crimes being committed. But he suggests that we ask why he invested his kids' money in a hedge fund that lost a bunch of money."

"You know about that, Laura?" Meredith asked. Laura was going to handle the financial questions.

"Yes, it showed up in the personal financial records. But Stanley had some of his own money in there, too, although he didn't lose a nickel. In fact, he made money. Is that what your man noticed, Randy?"

"Yes, but he also thought that there was a quid pro quo involved. It looks like Stanley invested in this loser fund because he was getting business from its manager."

"That's self-dealing," Laura said. "That could get him removed as a trustee even without a divorce."

"That's good to know, Randy," Meredith said. "Laura, be sure you get that into your questions. Oh, here they come." She rose and greeted Craig Fannin and his client as they entered the grim little room, just as if she was receiving guests at her own house. "Craig! Glad you could make it! You know everyone, I think?"

"I haven't met this gentleman," Fannin said, extending a hand to Carlton Hemingway, who introduced himself. "And I believe you've all met my client."

They all acknowledged Stanley with curt nods. Fannin, even as an opponent, was a charmer. Even Laura conceded that he was attractive, with a warm smile and a way of meeting gazes head-on that would be very effective with a jury. Stanley inspired no such warm feelings. He was a smallish, slightly built man, dressed fastidiously in imitation of *GQ* style, which he failed to carry off. He would not do particularly well with a jury, Laura thought, especially the female members of a jury. He was too prissy.

"Shall we begin?" Meredith said. "I see you've brought your own coffee, Craig—very wise. You have our prepared questions, of course."

"Yes."

"Well, then, if there are no objections, I suggest we get rolling." Meredith nodded to the court reporter, who from that point on began recording every word that was spoken. Meredith gave the date, time, and names of all the participants in the meeting, then turned the floor over to Randy Travers.

Travers cleared his throat. "Mr. Stanley, thanks for coming down. We're going to go over some of the information you gave us in your initial statement two weeks ago. You were out of town on the evening of May 8, is that correct?"

"That's correct," Stanley said, glancing at Fannin as if for approval. "I was in Charlotte, North Carolina."

Fannin opened his briefcase and took out some papers. "These are copies of my client's plane ticket and his hotel

room receipt. You'll see that they support his statement."
He gave copies to Travers and to Meredith.

Travers took a long look at the papers. "Your flight
arrived in Charlotte at seven-thirty P.M.?" he asked.

Stanley nodded.

"Please give your answers aloud," Meredith interrupted, "so they can be recorded."

"Sorry. Yes. At seven-thirty."

"And you checked into the Marriott at—let's see—
eight-oh-five P.M.?"

"If that's what the receipt says, yes; I don't remember
the exact time."

"And what did you do after that?"

"I ordered room service, and watched television. Oh,
and I called home as soon as I got to the room. I actually
made two phone calls home, but no one answered. I left
messages on the answering machine."

Fannin was ready to support his client again. "You'll
see the charges for his dinner and the phone calls on the
bill."

Laura craned her neck to look at the hotel record,
which Meredith pushed toward her. The bill listed the
time of the phone calls, as well as the numbers—both the
same, both in the 404 area code. She felt a vague sense of
disappointment; it would be awfully hard to fake a detailed
hotel record.

Fannin seemed to read her mind. "And here's a copy
of the answering machine tape. Shall I play it for you?"

"Please," Travers said.

Fannin inserted the miniature cassette into a tiny player,
and clicked a button. Stanley's voice sounded tinny and
small.

*"Hi, honey, it's me. I'm at the hotel. Room, ahh, 407. I guess
you're busy with the kids—I'll call back after they're in bed."*

Then some whirrs, and clicks, before he spoke again. *"Hi, it's me again. It's eleven-fifteen. I'm turning in now, but call me if you want to talk. Love you."*

"Was there a time and date stamp on the machine?" Hemingway asked.

"Yes," Fannin answered. "The first call was made at nine-fifteen, and the second, as my client indicates on the tape, at eleven-fifteen. I have the answering machine, with its original messages, at my office. I'd be happy to submit it to you."

"Please," Travers said. "Now, Mr. Stanley, tell us why you were in Charlotte."

"I had business there. I sell products from a couple of the banks and brokerages there to my clients—CDs, funds, partnerships. I go up there pretty regularly to meet with my contacts."

"I see. Mr. Stanley, was your business profitable?"

Stanley hesitated, and glanced at Fannin, who nodded. "Well, it's hard to say exactly. I'm a financial manager. I set up the firm about four years ago. There are a lot of, umm, up-front costs, you know—setting up an office, hiring, getting systems in place. And then there's marketing, you know, entertaining prospective clients and all that."

"But were you making money?" Travers said.

"Well, we had good cash flow, but no, I guess you would say we were still in the red. Technically."

"I see. And had you borrowed money from your wife to help start the business?"

"Yes, a little . . ."

"And from you children's trust funds."

"Once or twice. Look, I gave them all partnership units—it's not like I just took the money! It's perfectly normal. The other trustees knew about it, and no one objected."

"That's fine, Mr. Stanley," Travers said smoothly. "That leads me to your personal financial situation. You have a large mortgage on the Lakehaven house, I think?"

"Yes," Stanley said. "It's a large house. But in keeping with our income."

"In keeping with your income, or your children's trust fund income?" Hemingway interjected.

Stanley turned to him, angry. "It's the same thing. I am their trustee, and it is my job—as a trustee *and* as a parent—to give them an appropriate upbringing."

"We understand that," Travers said smoothly, "but the house is in your name and your wife's, not the children's names."

Stanley emitted a burst of air from his lungs, frustrated. "It's the same thing, dammit! Just what are you getting at anyway?"

"I'm not 'getting at' anything, sir. Is it true that your wife had asked you for a divorce?"

"No! And I don't give a damn what Lynette has told you—it's not true! Why aren't you questioning her?"

"James . . ." Fannin said, placing a warning hand on his client's arm. "Mrs. Stanley had not asked for a divorce. There were some rough patches in the marriage, but the Stanleys were working them out in good faith. They wanted to stay together for the sake of the children."

"That's not what Mr. Frank Watson says," Hemingway replied.

"Who is Mr. Frank Watson?" Fannin asked.

"He is the attorney Mrs. Stanley had contacted about a divorce, just about a month before her death."

Laura was surprised by this bit of information, but apparently not nearly so much as Stanley was. He rose to his feet. *"Bullshit!"* he shouted. "That's a damn lie!"

"I have here a statement from Mr. Watson, to the effect

that your late wife made an appointment with him to discuss the possibility of a divorce on April 17." Hemingway produced a piece of paper and waved it. *You go, Carlton!* Laura silently cheered.

Fannin extended his hand. "May I have a copy? Thank you. Now, Meredith, this line of questioning was not on our preapproved list."

"Gosh, Craig," Meredith said. "I didn't know a thing about this. But since it's on the table, shouldn't we explore a little?"

"Give me a moment to read Mr. Watson's statement." Fannin read over the page carefully, and put it down. "I see nothing here that indicates that my client knew about his wife's visit to this attorney. As I said, he was making a good-faith effort to restore the marriage. What his wife did without his consent or knowledge cannot be held against him."

Point to Fannin, Laura conceded.

"Let's move on, then," Meredith said. "Ms. Chastain has a few questions pertaining to the structure of your late wife's and your children's trusts, Mr. Stanley."

Laura had been assigned this part of the questioning because of her marginally greater knowledge of trust issues. She'd had a bit of family law experience at P&C, she warned Meredith, but wills and trusts were way beyond her expertise. "Just ask a few leading questions," Meredith had suggested, "and we'll see where they take us."

"Mr. Stanley, who are the trustees for your children?"

"Me, and my wife . . . was. Her father, her sister Lynette, and the family attorney, Bradley Mellott."

"I see. And who controls the investments made by the trust?"

"Well, all of us."

"No, I mean who managed the investment decisions day to day?"

"I did. I was the most qualified."

"Did the other trustees ever object to any investment you made?"

Stanley licked his lips and took a gulp of his coffee before answering. "Yes. Lynette did, regularly. But my wife always agreed with me."

"And Mr. Mellott?"

"He usually needed an explanation of what we were trying to do, but once I talked to him he was generally all right with whatever we did."

"Does that include an investment you made in a hedge fund last year that resulted in a substantial write-off?"

"Yes. Yes, it does. Not all investments are winners, Ms. Chastain." Stanley's voice was ringing with sarcasm.

"No, of course not, Mr. Stanley, but I was wondering how it is that your own personal investment in the same fund did *not* result in a loss." She folded her hands and looked at Stanley.

"Again, Meredith, I have to object—this wasn't on the preapproved list of questions," Fannin said sternly.

"But it would be nice to have an answer, wouldn't it?" Meredith said.

Fannin leaned toward his client and whispered something. Stanley whispered a reply. Fannin nodded. "My client says that the difference was in the timing of the investment—he invested his own funds before he placed any of his children's money in the fund. While he didn't have an actual *loss*, his return was far from what he had been led to expect by the fund manager. He withdrew his and his children's investments at the same time. Unfortunately, their investment had to be written down considerably, while my client's was marginally profitable—owing to the longer investment period."

It was a reasonable explanation—if you thought that putting your kid's money in a hedge fund was a reasonable thing to do. Laura pushed ahead. "Did you do any other business with the manager of that fund, Mr. Stanley?"

"A little, yes."

"Were your investments in his fund a quid pro quo for business consideration for your firm?"

"No! Absolutely not! Do you think I'd play that game with my own children's money?"

"I don't know, Mr. Stanley. Did Ms. Connell or Mr. Mellott ever object to these particular investments?"

"I don't remember. Lynette probably did—she objected to everything I did."

"Do you know what self-dealing is, Mr. Stanley?"

"That's out of line," Fannin boomed. "I insist that this line of questioning end right now."

"Okay," Travers said, unruffled. "I just have a few more questions, if that's okay." Fannin nodded his assent. "Mr. Stanley, who do you think killed your wife?"

Stanley gaped for a moment, and looked at Fannin, who nodded again. "I . . . I think it was a botched burglary. There's more than one housebreaker out there—just because you folks found one who *didn't* do it doesn't mean that someone else still out there couldn't have done this. In fact, I'm going to offer a reward—fifty thousand dollars for any information leading to an arrest and conviction. I figure that'll make up for your lack of interest in investigating my wife's murder."

"We always appreciate help," Travers said coolly. "Did you or your wife have any enemies?"

"Enemies? No! Are you saying this may have been a revenge thing?"

"No possibility can be overlooked."

"Well, I'm in a tough line of business—there may be some clients who were angry with me. But mad enough to kill Chrissie? I don't know ... It bears looking into, I guess."

Fannin straightened in his chair and snapped his briefcase closed. "I think that will do."

"We appreciate your cooperation," Meredith said. "If we have more questions, would you be willing to meet with us again?"

"On similar terms, yes, I suppose so," Fannin replied amiably. Then to the court reporter, he said, "This concludes the meeting. Please deliver transcripts to me, to Ms. Gaffney, and to Detective Travers. I think that's all." He rose, and Stanley followed him from the room.

"That went about as well as could be expected," Meredith said. "What did you think, Laura?"

"He seemed sincerely bereaved, and he had answers for everything. His alibi is pretty convincing."

"It's a lock," Travers conceded. "We move on from here to a killer-for-hire theory. I don't think there's anything in the revenge killing, but did you see how he went for it?"

Meredith nodded. "Are you really looking at his clients?"

Travers shrugged. "I like a family member in situations like this, but I've seen stranger things. But the sister is looking better and better to us." He flipped open his ubiquitous notebook. "Lynette Connell, age thirty. Lives with her father, Lester Connell, age sixty-eight, at 1022 Connell's Farm Lane in Marietta. She's got a record—one DUI, one misdemeanor possession of marijuana. That was about two years ago. Dad keeps her on a short string; apparently she's the wild one in the family. She went to the university but never finished her degree. She's never held a job, either, unless you count giving horseback riding lessons out at her father's place. She has a trust fund, like her sister's, but she doesn't have control of the income.''

"In other words, her motive is identical to James Stanley's," Meredith reflected.

"Yep. But there's another thing. Carlton, what about that stuff you got on Lynette's associates?"

"Not good folks, I'm afraid. In addition to her drug buddies, she had a boyfriend last year who is a registered gun dealer."

Laura managed to control her voice. "Did you find out where she was when her sister was killed?"

"Yes," Hemingway answered. "She has an alibi, too—she was away in Tennessee at a horse show. She was competing in one category and judging in another, so she was away from Tuesday until she heard about her sister on Friday. She's got receipts and witnesses who place her there the entire time she says she was."

"So," Travers said, "it seems that motive isn't the only thing Lynette Connell has in common with her brother-in-law. Iron-clad alibis must run in the family."

CHAPTER 8

Cheryl's voice was taut with irritation. "That *woman* is here again."

"Which woman would that be, Cheryl?" Laura asked.

"You know—Miss Thing," Cheryl sniffed. "She says that she has to see you right now."

She could only mean Lynette Connell, although Lynette was certainly not the only person capable of inspiring irritation in Cheryl.

"Tell her I'll be right with her." Laura hung up the phone and closed her eyes. This was an encounter she did not want to have—Lynette had to know that she had made Travers's short list of folks who were "good for" the murder. She probably saw Laura as an advocate for her innocence. *I shouldn't have talked to her in the first place,* Laura chided herself. *I'll just have to get rid of her.* She pushed back from her desk and walked to the lobby.

Lynette was standing by the reception desk, arms folded

across her chest. She was wearing an expensive-looking trouser suit, and her thick, dark hair was piled into an artfully disheveled "up-do." She was so effortlessly elegant, so wantonly beautiful. Laura felt a pang of envy, mixed with admiration.

Lynette, however, was not in the mood to be contemplated as an object of beauty. She started talking even before Laura reached her side. "What do you know about all this bullshit?"

"Hello, Lynette. This isn't the place. Let's go into the conference room."

"Uh-uh," Cheryl said. "It's being used. All day."

Laura sighed. "Let's go get a cup of coffee, then. I'll get my purse."

She guided Lynette to an out-of-the-way luncheonette where she hoped they wouldn't be seen. "I shouldn't be talking to you," she warned Lynette as they waited for their coffee. "You're the subject of a police investigation."

"Don't I know it? Everybody I've ever slept with, partied with, or just talked to seems to have been questioned by the cops—and that's a long list, believe me. And it seems that because I have a little marijuana bust on my record, I'm now the prime suspect in my sister's murder."

"Calm down, Lynette. You're not the 'prime suspect.' The police are just doing their job. Besides, you have an alibi, don't you?"

"Of course I do! Don't tell me that *you* think . . ."

"I don't think anything. That's the cops' job. But, Lynette, there are a couple of things that raise questions. You say that James wanted your sister dead so he could get hold of the income from the children's trusts. Well, you stand to benefit, too, as a trustee."

"How? How?" Lynette thumped the table in frustration. "If I killed Chrissie, James would become sole guard-

ian of the kids. I would be a trustee, same as I am now—
and I don't see a nickel of that money now, believe you
me!"

"But if James were convicted of killing your sister, you
would presumably inherit the guardianship."

"Oh, my God! Am I supposed to be that subtle? I not
only killed my sister, but I'm framing James for it? I wish
I'd have known I was this smart when I was flunking out
at the university."

Laura couldn't help but smile. "You have to understand
that a police investigation is a process of elimination,"
she said soothingly, quoting Amos's lecture to her nearly
verbatim. "They're looking at everyone. They're also looking at clients who might have had a grudge against James—
did you know that? You're not alone in this."

"Tell that to the people who were questioned about
me! The director of the horse show was appalled—I doubt
she'll ever ask me to judge again! And to dig up my old
boyfriends—that's going too far."

Laura swirled her coffee thoughtfully. *I should not be
having this conversation, but if I'm in for a penny, I might as
well be in for a pound.* "About the boyfriend—the one who
was a gun dealer . . ."

"See? You do think I'm a suspect! Well, for your information, Jesse is not a gun dealer—at least not the kind who
sells handguns to murderers. He sells high-end hunting
weapons, shotguns and rifles. Custom stocks and barrels.
You can ask my father—he's the one who introduced me
to Jesse. He bought a shotgun from him last year. We dated
for all of three months last summer. He turned out to be
a jerk, not unlike every other guy I've dated, and when he
found out that I don't have any money of my own, he
couldn't light out for the territory fast enough. Not that
I would have kept him around much longer anyway. Jesse

has some talent, but not enough to keep a girl enthralled more than a few weeks. No, as soon as he saw the lay of the land, he was outta there. I was mildly upset for about an hour."

"Did James know Jesse?"

"Jesse and James met a couple of times, and they seemed to get along fine. But I wouldn't say they were tight; Jesse couldn't do anything for James's career, and that's The Asshole's sole criterion for all his relationships: *How can this person help James Stanley?*"

"Lynette, when you called me a while back, you said you thought you knew where James might have gotten a gun. Was it from Jesse?"

Lynette hesitated. "Ye-es, I thought so at the time. But like I said, Jesse doesn't handle handguns."

"Surely he knows people who do, though."

She shrugged. "He goes to all those gun shows, and he's a social animal. The gun show circuit is a little bit creepy, and I'm sure he's met some shady types. But he would have told the cops if James had asked to be hooked up with a gun. Jesse wouldn't take a fall for anyone, let alone James."

"So, you've changed your mind?"

"I guess so. Besides, James didn't need to get a gun to kill Chrissie."

"Oh? Why not?"

"Because he hired someone to do it for him—can't you see? That's why he has this big elaborate alibi!"

Laura didn't want to point out that Lynette's alibi was just as "big and elaborate" as James's. She changed the subject. "Lynette, I really, *really* should not discuss this with you. But speaking of alibis, you were at the Nashville Classic, I guess."

"Yes—they told you where I was?"

"Not really; they just said you were in Tennessee at a horse show, and I figured it had to be the Classic. I'm from Nashville, and I rode in it a time or two."

"No kidding! I should have known you were a rider—you've got the build for it. Where do you ride now?"

"Nowhere, really. My good old horse is out to pasture up in Tennessee, and the way I work, it would be cruel for me to get another one—I couldn't ride regularly enough."

"Well, come ride mine! What do you ride?"

"I showed on hunter-jumpers, but I'll ride anything for fun. What do you keep?"

"Hunter-jumpers—mostly warmbloods, and a couple of thoroughbreds. I have a Belgian warmblood who'd be just perfect for you—you really have to come out to the farm! We have a great setup. I've just had the main arena rebuilt; it's gorgeous. We even have a Grand Prix ring—at least we call it the Grand Prix ring, although it's really just a paddock. But I can give you a good ride."

"I'd like to, after . . . when . . ."

"Oh, yes, when I'm cleared of my sister's murder. I forgot. Well, just give me a call." Lynette stood up. She seemed angry.

"I hope you're not taking this personally, Lynette. I have a job to do, and I'm kind of low woman on the ladder here. I'm not in control of the investigation."

Lynette's frown softened. "I know. I'm just—it's hard enough to lose your sister, but to have the police looking at everything you do . . . I'm frustrated. I wish the guys investigating me knew what it was like to lose someone you love this way—then they might go a little easier on their suspects."

Laura said nothing, but she thought of those terrible days and weeks after Tom's murder. She wanted to tell Lynette that she *had* been there, that she of all people could understand, but she couldn't bring herself to say anything. "It'll all be wrapped up soon," was all she could manage, with a weak and unconvincing smile.

"And then we'll ride," Lynette said.

"It's a deal."

The meeting with Lynette left Laura dispirited for the rest of the day. One of many things that was lacking in Laura's life was a close girlfriend, someone who shared her interests. She would very much have liked to take up Lynette's offer of a ride, for the sake of her company as much as for the joy of being back up on a horse again. Amos was a wonderful companion, but he was about as far from a girlfriend as hormones could make him. Laura's college and law school buddies were scattered from New York to California. She had tried participating in alumni events in Atlanta, but everyone who attended them seemed to be married, with children, living in the distant suburbs. And here it was, the Friday night before Memorial Day, and what was she doing? Cooking out at Amos's house. But Kenny Newton and his wife, Cindy, would be there—that brightened Laura's prospects a little. She didn't see nearly enough of Kenny these days.

"Laura, do you have a minute?" Meredith was poking her head around the doorway of Laura's cubicle, wearing an uncharacteristically solemn look on her face.

"Sure. What's the matter?"

"Fannin's had a press conference. Come into my office—I think we need to be private for this."

Laura had a sinking feeling in the pit of her stomach. *This is about my meeting with Lynette,* she thought irrationally. Of course no one could have known about it—especially not Craig Fannin, but Meredith seemed so stern that Laura figured she had to have done something to upset the boss. Her contact with Lynette was the only thing she could think of that was likely to cause trouble. "Look, Meredith, she came in here this morning and asked to see me. She's completely capable of making a scene. I thought it would be best just to listen to what she had to say . . ."

"Who are you talking about?"

"Lynette Connell. Isn't that what you want to see me about?"

"No—but, dammit, stop talking to her. I don't care what kind of scene she can make. I don't need Randy on my back." They had reached Meredith's office. Meredith shut the door and waved Laura into a chair. "No, I wanted to talk to you about Fannin's press conference. There's going to be some fallout, and I'd prefer that you hear it from me." She handed Laura a press release. "That was his opening statement."

Laura took the single sheet of paper and read.

> James Stanley, husband of Brookhaven murder victim Christine Stanley, has retained the firm of Craig Fannin and Associates to represent him. Mr. Stanley is cooperating with the Atlanta Police Department and the Fulton County district attorney's office in their investigation. Mr. Stanley is not a suspect at this time, according to the police investigators and Senior Assistant District Attorney Meredith Gaffney . . .

"Nice of him to reword our press release," Laura commented.

"Read on," Meredith said grimly.

> Mr. Stanley, although not under suspicion, met voluntarily with the investigating team this week to offer information. Mr. Stanley was in Charlotte, North Carolina, on the night of the murder. He provided the investigators with airplane

and hotel records confirming his whereabouts—it was clever of Fannin to avoid the use of the word "alibi;" no matter how innocuous the word was in reality, it implied guilt and suspicion—*at the time of his wife's tragic and brutal murder. "Mr. Stanley had no involvement in his wife's death," Craig Fannin stated categorically. "The police and district attorney have wasted a good deal of time, first in seeking a known burglar who was in custody at the time of the murder, and then in looking into my client's finances and his relationship with his wife. The police seem to have discounted the probability that the killer was not known to Mrs. Stanley, despite numerous signs of forcible entry into the house. Certain evidence collected at the crime scene and turned over to the state crime lab also seems to have been discounted. Mr. Stanley hired me to ensure that the investigation is kept on track and that the police and district attorney do not overlook any possible solution to this horrible crime. My client's only wish is to see the killer brought to justice, so that he and his children can mourn the loss of a beloved wife and mother in private."*

"Well, it's obnoxious, but we don't have any control over what Fannin says," Laura said. "Are you going to respond?"

Meredith shook her head. "To that? No. But there was a question and answer session after he read his little statement. I don't know exactly what was said, but Ilona and I have already fielded a couple of calls from reporters. Laura, he's making an issue of *you.*"

"Me? How? Is it Lynette?"

"Will you stop with the Lynette stuff? No, I'm afraid it's Jeff Williams again. And Tom."

"But no one said a word after I read our statement the other day—I thought they had forgotten all about me!"

"They probably had, but Craig seems to have given them a not-so-subtle nudge in your direction."

"But what does it matter? I mean, what happened with Williams has nothing whatsoever to do with Christine Stanley's murder."

"You would think not. And yet two reporters want to know about your emotional state. Judging from their questions, they seem to want you to be filled with remorse at Tom's death, and determined to prove your mettle by convicting James Stanley of murder."

"That's ridiculous! For one thing, I'm way down the chain of command on this investigation. For another—what business is it of theirs what my emotional state is?"

"None, really, but they're asking anyway. I laughed them off the phone, and Ilona 'no commented' them, but I'm afraid that you're going to be back in the spotlight for a day or two. Thank God it's Friday. Maybe they'll cool their jets over the weekend. What are your plans for the weekend?"

"Nothing special—Amos is kicking off the Memorial Day weekend with a cookout tonight. Kenny Newton and his wife are coming."

"Good. Maybe you should stay with Amos for a couple of days."

"I don't want to stay there! I want to be in my own bed, now that I have one again."

"Suit yourself, but think about it. I never saw the reporter who Amos Kowalski couldn't deal with."

"They probably won't even come after me, you know," Laura said.

"Maybe not. But if they do, I wouldn't talk to them if I were you. They've already got a story in their little heads: *Assistant District Attorney Has a Past*—that sort of thing. Just say nothing to them, and maybe they'll drop it."

In Laura's experience, "they" usually didn't drop it until every minute aspect of a story had been exhaustively examined. Maybe Meredith was right—Amos had been her shield and defender when it first happened. Maybe she should cower in his guestroom once again. "I'll keep my mouth shut," she said as she rose to leave Meredith's office. "What does Fannin hope to accomplish by dragging me into this?"

"Distraction, pure and simple. The more attention they pay to you, the less they pay to James Stanley."

"Great. Have a good weekend, okay?"

"I'll see you Tuesday."

Laura left the office with every intention of not thinking or talking about Christine Stanley's murder for an entire seventy-two hours.

CHAPTER 9

Kenny Newton was the one person Laura could always count on to take her mind off things—maybe because he was the only truly happy person she knew. Kenny thought his life was just perfect, and who was to say it wasn't? He loved his wife and their three bumptious children just as much as he loved his work as a private investigator—this despite having been attacked and injured by Laura's erstwhile crooked-cop client, the infamous, thankfully late Jeff Williams. Kenny hadn't allowed Laura to waste a lot of time in feeling guilty, however, and even though his limping walk, supported by a cane, was a constant, unhappy reminder of last December's events, Laura was always eager to see the big detective.

"Hey, shug!" he greeted her as soon as she stepped onto Amos's patio. "Lordy, you get better lookin' every time I see you! Doesn't she, Cindy?"

"Of course she does," Kenny's unflappable wife said

as she gave Laura a hug. "She could gain a pound or two, I think. You're not dieting, are you, hon?"

"No, I'm working for the district attorney—it's the next best thing to running a triathlon. What about you? You're looking mighty svelte."

"Finally got rid of the baby weight—just in time to chase the little rascal around the house all day."

"Oh, he's walking already?"

"No, he's *running,* everywhere, all the time. I never saw a child in such a hurry. Ken, did you bring the pictures?"

Laura and Amos performed the requisite ooh-ing and aah-ing that married couples expected of their single friends, aided by the fact that the three Newton children really were very attractive. The purpose of the ritual photograph display was, of course, to stir the hormones of the single friends to such a pitch that they would rush immediately out and book the church. Neither Amos nor Laura seemed particularly susceptible to the tactic, but Kenny hoped eternally.

When the pictures had been put up, and Amos and Kenny had lit the fire, Kenny settled down beside Laura and took a pull on his beer. "Look at that cat—I can't believe that Amos Kowalski lets a little kitty cat run his life."

"But Mr. Kitty is such a good boy!" Laura cooed as the cat in question jumped onto her lap. "Did you know that Amos has never given him a name? He just calls him Cat, so I call him *Mr.* Cat. Or Mr. Kitty, or Señor Gato, if I'm in an international mood."

"Isn't that sweet?" Kenny smirked. He was one of those men who pretended not to like cats. "So, I hear you're mixed up in this murder in Brookhaven."

"Yep. What do you think?"

"There's nothing like rich people when they get to killing each other."

"So you think money was the motive?"

"Is there any other?"

"Well, love, I suppose."

"I find that's usually pretty well tied in to money."

"You do not—you can't pretend to be cynical about love, Kenny Newton."

He laughed. "Okay, I'll qualify my statement: love and money in Northside Atlanta are often inseparable."

"So, you think maybe the husband did it?"

"I think maybe yes, he did. He's the most obvious candidate, and, sadly, it usually is the most obvious candidate in these domestic things."

"What about one of the husband's vengeful clients? He seemed to be good at losing other people's money."

"So why would an angry client shoot the wife—assuming he was mad enough to shoot anyone? No, I don't buy it. Is that what Randy Travers is looking at?"

Laura worded her answer carefully. Kenny was a former cop, and he undoubtedly knew Travers. "I think he's exhausting all avenues. There's really not a lot of hard evidence, and the husband has a very strong alibi."

"What? That he was out of town?"

Laura nodded. "His lawyer gave us copies of the plane ticket and the hotel bill."

Kenny snorted. "And Travers was satisfied with that?"

"Well, maybe not *satisfied,* but he's looking pretty carefully at Christine Stanley's sister, and the husband's clients. He doesn't seem too keen on going after the husband, unless he thinks Stanley hired a killer."

"Maybe, maybe. Has he checked out the alibi?"

"I suppose so, but it's pretty hard to dispute—there were phone calls on the hotel bill that match up to calls on the Stanleys' answering machine. He can't have been in two places at once, can he?''

''I can't say. Look, I don't want to criticize Randy— he's the best. But he's also taking early retirement. He's tired, and he's a little bitter, from what I hear, about the way he's been treated.''

''What do you mean?''

''Just that certain highly paid officers were offered retirement packages with the not-so-subtle message that if they didn't take them, they might not be able to stay in the jobs they were in—or even keep their rank. It's a 'cost-saving' program—a pretty shortsighted one, too. They're kissing off years—*decades*—of experience.''

''Wow. I thought he seemed kind of lackadaisical. But his partner's on the ball. Do you know Carlton Hemingway?''

''Never met the man. Nice name, though.''

''Isn't it? He seems to be carrying a lot of the work of the investigation.''

''Maybe he's verified that paper alibi, then.''

''What do you mean, paper alibi?''

''You think a plane ticket and a hotel receipt can't be faked? No, if you really want to eliminate the husband as the shooter, you gotta have someone reliable place him on that plane, and in that hotel, when he says he was there.''

''But the phone calls . . .''

''Please!'' Kenny said, waving away her objection. ''Look, if you were going to murder your wife, couldn't you cook up a clever scheme that would allow you to be in two places at once?''

Laura thought for a minute. ''Yes,'' she finally said. ''I mean, I don't know if I could cook up a clever scheme exactly, but James Stanley strikes me as the clever-scheme type."

"There you are, then. You just concentrate on how James Stanley could have been in two places at once. If he can't have been, then you go on and look at other suspects, or at a hired killer. But if you find that alibi's just paper after all, you might catch you a bad guy."

Laura needed no further incentive to break her resolution not to think about the murder. As she and Amos were cleaning up the dishes, Amos took note of her preoccupation. "I saw you and Kenny with your heads together," he said. "What were you talking about? Christine Stanley, I presume?"

"Yes. He's interested in the case. He thinks Randy Travers may be giving it short shrift. Did you know Travers was taking early retirement?"

"Yes, and I'm sorry about it. He's a good cop. But I don't think that he's capable of giving anything 'short shrift,' no matter how crappily he's been treated."

"Isn't it possible that he has a lot on his mind these days? Look at how this murder investigation has been handled so far. We wasted a week tracking down a phantom burglar who turns out to have been in jail. The victim's sister—who has her own alibi and no motive to speak of—seems to be a prime suspect, while James Stanley waltzes around Atlanta saying whatever he pleases."

"Your criticism is predicated on your belief that the husband is guilty. Randy can't afford to jump to conclusions like that. He knows that if he lets his mind get fixed on one possibility, others will elude him."

"But even you have to admit that the husband has the best motive!"

Amos sighed as he dried a platter. "Since when does

a killer need a motive? And there's another thing—Mere-dith tells me that the reporters are after you again.''

"They don't bother me."

"Just the same, I wish you would bunk here for a few days."

"No, but thanks. My phone number is unlisted and no one knows my new address. They can only find me at work, and to get to me there they have to go through Ilona and Meredith first. I'll be okay."

She spoke too soon. When she arrived home, Laura's answering machine was blinking crazily, loaded with messages from a newspaper reporter who apparently believed that if he called every ten minutes he had a good chance of getting an interview with her. She deleted all his invitations and imprecations, annoyed that he seemed to have had no trouble getting her unlisted number. He must have somehow obtained a copy of the supposedly sacred district attorney's office phone list. At least he hadn't been parked in front of her house, awaiting her return. Laura was reassured that she wasn't *that* great a story. But her conversation with Kenny was uppermost in her mind. She hustled back to her new study, which still smelled of fresh paint. Her briefcase sat on the desktop. She plowed into it, rustling papers until she produced what she wanted.

The photocopies of James Stanley's travel records on the night of the murder hadn't seemed very significant to her when Craig Fannin had distributed them in their meeting. She had taken for granted that Stanley had been where he said he was—the two phone calls that showed up on the hotel bill had been especially convincing. She had no more than glanced at the papers since. But now, in the light of Kenny's contempt of "paper alibis," there were a couple of things that struck her as odd.

There had to be at least twenty nonstop flights every

day between Atlanta and Charlotte, North Carolina; the two cities were the chief engines of economic growth in the Southeast region. So why had James Stanley booked a flight with a stopover in Greenville, South Carolina? To save money? Laura logged on to the Internet, and checked out a travel service. She sampled fares for nonstop flights to Charlotte, from the cheapest advance-purchase deal available to the full-price ticket. She repeated the process, adding a stopover in Greenville—it was hardly worth flying to Greenville, it was so close to Atlanta—and she found what she suspected: it cost *more* to fly to Charlotte through the connecting city than it did to fly directly. The reason, she knew, was simple economics: with a large supply of seats available from Atlanta to Charlotte, the airlines were eager to discount. But there was scarcely any traffic on the Atlanta-to-Greenville and the Greenville-to-Charlotte routes, so prices were higher, with few discount fares available. So there was no economic reason for Stanley to have traveled through Greenville. Could he have had a meeting there? He certainly hadn't mentioned it. Laura checked the flight times. If Stanley had scheduled a meeting in Greenville, it had to have been a fast one: there was less than a half hour between the arrival of the flight from Atlanta and its departure for Charlotte.

Laura felt distinctly satisfied with what she had found, despite the fact that it was after one A.M. when she switched off her computer and headed for bed. She knew, or thought she knew, how James Stanley had been in two places at once: he hadn't. He had gotten off that plane in Greenville and returned to Atlanta, where he killed his wife. There was, of course, the hotel record from Charlotte, and the phone calls from there to Atlanta—but these were only details. Laura knew she had her man.

CHAPTER 10

On Memorial Day weekend Laura had made no plans to honor the unofficial start of summer; holidays had a way of creeping up on her. She could easily have driven home to Nashville, but her parents were in Virginia, visiting her mother's college roommate. Laura's calendar was blank until Tuesday.

It was just as well, she reflected as she rose from her bed Saturday morning; she was eager to pursue her sleuthing. After a hasty breakfast, she flipped through the telephone directory, searching out the number of the airline that had carried James Stanley to Charlotte via Greenville. There was a benefit to its being a holiday weekend, from Laura's point of view: the airlines would be fully staffed, as if it were a normal workday. Airline employees lived in a curious inside-out world where everyone else's holidays were their peak stress-inducing times. *It's a pity for them,*

Laura reflected as she dialed the number, fully prepared to add to some airline employee's burden of work.

After hacking through the jungle of choices on the computerized switchboard, and running a gamut of uninterested humans, Laura was transferred to Operations. "Wendy Mays," a tired voice answered.

"Hello, Ms. Mays. This is Laura Chastain from the Fulton County district attorney's office . . ." she began.

"Oh, let me transfer you to Security," said Wendy Mays.

"No! I don't need Security. I need flight information . . ."

"That's 1-800-FLYNOW1," Wendy said helpfully.

"No, not that kind of flight information. I need to know the details of a flight from two weeks ago—when it actually took off and when it landed. And I need a passenger manifest," she added casually, knowing that she had as much chance of getting *that* without a warrant as she did of getting a date with Brad Pitt.

"Oh," Wendy hesitated. "That's not really in my area. Could you call back on Tuesday? I'm sure someone will be here who can help you then."

"No. This is in connection with a murder investigation. It's urgent."

There was a moment's hesitation, then capitulation. Laura knew that the magic words "murder investigation" were capable of getting results where none normally would be forthcoming. Most people welcome the opportunity to be part of something outside the scope of their everyday lives, and a real, live murder would make a great story at the dinner table. Wendy was only partially hooked, however. "I see. Well, how do I know you're for real? You could be just anyone, and *say* you're a district attorney."

"Of course. I could come down there," Laura volunteered, "and pick up the information in person. I could show you ID then."

Wendy surrendered. "Okay. Give me the flight numbers and the dates. I'll have to check with my supervisor about the manifest, though."

"That's cool. Maybe I can talk to her when I'm down there. Could you give me directions to your offices," Laura said, fumbling for a scrap of paper. She wrote down the convoluted instructions, and promised to be there in an hour.

Atlanta's Hartsfield International was a city unto itself. All the airlines had offices there, in addition to the offices of the air-freight companies, and the FAA, the security force, and the caterers. Laura wound through a maze of buildings looking for the address she needed, amazed at the sheer expanse of the place. She reached her destination without trouble, and pulled into a parking space marked Visitor. She had remembered to bring her official identification badge, which was a good thing, because the security guard inside the building seemed to suspect her of smuggling cocaine in her briefcase.

"I'm here to see Wendy Mays. She's expecting me," Laura explained.

Still suspicious, the guard dialed Wendy's extension. After about five minutes, Wendy herself appeared, a plump, cheerful blonde. "Oh, hey, Miss Chastain," she said. "I got the information you wanted. I mean, I got some of it, but my supervisor said uh-uh, no way to the passenger manifest. Sorry. She says she needs a warrant to let you see that."

"That's okay; I can always get one if I need it. What do you have?"

Wendy produced a report on several pages of paper. "Okay, this is not easy to follow. I highlighted the stuff I think you're interested in. Flight 1614 was scheduled to leave here at 5:50 P.M. on May 8. The actual time of departure was 5:56, and it landed in Greenville at 6:39 P.M. The connecting flight to Charlotte was scheduled to leave at 6:57, but you see here that it was delayed—that code means 'equipment problem.' It looks like they replaced a faulty electrical relay. The flight actually took off at 7:50 P.M., and landed in Charlotte at 8:23 P.M. Is this what you needed?"

"Wendy, I think I'm gonna kiss you!" Laura said. James Stanley's flight landed eighteen minutes *after* his receipt showed that he had checked into the hotel at 8:05. Laura's heart yo-yoed in her chest, and her hands shook.

Wendy shrank away from her. "Was the murderer on this flight?" she asked, whispering so the guard wouldn't hear.

"So he claims," Laura said, "but he can't have been! Wendy, you've been a big help. Tell your supervisor I won't be needing that manifest after all." She wrung Wendy's hand gratefully and took off, trying not to break into a run.

Back in the car, Laura took out her hated cellular phone. Talking on it always made her feel like a big, fat jerk—Meredith complained that there was no point in her having one, since she kept it turned off all the time. But she couldn't wait to get home to make this call.

"Homicide," a burly voice answered.

"Is Carlton Hemingway working today?" she asked.

"Nope," came the reply. "I can give him a message."

"Can you page him?"

"That depends on who's asking."

"Laura Chastain, with the Fulton County district attorney."

"Oh, I know you—you're the girl who killed Jeff Williams!"

"Well, yes, I am. I also won first place in the Tennessee

senior essay contest when I was in high school. I'd prefer to be famous for that, if it's all the same to you."

"No, it's just that I knew Jeff. He was a really bad dude."

"No kidding, Detective . . . ? I don't think I caught your name," Laura said.

"Sergeant Eldredge, Howard Eldredge. What do you need Hemingway for?"

"It's something that's turned up on the Christine Stanley murder. I think he'd want to know."

"That's Randy Travers's case—I could page him," Eldredge volunteered.

"No, this is something Carlton wanted me to follow up on with him," Laura fibbed, not wanting to deal with Travers.

"Okay, I'll page him. What's your number?"

Laura read it off the phone; she had never bothered to memorize it. "Tell him it's urgent, please."

"You got it."

Laura started the car and headed for the expressway that would take her back to town, hoping that she could get there before Carlton called her. She wasn't so lucky; the little phone cheeped at her while she was still on the interstate. Despite her often-repeated condemnation of people who tried to talk on the phone while they drove, Laura picked up. "Carlton? That you?"

"I got your page. What's up?"

She told him, as briefly as possible, her story, punctuated by the honking horn of the driver behind her. "Just go on and pass, Mister Man!" she said.

"Excuse me?" Carlton said.

"Not you. I'm on I-85, and I'm causing road rage. All I want to tell you is that I've found out that James Stanley's alibi is bogus—the records Fannin gave us have him checking into the hotel *before* his plane landed."

"You're kidding! Where did you get this?"

"Straight from the airline's mouth! I'm on my way back from their offices now. Where are you?"

"My place, just off Cascade."

"Mind if I drop by? I'm coming up on your exit."

"Sure, come on," he said, and gave her directions.

Carlton lived in an area populated by Atlanta's large and prosperous black middle class. It was a place few Northsiders visited, but Laura had no trouble finding the garden apartment complex where he lived. She parked her shabby car between a Lexus and an Audi. Carlton waved to her from his door. He was as neatly dressed on his day off as he was when he was working. Strains of jazz floated from the apartment behind him. "What are you doing investigating—and on a holiday weekend to boot?" he asked with a grin.

"I just got this idea, and I couldn't let it rest. Let me show you."

"Can I get you something? I just made a pot of coffee," he offered.

"Coffee would be great—I like a good bit of milk, if you've got it."

"Sure," he said, and headed into the kitchen, leaving Laura to survey his bachelor pad. It was neat as a pin, and dominated by stereo equipment. Carlton quickly returned with two mugs of coffee.

"Okay, here's the deal," Laura began. "Did you notice that Stanley made a stopover in Greenville on the way to Charlotte? I wondered about that—did he do it to save money? Obviously not, because that ticket actually cost him more than a nonstop flight would have. So I thought maybe he had a meeting in Greenville, but that didn't wash, either: the flight for Charlotte was scheduled to take off after less than thirty minutes on the ground. Then—

here's the kicker—I went to the airline to confirm the *actual* times of departures and arrivals. Look here." She showed him the report with Wendy's explanatory highlights. "The hotel record shows check-in at 8:05, but the flight didn't touch the ground until 8:23! He could not possibly have been there before nine at the earliest!"

Carlton took it in slowly. He surveyed the airline report carefully, comparing it to the photocopies of Stanley's ticket, which Laura had also produced. Then he nodded. "You're right. He's lying, unless the hotel record is in error. Let's see—could they have been off by an hour because of daylight saving time?"

"Nope. That changes in April. Surely they would have caught it before May 8. Anyway, it's 'spring ahead,' isn't it? Which would make his check-in time an hour *later*."

"It could be just a clerical error," Carlton said, still dubious.

"Think so? Then here's another brain-teaser: James Stanley says he checked in, went straight up to the room, and called home right away. But do you see when his first phone call home was made?"

"Nine-fifteen."

"I say we need to go up there and talk to the people at the hotel to find out for sure."

"I don't know. We're kind of short-handed, and Randy has a lot on his plate."

"Then you can go. I'll go with you. Meredith will give me the time off. It's just a day trip—come on, Carlton, we *have* to go!"

"I'll talk to Randy about it."

"You do that, but tell him that I'm driving to Charlotte first thing Tuesday morning—with or without you."

Carlton chuckled. "He's gonna love that. You give me

your home number, and I'll let you know if you have a driving companion."

They finished their coffee, and talked about work for a while. Pretty soon it was lunchtime, and Carlton suggested a trip to a barbecue place he knew. Laura agreed, and offered to drive. "Is that really your car?" Carlton asked, surveying the old Toyota dubiously.

"Yes. Why?"

"Let's take mine," he suggested, leading her to a shiny Nissan. "I know the way."

"You just don't want to be seen by your neighbors in a beater! Snob!" she accused him laughingly.

They lingered over Harold's spicy ribs and iced tea until well after two o'clock. Laura looked at her watch. "I should head on home," she said reluctantly. "This has been fun." It had been. It was the first time she had spent time with someone who knew nothing about Tom, or Jeff Williams and the whole horrible thing. Carlton didn't treat her like she was made of crystal that could shatter at any moment.

"We'll do it again," Carlton said. "And I'll call you about Tuesday. But one thing: if we do go to Charlotte, we take my car. That's nonnegotiable."

"Okay, okay—just as long as we go. See you then." She cranked up her shameful old wreck, and headed home happier than she had been in weeks.

CHAPTER 11

Gwinnett County lies to the northeast of Atlanta, with Interstate I-85 running through it like a vein that each morning bleeds half the county's population south to the city. Not so long before Laura had moved to Atlanta, Gwinnett had been an amiably slow place, dotted with small hamlets like Snellville and Duluth. Now, it was a terrifying object lesson in the evils of unregulated development. Strip malls, office parks, and tree-hating developers had turned the old fields and pastures into a carbon-monoxide-spewing knot of roads and acres of parking lots. Laura never passed through the place without wondering how anyone lived there and kept sane. People seemed to like it, though; the building boom was still going full tilt, despite the best efforts of irate residents. Still, if you wandered off the highways a bit, you could find a touch of the old Gwinnett, just as Laura and Carlton Hemingway found themselves early Tuesday morning, driving through a town in eastern

Gwinnett that still had some claims to rural credibility, if not charm.

"This is the kind of place that makes me nervous," Carlton said, gripping the steering wheel tightly. "They're not used to seeing a black man in a nice car out here."

"Oh, I don't think they're so backward—this is all suburban Atlanta now."

Carlton harumphed at Laura's naivete. "I'm just glad I have a badge. Where is this guy's house anyway?"

"The way I read the map, it's about a mile farther on this road; then we turn right onto Meeting House Road. He's at 1367 Meeting House."

They were on their way to visit Jesse DuPree, who had been out of town the previous week and unavailable for an interview. Randy Travers had reluctantly given permission for the expedition to Charlotte only on the condition that they stop off in Gwinnett and talk to Jesse on the way. They were traveling east on a two-lane state road lined by small brick ranch houses with scraggly lawns that were home to chipped birdbaths, powerboats on trailers, and the occasional sleepy yard dog. They had left the new subdivisions, with their malls and minimansions, back to the west.

"Here's the turnoff," Laura said. "Slow down and let me look for the address."

Jesse DuPree's house was as modest as its neighbors, but the presence of a black BMW in the drive announced that its resident had aspirations, possibly of the wrong kind. "Here we are," she said. "Gun business must be pretty good," she added, inclining her head at the car.

"Probably on lease," Carlton sniffed. "Probably spends his whole paycheck on it."

Laura laughed. "Carlton, you are a hard man."

"Well, just look at this place—run down, no grass in

the yard, old washing machine in the side yard. If he could afford that car, wouldn't he live in a better place?"

"I bet this is his mama's house," Laura said. "He probably looks after her. Come on, we're wasting time speculating anyway."

They approached the front porch after crossing the bald front yard. Jesse answered the door before they could knock. Laura remembered what Lynette had said about Jesse's "talents"—she could see now what Lynette had meant. Jesse was one good-looking country boy, with black curly hair and eyes as blue as the neon in a beer sign. His spanking white T-shirt was just tight enough to hint at a muscular form beneath, and he stood with the hip-cocked confidence of a man who knew just where his own talents lay. "Hey," he said, flashing a friendly grin. "I've been waiting for you; I didn't want you to ring the bell—my mama's still asleep." Laura poked Carlton with her elbow.

Jesse led them into the small but neat living room and offered coffee, which Laura accepted and Carlton refused. Jesse continued talking cheerfully from the kitchen. "I sure am sorry that y'all had to come all the way out here. I wish I'd a known last week that you wanted to talk to me. I surely would have come downtown to see you before I went to Florida. 'Course, I knew about Lynette's sister being killed before I left, but I had no idea that y'all would think she had anything to do with it." He reappeared with two mugs in his hands. "You sure you won't have coffee, Detective? Anyway, that is why you're here, I guess—to ask me about Lynette."

"In part, Mr. DuPree," Carlton said, not falling for the charm. "We need to know a few things about you and your relationship to the Connell family, too."

Jesse shrugged as he sat down. "Not much to tell. The old man bought a rifle from me 'bout this time last year.

It was a custom job, so I had to go over there and see him several times. That's how I met Lynette. Have y'all met her?" They both nodded. "Well, then you don't need me to explain why I wanted to get to know her better. She's the best-looking gal I ever dated, that's for sure." He grimaced in mock regret. "She didn't have much use for me, I guess. We went out a few times—I even went with her to a couple of her horse shows. But I didn't mix very well with her horse friends. Except the ones who hunted—they thought I was all right."

"Did you meet James Stanley through your acquaintance with Miss Connell?" Carlton was speaking with stilted formality, in contrast to Jesse's drawling candor.

"Sure, a coupla times. He's got a corncob the size of a white pine up his . . . Sorry, miss," he said with a wink. "He didn't have any use for me a'tall. None a'tall," he reflected, seeming to muse on the injustice of it. "I don't have much money, and James does like money. Hell, don't we all? But he *really* likes the stuff. Soon as he found out I was just an old cracker from Gwinnett, he was done with me." Another wink. "Not that I minded. I got no use for a man who doesn't hunt, and James Stanley definitely ain't the hunting type."

"Did James Stanley ever approach you about buying a gun?" Carlton asked.

"No, not really. I showed him a few pieces, and he seemed interested, but he never bought one—not from me anyway. I don't deal in handguns in a big way—just a few pieces of historic interest. Lemme show you what I mean." Jesse rose and crossed the room to a locked steel safe. He unlocked it and produced a box. "This is about the only handgun I have in stock now," he said as he opened the box. Inside was a leather-holstered gun of incredibly evil appearance. "It's a Walther P-38, a genuine

Nazi sidearm." He withdrew it from the holster and displayed it. "You ever seen one of these? I get my hands on one from time to time—lotta old vets out this way brought these back from Europe. When they die, the widows call me about selling the guns."

"Was this the kind of gun James Stanley looked at?" Laura asked.

"Something similar. I believe it mighta been Soviet, World War II vintage. Those are rarer." Jesse hefted the gun one last time, then replaced it in its box.

"Do you know if he contacted any other dealers?" Carlton asked.

"No. That's not to say he didn't. I just don't know. I could ask around if you'd like."

"That won't be necessary. Laura, did you have any questions for Mr. DuPree?"

"Call me Jesse, please. Mr. DuPree was my daddy, and he's dead." He grinned in a way that Laura supposed might be charming, maybe after a couple of drinks.

"Yes. I'd like to know if Lynette Connell ever discussed her sister's marriage with you."

"Sure. She hated ol' James. Talked about it all the time. It made her madder 'n hell that he was spending her daddy's money on country clubs and that big house. Didn't seem to bother the old man any, but Lynette acted like it was her money."

"I see. Did she ever tell you that her sister was thinking about leaving her husband?"

"Nope. I only met Christine a time or two. She was a real sweet girl—short and blonde, didn't look a thing like Lynette—but it never struck me that she was unhappy with her husband. Not that he was any prize, of course, but I can usually tell when a woman's not being taken care of. She didn't strike me as particularly unhappy in that department." He grinned at Laura.

Carlton cleared his throat. "Mr. DuPree, would you tell us where you were on the night of May 8?"

"Sure. I was out at Foley's—that's a bar in Dacula."

"Can you remember when you arrived there?"

"I had dinner there, so it was probably about eight. Then I went to the bar and watched the baseball game for a while."

"Anyone with you?"

"Not at first," Jesse leered. "But I went home with a gal. You want her name? It's Deanna Sutton. I don't have her home number—lost it—but she works at the checkout at the Publix on Hamilton Mill. She's probably there now," he added helpfully.

Carlton stood up, and Laura followed. "One more question, Mr. DuPree," Carlton asked. "What size shoe do you wear?"

"Eleven and a half," Jesse said with a lewd wink in Laura's direction. He stuck a Gucci-loafered foot up in the air. "Want to check?"

"No, thanks," Carlton said. "That's all I have for now, Mr. DuPree, but we may need to talk to you again." He handed Jesse one of his cards. "Be sure to call me if you plan to go out of town again."

"Will do. And you call me any ol' time, you hear?" He addressed this to Laura. *It must just be a reflex with him,* she thought. *If it's female, he flirts with it.*

"We'll do that," she said, and they left.

Carlton backed the car carefully from the driveway. "What did you think?" Laura asked him.

"Not much. These people sure are good at collecting alibis, aren't they?"

"His seems to fit him pretty well. He doesn't deal in

handguns—I guess that kind of lets him off the hook, too."

"Not necessarily. Those European sidearms are all nine millies. The ballistics guys at the crime lab are having some trouble telling what kind of weapon fired the bullet—could be that it was an antique. I'll give 'em a call when we get to Charlotte. In the meantime, I guess we should stop by that grocery store and talk to that girl who slept with DuPree."

"We can get there without getting back on the Interstate," Laura said, surveying her map. "Head west on 20 to 316, then go north to Hamilton Mill Road."

The parking lot of the Publix was crowded, even on a weekday morning. It looked like an SUV dealer's lot. "What do these people think they need these tanks for?" Carlton groused. "I can't even see around the damn things to find a parking place. Do they think the Ice Age is coming back? Do they go moose-hunting on the weekends?"

"I think they only thing they hunt is a good cappuccino," Laura said. "There's a spot. You want me to come with you?"

"Yes. I don't want to know what these people would say to a black man coming in, asking to talk to a white girl."

"A, you don't know that she's white ..." Carlton snorted in disagreement, and gestured to the all-white shoppers. "And B, you are just too paranoid about the suburbs. I came into your neighborhood, didn't I? I didn't think that I was going to be jumped by gang members."

"Of course not—not where I live!"

"Well, this is where these people live. They're not wearing sheets, Carlton."

Carlton snorted again and let Laura enter the store ahead of him. They took a moment to orient themselves to the cavernous interior of the store. There was nothing like a new suburban grocery store, complete with cafe, bakery, deli, salad bar, pharmacy, and florist. "What if you just want a can of corn?" Carlton mused. "There's the office. Let's find a manager."

A young man with a lush mustache confirmed that Deanna Sutton worked there, and that she was working her shift. "But I can't take her off her register until her break, which is in about five minutes. Can you wait?"

"We'll get some coffee," Laura said. "Send her to the cafe when she gets off, if you don't mind."

Deanna Sutton, when she shuffled into the cafe, was a surprise. Laura had been expecting big hair and long nails, but Deanna was fully Goth—in a Gwinnett County sort of way. Her shingled hair was dyed dark as a raven's wing, streaked with magenta and center-parted. She sported a pierced nostril. Her black "Dead Can Dance" T-shirt looked odd beneath the cheery green apron she wore. "You wanted to talk to me?" she sighed.

Carlton flashed his detective's badge. "Carlton Hemingway, Atlanta Police Department. And this is Laura Chastain with the Fulton County district attorney's office. We'd like to ask you some questions about your whereabouts on the night of May 8."

"May 8. When was that?"

"Two weeks ago," Carlton said, exasperated. "It was a Thursday night."

Deanna did some mental calculating. "Oh. Yeah. Me and my friend went to Foley's."

"Did you meet anyone there?"

"Yeah. Jesse something."

"And did you spend some time with him?"

"Yeah. We went back to his place. I live with my mom.

So does he, but she's so old she doesn't care if he has people over. What did he do?"

"Nothing. Did you spend the whole night with him?"

"From about ten o'clock, yeah. I thought he was cute, but he turned out to be *such* a redneck. God."

Carlton looked at Laura and rolled his eyes. "I think that's all we need. Give me your home address and phone number, in case we need to contact you again. And here's my card."

Back in the parking lot, Carlton laughed. "What do you think her problem is?"

"Rebel without a cause. She's stuck here in Dacula, dreaming of the Yorkshire moors."

"I wonder what'll happen to her."

"Not much."

They got back in the car, secured their coffee cups, and headed for the Interstate. Charlotte was about a four-hour drive from where they were. "Would you mind some music?" Carlton asked

"Bring it on," Laura replied.

Carlton slid a CD into the player, and a few tinkling piano notes sounded. A familiar tenor voice started singing. "Bet you don't know who this is," Carlton said, pleased with himself.

Uh-oh, Laura thought—*another jazz fan. Only one way to deal with 'em.* "Nat King Cole Trio—Nat on piano and vocals, Oscar Moore on guitar. I forget the bass player's name. This recording was made in the McGregor studios between 1941 and 1945 as a radio transcription." Hemingway looked so crestfallen that Laura had to laugh. "Sorry, I'm cheating—I've just been lectured on Nat's early career by another fan. You know Amos Kowalski?"

"He's in Sex Crimes, yeah. Are you and he . . . ?"

"No," she said, too vehemently. "I mean, he's a great

friend, but I recently lost someone, and I'm not back in the game just yet."

"Yeah, I remember when all that happened. It's a shame they had to drag all that up again. It's got nothing to do with the case you're working on now."

"What do you mean, drag it back up?"

Carlton looked stricken. "You didn't read the paper this morning?"

"No. I have it in my briefcase. Oh, my God, are you saying they printed something?"

"It's no big deal, really. Just Andy Martin's column, and no one reads that."

"You did," Laura said grimly as she fished her case off the backseat and pulled out the folded newspaper. Andy Martin wrote a column which usually appeared on the second page of the local section. Laura furiously ruffled through the paper to find it. There it was:

PROSECUTOR NO STRANGER TO MURDER

The murder of Christine Stanley shocked and horrified Brookhaven a few weeks ago, almost—but not quite—dimming the memory of another crime, equally horrible, that took place there just a few months ago. Now, in a strange coincidence, a major player in that earlier drama has become a central figure in the investigation of Christine Stanley's death.

It was a rainy night in December. Laura Chastain, a promising associate at the prestigious law firm of Prendergrast and Crawley, was preparing to celebrate her latest courtroom victory at the firm's annual Christmas party. Laura had won a dismissal of charges against Jeff Williams, an Atlanta detective accused of murdering a suspect in his custody. By the time the evening ended, Laura would know

*that her client was guilty of that murder and several others—
including the brutal stabbing death of Laura's mentor at
Prendergrast and Crawley, Tom Bailey. She would also
nearly lose her own life.*

The story went on to describe, in thrilling detail, what
had taken place on that night. Laura skipped over it; no
one needed to remind her of what had taken place in her
own living room. She read the last paragraph aloud in a
bitter tone.

*Laura Chastain lost everything she cared about that
night—her career, her lover, and her best friend. Her friends
expected her to give up practicing law, but they were wrong.
Laura Chastain, according to one former colleague, is determined to right the wrongs committed on that rainy night.
"I think she feels that everything that happened was prevent-
able, if she had just listened to the people around her,"
says this former co-worker. "She really didn't have enough
experience to take on a case like Jeff Williams."*

Laura felt heat rising in her face. Who at P&C would
dare speak to a reporter about her? Libby Arnold, of
course—that old cow would relish the opportunity to take
one more slap at her. Or maybe it was that prissy girl in
Securities—what was her name? It had to have been a
woman, at any rate. Her relationship with Tom—the professional one as much as the personal—had inspired much
envious gossip. She forced herself to read on through her
anger.

*Laura has now joined the Fulton County District Attor-
ney's office, where she can prosecute criminals who caused
others the pain she knows all too well. "I respect Laura*

Chastain," says Craig Fannin, who represents the husband of Christine Stanley. "She's a good lawyer and a fine person. I only hope that her need for revenge doesn't lead her to the wrong conclusion in this case."

Laura snapped the paper shut. "Revenge? Do I strike you as a woman on the hunt for *revenge*, Carlton?"

"Don't let it get to you," he said. "I thought the article was kind of nice—you came across well."

"I come across as a revenge-seeking head case! That's what Fannin wanted people to think, anyway."

"Fannin's just trying to distract everyone's attention from his client."

"Well, it won't work. What happened back then has nothing to do with this case—except that I think it makes me a better prosecutor."

"I think so, too. I think it's just a shame you had to go through all that. I know you miss your boyfriend. I'm real sorry it happened."

"So am I, Carlton. So am I," she said, turning her head to stare at the passing roadside as Nat sang a Johnny Mercer lyric.

CHAPTER 12

The road from Atlanta to Charlotte is not a beautiful one. Virtually the entire length of the Interstate between the two points is an exurban, semiindustrialized landscape of warehouses, office parks, motels, and outlet malls. The beauty of South and North Carolina is reserved for the traveler who departs from the main road. But if speed is paramount, the hapless driver has no choice but to soldier through the blight. There are some beauty spots along the way, of course, and the Big Peach at Gaffney, South Carolina, provides at least comic relief. All the same, Laura was glad when the sign announcing the exit that would take them to the Charlotte Marriott appeared by the side of the road.

The hotel itself was nothing out of the ordinary, a multistory pile of concrete and glass set between the airport and downtown. Laura and Carlton parked and emerged from the car cramped and wilted. "You got a plan for this?" Laura asked him

He shrugged. "Just to ask for the manager, I guess. Ready?"

"I'd like to powder my nose first. I'll meet you at the desk."

The lobby was dark after the glaring light of the late-spring day. Laura blinked and oriented herself. She found the restrooms without trouble and returned to find Carlton leaning on the check-in desk, tapping the case that held his shield impatiently on its faux marble surface. "They're getting someone to talk to us," he said. "I hope whoever he is that he's quicker on the uptake than the desk clerk."

As he spoke, the clerk reemerged from the office behind the counter with a middle-aged man who looked authoritative, if not impressive, in thick eyeglasses and the uniform Marriott blazer. "I'm Lloyd Batey," he announced. "I'm the assistant manager on duty now. Can I help you, Officer . . . ?"

"Detective Hemingway, Atlanta Police Department. And this is Laura Chastain with the Fulton County district attorney. I need to ask you a few questions about a guest who registered here on the night of May 8. Can we go someplace where we can talk?"

"Certainly," Lloyd Batey said graciously. "Come around to the side door and I'll let you into the office." The office was a ramble of desks placed in the open, and a cubicle for the assistant manager in the corner. The door to the general manager's office, Laura noted, was firmly closed against the noise and bustle. There was barely room for three adults in Batey's corner, but they managed to squeeze in. "Now, what can I do you for?" he asked amiably.

Carlton produced a copy of James Stanley's receipt. "Is this from your hotel?"

"Yes," Batey said, peering at it. "It surely is."

"Did you happen to be on duty when Mr. Stanley checked in?"

"No, no, I never work in the evenings. That night Ms. DeMarco would have been on duty. I could call her . . ."

"I don't think we need to do that just yet, Mr. Batey. We're curious about the time that's noted for the check-in." Batey peered once again at the document. "It says 8:05 P.M.—is that correct?"

"Yes."

"And does the record appear to have been altered in any way?"

"Well, it's not the original copy, but—let me look it up on the computer." He frowningly tapped at his keyboard. "Here it is. No, our record agrees with your copy—8:05 it was. What is this all about?"

"We're not sure. Could your computer's clock have been in error?"

"No."

"You sound very sure of that, Mr. Batey."

"I am, and I'll tell you why. Our wake-up call system is run off this same computer, and if it's off by as much as five minutes we catch hell." Lloyd Batey was very firm on this point.

"You couldn't have been off by exactly one hour because of daylight savings, or something like that?"

"No. If ever we do get off—and I can't say I remember a time when we ever have been—the error would be caught and corrected very quickly. No, if your Mr. Stanley says he was here at 8:05, he was." Batey settled back in his chair with a stubborn expression on his face.

Laura ventured a question. "Could someone have

changed the clock just for this one check-in—maybe as a special request from a good customer—and then changed it back right away, before anyone noticed?"

"No. That is, I doubt it . . . It seems to me that a systems manager would be the only one who would have the password to do that."

"Is there a systems manager working today?" she probed.

"Of course."

"Could you call him—or her? This is terribly important, Mr. Batey."

Lloyd pondered her request for a minute, then nodded. He picked up his phone and punched in an extension. "Wayne? Can you get up here to my office? I have the Atlanta police here asking some questions about our systems." He hung up. "Wayne'll be right up."

Wayne proved to be a lanky youngster in khakis and a plaid shirt. Laura supposed that the systems guys couldn't be persuaded to wear the polyester blazer and black slacks that the other employees sported, and she admired his independence. "Whassup?" he asked, glancing at her and at Carlton.

"This is Wayne Catrall. Wayne, these good folks want to know if the time stamp on a check-in could be altered."

"Sure," Wayne said. "If you have the password and can get into the systems files."

"Who has the passwords?" Carlton asked.

"Me, Danny Demopoulos—he works the night shift in Systems—and the general manager."

"No one else?" Carlton asked, skeptical.

"No one," Wayne said firmly. "Look, just tell me what the problem is and maybe I can help you better."

Carlton explained the discrepancy in the flight arrival and the check-in times. "Your record says the check-in was at 8:05, but the plane James Stanley took wasn't even on the ground then. The airline records can't be wrong—those times are from FAA reports. And Stanley also says that he called his wife as soon as he got into the room, but you can see his first call wasn't until nine-fifteen. We can't explain either discrepancy."

Wayne nodded. "I see. Lemme get at your computer, Lloyd." Lloyd yielded his seat to the younger man and plastered himself against the wall to make room. Wayne's fingers flew, and the computer responded with beeps and clicks. "I'm looking at check-ins just before and just after this one," he explained. "Nope, nothing unusual. Let me see . . ." He paused for a moment and resumed his communication with the machine. "Okay, here's something. I don't know if this is important. It looks like your guy Stanley checked in with one credit card, but presented a different one at check-out."

"What does that mean?" Carlton asked.

"Nothing, maybe. It happens all the time—they switch from their business to their personal cards, or vice versa. People are just funny that way. But here's the strange thing—he checked in on a card that's issued to James T. Stanley, but checked out on one that's in the name of James A. Stanley."

Laura felt her excitement growing. "Can you check the billing addresses for those cards?"

Wayne hesitated for the first time. "We'd have to call the issuer. I'd be happy to, if . . ." He glanced at Lloyd for approbation.

"I don't know," Lloyd said. "Those records are pretty private."

"Look, Mr. Batey," Laura said, "I appreciate your scruples, but this is a murder investigation. I can always get a warrant."

Once again, the words *murder investigation* worked their magic. Lloyd suddenly became a co-conspirator. "I don't suppose it would hurt. Wayne, would you make that call?"

"Sure." Laura shifted impatiently in her seat as Wayne looked up the toll-free numbers of the credit card issuers, and as he sweet-talked the operators. Amidst a lot of "uh-huhs"and "yeahs," he jotted down information. When he finally hung up, Laura was in a state of nervous tension. "Well," Wayne drawled. "Got something. James *T.* Stanley is from Winston-Salem, but James *A.* Stanley has an Atlanta address." He shoved the paper across the desk so that she and Carlton could see it.

Once Laura had been in a department store, standing next to a glass-sided escalator. Something had apparently caught in a seam of the glass panels, and in the moving treads of the stairs. As the stairs advanced and the stress increased, the glass panel shattered. Laura remembered how the cracks had spread across the pane, and the tinkling sound the fragments made as they crashed down on the marble floor. Her tension cracked and shattered just like that.

She jumped to her feet. "That's *it!*" she declared. "An accomplice!"

Wayne grinned. "No shit! Is this all for real?"

"It's very real," Laura said. "We're going to have to ask you two to say nothing about this, of course," she added, regaining her composure somewhat.

"My lips are sealed," Wayne promised. "Anything else you need?"

Carlton asked for a list of employees who had been on duty that night, and asked Lloyd if there was some way of determining which clerk had actually checked James T. Stanley into the hotel, and which waiter had taken his dinner up. Lloyd agreed to check the records, and Wayne headed back to his basement redoubt after shaking hands with Laura and Carlton. *The really nice thing about a murder investigation is that it brightens so many lives,* Laura thought ruefully. Now Wayne and Lloyd and Wendy Mays all had great stories—because to them, of course, it was just a story. They weren't dealing with the memory of Christine Stanley's blood-soaked family room, and the pitiful reminders of her last evening—a magazine and a pint of ice cream.

I'm doing it for you, Christine, Laura vowed. *I'm not going to let him get away with this.*

CHAPTER 13

Laura was beside herself in the parking lot. She tugged at Carlton's sleeve in her eagerness to get back in the car and head for Winston-Salem right away. Carlton was less keen on the idea. "Let's dial down a minute here," he urged her. "I want to call Randy and put him in the picture on this. If we go on up there, we might have to spend the night, and he might not be so thrilled about that."

"Oh, so he'd rather let a killer get away than pay for a night in a hotel? You can tell him *I'll* pay for it, if that's his beef."

"Don't be ridiculous—he won't buck at the cost if he thinks this thing is for real. Anyway, I'm not getting back on that highway until I have some lunch in me. Let's find a nice place to sit down and eat something; then we can call Atlanta. We'll get along much better if you let me eat regularly. I don't like to go too long between feedings."

Laura conceded, reluctantly, and they set off in search of a place to eat. Carlton rejected all the fast-food places, and recoiled in horror when Laura pointed out a Cracker Barrel Country Store. Finally, they were able to agree on a Shoney's. Carlton once again made a show of nervousness about being seen with a white girl, but Laura blew off his objections unsympathetically. "It's not Denny's, okay?" she said as she shouldered her purse and swung her legs out of the car door. "No one is going to think a thing about us, unless it's that we're two coworkers out for lunch. Now, come on."

Laura was right; no one paid them the least attention. After waiting patiently for five minutes, she grabbed the hostess and asked for a nonsmoking table. It was after the lunch rush, and the hostess seemed most unenthusiastic about seating two latecomers, regardless of their races. She led them wearily to a booth and plopped down menus in front of them, and they ordered as soon as a waitress approached. Carlton asked for the salad bar, but Laura ordered a bacon cheeseburger. "Road food," she explained.

"Oh, *that* makes sense—take in as many calories as you can while you're sitting immobile in a car all day," he remarked.

"You do it your way, I'll do it mine. Are you going to call Detective Travers?"

"May as well." Carlton produced a sleek cellular phone and dialed his boss. Laura nibbled her fries as she listened to Carlton's account of their day so far. He fell silent, apparently listening to Travers. Finally, he gave Laura a thumbs-up. "Okay, we'll go on to Winston-Salem and find this clown. Oh, one more thing—Jesse DuPree has an alibi; he was with a girl. But one thing did come out when we talked to him: he deals in antique weapons, especially Nazi and Soviet military sidearms. DuPree says Stanley was interested in buying a Soviet piece. That could explain why the ballistics don't match any known weapon. I'll call you again after we've seen this guy. If it goes late, we might have to spend the night up here." He refolded his little phone. "Happy now?" he said to Laura. "We get to drive some more."

"Carlton, I swear you sound as if you're not excited about this."

"I just don't like to get my hopes up. Of course I'd love to wrap this up, but I have misgivings. It just seems pretty stupid of Stanley to have involved a co-conspirator. He had to know the guy would talk if we found him—an accomplice has nothing at stake, but Stanley could go to the electric chair."

"Maybe he thought we'd just look at his hotel receipt and take his word for it."

"Maybe. You gonna eat those fries?"

"Yes. You gonna eat that lettuce?"

A short time later, they were on their way to Winston-Salem, which required more driving on the Interstate, although through slightly less ugly terrain. As they neared the city, Carlton fished out his phone and handed it to Laura. "We got his home and work numbers—call the work number first."

After some difficulty with the phone—apparently you needed to dial the area code first—Laura was connected to First Statewide Mortgage, which she assumed was James T. Stanley's employer. "May I speak to Mr. Stanley?"

"May I say who's calling?"

"He doesn't know me. I'm calling on a private matter."

"Just a minute. I'll see if he's free." After a moment the woman came back. "He wants to know what this is in regard of." Laura winced at the tortured syntax.

"Say it's about May 8. Tell him the Atlanta Police want to talk to him."

"Oh. Wait a minute."

It was less than a minute later that a male voice came on the line. "This is Jim," he said heartily.

"Mr. Stanley, my name is Laura Chastain. I'm with the Fulton County district attorney, in Atlanta. I'm in Winston-Salem with a detective from the Atlanta Police Department, and we would like very much to speak with you. Now."

"What's this all about?"

"Oh, I think you know, Mr. Stanley. Just give me directions to your office, and we can meet face-to-face."

Stanley complied. They weren't far from his office; Laura scribbled down the directions, and hung up.

"He pretended not to know what this was about?" Carlton asked.

"Yep. I think this is it." They pulled off the highway access road into the parking lot of an undistinguished, slightly shabby office park. "That's his company—First Statewide Mortgage." They parked and exited the car. "You want to do the talking?" she asked Carlton.

"Better let me. The badge always gets things going." They entered the offices through a glass door into a small lobby, covered in worn orange carpet. The receptionist, a chubby brunette wearing a purple tracksuit, sat at a metal desk covered with little office tchotchkes and cheap picture frames. A nameplate identified her as Candi.

"Are y'all the people who called a minute ago?" she asked, eyes wide.

"Yes. Mr. Stanley is expecting us." Carlton's voice took on a Jack Webb quality, Laura noticed, when the business was official.

"He says he'll be with y'all in a minute. Y'all want some coffee?"

"No, thanks."

There was nowhere to sit in the tiny lobby, so they didn't. Carlton leaned his muscular frame against the wall and looked pointedly at his watch. They waited almost ten minutes, no one speaking. The phone didn't ring once in that time. Finally, thudding footsteps sounded in a hall behind the receptionist's desk. Candi smiled nervously. "That's him. Y'all sure you don't want some coffee?"

They didn't have time to refuse; Jim Stanley burst into the already-crowded room. He was of medium height, with medium brown hair, thinning on the top. His gray off-the-rack suit was rumpled, and his tie was loose around his collar. His features were oddly blunt, almost simian; he was by no stretch of the imagination an attractive man. Laura guessed that he was in his midthirties, judging from the degree of hair loss and his softening middle section. "Hey," he said in a surprisingly deep voice. Not bothering with any ceremonies, he cocked his head back in the direction he had come from. "Let's go back here where we can talk in private."

He led them down the hallway, which was short, with only two doors opening from it. One, Laura presumed, was Stanley's office. The other was a small room containing a table and a few mismatched chairs. Stanley ushered them into this room and invited them to sit down. Files were stacked on the windowsill, the floor, and even on one end of the table. Jim Stanley made no effort to move them, so Carlton and Laura dragged chairs to the far end and sat down. Carlton spoke first.

"I think you know why we're here," he began.

"Yep. And you might as well stop talking right now. I've been on the phone with my lawyer, and he's on his way over here now."

"Surely that's not necessary," Laura said suavely. "We just want to ask a few questions."

"Yes, it's necessary. He'll be right along. Y'all will have to excuse me—I'm going to wait for him in my office. Did Candi offer you coffee?"

"Yes, thank you. We don't need anything. Really, Mr. Stanley, you're not a suspect in anything, and we have no intention of arresting you. We don't even have jurisdiction in North Carolina."

"We can sort all that out when Hoyt gets here. Won't be a minute." He gave Laura a wink and an ingratiating smile, and left the room.

"He's lawyering up? Why?" Carlton asked.

"He knows this is serious. Cops don't cross state lines just to talk about parking violations."

"What if he wants a deal before he talks?"

Laura shrugged. "I guess we give it to him. We don't want him—we just want James Stanley. This is going to get confusing, the two of them having the same name. This one calls himself Jim. I guess we'll have to, too. But what other evidence against James Stanley do we have? We need Jim's story."

"I think you're right. At least getting a co-conspirator to talk makes an easy case for you."

"If we have enough corroborating evidence to admit co-conspirator testimony."

"What does that mean?"

"Co-conspirators are notoriously unreliable—you can't just put one on the stand and have his testimony convict a defendant, especially in a capital case. We have to establish independently that a conspiracy existed. The check-in records at the hotel should be enough to satisfy the requirement."

"How do lawyers think up these things? It seems to me that a co-conspirator is almost as good as an eyewitness."

"Not always. There was one really famous case in England in the seventeenth century—a man testified against his mother and brother. He said they had all three killed a man who had disappeared. The supposed victim turned up a year or two after the three of them were hanged. John Masefield wrote a play about it."

"Why would someone do a thing like that?" Carlton asked, astounded.

"Who knows? Maybe it was a highly inefficient means of committing suicide, or of working out some family issues," Laura replied dryly. "Listen—I hear footsteps."

In the silence, they could hear murmured conversation in the hallway. A moment later, Jim Stanley reappeared in the doorway, followed by a highly groomed representative of the legal profession. Laura raised an eyebrow in Carlton's direction, hoping that he noted the glossy shoe and briefcase leather, the exquisite tie, and the expensive suit worn over the veddy British blue-striped shirt with white collar and cuffs. It was all at odds with the generally run-down and weary look of Jim Stanley and his office. This apotheosis of the legal profession flashed a white-toothed smile at Laura and Carlton. "Good afternoon!" he said heartily. "I'm Charlie Hoyt. Jim here says y'all want him to answer a few questions, and I thought it might be advisable for me to sit in. Y'all don't mind, do you?"

"Of course not," Carlton said. "But we really just have a couple of questions."

"Well, fire away, Detective . . . ?"

"Hemingway. And this is Miss Chastain, from the Fulton County district attorney's office."

Hoyt shook their hands, still smiling, and settled into a chair. His client followed suit. "Shall we begin?"

"Great. Mr. Stanley, did you check into the Marriott Hotel on Thursday night, May 8?"

Stanley and Hoyt whispered together before Stanley answered. "I can't answer that question."

"What do you mean?" Carlton said.

"Mr. Hoyt," Laura broke in, "is your client invoking his *rights?*"

"He has that right," Hoyt said, unruffled.

"But he's not in custody—we're on his premises, for pity's sake! Surely he can give us a yes or a no!"

"Let's cut to the chase," Hoyt said, still showing his crocodile teeth in a smile. "My client wants immunity."

"Immunity from *what?* He hasn't been charged with anything. Are you saying that he *could* be charged with something?"

"We make no admission, Ms. Chastain. Are you prepared to talk about an immunity deal?"

"Let's get hypothetical, shall we? Let's say your client assisted someone in the commission of a crime—let's say felony murder, for the sake of argument. Would he be willing to testify to his role in that crime if we gave him immunity on the conspiracy charge?"

"We want transactional immunity."

"Why? Exactly what did your client *do*, Mr. Hoyt? I'm acting on the presumption that he provided an alibi for a felon. Is there something I'm missing here?"

"No, you're not missing anything. We would simply be more comfortable with transactional immunity under the circumstances."

Carlton interrupted the debate. "Help me out here. What's transactional immunity?"

Laura answered him, her eyes fixed on Hoyt as she spoke. "Transactional means that we will not prosecute for any transaction referred to in Mr. Stanley's testimony.

In other words, if he tells us that he planned the murder and provided the gun, as well as the alibi, we couldn't touch him."

"That's correct," Hoyt said. "Without, of course, making any admission."

"What if your client played a material part in the commission of the crime? I could see us making a plea deal on a lesser charge—but immunity? Come on, Mr. Hoyt!"

"Those are our terms, Ms. Chastain. Otherwise, you can do this the hard way. Would you and your colleague like us to leave you alone for a few minutes to discuss our offer?"

"Yes. Please," she said. Hoyt and Jim Stanley left the room in a mild air of triumph.

"What's all this bullshit?" Carlton said.

"You heard him—he wants immunity from everything, not just a conspiracy charge. Normally, we would give 'use and derivative use' immunity, which means that we can't prosecute him for any charge arising from his own testimony. In that case, if we proved *independently* of his own testimony that Stanley played a larger role, we could go after him. But if we give him what he wants, we could find out he fired the damn gun and we'd have to let him go. He doesn't want to run the slightest risk of being prosecuted."

"Let's just get a warrant and arrest the sonofabitch, then."

"Then our case will be entirely based on the testimony of the hotel employees—which is inconclusive without this guy's story. If we arrest him, he pleads the Fifth and we get nothing."

Carlton frowned. "It seems to me that the worst case is that Jim Stanley did more than just provide an alibi—maybe he did plan the crime, or get the gun. We know that he couldn't have been the shooter, at least."

"How?"

"He has the alibi that James Stanley is claiming—remember? If we're right, it was *Jim* in the hotel room, ordering dinner and making the calls."

"You're right. But transactional immunity is a big deal—we very rarely grant it."

"What are you going to do?"

Laura sighed. "I'm going to talk to my boss. I can't make a call like this." She produced her cell phone and dialed Meredith's number. Meredith, of course, was away from her desk. Laura paged her. "Let's just hope she's not in court," she told Carlton. She tapped her pen on the table as she waited impatiently for a call that might take an hour to come. "Let's go back over the ground again before we say this immunity is really necessary. We keep on saying that there's no forensic evidence, but is that really true?"

"Practically. There are the slugs, but DuPree's Nazi guns are the best lead we've got on the actual gun. Other than that, there's just the footprint in the carpet—that's not going to send anyone to the electric chair—and the fibers that were caught in the door."

"What about those fibers?"

"The crime lab is underfunded and way backed up. It takes forever to get fiber analyzed, and then it's usually inconclusive. And there's really nothing else—the only fingerprints we found belonged to family members and known visitors."

"Hmm. 'Consider the strange behavior of the dog in the nighttime,' as a man once said."

"What's that supposed to mean?"

"In that case, the dog didn't bark when the house was burgled, because he knew the burglar. In this case, the burglar appears to have left no fingerprints—or maybe he did, and we just assume that they belonged there. And speaking of the dog, what about that dog killed with the same gun?''

"That's got me, I have to admit. Why would Stanley use the weapon he planned to kill his wife with to kill the dog? It doesn't make sense. It puts the gun in that neighborhood, when you'd think he'd be trying as hard as he could to convince us that he'd never so much as touched a gun.''

"That's true.'' The ringing of Laura's phone cut off further speculation. "Thank goodness it's you,'' she said to Meredith. "We have a helluva situation up here.'' She tried to explain as simply as she could, starting with why she was in Winston-Salem and not Charlotte. "So the good news is, we may have found our key witness. The bad news is, he wants a transactional immunity deal.''

"What's his involvement?''

"We don't know, but he's got himself a whole lotta lawyer. The guy must be costing him three hundred bucks an hour. He's not letting his client say anything until he has his immunity. I figure his story must be pretty damning, though. What should we do?''

"I guess we don't have a choice. What does Carlton say?''

"We've just been talking about our pitiful lack of evidence. I think we both agree that we need this guy.''

"And you can demonstrate that there was a conspiracy?''

"I think the hotel records show that.''

"Then give him what he wants. I assume you're staying up there tonight.''

"I think we'll have to. It's going to take some time to hammer out the details and get a statement. Better count me out for tomorrow.''

"Okay. Just keep me posted."

"I will. Thanks, Meredith." She ended the call and looked at Carlton. "All systems are go. Let's get that lawyer back in here and have us an immunity party."

Charlie Hoyt remained smoothly affable when he rejoined them. "I tell you what," he said. "It's after four o'clock now, and this is going to take us a while. Why don't we sketch out some terms for the immunity agreement, and I'll have it drafted overnight? Then we can all meet at my offices in the morning, finalize our agreement, and Mr. Stanley can give you a statement. I'll even have one of my girls transcribe it for you. How's that for an offer?"

"I think I'd prefer to draft the immunity agreement myself," Laura replied. "It will have to hold up in a Georgia court."

Hoyt grinned. "By a happy coincidence, I am a member of the Georgia bar. I've argued many cases in your fair state, Ms. Chastain. And I have a big ol' staff back at the office just waiting to do my bidding. I promise you you'll get a crack at redrafting it—if you still want to after you see it."

Laura looked at Carlton, who shrugged, as if to say, "It's your call." "Okay. Fine. Let's just get the main points down now, and we'll finish in the morning."

Two hours later, Laura and Carlton staggered into the parking lot. "Lawyers!" Carlton said. "It's every little thing with you people!"

Laura laughed. "Oh, that was just a warm-up. It'll be even better tomorrow. That Hoyt is a smoothie."

"He seems like an okay guy. It was real nice of him to give us the name of a good restaurant. I say we find a hotel, check in, and head for dinner."

"I am with you one hundred percent, Detective."

CHAPTER 14

I do attest and swear that this is a true and complete statement of the events that took place prior to and on the date of May 8, 1999, in Charlotte, North Carolina, to the best of my recollection.

Laura carefully folded the signed and notarized copy of Jim's statement and placed it in her briefcase. She wondered why she wasn't feeling more triumphant, given the victory that she held in her hand. But it had been a long day, and she and Carlton still faced the drive back to Atlanta—six hours, if the traffic wasn't too horrible—which would put them in the city around midnight. All she wanted was to put her feet up and have a drink, but that would have to be deferred; there was no chance of their spending another night in North Carolina. Neither Randy Travers nor Meredith would tolerate further delay.

The day had started at eight o'clock, when Laura and Carlton arrived at Hoyt's office in downtown Winston-Salem. They had made a quick trip to a Target the night before to pick up toiletries and other necessities. Laura was quite proud of the knit shell and scarf she had snagged at a bargain price, but Carlton had limited his wardrobe replenishment to underwear. "I don't discount shop," he had sniffed.

"You should. Some of those ties are just as good-looking as anything they have at Nordstrom," she had commented. Somehow, though, Carlton managed to look fresh and crisp despite wearing the same clothes he had traveled in the day before.

The offices of Marbury, Wright and Hoyt were as plush and elegant as Jim Stanley's had been shabby. An immaculately coiffed and tailored woman had escorted them into a conference room and asked them, in a pleasant Southern accent, to wait there for Mr. Hoyt. "Help yourself to coffee and pastries," she offered. A sideboard was spread with a lavish feast of muffins, Danish, bagels, and Krispy Kremes, which were native to North Carolina. Coffee steamed in silver carafes marked Regular and Decaf. Carlton made a move on the spread; they had skipped breakfast, at Hoyt's suggestion, and Laura was glad. This was far better than the buffet at the Hampton Inn. "Eat up," she said to Carlton. "It's all going on Stanley's bill. I wish we could make him pay for our expenses, too."

Hoyt and Stanley had kept them waiting in the conference room about an hour, during which time Laura consumed more coffee than was good for her. When they finally arrived, all apologies and smiles, she was wired. Hoyt presented his draft of the immunity agreement with a flourish for her review. "I think you'll find that it's just as we discussed last night."

It wasn't. It was lunchtime before Laura and Hoyt agreed on every word of the agreement. Laura was extra vigilant and nitpicked every detail. She didn't want to bring back some turkey of a deal to Meredith, so she concentrated on narrowing the immunity as much as she could—which wasn't much. At last, a secretary took a marked-up document away to produce a final copy. Sandwiches magically appeared, and they all ate again. At about one o'clock, they signed the immunity papers. Hoyt summoned a court reporter to make a transcript of Stanley's statement, which he was now prepared to give. Laura felt a sudden rush of anxiety—what if Jim Stanley had been more involved than they suspected? Had she let a murderer off the hook with the immunity deal?

Hoyt cleared his throat and began. "This statement is made by Jim Stanley at Winston-Salem on the twenty-eighth day of May, 1999, in the presence of Mr. Charles Hoyt, attorney for Mr. Stanley; Miss Laura Chastain, assistant district attorney for Fulton County, Georgia; and Detective Carlton Hemingway of the Atlanta Police Department. Mr. Stanley, please state your full name and address for the record."

"James Thomas Stanley, 1341 Brightleaf Circle, Winston-Salem, North Carolina."

"Detective Hemingway will now ask you some questions. Please answer as concisely and as accurately as you can. Detective?"

"Mr. Stanley, did you travel to Charlotte, North Carolina, on May 8 of this year?"

"I did."

"And did you register at the Marriott Hotel on May 8?"

"Yes, sir, I did."

"Why did you go to Charlotte on that date, Mr. Stanley?"

"I go there all the time. I'm a mortgage broker, and that's where the big banks are headquartered. I'm down there all the time talking to the mortgage servicing people."

"Did you have business with a bank on May 8 or 9?"

"No."

"Then why *did* you go on that date?"

"I went at the request of an acquaintance of mine."

"Could you name this 'acquaintance'?"

"Sure. James Stanley. He's from Atlanta."

"How did you come to know Mr. Stanley?"

"Well, that's kind of complicated. Like I said, I go to Charlotte a lot, and I always stay at the Marriott down there—it's close to the banks, and they have a good bar and restaurant for entertaining clients. One day—I guess this was about a year and a half ago—I showed up as usual to check in, and they told me that my room was gone—that someone had already checked into it. Well, you better believe I raised hell about that—I was a good, regular customer, and I wasn't used to that kind of treatment! Everybody runs around, they get a manager, and we come to find out that another fella with the same name as me had showed up. They thought *my* reservation was a double-booking, so they canceled it. They apologized, and gave me a room, and I thought that was it, but things kept on getting screwed up. I got his phone calls, and he got mine—things like that. Well, after I had dinner with a client, I headed for the bar, and I'm sitting next to this guy, just having a beer and talking, you know, like you do in these places—and wouldn't you know it's *him*—the other Jim Stanley! Except he goes by 'James.' We had a good laugh about the foul-ups."

"Was this the only time you met the other Mr. Stanley?"

"Oh, no. It got to be a regular thing with us—we'd always check when we got in to see if the other one was there. He came up a good bit, too, you see—he had business with the banks himself."

"So you became friendly?"

"I guess you'd say that."

"Returning to the evening of May 8, you say that you traveled to Charlotte at the request of James Stanley. Why?"

"One time—I guess it was about a year ago; that would make it about six months after we met—James said to me, 'You know, this name thing may come in handy someday.' I asked him what he meant by that, and he sorta smiled and said, 'Oh, you know—if one of us ever needed to be in two places at once,' and he kinda winked. Of course, I thought right away that he was fooling around on his wife. I knew he was married, but he didn't seem too happy about it to me."

"Did he ever tell you he was unhappy?"

"No-o, not in so many words—I just had a feeling. I'm married myself, and I know it's not a party all the time."

"Did he suggest at that time that you might cover for him someday?"

"Not directly. But he did joke about it a time or two after that."

"And did he ask you to travel to Charlotte and check into the Marriott for him?"

"Yes."

"When was this?"

"It was about a month ago. He called me at work, and we chewed the fat a little, and he asked me if I was planning any trips to Charlotte in the near future. I told him no—business has been a little slow—and he hemmed and hawed. Finally, he comes out with it—would I mind doing him a favor and drive down there on May 8 and check in? I was kind of reluctant. I figured he was cheating on his wife, and I really didn't want to be a part of that. But he kept after me, and said it was no big deal, that he just needed to go somewhere he didn't want his wife to know about.''

"Did he ask you to do anything else?"

"Uh-huh. I was supposed to check in around eight, and go on up to the room. He told me to order room service— he said he'd pay the bill for whatever I wanted—and that I was to make two calls to his number in Atlanta, one at about nine o'clock, and one about eleven. He told me to hang up as soon as anybody answered, or if the answering machine picked up."

"Anything else you were to do for him?"

"No. He said he'd be along later, and that I was just to stay there and go on to bed. He asked me to let him into the room when he did come, and said that he'd handle the bill with his own credit card when he checked out."

"And did he show up?"

"Yep. I think it was about four in the morning—I was a bit groggy, you can understand."

"How did he know which room to go to?"

"He rang me from the lobby, and I gave him the number."

"Did you have any conversation with him when he got to the room?"

"Hell, no—all I wanted was to get back into bed. He must have been tired, too, because he took his clothes off and got into bed."

"Was his behavior in any way out of the ordinary?"

Jim Stanley cocked an eyebrow at Carlton. "Other than running around in the middle of the night and asking me to pretend I was him? No, nothing *out of the ordinary*."

"How was he dressed?"

"Jeez, what kind of memory am I supposed to have? I guess he was wearing pants and a shirt—maybe khakis."

"Not a business suit?"

"No, I don't think so. I could be wrong."

"Was Mr. Stanley carrying anything?"

"Some luggage, I think, and maybe a briefcase."

"What happened in the morning?"

"I got up before he did—I had to drive back here and be in my office by nine. He was still asleep when I left."

"So you were not there when the police arrived to tell him that his wife had been killed?"

"No."

"Have you had any further communication with him since that date?"

"No. Wait—I take that back. He called me the next day and said thanks for doing what he asked me to do."

"Did he mention at that time that his wife had been killed?"

"No! I didn't know a thing about that!"

"Mr. Stanley, you didn't seem surprised to hear that a detective from the Atlanta Police Department was here to see you. Why was that?"

"Because I knew by the time you got here that she was dead—it was in the Charlotte paper, because he had supposedly been here when she was killed."

"You knew that his alibi was false, then. Why didn't you go to the police immediately?"

"I was scared. Hell, what was I supposed to do? I didn't sleep for about a week. Then I decided to get me a lawyer."

"And you retained Mr. Hoyt?"

"Not at first. I went to another guy, and I told him what had happened. He said he couldn't handle something like that. He gave me Charlie's name."

"But didn't Mr. Hoyt tell you that you had to go to the police right away?"

"No. I didn't call him until yesterday, when I heard you were on the way. See, I just thought I better let the trouble come to me, and not go out looking for it. I was scared that Stanley might come after me, and I was scared that I would be charged with murder myself if I went to the police. But Charlie calmed me down. He told me about immunity, which is why we're having this little talk now." He smiled broadly.

Laura, who had been listening in silence to everything Jim said, cleared her throat. "Let's go back over the details. James Stanley called you and asked you to impersonate him, in effect, by checking into the Marriott, and you didn't hesitate to do so?"

"I didn't say that—I thought it was fishy."

"But you did it out of the goodness of your heart, despite your reservations, as a favor to a friend?" Laura let a tinge of sarcasm creep into her voice.

"No, not exactly . . ." Jim trailed off, and looked at Hoyt.

"Did James Stanley offer you something for your trouble?" Laura asked. Jim Stanley nodded. "Please state your answer aloud for the record," Laura commanded him.

"Yes. He offered me money."

"How much?"

"Five thousand dollars."

"Five thousand dollars—for helping him cover up a marital infidelity? That seems like an expensive night on the tiles to me, Mr. Stanley."

"Well, uh, he offered me less at first, but like I say, business has been slow, and I was reluctant to do something dishonest . . ."

"So you dickered with him?"

"I wouldn't say I *dickered*, exactly—he just kept raising the amount while I *hesitated*."

"But when he said five thousand, you abandoned your scruples?"

Hoyt intervened. "Ms. Chastain, I don't see the point of your badgering my client. He's only trying to help you."

"And I'm only trying to understand why someone as naïve and well-intentioned as your client allows himself to be drawn into an enterprise that must have seemed suspicious, even to someone as naïve as he."

"Are you implying that my client had foreknowledge of the murder of Mrs. Stanley?"

"I am saying that he had reason to suspect that James Stanley had criminal intentions."

"Even if he did have such suspicions, how was he to have known that Stanley contemplated *murder*? Nothing in his prior acquaintance with the man led him to believe that he was capable of homicide."

"If someone offered me five thousand dollars, you better believe *my* antennae would be up."

"I am sorry that you seem to have an untrusting nature, Ms. Chastain. But whatever the case may be, my client's actions on the night of May 8, and subsequent to that date, are covered under our immunity agreement. No purpose is served by trying to force him to admit that he suspected that he was being made into an accomplice in a criminal conspiracy."

Hoyt was right, of course—Jim could sit there and tell them that he had known all along what James Stanley was up to, and they couldn't do a thing about it. But Laura didn't believe for a nanosecond that Jim Stanley was as ignorant as he pretended to be—you don't get a five-thousand-dollar payday just for being a good pal. A question occurred to her. "Mr. Stanley, have you been paid?"

"Yes. The five thou was wired to my bank account at Wachovia."

"Could we have a copy of the record of that transaction?"

"Sure. Charlie's got it right here."

"We'd be happy to provide you a copy," Hoyt said smoothly.

So Hoyt had known all along that his client had dirty hands—which was why he insisted on transactional immunity. Laura had the uneasy feeling that she had been out-lawyered, but she comforted herself with the assurance that anyone would have done what she had—even Meredith. Even Tom. Sometimes you had to sacrifice the small victories when you were after the big one.

"We've gotten off-topic," Hoyt said. "Do either of you have more questions for my client?"

"I don't," Carlton said. "Laura?"

"Not now. Can we stipulate that your client agrees to make himself available for further questioning at our request?"

"Certainly. And he will of course make himself available for all court proceedings."

"Thank you. I guess that's all."

"Then I'll have Marla type this interview up, and we'll review it and sign it—and you two can return in triumph to your native city."

And, after some lawyerly gee-hawing about the form of the document, to Carlton's disgust, that is what they did. They returned to Carlton's car in the gathering dusk, and began the long drive home in silence.

After about half an hour, Carlton spoke. "So how do you feel about this?"

"I don't know. I thought I'd be happier."

"Me, too. Why aren't we?"

"Because we don't like Jim Stanley, and we know that he's gotten away with something, scot-free."

"I guess you're right. But we couldn't have done it any other way—could we?"

"No. I've gone over it again and again, and he had us over a barrel. We could never have proved our case without Jim Stanley's testimony, and we never would have gotten that without giving him immunity. That doesn't make me like him one bit better, though."

"Me, neither. I feel like I need a good long shower."

They rode in silence for a few more miles. Suddenly, Laura cried out.

"What is it?" Carlton asked. "You just about scared the shit out of me!"

"The payment! The special master who's looking at Stanley's business would have found that payment! Damn!"

"So what about it?"

"I mean that we would have found Jim Stanley eventually, even if we hadn't found that the hotel record was screwy. Oh, God, I've been such a bonehead!"

"Whoa. Don't be so hard on yourself. We might never have noticed the payment—remember it was made *by* James Stanley *to* James Stanley. It would have looked like he was just shifting funds around his accounts."

"That's true," Laura said, only partly reassured. "But what if we *had* noticed it? We could have found Jim Stanley and implicated him *without* giving him immunity."

"He still would have taken the Fifth, don't you think?"

"A plea bargain could have gotten him talking. Well, there's no point crying over spilled milk. Although we *could* argue inevitable discovery and try to void the immunity . . ."

"Don't lawyer this thing too much, okay? We've got

James Stanley, and I'd like to see it stay that way. Look on the bright side, girl—you just caught yourself a killer. You should be feeling great right now."

"You're right, Carlton. It's just hard to celebrate something so completely, utterly sad."

CHAPTER 15

Meredith Gaffney put down Jim Stanley's statement and removed the wire-rimmed half-glasses she needed for reading. "What a story. What a damned *liar*."

Laura was startled. "You mean you think it's not true?" Panic washed over her.

"No, no, not that—just the bit about not knowing why Stanley wanted him to give him an alibi. He must have known James Stanley was up to something criminal."

Laura fiddled anxiously with the heart-shaped stone on the necklace she always wore. "I know. You don't get five-thousand-dollar paydays for innocent deceptions. And now I'm sorry I gave this creep the deal. Do you think we can get around it? I thought that we could argue that the payment from James to Jim would have inevitably led to the discovery of the conspiracy. We found the record of the payment, by the way—would you believe that the creep made it with funds from one of his kids' trust? Can't we void the immunity?''

"It's a long shot, at best. If we try to void the immunity on *any* grounds, this Hoyt guy will have us tied up in court for months. And I don't want to do anything fancy until after we get James Stanley indicted anyway. We'll go with what we've got. But if it makes you feel any better, I would have done exactly the same thing. Who knows if we would have smelled a rat just by looking at Stanley's bank records? We've got the real killer, and that's all that matters. Jim Stanley will get his someday, I'm sure."

"I wonder what Craig Fannin will do."

"Nothing, right away. He'll let us set a trial date, and he'll want to look at our case. We'll offer to take the death penalty off the table if he pleads his client."

"What if he doesn't?"

"He won't. And I'm ready to rumble if he is. What we have isn't perfect, of course—it would be great to get some solid forensic evidence placing him at the crime scene— but Craig's alibi defense is gone."

"Unless, of course, he places James somewhere other than the house *or* the hotel."

"Yes, that had occurred to me. This is going to be very interesting. Now, let's get our ducks in a row and get this thing in front of the grand jury next week. You'll need to get your witnesses subpoenaed and send notices to all the concerned parties."

"Who do we want to call as witnesses?"

"I think just the detectives, Jim Stanley, and the systems guy at the hotel. That'll be good enough for now. Let me know as soon as you get on the calendar, and I'll call Craig Fannin myself."

"Why?"

"Professional courtesy. He'll get a formal notification,

but he'll appreciate a phone call before the press gets hold of the story. Now get cracking."

The operations of a grand jury were mysterious to the uninitiated, and Laura was very uninitiated. Her limited experience in criminal defense had never included a grand jury indictment—even Jeff Williams's case hadn't gone that far. Everything Laura thought she knew was merely theoretical, and mostly incorrect. Luckily, there was an entire division of the district attorney's office that dealt with grand jury proceedings, and Laura was able to lean heavily on its expertise. She was soon deep in the arcane, ancient mysteries of the grand jury system.

The grand jury met only two days a week, so the assistant district attorneys who managed its caseload had to perform a sort of triage, taking the most pressing cases first. Christine Stanley's murder went straight to the front of the line, partly because the bill of indictment was for malice murder, the highest crime possible, but also partly because of sheer, sordid politics. *People* v. *James Allen Stanley* was scheduled to be heard by the jury on Wednesday, one week after Laura and Carlton had returned to Atlanta.

Meredith and Randy Travers had decided, given the high profile of the case, that the indictment should be obtained prior to an arrest warrant being issued for Stanley. "He's not a risk for flight," Meredith explained to Laura, "and it's always smart to proceed with caution before slapping the handcuffs on a taxpayer like Stanley. We don't want this to blow up in our faces."

That was fine with Laura, who was busy subpoenaing her witnesses and arranging for their appearances. She had to explain to Jim Stanley that a golf date could not take precedence over his appearance before the grand jury. He showed a tendency to pout about it, but she quashed his objections. Wayne Catrall, the systems genius from the Marriott, raised no objections at all to taking a couple of days off to fly to Atlanta and testify. Other than Travers, who would present the crime-scene evidence, those were all the witnesses they needed. Laura had made a halfhearted argument for calling Lynette Connell to testify.

"Nope. She's all hearsay," Meredith answered.

"But she's the best motive witness we have!"

"Randy is going to summarize the special master's report, and that should take care of the financial motive. We can also slip Christine's visit to the divorce lawyer into Randy's testimony."

"Wouldn't that be hearsay, too?"

"Not if I have a photocopy of the attorney's calendar to introduce."

"Oh. It's just that I think Lynette would make a great witness."

"At the trial, yes, maybe she would. But my theory on grand jury hearings is 'Less is more, and for God's sake keep it simple.' If the jurors want more, we can always give it to them, but I think that after they hear your boy Jim it'll be unanimous."

Laura had to be satisfied with that, and a promise that she could attend the proceedings, although she would not be allowed to enter evidence or question witnesses. She didn't mind; she was a great believer in learning by observation. For the rest of the week after she returned from North Carolina, she concentrated all her energies on making Meredith look good. This was a role Laura had rehearsed to perfection under Tom Bailey's tutelage—Meredith never needed to worry that Laura would forget to file an important document, or to notify a party to a proceeding. And Laura didn't pester Meredith with a lot of irrelevant questions; she knew that she could get answers from the clerks more quickly—and maybe more accurately. She did inform Meredith, though, when the notifications were sent out—including one to James Stanley in care of Craig Fannin. Fannin immediately called a press conference, preempting Marshall Oliver's planned announcement that his office was moving to indict James Stanley. Laura thought that they had given away a strategic opportunity by letting Fannin run the story. Meredith just laughed. "So what has Craig gained? Nothing. I think he's running a risk of painting himself into a corner with all this press coverage—he's going to look like a chump if he eventually asks us for a deal."

"I guess so, but I've started thinking of him as the enemy. *He's* the one who made it personal, after all—he should have kept my name out of it."

"It's never personal with Craig, believe me. He just likes to create distractions. You think Randy's bothered by all the stuff Craig's been saying about the investigation?"

"I don't think *anything* bothers Randy."

"And you should adopt his attitude."

Easier said, Laura thought as she returned to her work. She had a voice mail message from Lynette Connell, however, which gave her an entirely new problem to consider. Should she return the call? She decided that she could rely on her own discretion, and dialed the number. The phone was answered by a woman with a Spanish accent. "Miss Lynette is in the barn. I will transfer you to her."

Lynette picked up after a few more rings. "Hello?" she said, sounding breathless.

"Lynette? Laura Chastain. Did I catch you at a bad time?"

"No, of course not—I was just grooming a horse for a show tomorrow and he's giving me fits. I need a break. How are you?"

"Fine. You?"

"Okay. I hadn't heard from you in a while, but I did

hear that you're going to get an indictment of The Asshole. Nice going."

"How did you hear that?"

"His lawyer called Daddy—he said that we should probably count on taking the kids for a couple of days, to shield them from the publicity. I assume that James is also going to be in jail for a while."

"I don't know about that. He's probably bailable."

"Can't you keep him in until he goes on trial? They put O.J. away, didn't they?"

"O.J. proved that he was a flight risk—James hasn't done anything to make a judge suspect that he'll run off. Listen, I probably shouldn't be discussing this with you at all."

"Oh, come on—if his lawyer knows all about it, what's the big secret? Just tell me one thing: What did you get on him?"

"I definitely can't tell you that."

"But does it prove anything?"

"I think so, but that's up to the grand jury to decide," Laura said cautiously.

Lynette laughed. "Okay, I get it—I should mind my own business. Speaking of which, I heard you met Jesse."

"You talked to him?"

"He called me—Lord knows I wouldn't have called him. He thought you were cute."

"He's just one big hormone, isn't he? What else did he say?"

"Nothing really—just that he was glad he had an alibi."

Laura chuckled. "I met his alibi. A checkout girl at the Publix, with a nose ring."

"That's a bit off the main road for him. Still, I'm glad that he's not mixed up with James. I know—that topic is not open for discussion. Anyway, the real reason I called you was to ask you if you wanted to come riding this weekend.''

"Gosh, I'd love to, but I don't know if I should."

"Why the hell not?" Lynette sounded offended.

"Lynette, you *are* a witness in a criminal matter. There might be a conflict, or the appearance of a conflict. I wouldn't want to do the defense any favors. Let me run it past my boss, and I'll call you back.''

Laura felt slightly goofy approaching Meredith to ask for permission, in effect, to play with one of her friends. Meredith apparently saw nothing unusual in the situation, however. "I don't see why not. We're not calling her to testify in the grand jury proceedings, and I doubt we'll need her for the trial."

"Of course we'll need her! She'd be a great witness—why shouldn't we use her?''

"For one thing, I'm still expecting Craig to cut a deal with us once he hears what your witnesses have to say. But even if we do have a full-on trial, I'm not sure Lynette Connell would do us a lot of good. It's obvious that she has an ax to grind, and Craig might be able to do some damage to her on the stand."

"What kind of damage?''

"Oh, you know—she's a trustee for Christine Stanley's children, so she stands to gain from James Stanley's conviction. And there's that old boyfriend of hers—I'm not one hundred percent comfortable that he wasn't the source of the gun, alibi or no alibi. I'm not saying anything against Lynette as a person; I'm just afraid she's a little too messy to be useful to us. But the good news is that I see no problem with your socializing with her all you want to."

"She's really a very nice person," Laura said, a little defensively.

"I'm sure she is. And even if we don't call her as a witness, she can give a victim-impact statement at the trial."

"That's a good thought. Thanks, Meredith."

Laura called Lynette and accepted her invitation, on the condition that she be allowed to take a rain check until after the grand jury proceedings were concluded. That way, she felt she could avoid any awkward moments. After the grand jury indicted James, everything would be on the public record, and they could discuss it to their hearts' content.

After all the preparations, the actual grand jury hearing was anticlimactic for Laura—although she guessed that it was anything but for James Stanley. The jury returned a "true bill" against Stanley for malice murder after a brief deliberation. All the witnesses had been effective, especially Wayne Catrall, the computer expert. "Isn't he adorable?" Laura gloated to Meredith. "He's so self-assured—can you believe he's only twenty?"

"Is he? I thought he was much older. He's very convincing. I wish I could say the same of your star witness."

"Jim? What's the problem with him?"

"He's sort of smug, I think, and cocky. He smiles too much when he tells his story, like he thinks it's just a ripping yarn. I told him to try to keep in mind that this is about a dead woman and her two orphaned children, but I don't think I got through."

"Maybe he's just nervous—some people act strange when they're tense. I think he put the story over, though, don't you?"

"Oh, yes, the grand jury didn't have any trouble with his testimony. And we have time to work on him before a regular jury sees him. Overall, I'd say you done good, kid."

"Thanks," Laura said, foolishly gratified by the praise.

After the indictment was handed down, Randy Travers

swore out a warrant for Stanley's arrest. Craig Fannin had arranged for his client to surrender voluntarily, so that he would be spared the humiliation of being handcuffed and taken away from his home or office. Meredith had warned that they should be especially careful not to upset the Stanley children. She assisted Fannin in arranging a speedy arraignment and bail hearing. Fannin made a strong argument that Stanley's ties to the community and to his family would prevent his fleeing. Meredith countered that a million-dollar bond should back up Fannin's promise. The judge eventually agreed to a five-hundred-thousand-dollar bond, and James Stanley was free to go.

And Laura was free to visit Lynette without qualms about conflicts of interest. Saturday morning she drove to the Connells' farm in northern Cobb County, northwest of the city. Lynette had described her father's house as "a plain old ranch," but that didn't begin to do justice to the low, sprawling farmhouse that came into view as Laura rounded a bend in the driveway. She parked on the circular drive that ran in front of the house, hauled her saddle from the backseat of her car, and lugged it onto the wide front porch. The door opened before she could ring the bell, and a smiling woman in a housekeeper's uniform greeted her. "You are Miss Chastain?" Laura recognized the Spanish-accented voice who had answered the phone.

"Yes. I'm here to see Miss Connell."

"She is in the barn, miss. She says you should go on back there. Follow me, please."

Laura followed on through the antique-filled hallway and into a sunny room that looked out onto a landscape of fields and paddocks. It was hard to believe that she was only a few miles from some of the worst suburban sprawl in the country. The housekeeper opened a French door and pointed to a structure on the far side of the paddock. "There it is, miss."

"Thank you." Laura followed a gravel path that wound through flower beds to the barn. She found Lynette inside cleaning tack.

"Hey! You finally made it. You brought your own saddle? Great. I thought I'd get you up on Mica. His name was Orgueil de Flandres when we bought him, but we're just old rednecks who can't speak French, so we changed his name. Come on and have a look at him."

Mica was a huge silver-gray warmblood gelding. "I like his looks," Laura said. She reached forward to pet Mica's nose. The horse reared and rolled his eye back in its socket. "Ho, boy!" Laura said. "Lynette, I'm afraid this might be a little too much horse for me."

"Don't be silly—you can ride anything in this stable. Besides, what's the worst that can happen? You might take a spill."

And break my neck, and get my skull trampled in, Laura added, but Lynette was busy calming the huge horse, holding out her hand and clucking her tongue softly. The horse calmed, and thrust his nose into her palm and snuffled. "There, see how sweet he is? You wouldn't want me to put you up on some old mattress with feet—even if I had a wimpy horse. You'll love this boy." Laura was less sanguine, after more than a year out of the saddle, but she said nothing. She didn't want Lynette to think she was a wimp. Lynette entered Mica's stall and attached a lead rope to his bridle. Together they saddled him up and led him outside into a sunlit ring, which Laura noted was of championship caliber—no potholes or puddles to be seen. There were a couple of massive jumps set up in the center, which Laura immediately decided she would decline to attempt. "Get on up, and I'll get my horse and join you."

Laura led Mica to the mounting block and got up. The horse sidled and tossed his head, but Laura spoke firmly to him and set him at a moderate walk around the ring. She was gaining confidence, trying him at a trot, when Lynette joined her, mounted on a gorgeous chestnut mare. "This is Austen. Mean as a rattlesnake, but she can jump anything. How do you like Mica?"

"Love him. Do you show him?"

"Not yet—he's a little green. And I really don't have anyone to ride him regularly. I don't suppose you'd be interested?"

"I certainly would be. Can I try his canter?"

"Be my guest."

Laura rode happily for the next hour, taking Mica through his paces, and testing her own skills. She felt rusty and a little uncertain after more than a year away from the ring, so she declined Lynette's offer to set up a few easy jumps. "Another time," she said. "I'm going to be sore enough as it is just from riding flat—the last thing I need is to land on my butt."

She was pleasantly exhausted when Lynette suggested that they cool down the horses on the well-groomed track that ran around the largest paddock. "This is where I set up the Grand Prix course," she said. "We have a low-key show for my students here twice a year. It's fun for them, and I enjoy all the planning."

"This is such a beautiful place," Laura said. "I envy you—all this space, and so green."

Lynette nodded. "Daddy gets disgusted with the commuter traffic, and talks about selling, but I won't let him. I like being close to the city. Or I did, anyway, while Chrissie was alive. We haven't talked about what we're going to do after the trial. Maybe the best thing would be to take the children away from here, maybe out to Greene County or someplace like that. We have some land there."

"You're going to take the children if James is convicted?"

"Of course! That's what Chrissie would have wanted. His parents won't try to get custody. At least, I hope they won't, for the good of Matthew and Sara."

"Do James's parents live around here?"

"No, they're in North Carolina. There's no way Daddy would let those children go up there—except for visits."

"And if James isn't convicted?"

"What are you talking about? Of course he will be! You of all people should know that!"

"Funny things happen in the legal system, Lynette. There's no telling what a jury may do."

"I think that lawyer should plea bargain, don't you? He's got to know he can't win. James should just admit he's guilty and save everyone a lot of heartache."

"Craig Fannin might not see things that way. From where he sits, his case might look pretty good."

"How could it? You've *proved* that The Asshole did it!"

"Not exactly. I've proved that he lied about where he was that night, and that he conspired with someone to hide his whereabouts—but that doesn't prove he killed your sister. The investigation has to continue, even though we have an indictment."

"Why are you just telling me this now? I thought everything was taken care of, and now you tell me that he might get off!" Lynette seemed panicky.

"No, it would be naïve to assume that we had tied it up with a ribbon. Craig Fannin is no patsy, Lynette, and he's going to go to the limit for his client. He's going to argue that we don't know where James went that night, and he knows that right now we don't have proof that he came back to Atlanta. If I were in his shoes, I would argue that the evidence doesn't convict James beyond a reasonable doubt."

"That's so cynical! Don't you believe that James is guilty?"

"Of course I do, and I'm not cynical—just realistic. Look, the trial is scheduled for October—barring delays—and by then we should have a much stronger case. We may get the gun, which is really critical. The crime lab is working on some fiber evidence—we know what clothes James was wearing when he showed up in Charlotte. Maybe they can match the fibers they found on the broken door to them. And maybe Craig Fannin will decide it's wiser not to go to trial. All I'm saying, Lynette, is that you should be prepared for anything."

"I hear you. Let's put these horses up. Can you stick around a while? I'd like you to meet Daddy. I thought we could have lunch."

"Sure. Can I help with the horses?"

"Of course. You can wash 'em while I run out the rest of them. Care to muck out a stall or two?"

"It would be my pleasure."

Two hours later, a very sweaty Laura was introduced to Lester Connell. He didn't seem to notice, however, that her hair was a mess and her clothes were filthy as he extended a callused hand to Laura and greeted her, looking straight into her eyes. He looked more like an old farmer than a millionaire land baron, Laura thought. His face was a delta of wrinkles and his skin was sun-roughened and brown. They sat down on a patio overlooking the paddocks to eat lunch served by the housekeeper. They talked about horses for a while, but Lester clearly had other things on his mind.

"You're the gal who's prosecuting James?" he asked abruptly.

"Yes, sir."

He nodded. "Lynette's all for it. She never liked him. I say it doesn't matter anymore how we feel—I say what about the children? How's it going to be for them to lose their father and their mother?"

"It's a tragic situation, Mr. Connell, but we have no choice but to prosecute. You can't just let someone get away with murder."

"I understand. But I'll speak at the trial against the death penalty. I never was for it anyway. Foolishness. Those children will need help. A lot of help."

"We're going to do everything we can for them, Daddy," Lynette said, patting his hand.

Lester looked at his daughter sharply. "I'm seventy years old. I can't be a daddy to them."

"But I can be like a mother. I'll never take Chrissie's place, but I can try."

He shook his head sadly. "Nothing's like a mother. You know what is was like after your own mama died. No, you can say whatever you want to about James, but he's their daddy. Anyway you look at this, it's our family that loses. You go on and have your trial, miss. You do what you have to do. But I won't be celebrating."

PART TWO

SEPTEMBER

CHAPTER 16

Laura brushed her hand across her sweaty forehead, unwittingly smudging it with black dirt. Her hands were beginning to blister, even though she was wearing gloves. She wanted to stop, but she could see that Amos was nowhere near ready to quit. "Damn his energy," she muttered as she resumed jabbing at the rock-hard ground with her trowel.

They were working on Laura's "garden," which was a very kind way to refer to the weed-choked patch of ground behind her house. It had *seemed* like a good idea—Laura had imbibed many seed catalogs since she acquired a house—but now, in the heat of a September afternoon, the rewards of a blooming garden seemed as remote as Eden itself. Laura's task was to dig up the old flower beds in search of any ancient bulbs that had managed to survive years of neglect, while Amos roto-tilled the sparse lawn. He had offered her the roto-tilling job, but she had thought that digging up a few jonquils and the odd bearded iris seemed simpler and less taxing. She glared at his back as he zipped easily through another few feet of earth. He must have been aware of her scrutiny, because he stopped the machine, raised his protective goggles, and gave her a mischievous grin. "Getting tired?" he asked.

"This is impossible," she said. "I've been digging like a Welsh miner and I've only got about ten of them up."

"I told you to use the spade—you can't dig in this hard ground with that little thing. Want me to take a turn?"

"No. Let's just forget these old bulbs. I can order some new ones."

He shrugged. "It's your garden. I just thought you might like to save what you could of the old things. All they need is to be divided and given a little fertilizer, and they'll do better than anything you can get from a catalog."

"Well, let's stop and rest for a little bit. My back is killing me."

Amos nodded, took off his gloves, and disappeared into the house. He returned in a moment with two bottles of beer. "Here you go." They sat down at Laura's new patio table and sipped in silence for a few minutes.

"Amos, where did you learn how to garden?"

He shrugged. "Just picked it up when I bought my first house, I guess. I'm no expert, but I can get some things to grow."

"I can't even keep potted plants alive."

"That's why we're giving you a strictly low-maintenance garden. Once we get it planted, it should take care of itself—except for the occasional weeding, or fertilizing. Of course, you could get some insect damage, or maybe have problems with moles or rabbits . . ."

"Stop. You're exhausting me." She gazed out at what they had done so far. "It will be nice, though." The yard she had inherited might not have not been cared for, but it was nicely shaped, level, and it boasted a shapely, thriving holly tree in one corner. A lush bank of pink, red, and white azaleas had bloomed the previous spring without any prompting from her. It had potential. Amos had planned two simple rectangular beds and a small lawn— small enough, Laura had specified, to be cut with a push-mower. She refused to invest in a power mower—too sub-urban.

The beer perked her up sufficiently to allow her to watch patiently as Amos showed her how to dig up the dormant bulbs with a spade. They returned to work. Despite the heat, there was an end-of-summer feeling to the weekend—Labor Day was past, and Laura felt the pull of that back-to-school circadian rhythm, even though her summer had been far from leisurely. Crime, if anything, rises in the warm months, and Laura had been run off her feet covering for vacationing co-workers. She wasn't eligible to take time off herself until Christmas, although she had managed a few weekends in Nashville and a run to the mountains over the Fourth of July holiday—and she had ridden at Lynette's barn at every opportunity. She had even showed Mica in a flat class—no jumping—at one of Lynette's informal shows and done quite well. Not much of note had happened at the office, although she could look back in pride at how well she had performed the ordinary tasks. Meredith was giving her more responsibility all the time, and there were a couple of armed robbers and a carjacker who weren't going to be forming a Laura Chastain fan club anytime soon.

Always, though, at the back of her mind, was the James Stanley case. Everything else felt like a rehearsal for the big opening of the only trial anyone in Atlanta cared about. And yet the case had been strangely quiescent these months—too quiet, Laura reflected frowningly as she turned up the earth of her backyard. There had been some activity a few weeks earlier, which had whetted her appetite for more.

Carlton Hemingway had called her on a sullen August morning. It had been weeks since she had last talked to him. "Carlton! I thought you had been promoted or something! What have you been doing?"

"Nothing much. Just the routine cases—it seems like nobody has the energy to murder ingeniously during the summer. I've been looking for you at the courthouse, but I guess our paths just haven't crossed. Are you busy?"

"Not excruciatingly. Why?"

"The crime lab is ready to report to us on that fiber evidence. I thought you might like to tool out there with me and hear what they have to say."

A trip to the GBI crime lab would indeed be a welcome distraction, and Laura had agreed readily to meet Carlton downstairs in an hour.

The crime lab was located in Decatur, about a half hour's drive in Carlton's immaculate car. They chatted about this and that during the trip, but never mentioned the Stanley case. Although it was uppermost in both their minds, there was little they could say that wouldn't be just going over the same old ground.

At the crime lab, they were directed to the trace evidence section, where Carlton and Laura showed their IDs and asked to see Carla McNulty, who was produced and who proved to be a tired-looking woman in her late thirties. She greeted them in a pleasant Southern drawl, and asked them to step on back into her room, where she had set up a demonstration in anticipation of their arrival.

"I hope y'all aren't counting on this little bitty bit of

fiber to make your case, 'cause if you are, I'm afraid you're out of luck," Carla McNulty said with a shake of her head.

"No. We actually don't know what this fiber means," Carlton said. "We were kind of hoping you might tell us."

"I'll tell you what I know. What we have is a small sample—about six threads—of material that was found caught in the splintered wood surrounding a lock on a French-type door. There are two things I can tell you positively: one, that the splintering of the wood around the door lock was fresh. There was no dust or oxidation present which would have indicated that it had been broken some time earlier. That fits with the police theory that the intruder broke in through the door on the night of the crime. Second, because we know the lock was broken by the intruder, we can assume that the fibers were also left by the intruder—he or she brushed against the broken wood and caught a garment on the jagged pieces. Now, as to what we have here, I wish I could be more helpful. Step over to the microscope and take a look."

Carlton went first, screwing up his eye against the microscope. "It looks like two kinds of fiber," he commented as he stepped aside. Laura looked, and saw what appeared to be two threads twisted together, one dark and thick and one lighter and thinner.

"That's right," Carla said. "What you're seeing is a wool-and-acrylic blend of the type used to make suiting material. Unfortunately, we don't have a large enough sample to determine how the fabric was woven—if we had that, we might be able to trace it to a manufacturer. But I can tell you that, in all likelihood, the sample you're looking at comes from a gray tropical-weight wool-blend suiting."

"In other words, it's from one of possibly a billion gray suits?" Laura asked.

Carla laughed. "Make it two billion, and you've just about got it."

"But," Carlton said, "if Stanley had a suit made of material like this, we can link him to the fibers found in the door."

"He surely would have gotten rid of it by now," Laura said. "He would have realized it was torn."

"Not necessarily," Carla said. "This was a very small sample—it would have looked more like a snag, or an irregularity on the fabric, than a real tear."

Laura thought for a long moment. "Carlton, what did Jim say Stanley was wearing when he finally showed up at the hotel?"

Carlton consulted his notebook. "Khaki trousers and a sports shirt."

"Which means he changed his clothes," Laura said.

"Or that he wasn't at the crime scene," Carlton corrected her.

"No, he changed, because he was splattered with blood. He must have gotten rid of that suit somehow, just like he got rid of the gun."

Carla consulted her file. "I see that the firearms section determined that the shooter was about ten feet away from the victim. At that distance, he would have been spattered with very fine droplets—so fine that they would be almost invisible to the naked eye. He may not have known that he had bloodstains on him at all."

"So if we can find a gray suit belonging to our suspect, with a slight snag in the fabric and microscopic bloodstains on it, we can show he's the shooter," Laura said.

"I would say that's correct," Carla said.

Laura looked at Carlton. "I can get a search warrant for James Stanley's clothes."

"Let's do it, then," he replied. "Thanks a lot, Carla. We'll see you at the trial."

Laura waited with anxious high hopes while Carlton and a team of crime-scene technicians executed the search warrant, seizing every gray garment in Stanley's wardrobe while the suspect fumed and called his lawyer. There was nothing Fannin could do, however, and armfuls of expensive clothes were hauled away and taken to the crime lab. It only took a day or two for a discouraging report to come back: James Stanley owned nothing but one hundred percent wool suits, slacks, and sportscoats, although a great many of those were gray. The crime lab examined all the clothing for bloodstains anyway, but no one was surprised when they found none.

"He got rid of it, that's all," Laura said. "He wore his oldest, cheapest suit, and he ditched it before he got to Charlotte—just like he ditched the gun. We need that gun, dammit. How hard can it be to find out where he got an antique military sidearm anyway?"

"You'd be surprised," Carlton answered. "We're crosschecking registration records from all over the country, but the thing about a gun like that is that it might never have been permitted at all. Lots of soldiers brought them back from Europe and just stuck them away in their closets."

"Did James Stanley have a near relative—father, uncle, whatever—who served in Europe during the war?"

"No. His dad was in the Pacific, and neither of his uncles were sent overseas. We've thought of all of this already."

"How did he get the gun, then, if he didn't get it from Jesse and he didn't already have it?"

"I'm stumped."

And that was the last contact she had had with the

investigation. She hopped on the spade with all her weight, and wedged its blade beneath a chunk of earth. She plucked a bulb from the spadeful of earth, and plunged the shovel back into the hard ground as forcefully as she could. She was thinking about the trial and not about her garden at all. She had every reason to be confident in their case, of course, but doubts continued to nag at her. *We need to prove that he was in that house on the night Christine Stanley died,* she thought. *Without that, there's reasonable doubt, although a jury might not buy that a man would go to the elaborate lengths James Stanley had just to get a night out—faking a business trip and paying a co-conspirator five thousand dollars is pretty weird behavior for an innocent man.* Yes, that was certainly reassuring. *But why can't we link him to a gun?* Laura's foot slipped off the shovel, and she caught herself as she almost fell. *Jesse DuPree must know more than he's saying. We need to take a look at his financial records. James might have paid him to lie.* She rammed the spade into the dirt with unconscious violence.

"Whoa there. You look like you're trying to beat the ground to death with that thing." She hadn't noticed that Amos had turned off the tiller and was standing behind her.

"I'm thinking about James Stanley. That always brings out the animal in me."

"What about James Stanley?" Amos asked patiently. He had heard Laura go over every aspect of the case at least a thousand times, but he always pretended to be interested.

"The gun. Here we have this distinctive weapon, and yet we can't find hide nor hair of it. What does that make you think?"

"That James Stanley never owned the gun."

"What makes you say that?" she asked, dropping the spade and looking at him with interest.

"If he had bought a gun from that guy who dated the sister . . ."

"Jesse DuPree."

"Right. DuPree would have told you."

"Unless Jesse is also a co-conspirator. I was just thinking we should look at his financial records."

Amos shook his head. "The last thing a legitimate gun dealer wants or needs is to be caught up in a crime like this—although you should check into him. Who knows? He might be stupid enough to do it, and I admit it's one helluva coincidence that Christine Stanley was killed with a rare weapon of a type DuPree was known to deal in."

"And Travers has checked the records of every other dealer specializing in antique weapons in the country without turning up a thing."

"That's why I've come to the conclusion that James Stanley didn't own the gun at all, and that, in fact, he may have been in possession of it only long enough to commit the crime."

"That's a good point," Laura said, excited. "So what we need to do is look at every known gun of that type and determine if Stanley had access to it—starting with Jesse's stock."

"Correct. You know already that James Stanley didn't have a gun like that in his own family, so look at a wider circle. Friends? Clients? Did he know any gun collectors?"

Laura blanched. "Actually, his father-in-law collects guns—but I think they're just for hunting. I guess we should check that out. I wonder if Lester Connell fought in Europe?"

"There you go. Carlton Hemingway can get started checking it out first thing Monday morning. In the meantime, I can't till anymore until you finish digging these old flower beds. Or would you like me to finish for you?"

"Would you? I hate to be a wimp, but this is killing me."

Amos took the shovel, and fifteen minutes later he had recovered all the old bulbs that yard could yield. He looked into the bucket where Laura had tossed them. "It would have cost you a hundred bucks to buy that many. I'll just finish tilling so I can fertilize and seed the grass tomorrow."

Laura looked at her watch. "It's after six. I'll go take a quick shower and start dinner. Did you bring something to change into, or do you need to go home?"

"Nope. I brought some clothes. And I brought Scrabble," he added hopefully.

"Bring it on," she said.

CHAPTER 17

With James Stanley's trial only a few weeks away, Laura was not the only busy lawyer in Atlanta. Craig Fannin was not letting the grass grow under his feet, either—at least Laura assumed that it was Fannin who was behind the spate of news stories that began appearing in September. The first salvo was fired by the Atlanta *Constitution*, the morning paper, which printed a rehash of the case, heavy on sentiment but short on new revelations. Meredith even gave them an innocuous quote. Laura saw no cause for concern until one of the television stations ran a story alleging that her key witness had some experience of his own with the legal system.

Laura was no fan of the local news broadcasts, which hewed to the "if it bleeds, it leads" school of television journalism. She was always reminding herself that she should watch them for any references to the cases she was working on, but she was just as happy to let Ilona and her

PR crew do the dirty work. She was wallowing in her usual state of blessed ignorance when Meredith stuck her head into Laura's cubicle one fine September morning and asked, "Did you see the news?" with a wry expression on her face.

"No. Should I have?"

"Come on; I'll show you the tape. They got Jim Stanley's name."

"Not from us!" Laura said, half asserting, half questioning. As a matter of policy, no one from the district attorney's office would discuss grand jury testimony with anyone from the press. Craig Fannin, however, was under no such obligation.

"No, I'm sure it was Craig's doing. But that's not all they have." They entered the conference room, where a small television and VCR were hidden in a cabinet. Meredith punched the Play button on a remote and the handsome-but-empty talking head of news anchor Hank Morse appeared.

There are new developments to report tonight in the investigation of the murder of Brookhaven housewife Christine Stanley. Sources close to the investigation have informed the Live Eye news team that a key witness in the case has had some experience with the legal system himself. Here's Dorinda Lewis live with details.

The cameras cut away to a reporter standing outside the Fulton County Courthouse. "Why do they do that?" Meredith mused. "Why do they stand outside when nothing is happening?"

"I'm just glad they're not at James Stanley's house. Is this about Lynette?"

"Shh. You'll see."

Dorinda adjusted her earpiece and spoke into her microphone.

Thanks, Hank. The Live Eye has learned that a key witness against James Stanley has himself been in trouble with the law more than once. Jim Stanley of Winston-Salem, North Carolina, testified to the grand jury hearing charges against James Stanley that he had conspired with James Stanley to provide him with an alibi. It was the similarity in the two men's names that gave them the idea. Jim Stanley checked into a hotel in Charlotte, pretending to be the husband of the murdered woman on the night of her death. Police investigators discovered the ruse, and Jim Stanley was granted full immunity in exchange for his testimony. Our own investigation has revealed that Jim Stanley—that's the one in North Carolina, Hank, not Christine Stanley's husband—has a record of drug convictions. He's also no stranger to immunity deals, Hank. He was given immunity by the state attorney general of North Carolina in a fraud case two years ago.

How will this affect the case against James Stanley, Dorinda?

We're not sure, Hank. Right now we don't have a comment from the district attorney's office. James Stanley's attorney, Craig Fannin, gave us a statement, however. In it he says, "Immunity agreements are one tool that prosecutors have in their box, and I don't mind their use—as long as the testimony they elicit is fair and truthful. We plan to show that the second Mr. Stanley's testimony is neither of these things."

Sounds like things are heating up. We'll certainly be keeping our ears open on this case, Dorinda. Thanks for that report.

Meredith stopped the tape. "What do you think?"

"I think Craig Fannin hired a private detective."

"Me, too. Did you know any of this?"

"Of course not! I would have told you right away!"

"We need to get on top of this," Meredith said. "Call Randy Travers and ask him if he can put a man onto researching Jim Stanley's background. If he can't, I'll find some money to hire someone of our own."

"Do you think our case is hurt?"

"Not yet, but I've been waiting for a shoe to drop. Craig has been unnaturally quiet lately. But there's no cause for panic—James Stanley has a hell of a lot to explain, any way you look at it. But bring me details—I need details. We'll plan our next step when we know exactly what Craig has on our boy."

Laura hurried to do her boss's bidding. She called Carlton, not Randy, however, preferring not to get chewed out, which she anticipated Travers would do with relish. Carlton wasn't aware of the report on Jim Stanley. "It looks bad, Carlton," Laura said. "Of course, the news people were playing it for maximum effect. The drug convictions could be a couple of marijuana busts, and the fraud case—well, I don't see how that can have anything to do with us."

"It does show that Jim Stanley has a propensity for getting into trouble with the law—and that he knew about immunity deals anyway. That must have been his strategy all along—get us to come across with the free pass before he talked."

"Yeah. And so much for his argument that he didn't know James was up to no good. God, I'm beginning to hate Jim Stanley. I can't get past the feeling that I've let him get away with something."

"I wouldn't beat myself up—and I was there, too, remember. What we have to do now is get busy. Unfortunately, we're real busy over here. I don't think Randy can spare an investigator. What about your guys?"

"Always too busy to take on something like this. But Meredith said she might find the money to hire someone. Run it past Randy anyway—if he says no, we'll take it here. Meanwhile, do you have anything new on the gun?"

"Negative. We checked out Mr. Connell's collection—the old boy nearly blew a gasket when we told him what we were after—but it's strictly hunting weapons. We're running down every other possibility we can think of, but it's going to take a long time."

"I'd hate to go to trial without that gun."

"Can't you postpone the trial?"

"Nope. James Stanley has requested a speedy trial, which means it has to be in this session of the Superior Court. He seems to be in a hurry for some reason—usually they want all the time they can get." Laura sighed. "I'm getting a bad feeling about all this, Carlton. Give me a holler if you need us to take up the investigation of Jim Stanley's record."

Randy ultimately got Jim Stanley's sheet from the authorities in North Carolina, but it was short on detail. Meredith decided to hire someone to run down the story. Laura suggested Kenny Newton, since Meredith knew him, too. Kenny was only too happy to get a "real" job. "I've been peeping into too many bedrooms lately," he said. "I'm beginning to feel like a special prosecutor."

"Then this will be a welcome break for you; Jim Stanley is a whole different kind of sleaze."

"What you got on him so far?"

"His sheet says he has two busts for drug possession— one marijuana, the other not specified. He paid a fine and got probation on the marijuana charge, but he served time on the second charge."

"What about the fraud case?"

"That's not on the sheet, but I put in a call to the North Carolina attorney general's office. It seems that he was a minor player in a bank fraud. He helped one of his pals get a mortgage on a building that the guy didn't exactly own. Jim got immunity because they wanted his partner more than they wanted him."

"Fax over what you've got, and I'll head for Carolina in the morning."

"Isn't that a song?" Kenny answered in the affirmative by singing a few off-key bars. Laura hung up on him.

Laura was privately getting very uneasy about her case. It wasn't that she thought Fannin could really impeach Jim Stanley; if he could do that, he would have come out and done so, and not bothered with all this sneaking around to the press. And it wasn't the lack of forensic evidence; trials had been won on far less than she and Meredith had to go on. But the sum total was enough to keep her awake late into the night, staring at a crack in the ceiling that she really should have fixed weeks before. The wear was beginning to show in her face and in her mood, which was sharp and snappish, so much so that she nearly took Cheryl's head off when she got another call from the receptionist announcing that she had a visitor.

"There's a man here asking to see you," Cheryl said.

"Well, what's his name?"

"I don't know."

"It didn't occur to you to *ask* him, I suppose?"

She must have been intimidating, because Cheryl put

her on hold and came back a moment later and said, "It's someone named Jesse DuPree."

"I'll be right out." What was Jesse DuPree doing in downtown Atlanta in the middle of the week? It crossed her mind that he might have just stopped in to flirt with her, but she immediately dismissed the idea as too embarrassingly egotistical. She hurried to the lobby to see what he really did want. He was standing, hands in pockets, looking at the large color photographs of district attorneys past and present that adorned the walls. "Mr. DuPree?"

"Hey!" he said, smiling widely. "Boy, you don't have to be pretty to be the district attorney, do you? I'm glad you're here. You know, I wasn't sure I could just drop in on you, but I thought it was worth a try. I have something I need to tell you."

"Come on back to my office. Want some coffee?"

Jesse declined, and Laura led him to her cubicle and offered him a chair. He looked around, astonished. "They have you in one of these little old things? I pictured you in a big fancy office."

"I'm just a public servant. The big offices are for the defense lawyers. How can I help you?"

"I think I can help *you*, actually. See, I sold a weapon to Jim Stanley a few years ago."

"You *what?*" Laura was halfway out of her chair. "Why didn't you tell us this months ago?"

"I didn't know you were interested when we first talked. But I saw on the news that Jim is a witness for you. I thought you might want to know that he had a gun like the one James Stanley was interested in."

The situation became slightly clearer. "You mean you sold a gun to *Jim* Stanley, not James?"

"That's what I said."

"But how do you know Jim Stanley?" Laura's brain was reeling from the shock.

"I've known him for years—we grew up together. He's from Snellville, out in Gwinnett, you know, and we went to the same high school."

"Did you know that he knew James Stanley?"

"Nope. I haven't seen him in years, since before he moved to Carolina. But I recognized his picture when they showed it on the news." The Jim Stanley story had continued to be newsworthy, and one station had sent a camera crew to try to get an interview with him. All they got was Jim grinning and saying, "No comment," but they ran his picture for days.

"Hold on, Jesse—I want you to tell this to my boss." Laura buzzed Meredith, and told her she needed to see her right away. She hauled Jesse around to Meredith's office and sat him down. "Meredith, this is Jesse DuPree. Jesse, this is Meredith Gaffney. I want you to tell her exactly what you just told me."

Meredith listened as Jesse went through his story again. She was initially as confused as Laura had been, but Jesse patiently straightened her out. "This business of them having the same name is getting to be a pain in the butt," Meredith commented. "Mr. DuPree, do you have a record of his buying this gun?"

Jesse grimaced. "Not exactly. See, Jim really wanted that gun, but he was still on probation from one of his drug arrests, and it would have violated the terms. So, seeing as how he was an old friend, I kinda sold it off the books. Hell, it was an antique anyway, and it was before all this checking and waiting period," he added defensively.

Laura was too excited to express reservations. "That's not good, but we can live with it. You see what it means, don't you, Meredith? We can get the gun, and we can prove that James Stanley had access to it."

"I hope we can. Why didn't Jim Stanley tell us this to start with?"

"That's exactly what I'm going to ask him," Laura said grimly. "I'd like to smack him."

"I'll help. Let's get him on the phone."

They had to go through Candi again to get Jim, but he came on, cheerful as ever, after only a short delay. "Jim? This is Laura Chastain. I have you on speakerphone because I have two people with me—Meredith Gaffney, whom you met when you came down for the grand jury, and an old friend of yours."

"Hey, Jimmy," Jesse drawled.

"Who's that?"

"Jesse DuPree."

"Oh. Hey, Jesse."

"So you do know Mr. DuPree?"

"Uh, yeah. We went to school together."

"Is that all you did together, Jim?" Laura asked sternly.

"What do you mean?"

"I mean have you had any business dealings with Mr. DuPree? Have you ever *bought* anything from him, for instance?"

There was a long silence. "I think I'd like to talk to Charlie Hoyt before I answer that," Jim said.

"Oh, come on, Jim, you have transactional immunity. You can tell me that you gave James the gun *knowing* that he was going to kill his wife with it, and I can't prosecute you for it. You're bullet-proof, Jim—you have a 'Get Your Butt Out of Trouble' card you can use anytime." Laura was growing angry.

Meredith intervened before she completely lost her temper. "Mr. Stanley, this is Meredith Gaffney. Why don't you get your attorney on the phone and call us back?" She gave him her number and hung up. "No point in hollering at him. He might be able to help us. Tell me more, Mr. DuPree. When did you sell Jim Stanley this gun?"

"Must have been about three or four years ago—it was before the new law took effect, anyway, because, like I said, I didn't have to do a background check on him. It was all aboveboard from *my* side, although he could have gotten into a bunch of trouble for it. The gun he bought is a Walther P-38. It's an antique nine millimeter."

"Was the gun in working condition?"

"Oh, yeah. I got it from an old man who had traded for it in Europe when he was in the Army over there. He kept it mint."

"It's probably the murder weapon, then. Mr. DuPree, thanks for coming to us with this. We may need you to make a formal statement. Does Laura have your address and phone number?"

"I sure hope so," Jesse said with a wink at Laura as he rose to leave. "She can call me anytime."

"Thank you, Mr. DuPree," Laura said primly.

Meredith chuckled when Jesse was out of earshot. "He's a case. I've seen about a million boys just like him."

"I can't understand why Lynette ever dated him at all."

"Oh, he's plenty attractive."

"But what would you talk about with him?" Laura asked.

Meredith hooted. "You don't *talk* with a man like that! You can talk to your girlfriends, for pity's sake."

Fortunately, Meredith's phone rang before the boss could go any further down this ribald road. Laura knew it was Charlie Hoyt because Meredith slipped into her horse-trading lawyer mode right away. "Hello, Mr. Hoyt.

We're having a little problem down here and we were hoping that you could see your way to helping us out. May I put you on my speaker? Laura Chastain is with me.'' She hit the speaker button and replaced the phone in its cradle. "I'll let Laura tell you what we'd like from your client.''

"Hello, Mr. Hoyt,'' Laura said. "You've spoken to Jim Stanley?''

"I have him on hold on the other line. I understand that there's something about a gun. . . .''

"Yes. I have a man here who claims to have sold a Nazi sidearm to your client a few years ago. The ballistics people believe that the shots that killed Christine Stanley were fired from a similar type of antique gun. It seems possible that your client was the source of the gun that James Stanley used to kill his wife.''

"You understand, Ms. Chastain, that nothing I say will be binding on my client until I discuss it with him?''

"Of course.''

"Well, let's say that Jim Stanley can produce the weapon you're interested in for ballistics testing. I want it to be clearly understood that his failure to do so earlier will have no impact on the immunity agreement we reached.''

Laura looked at Meredith. They could make a stab at voiding the immunity by claiming that Jim Stanley perjured himself by giving incomplete information. Meredith didn't seem interested, however. She nodded, and mouthed, "Okay,'' to Laura. "We can give you that assurance,'' Laura said reluctantly. She believed that now, more than ever, they had an argument for voiding the immunity on the grounds of inevitable discovery, because if they had squeezed Jesse just a little harder, they might have found Jim Stanley by tracking the gun. But Meredith was the boss, and Laura didn't want to lose what little traction they had with Charlie Hoyt.

"Fine. Let me patch Jim in," Hoyt's disembodied voice said. There was a click, and Jim was back on the line. "Jim, why don't you tell the ladies what you just told me?"

"I lent James Stanley my gun, months ago. I had no idea he was going to use it to kill anyone—he told me he was interested in buying one, and he wanted to take it to a shooting range he knew of in Georgia. I . . . I guess I should have known when he came to me about checking into the hotel that he had something in mind, but, honestly, I had almost forgotten that he had the gun."

"Why didn't you tell us this earlier?" Laura said sternly.

"I didn't know if my immunity would cover it."

"Surely you could have asked Mr. Hoyt."

Charlie Hoyt broke in. "Ms. Chastain, you had ample opportunity to question my client. He would have answered questions about this gun fully and truthfully."

"If only I had known to ask," Laura said sarcastically.

"That's water under the bridge," Hoyt said. "I assume you'll want the gun?"

"Is it back in your client's possession?" Meredith asked.

"Yes. James Stanley returned it to him that morning at the hotel. I have suggested to him that he place it in my hands, and I will have it sent to you by courier."

Laura had a notion. "We have an investigator on the ground up there on, ahh, another matter," she said. She didn't want Jim Stanley to know that they had sent Kenny up there to check *him* out. "He can pick it up from Mr. Stanley this afternoon before he returns to Atlanta."

"Fine. Jim, can you arrange to turn the gun over this afternoon?"

"Sure. Just tell him to drop by the office. It's in the safe here."

Laura swallowed her bitterness and said polite good-byes to Hoyt and his client. To Meredith, however, she vented her frustration. "Just think—that damn gun was in the office all the time! Do you have any idea how much sleep I've lost over this, and all the time that idiot had it! God, I wish I had some reason to prosecute him."

"It would be nice, but let's keep in mind that James Stanley is the one we're really after. And now I think we really have him."

"There's still one thing I'd like to do."

"What's that?"

"Find out how James Stanley got from Greenville back to Atlanta that night. I figure he rented a car, and I think we should check out the rental car agencies. Carlton says Randy can't spare him, but I could go. I could do it this weekend."

"I don't know, Laura. You don't have a lot of experience investigating. I'd prefer to have the police do it."

"Can we get Kenny to do it?"

"Afraid not. I've used up most of my budget for outside investigators already, and I don't think it's such a crucial piece of evidence."

Laura had a sudden inspiration. "What if I can persuade Amos to go with me?" she asked. "He could do something like that in his sleep."

"If he's willing to give up his day off, it's fine with me."

"I know he'll do it," Laura said eagerly. "Amos is very interested in this case."

"He's interested in something, all right," Meredith said with a grin.

Laura reassembled her dignity and left without comment.

CHAPTER 18

"This is the gun that killed Christine Stanley?" Laura was peering into a box that lay open on her desk.

"Pending ballistics confirmation, yes." Kenny Newton shook his head sadly. "Ugly bastard, isn't it?"

"They all are to me. But thanks for picking this nasty thing up anyway. I'll get it over to the police this afternoon. Did you ask Jim Stanley if he had cleaned it? I'm wondering if we might be able to get prints off it."

"Yes, I did ask him, and yes, he did clean it. You'll have to make do with a match on the slug."

"Oh, well, I guess that was just wishful thinking. So what did you think of our boy Jim Stanley?" Laura leaned back in her chair and waited for Kenny's assessment.

"Jim Stanley? He's an operator—not a very good one, but an operator." Kenny flipped open his notebook. "I didn't expect to meet him in person—that was the cream in my coffee, let me tell you. First, I talked to the narcotics detective who busted him the second time. He says it was for possession of cocaine, about a gram. Jimmy ratted out his connection to get a light sentence. He has a propensity for making deals when he gets into trouble, doesn't he? As for the fraud charge—well, he might not have been so much guilty there as he was greedy. He hooked up with a developer who said he owned a piece of land and was going to build a strip mall on it. Jim got him a construction loan and a mortgage, but they failed to disclose to the lender that the land in question was an EPA clean-up site. Jim made a convincing case that he didn't know about the designation. Anyway, the developer took the loan proceeds and skipped out. Jim was left holding the bag, so once again, he cut a deal and helped them trace the guy. They recovered most of the money."

"In other words, he is no stranger to the legal system."

"Right. He's a crappy little guy, but I don't think that Fannin can use that to help his own client. He's got a solid story to tell your jury."

"I'm glad you think so. I've been worried half to death about the trial. It's just too big a coincidence, don't you think, that Jim Stanley knows Jesse DuPree?"

"It's a big coincidence, all right. But I put my giant detective brain on the problem on the drive home, and here's what I think: Jesse and Jim tell the same story about the gun, right? Which means that either they're both lying, or they're both telling the truth."

"Right. And if they're telling the truth . . ."

"Then it really is a big coincidence. *Two* big coincidences, really, if you believe that James Stanley met Jim Stanley completely by chance."

"But what if Jim and Jesse are *lying?*"

Kenny thought for a long moment. "If they are, it's Jesse who is the linchpin of this whole thing."

"Oh, I see—he would have to be the one who introduced James to Jim, because he knows them both. And he provided the gun. But why would they have turned the gun over to Jim Stanley?"

Kenny shook his head. "Maybe it's because Jim has immunity, and Jesse didn't want to take a chance on being charged with something."

"So Jim Stanley told you the same story we got about how he came by the gun, and how he gave it to James Stanley *months* ago?"

"Yep. And you'll love this: He asked me how long it would be before he got it back—he wants to auction it on the Internet."

"No! That little creep. Is he going to advertise it as a murder weapon?"

"That I cannot say. I doubt that would add to its value, so probably not. It's the Nazi associations that bring in the bucks."

"How much is it worth?"

"I couldn't say. A good nine-millimeter gun would go for several hundred bucks. The historic angle might boost the value of this one to a collector. If you want, I'll take it over to Travers for you—I was planning on dropping in over at Homicide since I'm downtown."

"I'd appreciate it."

"And I'll write up my report on Stanley and get it to you in a day or two."

"Right—and don't forget to send us the bill."

"Not to worry."

"Hey, Kenny, before you go, there's something else I want to ask you. I want to make this case as strong as I can, and I think it might be helpful to find out how James Stanley traveled from Greenville to Atlanta to kill his wife.

I thought someone should go check out all the car rental places in Greenville. What do you think?''

Kenny nodded. ''Makes sense. I would volunteer, but Meredith made it pretty clear that she can't pay me for more than two days.''

''And Travers says he can't spare a man, either. So I thought I'd go, and ask Amos to come along—you know, to flash the badge and all that.''

''Sounds like a plan. You talked to Kowalski yet?''

''No. I thought he might say it was a stupid idea.''

''Taking a road trip with you a stupid idea? Naw, he'll jump at the chance.''

''Don't you give me that innuendo, Newton. We're just friends.''

''Now. But after a trip to a magical romantic spot like Greenville, South Carolina, who can say what might happen?''

''Don't you have some work to do?''

''Just leaving. I'll talk to you soon.''

There was no real reason to run her plans past Kenny, except to see if he would react the way he had. Laura sighed in frustration; her relationship with Amos was going to be fraught with this tension for a while, until . . . *until he gives up or I give in,* she thought. She tried to sort out why it was that she couldn't let herself get involved with him, but she bogged down in her usual muddle. It came down to Tom Bailey, of course, a man with whom she had been romantically involved for a grand total of three weeks before he was killed. If she hadn't fallen in love with Tom, she might well have started dating Amos. But if she hadn't been involved with Tom, Tom would still be alive, and she would probably still be in love with him. Which led her to construct a syllogism: *If I hadn't started dating Tom, he would still be alive: therefore, I killed him.* It was nonsense, of course, but she couldn't convince her weary little psyche of that. She gave up worrying about it and called Amos.

"Whatcha doing?" he asked after they exchanged greetings.

"Little of this, little of that. Hey, Amos, I was wondering if you've got plans this weekend."

"Nothing I can't change. Why?"

"Would you be up for a trip to Greenville, South Carolina?"

"Why do you want to go *there*? Wait a minute—does this have anything to do with James Stanley?"

"Yes. I want to check out the rental car agencies, and see if we can prove that he got off that plane and rented a car."

"Isn't this a little bit of overkill? You've got a co-conspirator to testify, and now you've got the murder weapon. Isn't that enough to make your case?"

"If James Stanley was being defended by some chump just out of law school, maybe it would be. But he's being defended by Craig Fannin, and I don't want to take any chances. I know what I would do if I were in Fannin's shoes—I'd hammer away at the fact that we can't put James Stanley at the murder scene. If we had a fiber match, I'd be happy. But we don't, so I want that damn rental car."

"Okay, okay—what's my role in all this?"

"I want you to be a cop—show them your badge and ask the questions. I think we'll have better luck that way."

"I'll do it *if* Randy Travers says it's okay with him."

"Will you ask him? I'm afraid that if I call, he'll say no. I seem to get on his nerves."

"I'm sure you're imagining that. Where is Greenville anyway? Hang on a second—let me get out my maps." There was a rustling as Amos laid a map on his desk. "Greenville is about a two-hour drive from Atlanta, straight up I-85. We could drive up there Saturday morning and spend the afternoon asking around the rental places. We better plan on staying overnight—we can always come home if we luck into something, but we might need to try again Sunday morning. What's Greenville like?''

"I've only passed through it, but I don't think it's a real garden spot. There's probably a Holiday Inn or a Hyatt or something.''

"That's no fun. Let me see what's nearby—Asheville?''

"Too far.''

"How about Brevard? That's supposed to be pretty.''

Brevard was a small and pleasant mountain town near the point where North Carolina, South Carolina, Georgia, and Tennessee almost touched. "How far is it from Greenville?'' Laura asked.

"Looks like it's less than an hour. Why don't I try to find a nice place there for us to stay? That way we can get a decent dinner and see some pretty scenery, and the weekend won't be a total waste.''

"Okay, I guess,'' Laura said, but there was hesitation in her voice. Amos must have noticed it.

"I'll book two rooms, of course,'' he said casually.

"Oh—great. Sure you don't want me to do it?''

"No, just leave it to me. I'll call you back.''

Laura hung up uneasily. *Dammit, Kenny,* she thought, *I wouldn't have worried one bit about going away overnight with Amos if you hadn't put ideas in my head.* But to do Kenny justice, Laura knew that Kenny only said what she had been thinking herself. There was something between her and Amos, and it had to be resolved sooner or later. *But if he wants it resolved this weekend,* Laura told herself, *the answer will have to be no.*

She didn't have the luxury of worrying about Amos for too long, however, as Meredith buzzed her right away.

"More fun revelations from the press. Can you come in here?"

Laura found Ilona Crawford sitting in Meredith's office with a sour look on her face. "Here's Laura," Meredith said. "She can help us. Laura, Ilona has gotten a call from a reporter asking us to confirm some more information about Jim Stanley."

"I just talked to Kenny; I have the full story right here," Laura answered, happy to be on the ball.

"Good," Ilona said. "So we want to take the position that we've been aware of the divorce all along, and that it has no bearing on our case?"

"Wait a minute—divorce? We *don't* know about a divorce."

Ilona grimaced. "I thought you had sent a detective up there to check Stanley's background."

"To check his criminal record, yes, we did. But this is the first I've heard about a divorce. What are they saying?"

"It seems that Jim Stanley's wife has filed for divorce, and she talked to a reporter about her husband's . . . propensities."

"Okay, so how bad can it be? We know he has busts for marijuana and cocaine possession on his sheet, and that he was involved in a financial fraud—what more can the wife say?"

"Plenty. She's alleging domestic violence and spousal abuse. She paints a picture of a very unstable man. She also says that he's 'a pathological liar.' "

"That's for a psychiatrist to say, not a disgruntled spouse. Any substantiation of the claims of abuse?" Laura said, quickly moving in damage-control mode.

"Yes. Police reports, hospital records, photographs—the works."

Laura turned to Meredith. "This is Fannin's doing, isn't it? I guess we're really at war now."

"You said it. It's a bar fight, no holds barred."

"But none of this really impeaches Jim's testimony, does it? Yes, he's a jerk, maybe a violent, unstable jerk, but there's nothing in any of this to disprove his story."

"You and I know that, but will the public—the public which is going to make up our jury? Craig is trying to get as much as he can out there before jury selection begins."

"I say we can turn it around on him—we can show that his client was willing to make a deal with someone who is *clearly* a criminal."

"Maybe. But I think this gives us a hint of Craig's trial strategy. We thought that he was going for reasonable doubt—and he may be yet—but now I'm thinking that he's going to present an alternate theory of the crime."

"Such as?"

"Such as a conspiracy between Jim Stanley and Jesse DuPree."

Laura paused, thinking it over. "There's no reason for those two to conspire, unless he's going to say that Lynette Connell was a part of it."

Meredith nodded. "I'm afraid so. There are always going to be casualties in a war like this one. For now, let's help Ilona draft a statement that will show how supremely unconcerned the district attorney's office is with this sideshow."

In the end, they issued a statement that was long on bravado and short on contradiction, and the allegations against Jim Stanley led the six o'clock news. Laura didn't see it, however, because she was out in her backyard, planting bulbs in the newly dug flower beds and worrying about the weekend.

CHAPTER 19

There were many, many places to rent a car in Greenville, South Carolina—so many that, after six fruitless and frustrating hours of trailing from one agency to the next, Laura was ready to name Greenville the Car Rental Capital of the Western Hemisphere. Amos patiently pointed out that the city was located in the center of a tourist region, but the more he tried to calm her, the more irritable Laura grew.

Laura had started the trip with misgivings, which seemed to her now to have been prescient. What had seemed so necessary the other day now seemed of dubious value—she doubted that they would find proof that James Stanley had rented a car in Greenville, and even if they did, what would *that* prove? Fannin would have the same argument for reasonable doubt as he had before. The fact that he had rented a car didn't mean that Stanley had driven it to Atlanta, or that he had killed his wife once he got there. Her mood grew steadily gloomier as their search turned up nothing time and time again.

She hadn't been in the best frame of mind when they started out from Atlanta, after spending most of Friday night worrying as she tried to pack her bag. Suddenly, choosing clothes became a task of monumental significance. If she took a silk blouse to wear to dinner Saturday night, would Amos think that she was dressing up for him? On the other hand, if she just threw on jeans and a sweater, would he think she didn't care how she looked? She had never had these doubts before when it came to Amos. When he complimented her appearance, she had always taken it as a routine remark that any friend would make. Why was it different now? *Amos hasn't changed,* Laura thought. *Nothing that he's said or done has given me any reason to believe that he's pining for me.* What was it, then—Kenny's remarks? Meredith's? *Or,* Laura realized with a jolt, *is it me? Am I the one who's seeing Amos in a new light?* The thought left her even more discombobulated, so when Amos came by to pick her up Saturday morning she could hardly look him in the face.

"What's with you this morning?" he asked as he tossed her bag into the back of the Jeep. "Didn't you get a good night's sleep?"

"I slept fine," she replied. "I'm just anxious to get up there and get started."

"You might as well relax; worrying won't get us there any faster. Want to stop and get coffee on the way out?"

"Sure. There's a drive-through on Piedmont."

As they merged onto the expressway, coffees tucked into cup-holders, Amos jerked his head toward the CD player, one of the few alterations he had made to the old truck. "Pick out a CD. I brought some I thought you'd like."

"Nope. This time, I brought some of mine. We have Lyle Lovett and the Mavericks. Got a preference?" Laura had hoped that bringing along her own music would allow her to relax a little.

"*Country music?* You want me to listen to that stuff? It sounds like two cats in a bag, for God's sake."

"Not this. It's very sophisticated." She put a Lyle Lovett into the player. Lyle, however, turned out to be a poor choice, if the goal was to distract her from romantic preoccupations. Every other song was about rejection, which Laura thought was pretty rich, given that Lyle Lovett was a jillionaire music and movie star now, and that he had been married, albeit briefly, to the lovely Julia Roberts. He hardly seemed justified in complaining about his luck with women, in any case. Laura abruptly ejected the disc during one especially lugubrious song.

"Hey, why'd you do that?" Amos complained. "I was actually enjoying it."

"I want something more upbeat," she said, as she fumbled a Mavericks disc into the slot. "You'll like this just as well."

It was a better choice. Raul Malo sang about broken hearts and rejection, too, but over a bright Latino beat. The Mavericks could make a song entitled "All You Ever Do Is Bring Me Down" sound like a party. "How's this?" Laura asked.

"Okay, but I liked the other guy better."

"I just wasn't in the mood for him. Look at those horses!" They were out of the suburbs and passing through farm country.

"Uh-huh. Very pretty. How's your riding coming, by the way?"

"Great. I'm jumping—just little schooling jumps, but I'm getting the hang of it again."

"When are you going to let me see you on a horse?"

"I didn't know you wanted to. You can come anytime—Lynette would let you ride, too."

"No, thanks. I prefer to live. But I would like to see you."

Now, that was just the kind of remark that Laura would have taken at face value only a few short weeks earlier. Now, however, she replayed it in her mind until it nearly drove her crazy. She looked sideways at Amos, who was calmly concentrating on driving, and realized that she was right: *He* hadn't changed at all—it was *her* feelings that had changed. Somehow, over the summer, her shocked brain had relaxed its grip on Tom's memory and started living again—without Laura's permission. A wave of guilt broke over her. *He hasn't even been gone a year,* she reprimanded herself, *and you're already forgetting him.* She conjured an image of a sad and lonely Tom watching her driving up I-85 with Amos Kowalski, and the picture almost caused her physical pain. As bad timing would have it, the Mavericks launched into a song entitled "Missing You."

> *Though you're not here with me,*
> *I still want what used to be*
> *I need you so*
> *Oh don't you know I'm missing you?*

Laura batted tears away from her eyes. "What CDs did you bring?" she asked.

"Check the case. We can listen to this, though—I'm just kidding you. I really kind of like it."

"I'd rather hear something else." She flipped through Amos's CDs, chose Earl Hines, and changed the disc again. "Did you know that Carlton Hemingway is a jazz fan?"

"No. You've gotten to be quite friendly with him, haven't you?"

"A bit. I haven't seen much of him lately, but I think he's a nice guy."

"No truth to the rumors, then?"

"What rumors?"

"That you're dating him."

"Dating him? We had lunch a couple of times! Who starts these things?"

"There's nothing like a police department for starting gossip. I didn't think there was anything to it—he seems too young for you, in my opinion."

"Too young? I don't think he's more than a year or two younger than I am. And we have a lot in common." Laura had no idea why she was arguing in favor of a relationship with Carlton, a thing which had never crossed her mind. She had, in fact, relatively little in common with Carlton outside of the Stanley case. Not that he wasn't a great guy, but he lacked Tom's intellectual gravity, and Amos's general air of male competence, which was the most attractive thing about Kowalski . . .

There I go again, she thought. *I should just admit it: I am attracted to him.* She glanced sidelong at him again, and tried to see him in a new light. Amos was a big, muscular guy, and that was nice. He was in his late thirties, but he had good hair—*not that there's anything wrong with thinning hair,* she hastened to edit her own thought, *but Amos's hair is very nice.* And he had green eyes, and a nice smile, and he could do *anything* around the house, and he was a great cook . . . but mostly Amos was just *kind,* which in the final analysis was the most attractive quality of all.

Amos, luckily, was unaware of Laura's train of thought. He pulled a map from the center compartment and handed it to her. "We want to go to the airport first," he said. "See if you can tell which exit we should take."

They had crossed the South Carolina line sometime earlier, and Laura hadn't noticed. She unfolded the map and peered at the Greenville inset. "Okay, I see—just follow I-85 and we'll see the signs for the airport. What's the drill when we get there?"

"I'll flash the badge, but you can jump in anytime and ask questions. This is your trip, after all. I thought that we'd start by asking to see all the contracts from the evening of May 8 between, say, seven P.M. and midnight, on the assumption that Stanley would have taken a car out in those hours. There's no point in asking for contracts in his name—I'm assuming that the guy was smart enough to use a fake driver's license and pay cash."

"Maybe not—remember, he didn't expect anyone to be looking for him in Greenville."

"We'll see, then. Who knows? We may luck into what we're looking for right away."

"And then?"

"We'll get a copy of the contract. If it's in his own name, that's all we need. If it's under an alias, we'll need to find the clerk who dealt with him and see if we can get a photo identification. That's why I asked you to bring Stanley's mug shots. You did bring them, didn't you?"

"Of course. I also calculated the approximate mileage that he would have put on the rental car if he drove from Greenville to Atlanta, and then back to Charlotte. The record should show how far the car was driven by whoever rented it, I figured."

"Smart girl. Here's our exit."

They pulled off the highway and found the small but busy airport easily. Amos followed the signs to the rental car returns, and soon they saw a green National sign. "Might as well start there," Amos said.

Laura jumped down from the car as soon as it stopped, and tugged her sweater back into proper alignment. She was almost as excited as she was when she and Carlton had first discovered Jim Stanley. She waited impatiently as Amos put a blazer on over his sport polo and tan slacks. When he carried his gun, Amos wore a jacket of some sort to hide his shoulder holster. "Oh, come on, beauty bunny— you look fine!" she said, her impatience showing.

Amos smiled and shook his head. "Damn amateurs, always rushing. Let me give you a hint: it seems to help if you don't give a damn if they have what you're looking for or not. If they think it's too important, they get uneasy."

"Really? I've found that people love to be involved in a murder investigation."

Amos shrugged. "Maybe they just react better to your pretty face. Ready?"

They entered the building, and waited while the lone clerk on duty helped a customer. When the clerk was free, Amos approached the counter and casually flipped open the wallet that held his glaringly gold badge. "Hey. I'm Lieutenant Kowalski, from the Atlanta Police Department. Got a minute?"

"Sure," the clerk said, wide-eyed. He looked hardly old enough to drive the cars he was renting out.

"I'm looking for a particular rental contract. Can you help me with that?"

"I . . . I don't know. Maybe I should get my manager."

"Sure, that'd be great. I can wait." The clerk scuttled through a door, and a minute or two later a slightly older boy emerged.

"May I help you, sir?" he asked.

"I sure hope so. I'd hate to spend my whole Saturday

on this wild-goose chase," Amos said with a confiding grin. "What I need is to see if you have on your records a rental contract meeting certain specifications. Can you look up contracts by date?"

"Yeah."

"And time?" The manager nodded. "Okay, here's what we're looking for: a contract for May 8 of this year, taken out sometime after seven P.M."

"Name of the renter?" the manager asked, hands poised over the keyboard of the computer. Laura read his nametag: Erik Slaton.

"We're not sure. Maybe we should just look at a list of all of them."

Erik nodded, and began clicking at the keys. "Okay, here's a list of all the cars that went out that night after seven P.M. Should I print it out?" Amos nodded. He was somehow managing to look bored, although Laura's pulse was racing. In a few seconds, the printer had rattled out a sheet of paper, which the manager tore off and handed to Amos. Laura crowded in next to him and read the list. James Stanley's name did not appear on it.

"Can you look for any of these that were turned in at Charlotte, North Carolina?" Amos asked. More clicking ensued. Erik shook his head. "All local. Sorry."

Laura spoke for the first time. "Any that were turned in after midnight, and had especially high mileage?"

Click, click. "Nope. All of them stayed out at least twenty-four hours," the boy-manager said. "Sorry. What are y'all looking for, anyway?"

"We're interested in a particular individual," Laura said. "You didn't happen to be on duty that night, did you?"

"May 8?"

"It was a Thursday," Amos added helpfully.

"Oh. I wasn't here, but Donnie mighta been. Donnie!"

The first clerk reappeared, drinking a Mountain Dew. "Huh?"

"Did you work the three-to-midnight shift back in May?"

"Yeah. I just got day shift last month."

Erik jerked his head in Donnie's direction. "Ask him."

"Donnie, do you remember seeing a man who looked like this?" Laura asked, displaying an enlarged mug shot of a sullen James Stanley.

Donnie looked at the photo for a long moment, and shook his head. "I'm sorry, ma'am. They *all* look like that." It was true; James Stanley looked like any one of a million well-groomed professionals in his midthirties. Laura put the picture away with a sigh.

"Thanks a lot," she said. "You've both been very helpful."

Amos pulled out a card and handed it to Erik. "Give me a call if you find anything, or if Donnie remembers something." Erik's eyes widened as he read the card, which of course, said Sex Crimes on it.

Outside, Laura laughed. "He thinks we're looking for a sex fiend."

"He's probably more impressed by that than he would be by a mere murderer. Okay, next stop: Budget Rent-a-Car."

They went through the same drill at Budget, and Avis, and Hertz, and about a half dozen smaller companies at the airport. An assortment of Eriks and Donnies—and Shaunyas, and Darrells, and a host of other bored clerks—gave them the same answers. "Sorry, dude." "Nope, nothing here." "Everybody who was working that night has quit, man—this job *sucks*."

They took a break for lunch at a Wendy's, and then

started on the agencies located around town, with the same results. By five o'clock, they had only six places left to visit, but Laura was tired and discouraged. "Let's bag it for the day," she said. "I can't stand any more rejection."

"Welcome to the glamorous world of police work," Amos said with a grin. "Don't be so discouraged—*not* finding something is sometimes as good as finding something."

"Says you. Do you realize that if I can't positively prove that James returned to Atlanta, Craig Fannin can raise a reasonable doubt in the jury's minds? He's going to throw all kinds of pixie dust at them—including conspiracy theories involving Lynette Connell. I *need* this rental car."

"If it's out there, we'll find it—tomorrow. Let's head to the land of the white squirrel for the night."

"Huh? What's the 'white squirrel?'"

"I did a little research on Brevard—it's home to one of the few known colonies of white squirrels in North America. The whole town is a squirrel preserve."

"You're kidding. What do they do for garden club shows—displays of stems with the flowers chewed off?"

Amos laughed. "We'll have to ask. Look in the glove compartment—I printed out driving directions."

Laura navigated them out of Greenville and onto a mountain road that wound uphill to Brevard. The scenery was breathtaking. "I'm told that we should see Caesar's Head," Amos remarked. "We can stop tomorrow morning on the way back down—unless you're in a real big hurry to get back to Greenville."

"I'm not in that big a hurry," she said. But part of her did want the night to end quickly, so that she and Amos could get back to their regular stomping grounds and she could look him in the eye again without blushing.

CHAPTER 20

Brevard was a beautiful town, especially in the golden light of a late-September evening. Laura marveled at the collection of shingle-sided and white-columned mansions left from the days when Brevard had been host to presidents and potentates, while Amos gave her a brief rundown on the history of the place, gleaned from a North Carolina guidebook he had picked up at the big Borders store on Peachtree. Amos was always prepared.

"The town was founded in the early nineteenth century, but it was around the beginning of the twentieth century that it was in its glory. There are scads of tourist attractions around—lakes, mountains, trails. I guess the flatlanders used to come up here to get away from the hot summers. A lot of these big houses are bed-and-breakfasts now."

"Where are we staying?"

"Right here," Amos said, pulling into the parking lot

of a large white house with an inviting porch. "Does this meet with your approval?"

"It sure does. Is it very expensive?"

"That's not your concern. This is all on me."

"Amos, I can't let you . . ."

"Yes, you can. Now, hop on out and let's get checked in. There's still enough light for us to take a walk and see some of those white squirrels."

They carried their bags into the inn and were welcomed by the friendly owner. "You were lucky to get these rooms," she said. "I usually don't have last-minute cancellations. I'll show you upstairs." If she was puzzled at why a youngish couple were checking into separate rooms, she didn't show it. She had probably seen many stranger things in her career as an innkeeper.

Laura's room was pleasantly decorated, with a minimum of the flowered chintz that seems to be de rigueur at B&Bs. She was also glad that she had her own bathroom. Laura hated sharing a bath with strangers. She looked at herself critically in the mirror, and did a little patching up of her makeup before she rejoined Amos downstairs.

"Is your room okay?" she asked, suspecting that she had gotten the nicer quarters.

"It's fine. Yours?"

Laura nodded. "Do you have your own bath?"

"All the rooms do."

"Oh. Well, that's good. I hate creeping around the halls in a robe."

"Not half as much as I do. Hell, I don't even own a robe. By the way, I asked where we can see the squirrels, and they were kind of evasive. She said that the squirrels are shy of people. Shy squirrels—that would be a first. I think the whole thing may be a scam."

"That's a nice thing to do! They get us all excited about

white rodents and then tell us we might not see any after all.'' They headed outside nevertheless, undaunted in their determination to spot one of the snowy pests.

They followed a walking tour that their hostess had marked for them on a map. It took them past some fine houses, some of which were private residences, but more of which had been converted to inns and restaurants. They wandered into a small park with many oak trees. ''If we're going to see one, this would be the place,'' Laura said, scanning the branches for squirrel activity.

''I see a gray one,'' Amos said.

''Are the gray ones a protected species, too?''

''I guess so. Here's the restaurant where we have reservations. Want to read the menu? If we don't like it, we can always go somewhere else.''

The menu was very appealing, but expensive. Laura decided that she would pay the check, even if that meant secret negotiations with the waiter. They always brought the check to the man. Laura believed that even an incredibly rich woman like Madonna probably had to negotiate to get the check delivered to her, even when she was out with her pool boy.

Long shadows were falling, and Amos suggested that they return to the inn and change for dinner. As they crossed the park, Laura saw a flash of white scuttling up the side of a tree. ''Look! The great white squirrel!''

Amos and Laura watched as the white furry creature jumped onto a branch and disappeared into a canopy of leaves. '' *He piled upon the whale's white hump the sum of all the general rage and hate felt by his whole race from Adam down,* ' '' she solemnly intoned. ''Or should it be 'He piled upon the squirrel's white bushy tail . . . ?' ''

''Melville?'' Amos guessed.

"Uh-huh. Although I'm not really a fan. I bet everyone who comes to Brevard makes a *Moby-Dick* joke."

"I bet they don't," Amos replied. "You don't seem to realize, Laura, that you're 'smarter than the average bear,' so to speak. I've never met anyone as well read as you."

"I'm just a lapsed English major, that's all. You don't think I'm pretentious, do you, Amos?"

"Since when is it pretentious to be intelligent and show it? It's just a part of who you are. I wish I knew half as much as you do about literature and art."

"Literature and art don't seem very relevant to our line of work, do they? Sometimes I think I should just quit, go get a master's in English, and try to get a teaching job."

"You'd be a good teacher, but the world would lose a great lawyer."

Laura laughed. "Stop it—you're making me blush. I think it's getting too dark for squirrel-spotting. Should we head on back?"

They walked back to the inn in silence, Laura reflecting on what Amos had said. She used to love pulling out obscure quotations. It had been a game that she and Tom had played. He had been a great quoter, and Laura had always tried to keep herself stocked with a repertoire of mots justes, just so she could meet him on his own ground. She missed that. Amos was no dummy, but he was street smart rather than erudite. Laura didn't fault him for that; she just missed the intellectual camaraderie she had had with Tom. She returned to her room, wondering if she should tell Amos what she was thinking. No, she decided, it would just make Amos uncomfortable. He didn't want to hear about Tom. No one did, and Laura was determined not to make a bore of herself by saying "Tom this" and "Tom that" at every opportunity.

She took a quick shower, keeping her thick hair dry so

she wouldn't have to deal with it, and pulled out the outfit she had chosen to wear. She had brought her confidence-building black slacks, slinky and low-slung, which emphasized her newly slim hips, and a close-fitting white knit shell, through which the lace of her brassiere peeped. She topped it with a fitted watermelon-colored cashmere cardigan which made her skin glow. She paused for a moment before she took off the rose-quartz heart on a fine gold chain that she always wore. It was the last—the only—gift Tom had given her. It felt strange not to have the little heart nesting in the hollow of her throat; she had never taken it off since the day Tom had given it to her. Sometimes she hid it under scarves and collars, but she had developed a nervous habit of fingering it even when it wasn't visible. She thought about putting it back on, but she resolutely snapped closed its little box and reached for an oxidized-silver necklace from which pearls dangled every inch or so. She looked at it critically; it was new, bought on impulse just a few weeks earlier and never worn. She wondered if Amos would notice. He had never commented on the heart, but he knew that it had been a gift from Tom.

She finished her makeup and went to the lobby, where Amos was waiting. He was wearing a sports coat over a black polo sweater and slacks. He looked so good that Laura wondered, not for the first time, why it was that cops seemed to be either really well dressed or really poorly dressed, with no middle ground. She was glad—also not for the first time—that Amos belonged to the former group. They walked back into the warm night; Laura took off her sweater and draped it around her shoulders. They arrived at the restaurant early for their reservation, so they sat at the tiny bar and had a glass of wine.

"This seems like a nice place," Laura said. "Did you find it in the guidebook, too?"

"No. The people at the inn suggested it when I made the reservation."

When they were escorted to their table, Laura slipped the captain her credit card. "Please tell the waiter to bring me the receipt," she whispered behind Amos's back. She encouraged Amos to order a nice bottle of wine, knowing that she was paying. Dinner was excellent; Laura was able to get smoked brook trout, a favorite dish of hers, and Amos talked her into an extravagant dessert. He started to protest when he saw the waiter bring the check to Laura, but she waved him off. "Don't start with me, Kowalski. I think I need to go for a walk after that dessert. Are you up for it?"

He said he was, and they strolled around the streets they had explored earlier, now made mysterious by the moonlight. They were mostly silent, until Amos spoke. "Are you okay, Laura? You were awfully quiet at dinner."

"I'm fine. I guess I just have a few things on my mind."

"Like James Stanley?"

"Among other things."

"I've been a little worried about you lately. That's partly why I agreed to come here this weekend—I thought I could talk to you better away from work and all that. Look, Laura, I wouldn't blame you if you told me to shut up and mind my own business, but I think you should be getting some counseling."

"Have you been talking to Meredith?"

"No. This is something I've wanted to say for a long time. Laura, you had a horrible experience. I've been a cop for almost fifteen years, and I've rarely seen the kind of violence I saw that night. And yet you've just picked up and moved on, never saying a word. And I question the wisdom, frankly, of your taking a job with the district attorney. Maybe you *should* be teaching English.''

"You don't think I'm doing well in the new job?''

"Far from it. I think you're doing *too* well. I think you're sublimating everything into that job, and I don't think it's good.''

"Do you think the guy who wrote that column was right—that I'm bent on some kind of revenge?''

"That idiot? No, of course he wasn't right. He missed the boat completely. No, if anything, I think you're using the job—and the Stanley murder in particular—to avoid dealing with Tom's death.''

Laura threw up her hands. "Can nobody accept that Tom has nothing to do with this case? I'm just doing what I was trained to do!''

"Of course I don't think your every move is dictated by the way you feel about Tom. All I'm saying is that you're using the job as a cover, and as a way of delaying dealing with his death. Meredith should never have let you come to work for her so soon after it happened.''

"But what else could I do? I trained to be a lawyer— a very good one, thank you—for almost ten years. I'm not like one of those feisty gals on the Lifetime channel who picks herself up after a tragedy and starts a whole new life. What else could I do?''

"You could have taken some more time, Laura. You could have mourned a little longer.''

"Working hasn't kept me from mourning. Trust me.''

"I'll have to trust you on that, because all I can see from the outside is you working away, buying a new house, just like nothing happened.''

"Of course something happened! You think I don't remember it every single day? I miss Tom so much it *hurts,* but I can't bore everyone around me by talking about him all the time. People are sick of hearing about it!"

"That's what you don't understand, Laura—we're *not* sick of hearing about Tom, *because you never talk about him.* You never have. It's not healthy, and it's not right."

"But I can't talk about him. It doesn't feel right. As far as the world knows, we dated for a very short time. In fact, technically, I *dumped* him that night, before Jeff killed him. So you can see that public mourning would be ostentatious and inappropriate, I hope."

"But I'm not the public; I know what Tom was to you. I don't care how long you dated him. Why can't you talk to me? I was there that night, remember? It drives me crazy that you won't let me help you. I know I'm no substitute for Tom Bailey . . ."

"I don't need you to be! I don't *want* you to be! I just want you to be you."

"But you need things I can't give you. I can't talk about books and music. I can't drive you in a Bentley . . ."

"Is *that* what you think I want? I didn't care about Tom's money; you should know that. And so maybe you can't quote poetry at the drop of a hat. It was great that Tom could. It was like a game we had going for years, before we ever got romantically involved, but to be honest, sometimes it was more like a competition than a conversation. Maybe I don't want to be in top form all the time. Tom was like a walking Socratic dialogue. He was brilliant. He was a great teacher. And, yes, I loved him—I still do. But he's gone, and sometimes I get so confused. I want to move on, but when I try to, I feel guilty—like I'm betraying him. Sometimes I wonder if I can ever be happy again."

They had stopped by the little park where they had seen the squirrel. Amos silently put his arms around her, and she leaned gratefully into him. "I just want you to be happy, Laura," he said. "I'd like you to be happy with me, but I can understand what's holding you back. I'm willing to wait."

"I can't ask you to do that, Amos," she said, pulling away from him. "You're the greatest guy in Atlanta, and you deserve more than I can give you. You're wasting your time playing Scrabble with me and helping me with my house when you should be out there having fun."

"Being with you is my idea of fun. I'm thirty-seven years old, Laura, and I know what I want. I'm not going to find it in any stupid singles bar, or at the health club—I've got it right here. And I'm not giving up. You take all the time you need to, and if in the end, you tell me that you don't want me, I'll go away quietly. But if you do decide that you might be able to stand having me around, I'll be the happiest guy in Georgia. You understand what I'm saying to you?"

Laura nodded. "I do love you, Amos. You know I do. You're the best thing that's ever happened to me, and I don't deserve you."

"Yes, you do. Now, let's get back to the hotel. I need to get some sleep if we're going to finish with those rental car agencies tomorrow."

They walked back slowly, hand in hand, and said good night at Laura's door. She slept better than she had in a long, long time, waking only when the phone beside her bed jangled in her ear. It was Amos, already dressed and waiting for her downstairs.

Laura hurriedly showered and dressed, and went to meet him with her wet hair under a baseball cap. It crossed her mind that she was hardly presenting him with a romantic picture, but he'd seen her looking worse. No one could say they didn't have a high comfort level with each other anyway. They talked cheerfully at breakfast, as if they had made an unspoken promise not to mention what had happened between them the night before. At nine-thirty, they were on their way back to Greenville.

Laura insisted that they stop at the overlook at Caesar's Head, which commanded a view of the misty valley far below. There was just the slightest touch of fall in the air. "I bet this is beautiful when the leaves turn," she said.

"Yep. And I bet that road is one hellacious traffic jam all the way from Greenville."

"There's no traffic worse than leaf traffic," Laura agreed. "Seen enough?"

"Hey, you're the one who wanted to stop."

"And now I'm the one who wants to go to Greenville and finish up."

There were only a half dozen or so agencies left on the list, but they were well dispersed across the map of Greenville. They tried each one doggedly, with the same lack of success they had encountered on the previous day. Finally, at about three o'clock in the afternoon, Laura conceded defeat. "I give up."

"I never thought I'd hear you say that," Amos said. "There are some more agencies in some of the outlying towns. Want to try them?"

Laura shook her head. "It's no good. We're not going to find anything."

"At least you're no worse off than you were before," Amos offered helpfully. "It was never absolutely critical to your case, was it?"

"No, you're right. I just thought it would be nice."

"I say we get a late lunch and head home."

"I vote 'yes' for that plan."

They found a Waffle House. Waffle Houses were great favorites of Amos's, who, as a Yankee, had grown up deprived of their waffly goodness and six-way hash browns.

A friendly waitress took their orders. Laura took off her cap and shook out her hair. "How mangy do I look?" she asked.

"You're beautiful," he answered disingenuously. "I've never seen you look more lovely."

She swatted him with a menu. "I just hope I don't look as bedraggled as I *feel*. Do you hate me for ruining your weekend with this foolish mission?"

"This is the best weekend I've had in ages," he said. Just as she thought he was going to get sentimental on her, he added, with a twinkle, "You know I've been regrouting my bathroom tile. You're a definite improvement over that."

"Oh, am I? I'll take that as a compliment, since I know how much you do love a good grouting session. But I was just so *sure* we were going to find a rental car contract."

"We may have overlooked it. We made some assumptions that may have been invalid."

"Like what?"

"For instance, that James Stanley rented the car that night. He could have done it days earlier and left it sitting at the Greenville airport."

"I never thought of that. Do you think we should go back and . . .?

Amos cut her off. "There's another possibility that I think makes more sense."

"What is it?"

"Guess. It's as plain as the nose on your face."

Laura pondered frowningly for a few minutes before realization dawned. "He *flew!*" she exclaimed. "Why didn't I think of earlier? He just turned around and hopped on a plane back to Atlanta. Amos, why didn't you tell me this before?"

"You seemed so certain about the rental car that I

didn't want to question your judgment. It's your case, after all. But it did cross my mind that you were looking so hard at one possibility that you were ignoring all others.''

"You should have told me," she scolded him. "You knew we didn't need to come up here!"

He smiled. "Oh, I think we did, don't you?"

She reached across the table and took his hand. "We did. You're a devious bastard, Amos Kowalski, but I love you for it. Now, finish that sandwich and drive me back to Atlanta.''

CHAPTER 21

"So this is why I need a subpoena for the passenger manifests for those two flights," Laura said, breathless after presenting her case to Meredith first thing Monday morning. She was trying to convince her boss that they could prove that James Stanley had returned to Atlanta from Greenville on one of two Delta Airlines flights on the night of May 8.

Meredith looked doubtful. "The airlines are pretty sensitive about giving out that information. Are you sure it would be worth our while? They might fight the subpoena."

"Of course it's worth it! If we put James Stanley on one of those flights, we also place him *in Atlanta* on the night Christine was killed. I think it's critical."

"Okay, but what if he traveled under an assumed name? Are we supposed to run down every man on the flight?"

"If we have to. It won't be a long list—they don't fly

jumbo jets on the Greenville-to-Atlanta run, and some of the passengers are bound to have been women. It could turn out to be a very short list."

"All right, I'll get your subpoena. Or better yet, I'll have Marshall approach Delta's general counsel and see if we can get what we need *without* a subpoena. He's pretty sensitive when it comes to serving papers on the city's largest employers. Now that we've dealt with that little matter, I'd like to talk to you about how we're going to approach the trial." Laura sat down and poised her pen over her pad, and waited for Meredith to continue. "I realize that this is really *your* case, and I want you to know that I appreciate all the work you've done. I wish I could let you run with it by yourself, but it's just too big a case—there's too much at stake."

"I understand completely, Meredith. I didn't ever expect to take the first chair."

"Good. I just wanted to make sure that there's no misunderstanding. I think you're probably every bit as capable as I am of winning with a jury, but I wouldn't want to put you under that kind of pressure. Now, that said, I want you to play a very big role at the trial. I'll give the opening statement, but I want you to present the crime-scene evidence. We'll do that before we present any of the motive witnesses, and of course before we put Jim Stanley on the stand. I want you to set the scene for the jury. Take them inside that living room and make them see what you did."

"No problem. Who should we call—Travers, of course, but would you like to have Carlton Hemingway on the stand as well?"

"Hmm. No—not in the first phase. We'll call him and your computer buddy, Wayne Whatsis, before I call Jim Stanley. They can tell the court how we came to find the second Stanley. That way Jim's appearance will make more sense to the jury."

"Okay, we can call Randy, the ballistics expert, and the medical examiner. Then the motive witnesses. Are you planning to call Lynette Connell, or her father?"

"No. At least, not Lynette. You've met the father, though. How do you think he'd be as a witness?"

"On the plus side, he'd be powerfully emotional. But he's said all along that Christine never talked to him about the problems in the marriage."

"What about the financial angle—he lent money to James Stanley, didn't he?"

"Yes, and if you really made him get down to bare knuckles I think he'd tell the jury that he thought James was good-for-nothing. But there's one more thing to take into consideration: He thinks it's bad enough that those two children lost their mother. The idea of helping to send James to the electric chair is horrifying to him."

"So he might be an ambivalent witness. Well, we don't need that. I think I'll stick to the divorce attorney—what was his name?"

"Frank Watson," Laura replied, flipping through her notes. "I have his address and phone number here."

"Good. We'll call him and the special master, for the financial evidence. Come to think of it, I think I'll let you question the special master. You've got a more solid grasp of the money stuff than I do."

"I'd be happy to do it. Mr. Borden is an old buddy of mine from my Prendergrast and Crawley days. I know how to approach him; he's very methodical, you know."

"Better you than me—my eyes just about roll back in my head when I have to deal with numbers."

Laura reviewed her notes. "Let me get back to the

crime-scene evidence. When do you want to introduce the gun? And do you want Jesse on the stand?''

Meredith made a face. ''Yikes. No, I don't think we need Mr. DuPree—Jim Stanley can give the jury the provenance of the gun without him. I'd hate to give Craig a shot at Jesse.''

Laura nodded. ''That's what I was thinking. If Craig is going to go after Lynette, Jesse would be the way he'd do it. I'm betting that when we get his final witness list Jesse will be on it.''

''A pretty hostile defense witness, I would think. But back to the gun itself, I think it would be best if you had the ballistics expert identify it as the murder weapon. Then, when I have Jim on the stand, I'll have him cop to owning it and lending it to James Stanley.''

''Suits me. One more question on the crime-scene evidence: there were those fibers caught in the broken door. We weren't able to connect them to James Stanley, so I'm wondering if we want to bring them up at all.''

''No, I don't think we need to. Randy can get the broken door into evidence, and that's all we really need. The fiber evidence is inconclusive at best.''

Laura nodded. ''It might even be something that Fannin could use against us. I'd just as soon leave it out.''

''But, while we're on the subject, I guess we should turn over the crime lab report on the fiber evidence to Craig. I wouldn't want to be accused of withholding exculpatory evidence.''

''You don't think he'll be able to make use of it?''

Meredith shrugged. ''It's as ambivalent from his point of view as it is from ours. Why should he drag it in—unless he can connect it to another suspect?''

''I guess you're right. I do think that he's going to

present an alternate theory of the crime, so maybe he'll find some use for the fiber evidence."

"He'd better hurry up—the only defense notification we've had is the alibi he gave us at the conference."

When a defense team planned to argue that a defendant was not guilty of a crime for an "affirmative" reason, the defense was required to notify the prosecution of its intention. Then, the defense became responsible for proving its argument. Affirmative defenses included alibis, "mistakes of facts," "mistakes of law," diminished capacity, insanity, or, Laura's favorite, "impossibility" (for instance, if the gun alleged to have been used in a crime was not in working order when the crime was committed, and the defense could prove it).

Craig Fannin had filed notification of alibi defense months earlier, and had even moved for dismissal of the charges based on the evidence of the hotel record. Meredith and Laura had introduced Jim Stanley's statement and had the motion overturned. Fannin had been silent ever since, and Laura thought his silence was baffling. Surely he didn't expect his little media bombs about Jim, and her, to tip the scales in his favor. She felt pretty sure, based on his reputation, that he was cooking up something.

Her suspicions were confirmed a few days later, when she was having lunch with Kenny Newton. The conversation gradually worked its way around to the Stanley case, and Laura told Kenny, ruefully, about her wasted trip to Greenville. "We came up with nothing—and *then* Amos announces that he's thought all along that the guy took a plane."

"That Kowalski is a sly one—I told you he wanted to get you alone in Greenville. He knew all along you wouldn't find anything."

"I felt pretty stupid, I can tell you. But it all turned out okay. We're getting passenger manifests for the flights I think he might have taken. We have plenty of time to check them out before the trial opens."

"Let me know if I can help. And speaking of hiring private detectives, I've heard on the grapevine that Fannin is sparing no expense in that area."

"What do you mean?"

"He's hired at least three investigators that I know of."

"Three! I know he had a guy in North Carolina looking at Jim, but what else is he up to?"

"There's a guy checking into the victim's sister, Lynette Connell."

Laura nodded. "I knew he would go after her, but he won't get anything. What else do you hear?"

"He's hired a guy who usually investigates for litigators in civil liability lawsuits, especially airline disasters. Dan Crowder—ever hear of him?"

"No. Hmm. I thought Fannin was awful quiet. Evidently, he's got nothing, or we would have heard from him by now. As it stands now, all he can do is try to impeach Jim Stanley and make the jury believe that he's lying. I think he's going to draw them a picture of a conspiracy among Jim, Lynette, and Jesse DuPree."

"The gun dealer?"

"Yep. It won't wash, either—all three of them have corroborated alibis for the time of the murder. Juries don't like to have smoke blown at them. Maybe Craig will come back to the table and try to cut a deal before the trial starts. He's got plenty of time, and I wouldn't be a bit surprised."

"I'd sure hate to see you deprived of your first big trial," Kenny said with a grin. "I can tell you're just rarin' to go."

"You better believe I am—I've been rehearsing in my sleep for months. I can't wait to get at it."

"Amos will sure be glad when it's over."

"Why do you say that?"

" 'Cause then he can have your full attention."

Laura blushed. "Have you been gossiping with him?"

"Nope. Swear. It was Cindy. She wormed it out of him the other day."

"It's no big deal, really. We've just agreed to give it a try. I have a long way to go before I'm ready to pick my bridesmaids. I still feel like I owe something to Tom."

Kenny nodded. "I can understand that. You guys were together a long time. Just like I hope you and Amos will be."

"It's a dream come true for you, isn't it? You've schemed and planned this for three years."

"And now you've finally had the sense to see I was right."

"Lean over here a little closer, Ken."

"Why?"

"So I can *smack* you."

Smacking aside, Laura was happy that Kenny was happy. She had a special reserve of guilt feelings where he was concerned, no matter how often he reassured her that he didn't blame her for his limp or the cane he needed to walk. She blamed herself anyway. So much misfortune had flowed from that ill-starred first meeting with Jeff Williams, so many lives had been changed. It all seemed very long ago. The Laura who had so enthusiastically taken up Jeff's case was long gone, replaced by a somber drone. Amos had rekindled the first tiny spark of real life that Laura had felt for a long time. Still, every time she tried to lose herself in a happy daydream about Amos, she saw Tom's sad face. She didn't tell Kenny that. *Let him at least be happy,* she thought, *and I'm going to be happy, too . . . eventually.*

Prospects for happiness increased every weekend, when Laura loaded her saddle into the trunk of her car and headed for the Connells' farm. She thought about inviting Amos out to watch her ride the weekend following the South Carolina trip, but something inside her hesitated. She didn't want to explain him to Lynette. In the end, she made plans to have dinner with him Saturday night without mentioning riding, and she went to Cobb County alone.

Laura was now a familiar figure at the farm. Amparo, the housekeeper, and even Lester Connell, had begun to treat her as one of the family. She no longer knocked at the front door of the house when she arrived; she just parked her car around back, beside the paddock, and went into the barn. If Lynette wasn't there, she saddled Mica on her own and headed for the ring to warm him up. Lynette always came along eventually to ride with her, or to help with the jumps.

This Saturday, Lynette was nowhere in sight, so Laura parked next to a black BMW, heaved her saddle out of the trunk, and headed for Mica's stall. She was entering the barn, blinded by the slanting early-morning sun, when she heard a familiar laugh. *Oh, good, Lynette is in the barn,* she thought. She stepped past the curtain of light and saw something that shocked her to her core.

At the far end of the sunlit barn, with motes of dust floating in the air like glittering confetti, Lynette was standing close to someone, and talking in quiet tones. Laura could not hear what she was saying, but she saw who she was saying it to: Jesse DuPree.

Laura froze, not wanting to make her presence known. She realized that the sunlight was in Lynette's eyes, making Laura invisible from where she stood. Whatever she was saying to Jesse was making him laugh—Laura couldn't make out words, but she could hear him braying. Finally, after what seemed like an hour, but which was probably no more than a minute, he bent down and kissed Lynette— on the cheek, Laura thought, but she couldn't say for sure. Then he turned and left. Laura stood rooted to the ground. Lynette turned and took a couple of steps into the barn before she saw Laura.

"There you are!" she said cheerfully. "You're a little late this morning. We missed you last weekend. Did you have a good time?"

Laura had told Lynette only that she was going away for a couple of days, to explain why she wouldn't be riding. She hadn't mentioned the purpose of the trip, because she felt that discussing the trial with Lynette wasn't a very good idea, and she hadn't mentioned Amos because she wasn't ready to discuss him with anyone but Kenny. Now she stumbled over a routine answer to Lynette's question. "Oh, yes, I had a good time. It was great. I went to Brevard. In North Carolina."

"Really? I hear it's nice, but I've never been. I only seem to go to places that have horse shows these last few years."

"You should take a weekend off and go up there. It's very beautiful. They have white squirrels." *Should I say anything about Jesse?* she wondered while her mouth moved mechanically, carrying on an automatic conversation with Lynette. *What the hell was he doing here? They seemed very friendly for two people who had nothing in common but a brief fling that was over more than a year ago.*

She followed Lynette to Mica's stall, and chatted about this and that as she took him out and tethered him, put on his bridle, and saddled him up. Lynette was telling her about something Mica had done earlier in the week, when she was up on him, but Laura was having trouble following what she was saying. "Okay, he's ready. Check his girth before you mount. I'm going to ride Claudius today. I don't think you've seen him in the ring. I'm schooling him over three-foot jumps. You up for that?"

"Sure," Laura mumbled, tucking her hair under her helmet. "If Mica is."

"Great. The jumps are all set. I'll be right behind you."

Laura led Mica outside, positioned him next to the mounting block, and hauled herself into the saddle. The horse let out a gusty sigh, deflating his abdomen, an old horse trick that loosened the girth strap holding the saddle in place. "You rascal," Laura said as she bent down and took up another notch in the girth. "You can't fool me. I'm wise to your horse tricks." *But not to people tricks,* she thought. Seeing Lynette with Jesse had made her profoundly uneasy for reasons she couldn't define clearly. She had not been comfortable, however, since she learned that Jesse and Jim Stanley knew each other. *"The Jesse-Jim axis"* was what she called their oddly coincidental relationship, the sinister connotation of the joking nickname not lost on her.

"Walk on, Mica," she commanded, and the horse strolled into the ring, pretending to have no interest in the jumps. That didn't fool Laura, either; Mica was a demon over the jumps, and he loved them. Laura let her mind empty of everything but the rhythm of the horse, and by the time Lynette joined her, she was taking Mica around the ring at a fast trot.

Lynette warmed up her horse briefly, then stopped to explain how she had laid out the jumps. "Mica hates those artificial flowers, so I put a whole bunch on that first jump. Try him over it." Laura did; the horse balked a couple of times, but she finally got him over smoothly several times running. Lynette took a few jumps on her horse, and suggested that they ride around the track to cool down the horses. They rode in silence for a moment until Laura gathered up her nerve. "Lynette, was that Jesse DuPree?"

"Yes. You saw him? Why didn't you say hello?"

"You two seemed . . . preoccupied."

"Well, we weren't. He was just trying to charm the pants off of me, as usual."

"Is that why he came all the way over here?"

"No. What is this, an inquisition? He came to talk to Daddy about a shotgun, and he wandered out back to see me."

"He came to talk to your father at eight o'clock in the morning about a gun?"

Lynette looked surprised. "Jesus, Laura, you don't believe me, do you? I'm sorry, but it's true—everybody knows Daddy gets up at dawn. He's still a farmer at heart. And Jesse was on his way to Chattanooga, so we were on his way. Does that satisfy you?" Lynette looked and sounded angry.

"Yes, but I hope you understand why it concerns me."

"Frankly, I don't. I thought you told me that Jesse DuPree has nothing to do with the case. I didn't know that I should be throwing him off the property every time he showed his face."

"Jesse may not be directly involved, but don't forget that he was the source of the gun. My God, Lynette, do I have to spell it out for you? James's attorney is a piranha, and he'll attack anything that moves. Please don't give him any more reason than he already has to go after you."

"What reason does he have to go after me?"

"For one, he can spin a nice theory about a conspiracy among you, Jim Stanley, and Jesse to kill your sister and frame James Stanley for it."

"That's ridiculous! He might as well say Daddy was in on it, too!"

"Don't think for a minute that he wouldn't. You have to avoid any appearance of an ongoing relationship with Jesse DuPree, Lynette, and your father should, too. You don't understand what a lawyer like Craig Fannin can do with a few facts and a little innuendo. Don't play into his hands."

"It seems to me that you're not as confident in your case as you ought to be. I thought you people had James cold, but now I guess we might not get justice for Chrissie after all. I guess it's just the *system*, and you're a part of it."

"I understand why you're angry, Lynette, but I wish you wouldn't turn it on me. I'm just telling you how it is. I'll go home now. Maybe I shouldn't come out here anymore."

"No, don't say that! I'm sorry, Laura. I didn't mean to imply anything. I know you're doing the best you can. I'll tell Daddy that he can't let Jesse come here until after the trial. And please, please, don't stop coming to ride with me—I look forward to Saturdays so much!"

Laura saw that Lynette had tears in her eyes. She leaned across and squeezed her hand. "It's okay. We're almost through it, and life will be back to normal very soon." If only she could believe her own soothing words.

CHAPTER 22

Judge Claudia Penfield peered through her bifocals at the panel of prospective jurors. "Ladies and gentlemen," she began in her deep, Southern-accented voice, "thank you for being here today. You have been selected as potential jurors in the trial of James Stanley for the murder of Christine Connell Stanley, his wife. We will now begin a process known as voir dire, which means 'to speak the truth.' You have already completed a questionnaire about your background. I will now ask each of you a number of questions which will help us to determine if you are able to serve impartially in the matter of *People* v. *Stanley*."

Jury selection had begun. After all the months of waiting and worrying, they were finally seated in an actual courtroom, presided over by Judge Claudia Penfield, the first woman and the first black to serve as a Superior Court judge in the State of Georgia. She had been on the bench almost thirty years; at least two governors had tried to appoint her to the State Supreme Court, and Lord knows how many times she had been asked to run for attorney general. She was a Democrat, but the Republicans had asked her to be their candidate for Congress. She was always short-listed for federal judgeships, too, but she said no to everything. The Fulton County Superior Court was her kingdom, and she was its undisputed queen.

Meredith said they were lucky to have had the trial land on Judge Penfield's calendar. "She has a low tolerance for theatrics, and she never lets cameras into the courtroom." A coalition of television stations had already filed suit to be allowed to broadcast the James Stanley trial, but both the district attorney's office and, to Laura's surprise, Craig Fannin had submitted briefs opposing the cameras. Laura guessed that was Stanley's wish, and not his attorney's— Craig Fannin had never met a camera that he didn't love.

They were now considering a panel of forty-two prospective jurors, or "venirepersons." Laura liked that word. It was based on the Latin verb "to come," because the venirepersons came in response to a summons. During *voir dire*, panels of venirepersons were selected by lottery; then they were culled by a long and sometimes tedious process of questioning by the judge and the attorneys. In this case, the two sides would go through as many venirepersons as it took to select twelve jurors and six alternates. If they exhausted the initial supply of forty-two, more would be called. It could take two days or two weeks to select eighteen objective citizens.

Laura was watching Fannin closely, trying to determine what he was looking for in the jury. The defense in a death penalty case was allowed twenty "peremptory strikes," which allowed them to dismiss an apparently unbiased juror without specific cause. The prosecution had half as many strikes. Laura and Meredith were less concerned about the composition of the jury than Fannin seemed to be. They had a good story to tell, with strong witnesses. Meredith didn't believe in trying to finesse the selection process too much. "What good does it do, unless there's some really explosive issue involved, like race or abortion?" she had said when Laura asked whether they should consider asking Marshall to stretch the budget for some jury consultants. "I think we can trust the common sense of Joe and Josephine Six-pack on this one."

Craig Fannin, however, had hired some expensive-looking consultants to sit behind him and whisper in his ear. Laura knew what they were telling him; they had used jury consultants all the time at P&C. Drawing on opinion polls and demographic research, they would construct for Fannin an ideal juror, which in this case would probably be a professional male.

There were two consultants, one a balding man and the other a sharp-featured young woman who seemed to be the shot-caller. They were marshaling the defense's copies of the jury questionnaires, looking for any detail which might be cause for closer questioning. The woman would occasionally whisper something to her colleague, and he would scurry out of the room, returning a few minutes later with a piece of paper. She tapped steadily on the keys of a laptop computer, which she would turn and display to Fannin from time to time.

Judge Penfield was beginning her questions to the panel, beginning with an mild-looking man whose questionnaire identified him as retired tax assessor. "Have you, Mr. Bennett, formed and expressed any opinion in regard to the guilt or innocence of Mr. Stanley?"

"No, ma'am."

"Have you any prejudice or bias resting on your mind either for or against the accused?"

"No, ma'am."

"Is your mind perfectly impartial between the state and the defendant?"

"Yes, ma'am, I hope so."

"Are you conscientiously opposed to capital punishment?"

Mr. Bennett paused before he answered. "No, ma'am, I reckon it's the law."

"Thank you, Mr. Bennett. Mr. Fannin, do you have any questions?"

Fannin rose and asked a series of questions about Mr. Bennett's work, his family, and his background. "Have you ever had a close friend or relative who was the victim of a violent crime, Mr. Bennett?"

"No, sir."

"You were a tax assessor for Fulton County. Are you familiar with the Brookhaven neighborhood?"

"No, sir, not really. I worked in south Fulton mostly."

And so on. Laura could see no particular pattern to Fannin's questions. Meredith had only one or two queries for Mr. Bennett before they moved on to the next veni-reperson. The pattern was always the same: the judge asked the statutory questions first. Only twice did a prospective juror admit an outright bias. Judge Penfield dismissed both of them "for cause."

Laura noticed, as more people were questioned, that Craig Fannin was particularly anxious to know how the women on the panel felt about violent crime, especially the mothers. He obviously didn't want jurors who could identify too readily with Christine Stanley. He questioned the men more about their feelings about money; Laura deduced that he was concerned that James Stanley's profession and his family's wealth might arouse hostility in a workingman. *It doesn't seem that he really needs those consul-*

tants, she said to herself after the first few people had been questioned. She hadn't seen anything yet.

When Fannin rose to his feet to question Mrs. Henry Morse, a silver-haired Buckhead matron, Laura saw the first evidence of serious activity by the consultants. "Mrs. Morse, you and your husband belong to the Capital City Country Club, is that correct?"

"Yes, it is."

"Did you know that James and Christine Stanley were also members there?"

"Yes."

"Did you ever meet the Stanleys there?"

"No. It's a very large club. There were a lot of new people that we, well ... I'm a good bit older than Mr. Stanley. I never met him or his wife, and I'm certain that my husband didn't."

It was impossible to miss Mrs. Morse's implication: *I wouldn't be caught dead hobnobbing with a* nouveau-riche *so-and-so like James Stanley.* Laura noticed that the back of James's neck was turning red. He had probably dealt with his share of Mrs. Morses in his attempts to reach the aerie of Atlanta society. He whispered something to Fannin, who spoke to the pointy woman. She nodded, and said something to her associate that sent him scurrying out of the room.

Fannin continued to question Mrs. Morse. "Did you ever hear anything about the Stanleys at the club that might affect your judgment in this trial?"

"No. Of course, people talked about the murder—it was shocking. But I have an open mind."

The bald jury consultant came back, and the pointy-faced woman was displaying her laptop's screen to Craig, who nodded and turned back to jury box.

"Mrs. Morse, you say that you had no personal acquaintance with James Stanley, his late wife, or any member of their families. Is that correct?''

"Yes, it is.''

"Mrs. Morse, you're active in a number of civic organizations—is that true?''

"Yes, I suppose I am.''

"Are you a member of a group called Atlanta Neighborhoods?''

"Yes.''

"And you serve on the board of directors of Atlanta Neighborhoods?''

"Yes.'' It was clear from the tone of her voice that Mrs. Morse had no idea where Fannin's questions were leading. Laura was equally baffled; she exchanged raised eyebrows with Meredith.

"Mrs. Morse, do you recall testifying at a zoning board hearing about six years ago?''

"I have appeared before the Zoning Board many times.''

Fannin turned back to the defense table, and the pointy woman handed him a piece of paper. "Let me read you something, Mrs. Morse. *This neighborhood was intended to have relatively modest homes on large wooded lots. It is neighborhoods like Brookhaven that give Atlanta its charm, and its nickname the 'Tree City.' If this petition for a variance is approved, three houses, none in keeping with their neighbors, will take the place of one. Some thirty mature trees—irreplaceable trees—will be sacrificed, all in the name of greed.'* Do you recall making this statement?''

"Ouch,'' Laura said under her breath. She had a new appreciation for the value of jury consultants.

Mrs. Morse's face was impassive. "Yes, I believe I remember making that statement.''

"And do you remember the name of the property owner who filed for that zoning variance, Mrs. Morse?"

"Well, yes, it was Mr. Stanley, now that you bring it to my memory. But I never met Mr. Stanley—I didn't even remember his name! There must be dozens of James Stanleys out there!"

"You can say that again, sister," Meredith muttered.

Fannin turned to Judge Penfield. "Your Honor, the defense asks that this juror be dismissed for cause."

"So ordered. Mrs. Morse, you may go."

Meredith rose to her feet. "Your Honor, with all due respect, an old zoning dispute hardly amounts to an animus against Mr. Stanley."

Fannin cut in quickly. "I disagree with my learned colleague. Mr. Stanley recalls that the dispute was extremely acrimonious and adversarial. Seating her would be clear error, Your Honor."

Judge Penfield nodded. "Quite right. We wish to avoid even the appearance of a conflict. Thank you for your time, Mrs. Morse."

Mrs. Morse stood trembling with indignation and humiliation in the jury box. "Your Honor, I'd like to say something. May I say something?"

"No, Mrs. Morse."

"But he—that man—he implied that I was *lying!* What I said was absolutely true; I did not until this moment connect Mr. Stanley with that teardown in Brookhaven. How was I to know it was the same James Stanley? I resent the implication that I was hiding something. And if that man thinks for one minute that I would let something like a zoning dispute affect my judgment in a *murder* trial. . . ."

"Yes, Mrs. Morse. I understand your feelings, but I don't think that Mr. Fannin meant to imply that you were being dishonest in any way. We are only trying to avoid the appearance of impropriety." Mrs. Morse left, head held high.

Judge Penfield looked at her watch. "As it is almost one o'clock, this seems like an opportune time to call a recess for lunch. All parties will be back in this courtroom at one forty-five." She banged her gavel, rose, and left in a magnificent swish of silk.

Meredith turned to Laura. "And now you see, my young apprentice, what Craig Fannin can do to a witness. Speaking of which, at the rate we're going, we should have a jury empaneled by Thursday, which means that with any luck we may get to make opening statements on Monday. I want you to get Jim Stanley down here this weekend so you can begin to review his testimony. We'll need him to stay the entire length of the trial."

"Where do we put out-of-town witnesses?"

"One of those suite hotels. Talk to Regina Alvarez when you get back to the office. She coordinates all that."

Voir dire continued, as Meredith expected, for another three days. Craig Fannin didn't get another chance to repeat the tactics he had used to strike Mrs. Morse, but he did manage to persuade Judge Penfield to strike five more jurors for cause, and he expended all twenty of his peremptory strikes.

When the dust settled, Meredith and Laura were pleased with the composition of the jury. There were three retired men on the final panel—two white, one black, all professionals. There were four single, childless workingwomen, two white and two black. Two more white men, an accountant and a car salesman, were seated, and two young black men, a substitute science teacher and an auto-parts store manager. The six alternates were similarly diverse—but there were no married women with children on the panel.

"Do you think that Fannin got what he was after?" Laura asked Meredith.

"Who can say? None of them have any obvious axes to grind, and they all seem to have common sense. But if Craig wants to sell them a conspiracy theory, it might be the wrong group. If, on the other hand, he wants to make a complex argument for reasonable doubt, he's got a good jury to tell it to. Or they may be smart enough *not* to buy it. I find that it's the weaker juries that overemphasize reasonable doubt—they seem to forget the word 'reasonable.' But there's a funny thing about juries: sometimes both the defense and the prosecution think they have the ideal jury. I guess that's how you can tell they're really impartial."

Laura nodded. "There doesn't seem to be anyone on the jury with an emotional stake in the outcome. They'll decide it on the facts, and I think they can tell smoke from fire. By the way, Jim Stanley is coming down on Saturday morning. I'm meeting him at the airport. I'll take him to his hotel, and we'll start to go over his story. I thought we could all three get together at his hotel Sunday afternoon and you could play Fannin, and prepare Jim for some rough questioning. I don't think I can do that part."

"I can. And I am very much looking forward to leaning on Jim Stanley for a few hours."

CHAPTER 23

"What a dump," Jim Stanley said as he looked around the lobby of the downtown hotel where the district attorney's office had arranged for him to stay.

"The Ritz was booked," Laura said.

"I'm not blaming you," Stanley replied as Laura's facetious remark sailed over his head and out of sight.

Laura had picked Jim up at the airport an hour earlier, and she was already tired of his complaining about the inconvenience of coming to Atlanta. What was most galling was that Jim was her star witness, and he knew it. All Laura's hopes of finding some nice, clean witness—someone who hadn't conspired with James Stanley, someone who had never met Jesse DuPree—had evaporated when the passenger manifest for the Greenville-Atlanta flights turned up no one who could be James Stanley, and no one who remembered seeing him on either plane. They were stuck with Jim's imperfect record for truth-telling, and Laura was stuck with him on a Saturday brilliant with the dying embers of the summer sun.

"Let's get you checked in and then we can start to work," she said, seized by a sudden desire to get it over with.

"I could use some lunch," Stanley said.

"They have a coffee shop here. We can get sandwiches and take them up to your suite."

"Didn't we pass a Friday's? I could use a beer, too."

"You'll have to get one later. We have to get some work done, and we have to do it in private—either in your suite or in my office. Let me get you checked in, and then we'll get something to eat." Laura left Jim standing in the lobby, and went to the registration desk. "You have a room for Mr. Stanley, booked by the Fulton County district attorney's office."

"Yes, miss. Room 349."

The clerk handed Laura a small paper wallet containing two keys. Laura thrust it into the pocket of her ratty barn jacket as she spoke to the clerk. "I'll sign for the room. We're paying for the room only. There should be a block on the phone, and on room service, and laundry and things like that."

"Yes, miss. I'll need Mr. Stanley's credit card for those services."

Laura turned and beckoned Jim to the counter. "You'll have to pay for your own phone calls. We'll reimburse you up to twenty dollars a day in meal allowance—keep your receipts."

Jim handed over his credit card, but he started to pout. "I think you people should pay for everything—you're dragging me down here for God knows how long, and you won't even pay for my phone calls. That stinks."

"Do I need to remind you that we have the power to

compel you to testify, Mr. Stanley, and to hold you in contempt if you refuse? We could have subpoenaed you and made you pay your own way. As it is, I think we've been downright generous to you." *We could have tried to void your immunity and put your sorry butt in jail, too,* she thought, wishing more than ever that they had at least attempted to do just that.

"I'm not saying it's your fault," Jim said ingratiatingly. "It's just hard on a man to be away from home for an indefinite length of time."

"I bet it is," Laura said, thinking of the charges Jim's wife had made against him. "Let's get some sandwiches and go upstairs. Here's your key." She fished the key from her pocket and gave it to him.

They ordered sandwiches to go at the counter of the cheerful coffee shop. Laura asked for two cups of coffee to fuel her for the upcoming ordeal. On a generous impulse, she paid for Jim's meal, too. "I'll expense it," she said. "Come on, let's shake a leg. We can get this done in a couple of hours if we concentrate."

The suite—really a glorified hotel room with a half-wall separating a sitting area from the bed and bath—was pleasantly, if blandly, decorated. "Give me a sec to hang up my things, and I'll be right with you." Laura could hear Stanley fussing around in the other part of the suite. The toilet flushed, and she heard running water. She was suddenly uncomfortable and wished that she had insisted that they go to her office, but it was too late now.

Jim, now jacketless, returned to the sitting area where Laura had unpacked the sandwiches and drinks onto the coffee table. Jim sat down on the sofa. Laura took the chair to his right.

"So, what do you do for fun in this town?" he asked as he popped the tab on his Coke.

"I prepare witnesses for court appearances," Laura responded.

"Don't be such a stick in the mud! If I'm going to be stuck down here for God-knows-how-long, I'll have to have some fun. You don't expect me to stay cooped up in this crummy room, do you?"

"What you do on your own time is up to you—as long as you stay out of jail and away from reporters."

"You mean I can't talk to the press?"

"*Absolutely,* you cannot talk to the press. Too much has been leaked out already, and I don't want any more surprises. Your only comment is 'no comment.'"

"Why are you so hostile?"

"You think this is hostile? Wait until you see me in a courtroom. Now, I'm just trying to get some work done here so I can go home."

"You hardly said a pleasant word to me all the way from the airport," he said accusingly.

"I'm not here to be your buddy, Jim. This is work." Laura was trying to maintain a strictly professional atmosphere, but the truth was that she didn't like Jim Stanley. She hadn't liked him from the first time they met. There was something sleazy about him. Laura would believe almost anything bad that was said of him—and yet she was depending on him for virtually her entire case against James Stanley. The situation was profoundly uncomfortable for her. She wished that Meredith was here; her presence might at least keep Jim from looking Laura up and down in that appraising way. "Let's get going. Since you've had a little bit of experience with the law, I assume you have a general idea about what goes on in a trial."

"I've never had a trial," Jim said, a note of pride in his voice.

"No, I guess you haven't. So, here's how it's going to

be: The trial begins with opening statements from both sides. Then the prosecution presents its case. We call a witness and question him; that's called direct examination. Then the defense questions him—that's cross-examination. Then we get to ask a few more questions in rebuttal. We plan to call about half a dozen witnesses ahead of you. That could take anywhere from two days to a week. Maybe longer, depending on how the defense handles our witnesses."

"Why'd you get me down here so soon, then?"

"I said, it *may* take that long. And you're here now because I won't have time to deal with you after the trial gets underway; I'll have too much else to do, and I'll be in court all day."

"It'll be fun to watch you, at least," he said, leering slightly.

"No, Jim, you're not going to be in the courtroom. You're going to be sequestered in a witness room at the courthouse, waiting to be called. I suggest that you pick up some books and magazines to pass the time. There won't be much to do in there except talk to the other witnesses."

"Jesus. Who *are* the other witnesses?"

"Mostly cops," Laura said breezily. "And a lawyer. I'm sure you'll like all of them."

Jim slumped back onto the sofa. "I didn't think it would be like *that*. I was kinda pumped about seeing a real trial."

"You'll see plenty. I expect that we'll have you on the stand for the better part of a day, and Lord knows how long Craig Fannin is going to keep you up there."

"Who's he?"

"He's the defense lawyer. He's going to try to destroy you, which brings us back to why we're here right now."

"Okay," Jim said with a resigned sigh. "Where do we start?"

"When you're called to the stand, the jury will already have heard all the details of the crime from the police and the crime-scene witnesses. We're going to let the ballistics expert introduce the gun into evidence. Carlton Hemingway—you met him in Winston-Salem—is going to set up your testimony by describing how we found you. You'll be sworn in, and Meredith Gaffney will question you."

"I thought *you* would."

"Nope. This is too important. I'm new at this, but Meredith has years of experience. Now, when she—or Fannin, or the judge—asks you a question, give the shortest answer possible. If you're asked a yes-or-no question, answer 'yes' or 'no,' period. If the questioner wants more, he'll ask for it. That's *especially* important when Fannin asks you a question."

"Why?"

"Because he'll be trying to discredit you, and the more you talk, the better his chances. Let's say he asks you, *'Mr. Stanley, why did you think James Stanley offered you five thousand dollars to check into a hotel in his name?'* What would you reply?"

"I'd say, *'I thought it was real important to him that I be in that hotel.'*"

"Wrong. That's too much information, and, anyway, it's speculative. Fannin would take that answer and run with it, and he'd make it seem to the jury that you knew that James was planning to murder his wife. Now try again. *'Mr. Stanley, why did you think James Stanley offered you five thousand dollars to check into a hotel in his name?'*"

"I have no idea."

"Much better. That's not really what I want to work on

Paul

45 3526 2999 home

45 3520 5913

today, though—Meredith is going to play defense attorney and give you a good going-over tomorrow. Then you'll have a much clearer idea of what it's like to go up against a lawyer like Craig Fannin."

"What's the big deal about him? I've dealt with a fair number of lawyers, you know."

"I doubt you've ever dealt with one like Craig Fannin. He's a turbo-charged, heavy-duty, all-wheel-drive lawyer. He will run right over you and leave you wondering what the hell hit you."

"Oooh, I'm scared."

"You should be. Now, let's get back to work on the basics. State your name."

"Huh?"

"State your name for the record."

"What record?"

"Jim, get with it—we're talking about your testimony. I want you to tell the court your *name*."

"Oh. Jim Stanley."

"No."

"Whaddaya mean, no? I know my own name."

"Your name is *James* Stanley."

"I get it—you want the jury to pick up on the same-name thing. Okay, *James T. Stanley*. How's that?"

"Fine. And where do you live, Mr. Stanley?"

"Winston-Salem, North Carolina," he replied cautiously, unsure whether Laura was going to jump on him again.

She nodded. "What line of work are you in?"

"I'm a mortgage broker?" he said, raising his inflection at the end of his statement.

Laura tried not to smile, but it was funny. "I'm not trying to trap you, Jim. Just give straightforward answers. Does your business require you to travel much, Mr. Stanley?"

"Some, yes."

Laura nodded and continued. "And do you visit Charlotte, North Carolina, from time to time?"

"Yes. There are a lot of banks there . . ."

"No! Too much information. Try again. Do you visit Charlotte, North Carolina, from time to time?"

"Yes."

"Did you often stay overnight in Charlotte?"

"Sometimes."

"How often is 'sometimes?'"

"Maybe twice a month."

"Okay, you're getting the hang of this. You'll be asked about the hotel, and how often you stayed there, and Meredith will gradually lead you up to the story of how you met James Stanley. Don't anticipate her; she's going to go slowly for a reason. Let her draw out the details. Let's try it. *Is there a particular hotel you stay in when you visit Charlotte, Mr. Stanley?*'"

"Yes."

"Okay, you can be a little more forthcoming there. You can give the name."

"Yes. The Marriott."

"Why do you stay there?"

"Because it's a good location."

"Is the service there good?"

"Yes."

"Always?"

"Usually."

"Have you ever had any problems at the Marriott?"

"I get it—this is where I tell about the time they screwed up the reservations."

"Exactly. Have you ever had any problems at the Marriott?"

"Only once."

"Okay, this is good. I want you to be prepared, though, for Fannin to jump in with objections from time to time. Right then, he might say, *'Objection, Your Honor—relevance.'* If he does break in, just sit tight and let us hash it out. Never try to answer the objection yourself. All right, where were we? *Did you have a problem when you tried to check into the hotel on July 15, 1998?'"*

"Yes."

"What happened?"

"They didn't have a room for me."

"Why not?"

"They had given it to another James Stanley."

"That's your big moment—make it count. Meredith will go on and pull out the details, how you met the other James Stanley, and all that. Then she'll ask you if you see James Stanley in the courtroom."

"Will I?"

"Yes. You just tell her where you see him sitting. Then she'll return to questioning you. She'll ask you if you met James Stanley again, and how often. She'll ask if the two of you ever discussed making use of the similarity in your names. She'll ask you for details of those discussions, and then she'll ask if James Stanley asked you to check into the hotel for him on the night of May 8. That's another big moment—answer it with a simple yes or no." Jim nodded solemnly. "She'll pull the details out of you—when he told you to check in, what you were supposed to do. Don't volunteer anything; wait until you're asked. For instance, when she says, *'What did James Stanley ask you to do after you checked in?'* give only the *immediate* answer."

"Like, *'He asked me to go up to the room and wait until he showed up?'"*

"Exactly. She'll ask if he wanted you to do anything else, and you say . . ."

"Yes."

"What else did he ask you to do?"

"Order dinner, and make two phone calls."

"Good. Then she'll ask you what happened when he showed up—if he said anything to you, what he was wearing. *What did the defendant say to you when he arrived at the hotel room?*'"

"That he was tired. He took off his clothes and got into bed—there were two beds in the room."

"Too much data, Jim."

"But he didn't get into bed with *me*."

"No one cares. Now, what did he say?"

"That he was tired."

"And what did he do?"

"Went to bed."

"Okay, that'll pretty much get out that part of the story. Then it's going to get sticky."

"Why?"

"We have to deal with the gun, and what you knew about his intentions. Let's give it a try. *Mr. Stanley, do you recognize this gun?*' Remember, the gun has already been introduced into evidence, but the jury has no idea it belongs to you."

"Yes. That's my gun."

"Did you ever lend this gun to anyone?"

"Yes."

"To whom did you lend it?"

"To James Stanley."

"Okay, she'll probably ask you to point him out again for the record. *Why did you lend the gun to Mr. Stanley?*'"

"He said he was interested in military pistols. I told him I had one. He asked to see it, and then he asked if he could borrow it. Is that too much?"

"No, that's okay. Meredith may phrase the question differently. *'When did you lend the gun to James Stanley?'*"

"Maybe last November or December. I don't remember."

"Did you think it was odd that he asked to borrow a gun?"

"No. He seemed to know a good bit about the gun. I thought he was a collector."

"Okay, that's good. She may ask a few more questions—like did you know that the gun was in working order, was it loaded when you gave it to Stanley? That part is pretty straightforward, but it leads us up to the tough stuff: *'Mr. Stanley, did you wonder why James Stanley offered you five thousand dollars to pretend to be him for one evening?'* That's the crux of your testimony—your answer will determine in the jury's eyes how reliable you are."

"What do you want me to say?"

"I can't tell you what to say."

"Oh. How about *'I thought he was having an affair?'*"

Laura sighed. "That might have to do. You knew, didn't you, that he was planning to kill someone?"

"Of course not!"

"You lent him a gun, and gave him an alibi, and you didn't know he was planning a murder? Come on, Jim, it's just you and me here. Why don't you just tell me what you really thought?"

Jim narrowed his eyes, cagily. "You won't use it against me?"

"How can I? You have 24-carat immunity. And I can't testify, and even if I did, anything you say to me here is just hearsay. And I just want to know what you *thought*. Thoughts aren't criminal."

"Okay, then, I'll tell you—not to go out of this room. I thought James wanted to kill the old man."

"What old man?"

"You know—his father-in-law. He was always bitching about him. He said he couldn't wait until the old son of a bitch died, so he could get some real money behind his business. *That's* how the subject of the gun came up—he said the old man collected guns. I mentioned that I had a Nazi piece that I was looking to sell. The thing's worth more than a grand, you know, and I was a little short of cash. He told me he'd take the gun down to Georgia and show it to his father-in-law. I saw him a couple of times after that and asked him if the old man wanted the gun, and he said that he hadn't made up his mind. Then, when he asked me to check into the hotel, I thought I had it all figured out." Jim smiled at his own canniness.

"What did you figure out?"

"That he was going to kill the old man, and stage it as an accident or a suicide, using that gun."

"Why not use one of Mr. Connell's guns?"

Jim shook his head. "They were kept in a locked gun room. James couldn't get in there. I figure James held on to that gun for a while trying to work up the nerve to do it. You could have knocked me over with a feather when you told me he had killed his wife."

Laura frowned as she tried to take it all in. "At least it's logically consistent. I'll tell Meredith about it. She'll lead you through it. I think it makes you much more credible. Yes, it's good."

"Wait! I thought you said it was between you and me—not to leave this room."

"Oops. I lied. You'll have to tell that story to the jury now." Laura had realized that Jim Stanley was a one-man *Rashomon,* able to provide multiple versions of the same event, depending on his audience. She had decided, after one too many surprises, that she should meet him on his own ground, and if that meant playing with the truth, so be it. Besides, if she let him say something else on the stand, she would be suborning perjury.

Jim looked indignant for a moment; then he laughed. "Taste of my own medicine, huh? You're a smart gal."

"You're right about that. Okay, we're done here. I'll pick you up at about eleven tomorrow morning. That'll give you time to go to church. We'll need you for four or five hours, so don't make any plans for the afternoon." She gathered her papers and prepared to go.

"You're leaving?"

"Yep. It's after four, and I have plans for tonight."

"Big date?"

"Dinner with a friend."

"Care if I tag along?"

"I don't think that's appropriate. Don't you know anyone down here? I thought you grew up in Georgia."

"I don't have a car. I guess I could call Jesse DuPree."

"Oh, no, you don't. Why don't you take in a movie? Take a cab to Buckhead. I'll make sure you're reimbursed. Just for pity's sake, don't call Jesse."

Jim grinned, conscious of having scored a point. Laura stood up, put on her jacket, and made for the door. "Don't get into any trouble—your immunity only applies in the Stanley case." She left the hotel quickly, eager to get into the fresh air. She headed for home, and dinner with Amos.

CHAPTER 24

The trial of James Allen Stanley for the murder of his wife opened on a crisp Monday morning in October. A front had moved in from the plains, bringing with it the first nippy breeze of fall and shooing the last of the summer's humidity away. It was as if even the weather knew that it was time to get serious.

Laura woke early from a restless night and was unable to return to sleep. After an hour or so tossing in the greenish glow of her clock's electronic display, she decided to shower and get dressed. She had already picked her clothes carefully. Of course, if the trial dragged on for weeks, she would eventually work her way through her entire working wardrobe, but for today, she wanted Full Battle Dress. She took her favorite black suit from the closet, and a creamy silk blouse. The skirt hit in just the right place—not so short that she would look like a television lawyer, and not so long that she would appear frumpy. She opened a fresh package of nude pantyhose, and put on her best underwear—not her best *date* underwear, but her most *serious* bra and panties. The black pumps she selected had heels just a smidgen higher than her everyday pair. She wore minimal jewelry; Tom's necklace would be hidden by her collar, so she put on her grandmother's pearls and a matching pair of stud earrings. Makeup had to be light and neutral—no eyeliner, and only a little gray shadow. No blush, and light pink lipstick. She had had her nails done Saturday before she met Jim Stanley at the airport, in a barely there pink like the inside of a seashell.

When she had fully armored herself, she looked at her watch. It wasn't even six o'clock yet, and she didn't plan to meet Meredith at the courthouse until eight. She retrieved the paper from the front yard, made coffee, and toasted a bagel. She dozed off over the paper, and awoke with just enough time to make her rendezvous with the boss. *Wouldn't you know?* she thought as she backed the car out of the driveway. *Up all night, and I'm running late.*

She met Meredith in the parking lot. Her boss looked at Laura approvingly. "Dressed to convict, I see."

"Mm-hmm. And I see you've opted for the up-do."

"Hey, I'm a blonde with big boobs. If I didn't wear my hair up in court I'd never get a conviction."

If anyone overheard them, they might have been shocked at their callous attitude toward something as solemn as a trial, especially a trial in which a man's life was at stake. But all professions have a tradition of dark humor—gallows humor, literally, in the case of trial lawyers. It was a way of keeping a psychological distance from a tough and sometimes harrowing job. Laura had lost count of the times Tom Bailey had made tasteless jokes completely out of keeping with his character, things he never would have said to anyone but another trial lawyer.

When they arrived in the courtroom, Craig Fannin was already there with James Stanley and two associates Laura had not met before. Meredith strolled toward him and greeted him as if it were an ordinary day. Laura followed and was introduced to the associates. Craig greeted her warmly, but the assistants eyed her warily. Laura made a point of being extra-casual and friendly with them, just to prove to herself that she had no personal stake in "beating" them. *It's not a beauty contest, Laura,* she could hear Tom saying. *It's business.* Of course, Tom had never tried a murder case. Laura tried not to look at James Stanley, but it was hard. He was neatly dressed, as always, but he was staring straight ahead, his hands folded in his lap. He looked calm, but Laura could see that he was pressing his hands together so tightly that the knuckles were white.

The courtroom was filling up with reporters and spectators, and there was a low hum of voices. The bailiff came in and placed some things on the judge's desk, and then left again. Laura arranged her own things on the prosecution table: legal pad, pens, and the hefty box of files that she had helped Meredith haul in from the parking lot. She saw Lynette and her father taking a seat in the row behind the prosecution table. *This is going to be hard for Mr. Connell,* Laura thought sympathetically. *Whatever the outcome, he loses.* She waved to Lynette but didn't approach her to speak. She didn't have time; she needed to speak with Randy Travers, but he wasn't there yet. She did see Megan Carney, though, coming through the great double doors with a huge artist's portfolio in her hand. "The exhibits are here," Laura said to Meredith.

"Good. Have you had a chance to check them?"

Laura shook her head. "They were still working on them over the weekend. Should we take a look?"

"Yes. I wish Randy would get here before the proceedings start so he can check them. Hello, Meggie. Let's see what you've got."

Megan was a freelance graphic designer with one of the more unusual jobs in her field: she designed exhibits for trials. Prendergrast and Crawley had used her, and the district attorney's office did, too. There weren't that many designers who understood the requirements of a courtroom. "Hello, lawyers," she said, opening her portfolio and producing four foam-backed boards. "I've got them all, but there's time to make changes if you need them."

Laura flipped through the displays. The one that particularly concerned her was the floor plan of the Stanley house, with the positions of the important details marked. She was surprised that Megan had represented the position of Christine Stanley's body with the outline of a human figure. She had expected an X.

"Is it okay?" Megan asked anxiously. "That's the first one you'll be using, so I don't think there's time to alter it."

"It's fine. It's just that the body—well, it's a little macabre."

"That's how Meredith likes it done, right?"

"Right," Meredith answered, surveying a board on which were mounted black-and-white crime-scene photos. "These blew up well. What else? Oh, the ballistics. Good job."

"Thanks. Beep me if you need me. 'Bye." And Megan was gone, but Randy Travers took her place.

"Good," Laura said. "I wanted to catch you before they sequestered you. Here are the house diagram and the crime-scene photos. Take a look at them."

Travers had dressed up for court, in a baggy blue suit and a white-on-white striped shirt, with a wide gold tie. The jury would look at him and see "cop" personified, and Laura supposed that was all right. He gazed at the exhibits, and grunted his approval. "You'll be the first called after the opening statements," Laura said. "I hope we can get through your testimony today."

"Me, too. See ya later," he said, and walked off.

"I can't get over the feeling that he doesn't like me," Laura said as she watched him leave the courtroom.

"He doesn't like anyone much these days," Meredith said. "And you did more or less take over his investigation."

"With Carlton! Carlton was always with me!"

"I know, I know. Oh, here's Judge Penfield."

The bailiff announced the judge, who made a stately entry and gaveled the courtroom to order. "Please summon the jury," she commanded. The jurors filed in, led by a Fulton County sheriff's deputy. They had been in this room before, but the atmosphere today was charged as it had not been the previous week during voir dire. They looked appropriately awestruck today. "Have you selected a foreperson?" Judge Penfield asked.

"Yes, Your Honor," replied one of the jurors Laura had liked the best, a retired black man who had worked for the power company. "I've guess I've been elected."

"Very well. The bailiff will administer the oath to the jurors."

The bailiff did. Then he proceeded to read out the charges in solemn, ringing tones, and the trial was officially underway. Laura caught her breath as Meredith rose to give her opening statement. The boss walked confidently around the prosecution table and stopped before the jury box. As she took those few steps, Laura could hear the courtroom preparing itself to listen. There was a soft intake of breath, and a rustle of bodies settling deeper into the hard seats. Then, in the dead, absolute silence that followed, Meredith began to speak.

"Ladies and gentlemen of the jury, I want to thank you, right now, before this trial starts, for what you are about to do. There is no more solemn duty that a democracy demands of its citizens than that of sitting in judgment of another citizen's life. Right now, if you'll permit me to do a little mind-reading, I imagine that some of you are a little uneasy about that responsibility. I imagine that some of you are asking yourselves, *'How can I judge another person? What qualifies* me *for this onerous duty?'* You might even find yourself thinking, *'What if that were me—what if I were the defendant in this case? Would* I *want to be judged?'* These are natural questions.

"We live today in a culture where tolerance is considered *the* prime virtue. And it is a virtue; I would never dispute that. But how far will we go in our tolerance? Will it keep us from judging anyone, anytime? Take as an example Adolf Hitler. Surely we can all agree that here was a man truly unworthy of his humanity, a living embodiment of evil. *Of course,* you may be thinking now, *Adolf Hitler was the most evil man ever to have lived. No problem there.* And yet, when a high-school teacher recently asked his students what they thought of Hitler, some of them— not all of them, thank God—said that they didn't feel 'qualified' to sit in judgment of him. Maybe, these children said, if they had been in his shoes, they would have become Hitler themselves.

"Well, ladies and gentlemen, I hope you think more highly of yourselves that *that.* I believe that none of us would like to think that he or she has the potential to become a Hitler. But I think I understand what those naïve students were driving at, don't you? We define our humanity in terms of our ability to empathize with others. We live in fear of losing that ability to empathize, fearing that if we do, we might become less than human ourselves. *So how can we judge someone else?*

"Part of our reluctance to pass judgment comes from that sense of common humanity. We have a wonderful capacity for empathy that allows us to project ourselves into another's position. Most of us have said at one time or another, *'There but for the grace of God go I.'* When we open the newspaper in the morning, we feel instinctively the pain of the parents who have lost a child in an accident, or the agony of victims of some faraway natural disaster. And we say, *'There but for the grace of God . . .'*

"But there have to be limits to our ability to empathize. When we read, in that same newspaper, a story about a brutal, senseless crime, our empathy dries up—our empathy for the perpetrator of that crime, at any rate. We cannot project ourselves into his shoes. We cannot conceive of ourselves brutalizing another person, especially a person we love. Of course we pity the person who causes harm by accident. Maybe we even identify a little bit with someone pushed beyond the limits of human patience who lashes out violently. But it is impossible to identify or empathize with a person who deliberately and methodically plans a crime. Of that person we say, *'How could he do that?'* In short, we judge. Someone who would do that is not us— he is The Other. We cannot empathize with him, because he has forfeited his own humanity.

"And that, ladies and gentlemen, is where you will find the strength and the courage to do your duty as jurors in the trial of James Allen Stanley for the murder of his wife. Here is a man who planned, carefully and cleverly, to kill his own wife, the mother of his two young children. And he did it out of greed. He did it for *money*.

"Christine Connell Stanley was a beautiful young woman. She loved her family, especially her two children,

Matthew and Sara. But her marriage was not happy, and it had not been for a long time. She and her husband disagreed about the importance of money. Christine wanted to live simply, as she always had, despite the fact that she was rich—very rich. James Stanley, her husband, wanted to live the life of a rich man. He wanted a big house, and a country club membership, and fancy cars. He already had the love of a beautiful family, but that wasn't enough for him. And when Christine Connell Stanley grew so unhappy that she began to think about leaving him, James Stanley realized that he would lose all that lovely money. That is when he began to plan, and to calculate.

"In the coming days, you are going to hear a horrible story. You are going to hear some painful details, and you will be asked to look at some pictures that will make you profoundly uncomfortable. But nothing that you will be asked to contemplate will be as terrible as what we will tell you about why this crime took place, and how carefully it was planned and carried out.

"You will need to pay attention to the facts in this case. They are fairly straightforward. We're not going to drag in a lot of scientific testimony, and we're not going to ask you to understand the mind of this brutal killer. We only ask that you listen carefully, and keep the simple facts in your mind.

"You may hear some of those facts disputed. You may hear the term 'reasonable doubt' thrown around. I ask you only this: remember that the doubt must be *reasonable*. Don't let yourself be led astray by fancy theories. Don't ignore facts and allow doubt to grow in your minds, because if you follow those facts, you will have no doubt that James Stanley killed his wife.

"Thank you."

As Meredith spoke, Laura relaxed. The anxiety that

had kept her awake most of the night slowly ebbed away. The trial had begun, and she could stop second-guessing herself about what more she could have done to strengthen the case. They had to go with what they had—and what they had was good. Meredith's experience was showing in every gesture she made, and the jury couldn't ignore the facts that they were about to hear. Craig Fannin might be a great courtroom duelist—and Laura hoped that he was, because she did love a challenge—but he couldn't overcome the truth. Meredith returned to the table, and raised her eyebrows in a silent query. Laura gave her two thumbs-up under the table. "He's halfway to prison," she whispered.

Craig Fannin scraped the legs of his chair on the floor as he pushed back from the defense table and stood. He walked carefully to the same position that Meredith had just abandoned, his tread firm. He gave the jurors a warm smile. "Good morning, ladies and gentlemen. Thank you for being here today.

"I've been a trial lawyer for almost twenty years—and yes, I know all the lawyer jokes. We lawyers don't get a lot of respect, and maybe sometimes we don't deserve it. But I love my job. It's the most satisfying job in the world. You know why? Because every day, I look for the truth, and there's nothing more satisfying than finding the truth.

"Every time I take a case, I see it as an opportunity to solve a puzzle. Somebody comes to me with a problem—and if he's coming to me, it's a bad one. He tells me his story, and I listen. Just like you're going to listen to a story in this courtroom.

"And that's one thing you folks will have in common with me: to us, this is just a story. None of us were there when the events we're going to hear about took place. None of the prosecution witnesses were there, either.

They'll all be telling *part* of the story, but there are only two people who know the entire tale: Christine Stanley and the person who murdered her.

"Right about now, I bet you're wondering, '*So how are we supposed to get the whole story of what happened that night?*' That's exactly what I asked myself when James Stanley came to me. '*How can I find the truth of what really happened?*'

"One thing that I've learned in twenty years of lawyering is that you don't just cobble together a fact or two and serve it up as a case. No, before you make a case, you have to get *all* the facts in front of you, and you have to make use of *all* those facts. It's like doing a jigsaw puzzle: You lay out all the pieces on the table, and you turn them right side up, and you sort them by shape and color. *Then* you start to assemble the puzzle. If you don't do all that sorting, you'll be starting without a clear idea of what you're doing. You may find a few random pieces that stick together, but you won't know where they go in the larger picture. Put together enough random pieces, and you may even get a picture—but it might not be the right one. You can force some of the pieces to fit together, and you can leave out the ones that don't seem to go anywhere. Maybe you'll get a rough idea of what the puzzle-maker intended the picture to look like, or maybe you'll get a different picture entirely.

"When James Stanley came to me with his problem, I started laying pieces out on a table. Since last May, I've been collecting those pieces. When I finally had all the pieces, I was able to put together a picture. It's a very ugly picture, I'm afraid. But it's a very *different* picture from the one the prosecution has put together.

"'*Now, how can that be?,*' you might ask. '*Surely we're all dealing with the same set of facts.*' Well, yes, we are, but the prosecution has chosen to use only *some* of the facts in building its case. When a fact didn't fit their theory, they simply discarded it. And by pounding and mashing what was left into place, they put together a pretty good picture of their own.

"But you know and I know that 'pretty good' isn't good enough in this case. James Stanley has been accused of murder, and the penalty, if you find him guilty, is life in prison without the possibility of parole—or death. I'm sure that before you make a decision like that, you'll want more than a 'pretty good' idea of what happened that night in May.

"I think I told you that the picture I got when I put all the pieces together was not a pretty one. In fact, it's downright ugly. It's ugly because someone has committed the most heinous crime that we know of, murder. Worse than that, someone has very cleverly planned this crime to make it appear that it was my client who is the murderer. Ladies and gentlemen, I am relieved to tell you that he is *not*.

"Mrs. Gaffney asked you to listen. Please do. Please listen to everything that is said in this courtroom. And when you've heard it all, and when you've seen all the pieces of this puzzle in their proper places, you will know who killed Christine Stanley. And it will not be James Allen Stanley."

With a curt nod, Fannin spun around and returned to his seat. Meredith turned to Laura. "Your turn," she said. "*Vaya con Dios.*"

CHAPTER 25

A short while later, Laura sat down, very pleased with herself, and very, very pleased with Randy Travers. Travers had managed to shuck his weary cynicism for more than two hours while Laura questioned him about the events of May 8. He had even joined her in front of Megan's diagram of the house, and pointed out the position of various objects. They were a team, and a good one. And Randy was, well, *incredibly credible,* Laura thought paradoxically.

The jury had listened closely as the experienced detective took them inside the Stanley house and re-created the events that took place there. The jurors craned their necks and took in every word, every syllable, he spoke. They cringed, Laura noticed, when the actual crime-scene photos were shown, but she noticed at least one juror taking out a tissue and dabbing at her eyes when Travers described the container of melted ice cream. He even made the nonexistent fingerprint evidence seem compelling.

Laura sat down next to Meredith, who patted her arm warmly. "You done good," she whispered. "Craig's going to have a hard time with Randy." As she spoke, Craig Fannin and one of his young associates rose from their seats. The associate lugged a foam-board exhibit to the easel where Laura's exhibits still rested. The bailiff removed the prosecution's boards, and Laura was surprised to see that Fannin was replacing them with a diagram of the house exactly like her own. "That Megan— comforting the enemy," she muttered. But another look told her that the diagram was not *exactly* the same. Megan had added two large red arrows, one pointing to a spot on the floor in front of the body, another to the French doors in the kitchen. They were labeled "shoe print" and "fibers," respectively. Laura knew immediately where this was headed.

Fannin greeted Travers as an old friend, and Laura was pleased to see a mulish look cross the detective's face. "Hello, Detective. I'd like to go back over a couple of points in your testimony if I may." *As if he needs to ask permission to cross-examine,* Laura thought. Travers nodded his assent.

"Detective Travers, when you examined the crime scene, you say that you found no sign of an intruder in the house, other than the broken lock on the doors in the kitchen."

"That's correct."

"And yet, Detective Travers, didn't you find a shoeprint in the carpet in the family room?"

"There was a faint print, yes."

Fannin walked to his exhibit. "The mark was here, was it not?"

"Yes, approximately."

"About eight feet from where the body lay."

"Yes."

"Did the crime-scene team take the measure of that print?"

"Yes, they did."

"And what size was it?"

"It was about twenty-nine centimeters long."

"And what size shoe does that equate to?"

"A ten."

"A men's ten, is that correct?"

"Yes."

"I see. Detective Travers, what size shoe does the defendant wear?"

"An eleven. Men's."

"Detective Travers, do you know the equivalent woman's size?"

"About a ten and a half or an eleven."

"Hmm. That's large for a woman's shoe, isn't it?"

"Yes, I suppose so. I'm not an expert."

Fannin smiled graciously. "And yet you knew immediately when I asked, what size woman's shoe equated to a men's ten."

"Yes."

"Did you look into that for some reason, Detective?"

"Yes. You can't tell what sex someone is just by looking at a shoe print, Mr. Fannin. We had to consider that a woman or a man might have made that print."

"Yes, of course. Did you determine what size shoe Mrs. Stanley wore?"

"Yes. Eight and a half."

"And the cleaning lady?"

"Seven and a half."

"Did you find in your investigation *any* woman who wore a size ten and a half or eleven shoe?"

"Objection, Your Honor—relevance," Laura said, standing.

"Your Honor, I am trying to determine why the police didn't think that the shoe print was important."

Judge Penfield nodded. "Objection overruled. You may continue."

"Thank you. So, Detective, were there any women connected with the investigation who wore a shoe of that size?"

"Yes. One."

"And who was she?"

"The victim's sister, Lynette Connell. But we . . ."

"Thank you. Now, Detective, I'd like to turn your attention to the second spot marked on this diagram. Can you see where the arrow is pointing?"

Randy looked at Laura for a split second before he answered. She nodded reassuringly; Fannin had managed to introduce Lynette's name without allowing Travers to exonerate her, but Laura could easily correct that in her redirect examination

"Yes. It points to the kitchen doors," Randy said in answer to Fannin's question.

"It was the lock of those doors that was forced, was it not?"

"Yes."

"Detective Travers, did the crime-scene team find anything caught in the splintered door?"

"Yes."

"And what was that?"

"A few fibers."

"This is a report prepared by the Georgia Bureau of Investigation Crime Lab," Fannin said, displaying a document. "I request permission to enter this report as Defense

Exhibit B. Now, Detective, could you read the highlighted section on that page?"

" *'Approximately six fibers measuring six to ten millimeters each were discovered in the splintered wood around the door lock. Examination showed these fibers to consist of gray wool and polyester fibers twisted together in a manner consistent with wool-blend fabrics of the type used to make garments, especially suiting material. The sample was not large enough to permit further identification.'* "Travers handed the report back to Fannin with no comment.

"Detective, did you examine Mr. Stanley's wardrobe to see if he owned a garment made of material matching the fiber sample described in this report?"

"Yes."

"And what did you find?"

"We found no wool-blend garments. But . . ."

"Thank you, Detective. Did you look only at Mr. Stanley's wardrobe, or did you examine clothing belonging to other suspects, as well?"

"Only Mr. Stanley. By that time he was indicted . . ."

"So you didn't look at clothing belonging to Miss Connell?"

"No. She was not . . ."

"Thank you, Detective. I'd like to turn your attention now to the fingerprint evidence. You told the court that the fingerprint team found no prints except those belonging to the family, the cleaning lady, and frequent visitors. Is that correct?"

"Yes."

"And how was this determined?" Fannin asked patiently.

"The latent evidence team got elimination fingerprints from all the family members, and the others whose prints we might have been expected to find."

"Did you find any prints on the kitchen door, or on the broken lock?"

"Yes, there were a number of prints on the handle and the plate surrounding it, all belonging to family members."

"Did you also find prints on the burglar alarm control panel?"

"Which one?"

"Either of them, Detective."

"Yes, there were prints on the panels in both the front hall and in the kitchen."

"You have testified that the latent evidence team took prints from all the family members, the cleaning lady, and close friends who may have visited the house in order to eliminate prints they might have left. Is that the case?"

"Yes."

"Did you, or someone from your team, fingerprint Lynette Connell, Christine Stanley's sister?"

"We did."

"And did you find any of her fingerprints in the house after the crime?"

"Yes, several sets."

"And would you mind telling us where they were located?" Fannin asked the question casually, with his back half turned to Travers.

"May I refer to my notes?"

"Certainly."

Randy riffled through his notebook. "Lynette Connell's prints were found on the refrigerator door, on the taps on the kitchen sink, on the kitchen door . . ."

"Wait just a moment, please. Her fingerprints were on the *broken* door?"

"Yes. Actually, they were on both kitchen doors—the French doors that led to the patio, and the swinging door that led to the dining room."

"I see. And were Miss Connell's prints on the burglar alarm control panel, as well?"

"Yes."

"Both control panels?"

"No, only the one in the kitchen."

Damage. Laura sensed it. She could also sense Lynette's eyes boring into the back of her head, willing her to turn around. Laura couldn't. She rapidly collected her thoughts, and scribbled a note to Meredith. *I can handle all this on redirect.* Meredith nodded; she didn't look overly concerned.

"So we can conclude that Miss Connell had been in the house shortly before the murder?"

"In all likelihood, yes. But she frequently . . ."

"And let me clarify something, Detective. Did Miss Connell stand to benefit in any way from her sister's death?"

"Not directly."

"But indirectly . . . ?"

"She was a trustee for Mrs. Stanley's children, along with Mr. Stanley, Mrs. Stanley, and a family attorney."

"The trustees for the children have control of quite a large sum of money, isn't that true?"

"I'm not sure. I didn't examine the financial records personally."

"But you must have discussed them."

"No," Randy said, digging in his heels. "The court appointed a special master to look at all that stuff. I have no idea what the specifics of those trusts are."

"I see. But if Mr. Stanley is convicted of his wife's murder, the trust would presumably be removed from his administration."

"Is that a question?"

"Yes. Who would be trustee for those children if Mr. Stanley was not available?"

"I don't know."

Fannin gave up that line of questioning, but he quickly wound up for another run at Lynette. "Detective Travers, in your investigation, did you find that Miss Connell had a police record?"

"Objection, Your Honor—relevance," Laura said. She and Meredith agreed that she would handle objections when one of "her" witnesses was on the stand.

"Your Honor, the defense is trying to determine whether the police considered suspects other than Mr. Stanley," Fannin explained.

"The prosecution questions whether the existence of other suspects is relevant, Your Honor," Laura countered.

"It is, if the police investigation was inherently flawed and biased," Fannin retorted.

"Do you have some evidence of bias, Mr. Fannin?" Judge Penfield asked.

"I believe that the failure of the police to investigate subjects other than Mr. Stanley is prima facie evidence of bias, Your Honor."

"That's ridiculous, Your Honor—Detective Travers *did* investigate Miss Connell, and a number of other individuals in connection with the case, and he has already stated that he did so."

Judge Penfield sighed. "I'll disallow your last question, Mr. Fannin, but you may ask if the detective investigated specific subjects."

"Thank you, Your Honor. Detective, was there a point in time when you considered Miss Connell a suspect in her sister's death?"

"There was a time when I considered *you* a suspect, Mr. Fannin. I never overlook any possibility."

Fannin smiled. "And yet you didn't fingerprint me, or

question my associates. Did you question Miss Connell's associates?"

"Yes, we did. We investigated her thoroughly and exonerated . . ."

"Thank you, Detective. That's all I have for now," Fannin said serenely.

Laura was on her feet, with no prompting from Meredith, before Fannin had sat down again. "Your Honor, the prosecution would like to question this witness again."

"You may."

Laura stepped to the witness box, careful not to block the jury's view of Travers. She was going to take it point by point, although it was hard not to deal with the insinuations against Lynette right away. "Detective, you have testified that the shoe print found in the Stanley family room measured twenty-nine centimeters. Is that an exact measurement?"

"No. The print was blurred and indistinct."

"Could the shoe that made it have been larger than twenty-nine centimeters long?"

"Yes. Or smaller."

"So you didn't regard that shoe print as reliable evidence?"

"No. There was no distinctive tread pattern, and no way of telling when the print was made. The room had been vacuumed early that morning, and several people had been in the room since, including James Stanley, the defendant."

"Thank you. Now, Detective, you read to the court the crime lab report on the fibers found in the broken door. Did you find a garment that matched the description of those fibers?"

"No, we did not."

"But you did look at Mr. Stanley's wardrobe, did you not?"

"Yes, but there was nothing made of that type of fabric."

"You looked only at Mr. Stanley's wardrobe. Why was that?"

"Because he had been indicted by the time we received that analysis of the fiber evidence. We had no other suspects."

"I see. Detective, you testified that the gunman stood approximately six to eight feet from Christine Stanley as he shot her. Would he have been splattered with blood at that distance?"

Fannin hopped up. "Objection, Your Honor—the witness is not an expert in ballistics."

Laura was quick to counter the objection. "Your Honor, Detective Travers is a veteran of twenty years on the homicide squad. He is very familiar with firearms and the damage they do."

"I'll allow it," Judge Penfield said. "Answer the question, Detective."

"Yes, he would have been splattered with fine drops of blood. The gun was a nine millimeter, which uses a high-velocity cartridge. When it meets the target, it causes 'blowback.' Very close to the target, there would be a great deal of blood. Farther away, the droplets of blood would have been very fine."

"Would they have been visible to the naked eye?"

"Probably not."

"Could they have been detected by a lab, using a microscope?"

"Oh, yes. Very easily."

"So, if the shooter knew about blowback, he may have known to dispose of the garments he wore, despite there being no visible bloodstains on them?"

"Objection, Your Honor—calls for speculation." Fannin had been waiting for an opportunity to cut Laura off.

"I withdraw the question. Detective, you testified that at one time you considered Lynette Connell, the victim's sister, a suspect in her death. Is that correct?"

"Yes."

"And did you investigate Miss Connell?"

"Yes, and her associates."

"What did your investigation find?"

"Miss Connell had a corroborated alibi for the night of the murder. She was at a horse show of some kind in Nashville, Tennessee. She ate in a restaurant with three people who all gave affidavits that they had been with her. Miss Connell also produced restaurant and hotel receipts."

"I see. Did you consider the possibility that Miss Connell may have hired a gunman?"

"Yes. Miss Connell had an associate, a former boyfriend, who deals in guns. We thought he might be involved."

"And was he?"

"No. He also had an alibi, which we were able to corroborate."

"And so your investigation showed that Lynette Connell had nothing to do with her sister's murder?"

"Yes. We also uncovered evidence that James Stanley had been involved in the crime. We confirmed Stanley's role, and that served to further exonerate Miss Connell."

"Thank you. I have no further questions for this witness at this time," Laura said. She returned to her seat, and got an under-the-table low five from Meredith.

"Would counsel for the defense like to reexamine this witness?"

"Not at this time, Your Honor."

"You may step down, Detective Travers. Please remain

available throughout the trial for recall. Call the next witness, please."

The next witness Laura called was Carl Bellamy, the GBI Crime Lab ballistics expert, veteran of many trials. He very carefully, almost lovingly, walked the jury through the procedures he used to identify the weapons used in crimes. They could have passed a test on it afterward. Then he delved into the specifics of the gun that was used to kill Christine Stanley. He told them why he had suspected a European military gun, an old one, from the beginning.

When Laura introduced the actual gun, Bellamy gave a short lecture on the history of the Walther P-38. Fannin interrupted, objecting that the testimony was irrelevant, but Judge Penfield overruled him when Laura argued that it was important for the jury to know that the witness was very familiar with the gun used to kill Christine Stanley.

Bellamy also confirmed what Randy had said about "blowback" of blood from the impact of the slug. To Laura's delight, he thought that the blood might even have been visible on the shooter's clothing, making it, Laura was quick to point out, more likely that the killer would have destroyed his clothing. By the time Carl stood by the enlarged pictures of the slugs removed from the crime scene, the jury was following his every syllable. *He should have been a teacher,* Laura thought. *And, God, I'm glad he's on my side.* She beamed at him when she was done with her questions.

Fannin approached the witness box with a thoughtful expression on his face. "Mr. Bellamy, you testified that the slugs from the crime scene were, with ninety-eight percent certainty, fired from the gun presented by the prosecution."

"Yes, that was my testimony."

"And you also testified that this same gun was used to

kill a dog near the Stanleys' home some weeks before the murder. Is that correct?''

"Yes."

"Mr. Bellamy, did it strike you as odd that someone shot a dog with this gun?"

"It struck me as sadistic and unnecessary."

"Exactly. *Unnecessary* is exactly the word I was searching for. Does it not seem curious to you, Mr. Bellamy, that someone planning a murder would use the gun he planned to kill his wife with to kill a *dog?*''

"Objection—calls for speculation." Laura was quick to intervene.

"I only asked Mr. Bellamy for his opinion, Your Honor."

"The objection is sustained," Judge Penfield said.

Fannin returned to face Carl. "I'll rephrase the question: Mr. Bellamy, don't you think it's odd that the killer used the same gun in both these crimes, thus allowing us to place the gun in the Stanleys' neighborhood weeks before the murder?"

"I wouldn't know," Carl answered. "I've never killed anyone."

Meredith poked Laura under the table and waggled her eyebrows in delight. Fannin gave up the line of questioning, and Carl left the stand in triumph. Laura wondered, though, if Fannin's question had been such a blunder. He had managed to point out one of the most illogical aspects of the crime, one that Laura had not been able to get comfortable with herself. But Carl had done a good job deflecting Fannin's speculation, and she was content to let his testimony stand without further questioning.

Laura was so absorbed in the trial proceedings, and so adrenaline-fueled, that she was shocked when Judge

Penfield gaveled the proceedings closed for the day. She and Meredith were conferring, heads together, when Laura felt a touch on her shoulder. It was Lynette.

"I just want to say thanks," she said. "I can see why you didn't want me on the stand—I would have come out of the chair and strangled that sonofabitch."

"He took a lot of shots at you, but they all went wide, I think," Laura said. "Just be prepared for more of the same—especially when the financial testimony is introduced."

CHAPTER 26

"Mr. Borden, you reviewed the financial records of James Stanley's firm, James A. Stanley and Associates, did you not?"

"Yes, I did."

"And did you also review the personal financial records of James Stanley and his late wife Christine Connell Stanley?"

"Yes, I did."

"Could you please tell the court how you conducted your review?"

Laura was presenting her last witness. When William Borden, the special master, finished his testimony, only Meredith's three witnesses—Carlton Hemingway, Wayne Catrall, the Marriott's computer jockey, and Frank Watson, Christine Stanley's divorce attorney—remained before Jim Stanley took the stand. Laura was questioning Borden slowly and methodically, as his testimony was going to be the hardest for the jury to follow, and, frankly, the least exciting. Borden was a great choice as special master, but he left much to be desired as a witness, having a tendency to use expressions like *"within the meaning of the act,"* and *"pursuant to our mandate."* But there was no doubting his honesty or his thoroughness. Meredith called him "Mr. Probity." "Kind of makes you understand what they mean by éminence grise, doesn't he?" she said, eyeing the gray suit, white shirt, and red tie that he wore every day.

Laura was hoping that she could lead him through his testimony in less than two hours. She had no idea what Fannin was going to do with him on cross-examination. There was always the risk that Fannin would try to numb the jury by keeping Borden on the stand hour after hour, while the details of the crime receded from the memories of the jurors, but Laura and Meredith had decided that it was a risk worth taking. Putting him on earlier would have meant that the impact of his testimony would have been dissipated, and, besides, if Borden's report slowed down the trial a bit, Meredith could always jump-start it again with Carlton's testimony.

Borden cleared his throat and prepared to answer the question. "We reviewed records of Mr. Stanley's firm, of which he was managing partner, from its inception in 1994 to the present. We also reviewed his personal financial records, and those of his wife and children, for the same period."

"And did your examination also include a review of the trusts in the name of the two Stanley children, Matthew and Sara?"

"Yes, it did."

"Please explain to the jury what business the firm of James A. Stanley is involved in."

"James A. Stanley and Associates is a financial advisory

and management firm which specializes in managing the assets of high net-worth individuals. Mr. Stanley—there are no associates—solicits funds from individuals, and invests them in various instruments and enterprises."

"Such as?"

"The investments range from publicly traded securities, to partnership interests—for instance, real estate, and restaurant partnerships. He also markets financial products for certain banks and insurance companies—certificates of deposit, annuities, and the like. He also places client funds with financial funds, such as mutual funds and hedge funds."

"Is Mr. Stanley required to have any special licenses or certifications to provide these services?"

"Oh, yes. These are highly regulated businesses."

"Are Mr. Stanley's qualifications all in order?"

"Yes, so far as we could tell."

"How many clients did the firm of James Stanley and Associates have?"

"In addition to the trust funds belonging to his two children, Mr. Stanley had approximately ten clients."

"Who was his largest client?"

"The two trusts were by far the largest clients."

"Is there an inherent conflict of interest in Stanley's role as a trustee and in his role as an investment manager?"

"No, not as long as his role was fully disclosed to the other trustees, which it was."

"Mr. Borden, could you summarize for the jury, in layman's terms, what you discovered in your investigation of the firm of James A. Stanley and Associates?"

"There were numerous irregularities in the management of the affairs of James A. Stanley and Associates. In some instances, client funds were received and not segregated from the firm's general operating funds. More seriously, Mr. Stanley did not disclose to his clients certain fiduciary arrangements he had with some of the partnerships and funds in which he invested their monies."

"Such as . . . ?"

"In particular, Mr. Stanley had an arrangement with a so-called hedge fund. . . ."

Laura had to stop Borden and ask him to explain what a hedge fund was. She had to stop him numerous times, in fact, to explain the esoteric terms he used, like "self-dealing." Finally, when Borden had spelled out the whole story of the hedge fund, Laura took a stab at summing up in terms that would say to the jury *James Stanley was crooked as a kudzu vine.* "So, Mr. Borden, if I understand it correctly, Mr. Stanley invested client funds—and that includes his children's trusts—in this hedge fund that paid him what amounts to a kickback. Is that correct?"

"Objection, Your Honor. The term 'kickback' has no legal meaning here." Fannin had been quiet up to this point.

Laura didn't wait for Judge Penfield to rule. "I'll rephrase the question, Your Honor. Mr. Borden, was Mr. Stanley allowed, by the laws and regulations governing his profession, to have a financial interest in the investments he sold to his clients?"

"A financial interest, yes. He could make an investment. But he could not receive a commission from any firm in which he invested client funds without disclosing that arrangement to his clients."

"Did he receive commissions from this hedge fund?"

"Yes, he did."

"And did he disclose this commission from the hedge fund?"

"No."

"Would you say that this action was illegal?"

"Yes. In fact, I have forwarded my report to the regulatory authorities for action. I have cited his dealing with the hedge fund as well as his mismanagement of client's funds that should have been held in escrow pending investment. Either offense is sufficient to cost him his licenses."

"I see. Would loss of his license have caused his removal as a trustee of his children's money?"

"No. You must understand, Miss Chastain, that Mr. Stanley wore two hats, as it were, with regard to the trusts. First, he acted as a trustee, which is to say that he, along with his fellow trustees, was responsible for the prudent investment of the funds to ensure the maximum benefit to the children, Matthew and Sara. In addition to those duties, Mr. Stanley, in his capacity as an investment manager, was hired by the trustees to make investments for the trusts. The two roles were separate."

"I understand. So, if he lost his license, he could remain a trustee, but he could no longer manage the trust funds."

"Yes."

"How much would his firm lose in income if that were to happen?"

"James A. Stanley and Associates received a fee of approximately 1.75 percent per annum on assets managed for the trusts. That equates to about three hundred fifty thousand dollars per annum."

"What effect would loss of this income have had on the firm?"

"It would have been disastrous. The firm would not have been able to meet its overhead, such as rent and salaries."

"Bottom line, Mr. Borden, what kind of financial shape was Mr. Stanley's firm in?"

"The firm consistently lost money, largely due to high overhead expenses."

"Such as . . . ?"

"Lavish offices, exorbitant travel and entertainment expenses, for the most part, as well as some investment losses. Mr. Stanley had all but exhausted the firm's original capital. That is why I believe he sold partnership interests in his own firm to his children's trusts—to raise more capital."

"Anything illegal about that?"

"No, not if it was done with the knowledge and approval of all the trustees."

"Was it done with that approval?"

"Yes. That, of course, does not mean it was a good investment of those trust funds."

"Was James A. Stanley and Associates a good investment?"

"No. In my opinion, the firm was near insolvency and required an additional capital injection of some two million dollars in order to continue operations."

"Mr. Borden, without the benefit of continued income from the trusts, would Mr. Stanley's firm have been bankrupt?"

"Objection. Calls for speculation," Fannin interjected.

"Sustained." Judge Penfield sounded weary. Laura hurried to sum up.

"I'll rephrase the question. Could Mr. Stanley have continued to operate his firm without the management fee paid to him by his children's trusts?"

"No, not without a capital injection from some other source."

That was what Laura had wanted the jury to hear and to understand. She turned from the problems of James A. Stanley and Associates to the personal finances of the

Stanleys, which were an ugly jungle of tax problems and past-due bills. She wanted to make sure that the jury understood Stanley had been using his children's income from their trusts to fund both his business and personal expenses. "I'd like to turn your attention now, Mr. Borden, to the 'second hat' that the defendant wore as a trustee. Was the defendant paid for his work as a trustee?"

"No."

"He derives no financial benefit from those trusts?"

"Yes, in fact he does. As the guardian of Matthew and Sara Stanley, he is able to direct the expenditure of the trust income. The income was technically Matthew and Sara's, but, as they were minors, their parents used the income to provide housing, schooling, and all other necessities. As Mr. Stanley lived in the same house his children did, he could be said to have benefited from the trust income."

"And how much income would the trusts pay out each year?"

"The trustees voted the annual disbursements based on investment performance and the needs of the children. Last year, it was somewhere in the neighborhood of five hundred thousand dollars."

"That's in addition to the income received by the firm of James A. Stanley and Associates?"

"Yes."

"You have said that Mr. Stanley would continue as a trustee even if he was removed as manager of the trust funds. Is that correct?"

"Yes, he would, unless the other trustees voted to remove him for cause."

"What would constitute cause?"

"Financial malfeasance, fraud, or conflict of interest, primarily. Also incapacity, or conviction of a felony."

"So, even though the loss of his investment license would not necessarily have cost him his role as trustee, he could be removed for other reasons?"

"Yes."

"What about in the case of divorce? Would he remain as a trustee if he and Mrs. Stanley divorced?"

"No, that is a term of the trust indentures. If Mr. and Mrs. Stanley divorced, Mr. Stanley would be removed as a trustee."

"Could the defendant have continued making mortgage and tax payments on his Brookhaven residence without the children's income?"

"No."

"Could the defendant have paid the annual dues of his country club without the income from his children's trusts?"

"Again, no."

"In short, Mr. Borden, you would say that the defendant would be materially harmed financially if his wife chose to divorce him?"

"Objection. Calls for speculation."

"No, Your Honor, actually it does not call for speculation." Borden was addressing Judge Penfield directly. "It's a matter of fact: Mr. Stanley's expenses far exceeded his own income, even the children's income from the trusts in some years. Without that income, he would have needed to make major changes in his lifestyle."

"Thank you, Mr. Borden. We'll accept that as your answer. However, I must ask you to remember that you are a witness in this matter, not an attorney. Please refrain from responding to Counsel's objections," Judge Penfield said, smiling. "You may continue, Miss Chastain."

"I have no further questions for this witness at this time," Laura said, relieved that she could sit down again.

Fannin approached the witness stand with a smile. "You've been on the stand quite a while, Mr. Borden. I won't keep you too much longer. I'd like to thank you for giving us such a clear picture of the financial arrangements that Mr. and Mrs. Stanley had made for their family. Let me clarify something: If Mr. and Mrs. Stanley had divorced, you say that Mr. Stanley would have been automatically removed as a trustee for his children?"

"That is correct."

"And would his firm have been removed as the manager of the trust funds if he and Mrs. Stanley divorced?"

"Not automatically, in the case of divorce. However, the loss of his business licenses would have forced his resignation from that job."

"Yes, but the mere fact of his divorcing would not cost his firm the trust business?"

"No, it would not."

"And what about the income from the trusts—as father to the two children, would he still have had some say over the expenditure of that money, even if he were not still a trustee?"

"That would depend entirely on the terms of the divorce settlement, and that is an area outside my expertise."

"I understand. But what I want to know is, if, in your opinion, a divorce would have automatically meant financial disaster for Mr. Stanley?"

Borden thought for a minute. "No, it would not have, automatically."

"Of course, there is no possibility of a divorce now. How does the death of Mrs. Stanley affect the trusts?"

"The terms of the trust call for the replacement of a deceased trustee by the vote of the remaining trustees."

"That would be Mr. Stanley, Lynette Connell, her father Lester Connell, and their attorney, Mr. Bradley Mellott?"

"Yes."

"If Mr. Stanley is sent to prison, would he be removed as a trustee?"

"Yes. Conviction for felony would result automatically in his removal."

"And what about the status of his guardianship of the children? Would that change?"

"Yes. He could not fulfill a guardian's duties if he were imprisoned."

"Who would be the guardian?"

"That would be determined by the courts, in all likelihood."

"Would Miss Connell be a candidate?"

"Certainly, I would think so. She would have standing to petition for custody of the children, at any rate. Again, my review was not conducted with a view to answering these questions . . ."

"That's all right, Mr. Borden. We accept your expertise in these matters. If James Stanley went to prison, and Lynette Connell became guardian to his children, would Miss Connell direct the expenditure of approximately half a million dollars annually in trust income?"

"Whoever assumed the guardianship of the children would have that power."

"That's an enormous financial benefit, is it not?"

"Objection. Asked and answered, Your Honor," Laura said.

"I withdraw the question. Thank you, Mr. Borden. I have no further questions."

"Does the prosecution wish to question this witness again?"

"Yes, Your Honor," Laura said.

"It's after one o'clock, Miss Chastain. If this is going to take long, I would prefer to resume after a break for lunch."

"I have only a few questions for the witness."

"Go ahead, then."

"Thank you. Mr. Borden, you have said that a divorce from the victim would have damaged the defendant financially. If he had lost custody of the children in a divorce, would he have continued to be able to spend trust monies on his housing and his other expenses?"

"Probably not."

"Mr. Borden, as it stands now, after the death of his wife, is Mr. Stanley the sole guardian of his children?"

"Yes."

"And as such, is he the sole arbiter of how the trust income is spent?"

"Yes."

"And would you say that he is better off as a widower than as a divorced man?"

"Objection, Your Honor! That's an outrageous question!" Fannin was almost shouting.

"Sustained. Watch yourself, Miss Chastain," Judge Penfield said sternly.

"Yes, Your Honor. Thank you, Mr. Borden. I have no further questions."

Judge Penfield picked up her gavel. "We will adjourn for forty-five minutes. Please return by two o'clock."

"That went well," Meredith said.

Laura looked at Meredith anxiously. "Do you really think so? I thought we did a good job of making James look like a greedy yuppie, but we didn't get the motive across clearly. And Fannin got in a couple of licks at Lynette."

"Don't worry. The divorce lawyer will take care of that.

He's going to tell the jury that Christine was primarily interested in getting her children's money away from James. At least, that's what they're going to hear when I question him. And don't forget that the jury hasn't heard from Jim Stanley yet. We've still got our ace in the hole.''

CHAPTER 27

The "ace in the hole" stood before the judge with a grin on his face, his eyes scanning the courtroom, as he took a solemn oath to tell the truth. *You would think that Jim Stanley testifies in murder trials every day of his life,* Laura thought ruefully. At least he had bought a new suit for the occasion, although it didn't fit any better than the disreputable old gray one he had worn when Laura first met him.

Meredith approached the witness box, and began her questioning. "Please state your name."

Jim looked pleased. He could handle *that* one.

The jury knew already who Jim Stanley was, because Carlton had testified to his existence the day before. Laura had expected that to be one of the more combative episodes of the trial; she had expected Fannin to make every effort to discredit what Carlton—and Wayne Cattrall— had said, but he didn't. He had only a few questions for

Carlton, and none for Wayne. They had flown through both witnesses' testimony in less than three hours. That didn't make Laura feel any better, because she knew that Fannin was keeping his powder dry for his assault on Jim Stanley. The big guns wouldn't be silent for long.

Meredith walked Jim through his background testimony—where he lived, what he did, how often he traveled to Charlotte and where he stayed when he was there. Jim seemed to remember what Laura had tried to drill into him, and he kept his answers short and direct. Laura had never really worried about how he would respond to Meredith's questioning, but she was still shuddering at the memory of the debacle that had taken place when Meredith, playing the role of Craig Fannin, had grilled him in a rehearsal for the trial. Jim had lost his temper several times, but worse, from Laura's point of view, was his tendency to overanswer leading questions. "Don't give me a paragraph when a sentence will do!" Meredith had warned. But Jim hadn't been able to master his desire for self-justification. "We'll just object a lot," Meredith said to Laura at the end of a long day. "At least it'll break up the flow."

Meredith was getting to the meat of the matter. "Let me make sure I understand the sequence of events, Mr. Stanley," she said. "After you and James Stanley discovered the mix-up in your names, who suggested that the coincidence might be useful to you at some point?"

"That was him. He said it was nice to have a double-ganger."

"A doppelgänger?"

"That's right—it's German."

"I see," Meredith said. "And the defendant at some point actually did suggest to you that you should pose as him on a certain date?"

"Uh-huh. He wanted me to be him last May 8."

"When did he propose this plan to you?"

"It was around the middle of April. I remember because it was tax time, and I was a little short of funds."

"Did the defendant offer to pay you for cooperating in this little ruse of his?"

"Well, not exactly. Not at first."

"You mean that it was *you* who suggested that he pay you?"

"More or less."

"Is that a 'yes,' Mr. Stanley?"

"Yes, it is. I asked him for money."

"How much money?"

"I didn't exactly specify an amount. I just kind of hinted that I could use some dough."

"Did the defendant suggest an amount?"

"Yes. He offered me five hundred dollars."

"Did you accept?"

"I told him I needed more—I told him about my tax situation."

"In other words, you negotiated with the defendant."

"Yes."

"And what price did the two of you finally agree on?"

"Five thousand dollars."

Laura watched the jury for their reactions. Jim was making himself appear shameless, but she hoped that his misplaced candor would at least convince them that he was telling the truth.

Meredith turned away from Jim and faced the jury. She took a couple of steps toward the jury box as she phrased her next question. "What did you do to earn this five thousand dollars, Mr. Stanley?"

"Well, for starters, I showed up at the Marriott . . ."

"Go on. What time did you arrive there?"

"It was around eight P.M."

"Did the defendant specify the time you were to arrive and check in?"

"Yes, he did."

"Did he say why?"

"Yes, it was because that was when his plane was supposed to land."

"Did you check in under your own name, or under that of the defendant?"

"The reservation was in *his* name—that's James *A.* Stanley, and I'm James *T.* Stanley—so I just said I was 'James Stanley.' I gave them my credit card. They didn't notice the difference in the name."

"What did you do next?"

"What he—the defendant—asked me to do. I went up to the room, ordered some dinner, and made two phone calls to his home number."

"Did anyone answer the phone?"

"No. I hung up as soon as the machine picked up."

"Did you do anything else?"

"Nope. I mean, not anything else that he asked me to do. I watched a movie, and I had a couple of beers from the minibar. That's it."

"And did the defendant show up at the hotel that night?"

"Not that night—the next *morning,*" Jim said precisely.

"What time the next *morning* did the defendant arrive?"

"I'm not sure. Maybe five A.M., maybe later. He woke me up, because he had to call up from the lobby to get the room number. He didn't have a key."

"Of course. Did you talk to him when he came to the room? Did you ask him where he had been?"

"No. I went back to bed. There were two beds in the room." Jim always insisted on the two beds being there—

as if anyone suspected that he and James had indulged in a little man-on-man action.

Laura let her attention wander from Meredith and Jim back to the jury. They were intent, still paying careful attention to what was being said. After almost four days of testimony, that was good. And they didn't appear to be revolted by Jim, which was even better. Laura glanced over at the defense table. James Stanley's face was blocked from view, but she could see that Fannin was relaxed back in his chair, his hands jammed into his pockets. His associates were taking notes furiously, stopping every so often to talk to their boss, but Craig might have been watching a movie, he was so stoic.

Meredith was now moving on to the sensitive topic of the gun. They had decided, after a long debate of the pros and cons, that it would be best not to examine Jim about where he had bought the gun. Fannin had Jesse DuPree on his witness list, and this was a cause of much consternation to Laura, but Meredith was sanguine. "All Jesse can do is introduce more innuendo about Lynette, and we can object Craig into the ground on *that*."

Meredith had retrieved the gun from the exhibit table, and was displaying it to Jim. "Mr. Stanley, do you recognize this gun?" she asked.

"Yes. It's my gun."

"Your gun!" Meredith acted surprised, in order to emphasize to the jury that *this* was indeed a big surprise. "Mr. Stanley, this was the gun that was used to kill Christine Connell Stanley, the defendant's wife. How did it come to be used in a crime?"

"I had no idea that was what he wanted it for!"

"What *who* wanted it for?"

"Him—the defendant. James Stanley."

"Did you sell this gun to the defendant?"

"No, I lent it to him."

"Are you in the habit of lending guns to people, Mr. Stanley?"

"No, but I was *trying* to sell it to him. See, I bought it about five years ago. I thought it was neat." Turning to the jury, Jim said earnestly, "It's a Nazi gun, you know. I thought it would be a good investment."

"So you owned it for several years?"

"Uh-huh. And I mentioned to the defendant that I had a valuable gun I wanted to sell. I needed a little cash."

"Did he express an interest in buying it?"

"Not for himself. He said his father-in-law might be interested in it—he said the old man had a gun collection."

"So you let him take the gun to show to Mr. Connell?"

"Yes."

"When did this take place?"

"A few months before . . . maybe November. Or maybe it was December—I needed a little extra money for the holidays, I remember."

"And did you discuss the gun with the defendant at any time after you lent it to him?"

"A couple of times. I told him that if his father-in-law didn't want it, would he please give it back to me, so I could get some money for it."

"But the defendant never returned the gun to you?"

"No, he didn't," Jim said sadly.

Meredith replaced the gun on the exhibit table, and walked back to the witness stand. She folded her arms and looked at Jim for a long moment. "Mr. Stanley, I want you to be completely honest with this court. You have said that you took five thousand dollars from the defendant to pose as him for one night. You have said that you loaned him a gun. Mr. Stanley, did it never occur to you that the defendant was planning a criminal act?"

"Not killing his *wife*, for God's sake—I wouldn't have had anything to do with that!"

"But why did you think the defendant wanted a weapon, and an alibi?"

"I ... I thought maybe he was planning to kill his father-in-law—but, Christ, I didn't think the little squirt had the guts to do something like that!"

"In fact, you tried deliberately *not* to inquire too closely into the defendant's motives, didn't you, Mr. Stanley?"

"Yes. I mean, I didn't ask and he didn't tell."

"Do you realize that you acted as an accessory to murder?"

"I didn't, not knowingly!" Jim was growing agitated.

"Whether knowingly or not, you did. Mr. Stanley, why are you testifying today?"

Jim hung his head, and Laura was surprised to see that he was *crying*. "I ... I knew something was wrong when that detective and Miss Chastain came to see me—I knew he had done something bad, as soon as I heard they were from Atlanta. I had to tell them what I knew. Oh, God, I'm sorry—so sorry! I never would have done it—oh, God!" He was crying quite hard now, and so were a couple of the jurors. "I want to say to her family—to Christine's family— how sorry I am. I know they can never forgive me, but I want them to know I'm sorry. . . ." His voice trailed off into broken sobs.

This was more than either Laura or Meredith had expected from Jim, and it was great. Any doubts about Jim's character and veracity the jury might have had would be swallowed up by this performance—and Laura didn't doubt for one minute that it *was* a performance, carefully planned. She felt partly responsible for the theatrics, because she had warned Jim that his answer to the critical question of what he knew and when he knew it would determine his credibility in the eyes of the jury. All the same, she never expected the pageant of grief and guilt that was unfolding on the witness stand. Trying not to look triumphant, she sneaked a glance at Fannin. His face was twisted in a wry, cynical smile.

"Would the witness like to take some time to compose himself?" Judge Penfield asked.

"Your Honor, I have no further questions for Mr. Stanley at this time," Meredith said.

"Then's let's take a five-minute recess so that the witness can collect himself before Mr. Fannin begins his cross-examination."

Meredith returned to the prosecution table, one eyebrow lifted in inquiry. "Don't look at *me*," Laura said. "I had nothing to do with it."

"I guess our friend has seen one too many Bette Davis movies. I think it was effective, anyway."

Laura nodded. "But now Craig Fannin is going to give him something to cry about, to borrow a phrase from my mother." A bailiff was ministering to Jim with water and tissues. Jim was managing a weak smile, darting glances at Laura and Meredith every few seconds as if looking for approbation. It was not forthcoming. Fannin was conferring with his associates and a casually dressed man whom Laura had not seen before. He was expostulating to the lawyers while pointing to a piece of paper he held in his hand. As the bailiff reentered the courtroom to announce Judge Penfield's return, Fannin nodded to the man, and said something. The man nodded in return and left the courtroom. Laura didn't have time to worry about what was up, however, as Judge Penfield was gaveling the courtroom back into order. "Your witness, Mr. Fannin."

Craig Fannin ambled casually toward the witness stand. "Feeling better, Jim?"

"Yes, thank you," Jim replied weakly, shifting his eyes away from Fannin's cool gaze.

"That's good, because I have some questions for you, Jim, and I'd like some straight answers. You're not here today because you think it's the right thing to do, are you?"

"I don't know what you mean." *Good, Jim,* Laura thought. *Just like we told you: buy time by making him repeat the questions.*

"Oh, I think you do know, Jim. What was it that induced you to come here today and testify against James Stanley?"

"The detective and Miss Chastain, they came and told me what had happened. I just had to tell them what I knew."

"But you didn't tell them anything at first, did you, Jim?"

"I don't understand the question."

"Oh, come on, Jim, don't be disingenuous. You negotiated with Miss Chastain before you would talk to her, didn't you?"

"I called my lawyer, if that's what you mean. He told me . . ."

"Cut the act, Jim. You're no virgin."

"Objection, Your Honor," Meredith cried. "He's characterizing the witness."

"Sustained. Watch yourself, Mr. Fannin."

"Thank you, Your Honor. Jim, isn't it true that you are testifying today under an immunity agreement with the district attorney?"

"Yes." Before the trial, Jim had showed a tendency to try to justify himself whenever the question of the immunity came up. Laura was glad that he was sticking to monosyllables now.

"And isn't it true, Jim, that you've testified under immunity deals in the past?"

"That was different . . ."

"No, that was the same thing. You're quite a negotiator, aren't you, Jim?" Fannin managed to make "negotiator" sound like "orphan-robbing, nun-raping dirtbag."

Meredith caught the tone, too. "Objection, Your Honor—counsel is continuing to characterize the witness."

"Your Honor, I don't see how asking the witness about his negotiations with the district attorney amounts to a characterization."

"Possibly not, Mr. Fannin, but I will ask that you watch your tone of voice."

"Thank you, I will." He turned back to Jim. "You had been expecting a visit from the Atlanta Police Department for quite some time, hadn't you, Jim?"

"No, I didn't think that he had gone through with it . . ."

"Oh, really?" Fannin wheeled around and strode to the defense table, where he plucked a sheet of paper from the waiting hand of one of the associates, all in one smooth, balletic pass. "Would you read the highlighted portion of this statement for the Court, please?" He handed the paper to Jim.

Jim peered at the page, frowned, and began to read quickly, slurring the words.

Detective Hemingway: Mr. Stanley, you didn't seem surprised to hear that a detective from the Atlanta Police Department was here to see you. Why was that? Stanley: Because I knew by the time you got here that she was dead—it was in the Charlotte paper, because he supposedly had been here when she was killed. Hemingway: You knew that his alibi was false, then. Why didn't you go to the police immediately?

Stanley: I was scared. Hell, what was I supposed to do? I didn't sleep for about a week. Then I decided to get me a lawyer.

Jim looked up at Fannin.

"Was that an excerpt from the statement you gave to Miss Chastain and Detective Hemingway when they interviewed you in Winston-Salem?"

"Yes."

"So you knew days—*weeks*—before the detective and Miss Chastain arrived that Christine Stanley had been killed. Is that correct?"

"I was confused . . . I thought . . ." Jim was floundering badly, having been caught in what amounted to a lie. *Come on, Jim,* Laura thought. *It's just a small inconsistency. Brazen it out—God knows you know how to do that.*

As if he could read Laura's mind, Jim suddenly straightened in his seat. "No, I didn't come forward right away. I was scared. I've been in trouble with the law before, Mr. Fannin, and I knew what it would mean if I was to get involved again. I *wanted* to go to a lawyer, I really did . . ." Here, Jim turned a tormented face to the jury. "But do you know what those lawyers charge? I'm not rich . . . I didn't know what to do."

"It seems to me that you knew *exactly* what to do, Jim. You waited until you got caught, and then you started negotiating, just like you did when you were caught before . . ."

"Objection, Your Honor, he's badgering the witness, and the witness's past criminal record is not relevant."

"I disagree, Your Honor," Fannin said. "Jim Stanley is a veteran of the justice system. He knows as much about immunity as you and I do."

"I doubt that, Mr. Fannin," Judge Penfield answered

tersely, "but I accept your argument. You may continue this line of questioning, *without* badgering Mr. Stanley."

"Thank you, Your Honor. Jim, how many times have you been arrested?"

Jim paused and glanced at Meredith, evidently hoping for an objection. None came. "Two times," he answered.

"And what were the charges on each occasion?"

"One, possession of marijuana. The second time, possession of cocaine."

"You were convicted of both offenses, were you not?"

"Yes. I pled guilty both times, and I paid a fine for the grass, and served a sentence for the coke."

"Wasn't there a third arrest, Jim?"

"No," Jim replied firmly. "I was questioned in a business matter, but never arrested."

"You weren't arrested because you arranged to testify against a co-conspirator under a grant of immunity, isn't that so?"

"There was no conspiracy. I was as much a victim as the bank was . . ."

"If there was nothing to charge you with, why did you need immunity?"

"They had the facts wrong," Jim answered stubbornly. "I didn't do anything wrong."

"But you did negotiate an immunity deal, didn't you, Jim?"

"My lawyer did, yes."

"Is that how you learned about immunity?"

Jim shrugged. "I guess so."

"So that when Detective Hemingway and Miss Chastain appeared on your doorstep, you were waiting with a plan, is that right?"

"Objection, Your Honor—asked and answered," Meredith intoned.

"I'll withdraw the question. Jim, you knew that prosecutors will offer immunity to certain witnesses to get the testimony they need to convict someone, don't you?"

"Yes, I know that."

"And you knew that you could craft an immunity that would protect you even if you had played an active role in a crime, did you not?"

"Yes, I guess so."

"And that is why you agreed to come here today and, under immunity, tell the story that you and your co-conspirator cooked up, isn't it?"

"I don't understand what you're asking."

"Really? Then I'll make it simple for you: You agreed to come here and tell lies about my client, James Stanley, because you knew that under your immunity deal you couldn't be convicted of conspiring to kill Mrs. Stanley. Is that simple enough?"

"Objection, Your Honor," Meredith said. "Badgering the witness."

"Badgering, Your Honor?" Fannin said. "I'm merely stating the facts."

"Sustained," Judge Penfield said.

There was activity at the defense table; the casually dressed man had returned and was conferring with one of the associates. James Stanley was leaning in to hear what they were saying. None of them was following the exchange between Fannin and Jim Stanley.

Fannin rephrased his last question. "Did you participate in a conspiracy to kill Christine Stanley?"

"Not knowingly—I've already said that."

"Who is Jesse DuPree?"

Jim looked startled, although he had been prepared for this line of questioning. "Jesse DuPree? He's a guy I went to high school with."

"And did you buy a gun from Jesse DuPree?"

"Yes."

"What kind of gun?"

"That gun," Jim answered. "The murder weapon."

"Oh, I see. So Jesse DuPree knew you had this gun?"

"I guess so," Jim said, puzzled.

"Did you ever meet Lynette Connell, Christine Stanley's sister?"

"No."

"Did Jesse DuPree ever discuss her with you?"

"No." Out of the corner of her eye, Laura could see more activity at the defense table. The casually dressed man was not there any longer, but one of the associates was signaling to Fannin. He acknowledged the signal with a slight incline of his head, and turned back to Jim to continue his questioning. "Really? If you've never met Lynette Connell, how did you come to be involved in a conspiracy with her and Jesse DuPree to kill Christine Stanley, Jim?"

"I'm not involved in any conspiracy!"

Fannin shook his head. "Why are you lying to this court, Jim?"

"Objection, Your Honor. Counsel is making unsubstantiated allegations," Meredith said.

"I can substantiate them, Your Honor," Fannin said, "if Your Honor will allow it."

"Please make yourself clear, Mr. Fannin."

"I have evidence that the witness is not telling the truth, Your Honor. I would like to introduce this evidence now to impeach him."

Laura gripped the table to prevent herself from sliding underneath it. Meredith turned to her and spoke; Laura heard her voice as if it was coming from a long way away, from the bottom of a deep well. "What does he know, Laura? What does Fannin have?"

"I don't know," Laura managed to say. "I don't know."

CHAPTER 28

Judge Penfield's chambers were as austere and grand as the judge herself, but there was scarcely room for all the participants in the meeting taking place there. Meredith, Craig Fannin and one of his associates, James Stanley, and a bailiff sat where they could. Laura remained standing by choice. Judge Penfield folded her hands on her desk. "I'm listening, Mr. Fannin."

"Thank you, Your Honor. As you know, my client has maintained all along that he is innocent of the charges against him. At his suggestion, I hired private investigators in an attempt not only to *disprove* the prosecution's case, but also to *prove*, beyond all doubt, that he is, indeed, innocent. The prosecution's case consists largely of the testimony of Jim Stanley to the effect that Jim Stanley provided my client with an alibi for the night of his wife's murder. The prosecution's presumption is that, because they could prove that he was *not* where he said he was, he

was in fact *in his own house*, killing his wife. I immediately
seized on the logical inconsistency in that theory, which I
am sure hasn't escaped Your Honor's attention, either.

"The mere fact of James Stanley's not having been in
Charlotte, North Carolina, when he claimed to have been
is not in itself proof that he was in his house, or even
in Atlanta. I took Mr. Stanley's case believing that the
prosecution had not—and *could* not—prove its case
beyond a reasonable doubt. I told my client that these
were the grounds on which I would defend him. Instead
of being reassured, however, Mr. Stanley grew very angry
with me. He told me that he didn't *want* to be acquitted
because there was only a 'reasonable doubt' of his guilt;
he wanted to be exonerated because the *facts* showed that
he was innocent. He has never once wavered from his
contention that he *did* arrive in Charlotte, and that he *did*
check into that hotel room. Moreover, he is adamant in
insisting *that he has never met this man Jim Stanley in his life*,
let alone planned a crime with him.

"I told my client that, ideally, we would establish his
innocence beyond any doubt, but that with the facts at
hand as the trial date approached, he might have to be
content with my original strategy. He suggested that we
hire private investigators to prove that he was where he
says he was—in fact, that he was *in that hotel* when the
murder took place. Mr. Stanley told me that he *had* taken
the second segment of his flight that night, that he *had*
arrived in Charlotte, and that he *had* checked into the
hotel, just as he has said all along. He recalled a curious
incident, however: when he attempted to register, the hotel
clerk said that he was already checked in. The hotel clerk
insisted that the record was not in error, and gave him a
key to his room—without asking for his credit card.

"Mr. Stanley dismissed the error from his mind, and

went about his business—ordering dinner, calling home, and going to bed. He was preparing for a morning meeting when the Charlotte police arrived and told him that his wife had been killed.

"While I never for a moment doubted my client's veracity, I was skeptical about our ability to prove his story. We seem to have been in a he-said, he-said situation. However, when the prosecution witness, Jim Stanley, began his testimony, both my client and I listened carefully for any inconsistencies in his story which might prove it false. Under examination by Mrs. Gaffney, he made a statement that excited my client tremendously. Jim Stanley said that he had been awakened very early in the morning by my client, and that he had admitted him to the room, where they both went to sleep *in two beds*. My client was sure that there had been only one bed—a king-size one—in the room. We have managed to verify that with the hotel, and we can prove our contention. This proves that Jim Stanley was never in that hotel room, and it further proves that his entire story is false. I believe that Jim Stanley was part of a conspiracy not only to kill Christine Stanley, but also to frame my client for it. Your Honor, I move that this witness be impeached and that a directed verdict of acquittal be entered."

"Whoa!" Meredith said, holding up her hand. "Just a doggone minute—this is a nice story, but we're not buying it yet. We need a chance to examine the evidence and come to our own conclusions."

"I agree with Mrs. Gaffney. While your story is compelling, Mr. Fannin, the prosecution must be allowed time to assess its position. I'll grant a continuance until tomorrow at noon . . ."

"Your Honor, may I respectfully request more time?

We may have to send an investigator to Charlotte, and tomorrow is Friday," Meredith pointed out.

"Yes, so it is. I'll grant a continuance until Monday morning at eight A.M."

"Your Honor, this is onerous for my client. We would be happy to allow them time to examine the new evidence, but three days is too much time. My client is under a cloud, Your Honor, and he wishes it removed as speedily as possible so that he can pick up the pieces of his life," Fannin concluded dramatically.

"Your client is not incarcerated, Mr. Fannin, and I fail to see what difference three days will make if he is ultimately acquitted," Judge Penfield replied tartly. "The continuance is granted. Now, if you will all return to the courtroom, we can formalize this decision and adjourn until Monday." Dutifully, the participants returned to their places in the courtroom, where the spectators were buzzing. As soon as the jury filed in, Judge Penfield gaveled the humming room to order, announced the continuance, and gaveled the proceedings closed. Laura gathered her things robotically, and followed Meredith like a duckling toward the door. Fannin intercepted Meredith. "Got a minute? Good. Here's our report. You can check it out, but I think you'll find it's good information. We used Dan Crowder—you know him? He used to be with the Atlanta Police Department."

"We still need corroboration," Meredith replied evenly. "But thanks for the info."

"Good luck," Fannin said, sounding sincere, and not appearing to enjoy his advantage. No matter how adversarial the proceedings might get, a good lawyer didn't make it personal. Meredith wouldn't celebrate in front of her opponent, and Tom Bailey wouldn't have, either. "Have

316 / *Lelia Kelly*

a good weekend, Craig," Meredith said, like an honorable duelist.

"You, too," he replied. "Don't work too hard." He and his crew disappeared out the door, leaving Meredith and Laura standing in the emptying courtroom.

"Meredith, I don't know what went wrong . . . I'm so sorry. I really screwed up this time. Why did I ever believe a single word Jim Stanley said?" Laura finished on a note that fell somewhere between a sob and a wail.

"Oh, no—none of that," Meredith said, putting an arm around Laura's shoulders. "We don't have time for that. We have work to do, and lots of it." She began steering Laura toward the doors. "I want you to get Kenny on the horn. We need to verify this thing independently, or debunk it, one or the other. Tell him we'll pay for everything—I'll find it in the budget somehow. And I want Randy and Carlton brought up to speed. They need to jump on Jesse DuPree with both feet. But most of all," Meredith said as she propelled her shattered assistant into the hall, "I want Jim Stanley. He disappeared right quickly—did you notice that? Find him. I want to see him in my office *now,* in handcuffs if necessary. And if we have to take him over to Homicide and keep after him all night, that's what we'll do, until he tells us the truth—if he's capable of telling the truth." Laura nodded mutely, and Meredith hugged her tighter. "Don't fall apart on me, Laura. Focus—I need you now."

"But, Meredith, I'm the one who screwed up this whole thing, right from the get-go. I knew there was something about the way he insisted on there being two beds—how could I have overlooked something like that?" she moaned.

"How? My God, it was one tiny detail buried in one of the most complicated cases I've ever seen. And I'll tell you something else: I'm not convinced that catching Jim Stanley in an *error*—if that's what it is—exonerates James Stanley. It certainly doesn't automatically incriminate DuPree and Lynette Connell anyway. I think it's time that we got the facts together and looked at them in a new light."

They were in the main hallway now, heading for the elevators. Laura was listening to Meredith so intently that she didn't see Lynette Connell hurrying toward them.

"What is going on?" Lynette demanded. "What happened in the judge's office? What's a continuance?"

Laura looked from Lynette to Meredith, unable to speak. Meredith answered for her. "The defense has introduced some new evidence, Miss Connell, which may affect our case. I'd like you to make yourself available for questioning tonight and tomorrow—and all weekend, in fact."

"Yes, of course I'll be available—but what does all this mean? Daddy's still sitting in the courtroom; I think it's been too much for him. I'm taking him straight to the doctor, but what should I tell him?"

"Tell him just what I told you—there's been some new evidence uncovered, and we're stopping the trial until it can be thoroughly checked out."

"Is it evidence for or against James?" Lynette persisted.

Meredith looked at Lynette intently for a moment. "If verified, this evidence would tend to exonerate him." Laura saw that Meredith was watching Lynette closely as she spoke, gauging Lynette's reaction.

Lynette's face, frantic with worry about her father, gave nothing away. "Daddy will be glad to hear that," she said. "He's been all torn up for weeks about this. Laura, will we see you Saturday?"

"Probably not," Laura said awkwardly. "I have a lot of work to do."

"I see," Lynette said, a chill in her voice. "Well, call me if you change your mind, or if you need me for anything." She turned and disappeared down the hall.

"Don't worry," Meredith said when they boarded the elevator. "She may not be involved. And if she is—well, she fooled all of us, Randy Travers included. Come on, let's get in gear. I have to run home and get my ducks in a row there. Go back to the office and take care of everything for me, will you? I'll be down in a couple of hours. I guess we'll be having pizza for dinner tonight." Meredith clattered away, and Laura slumped toward the office.

Meredith was right to push Laura out of her stupor; once she threw herself into activity, she quickly got over the numbing shock. A grim determination took its place. She paged Kenny Newton first, and told him what had happened. He was sympathetic, and agreed to fly to Charlotte immediately. "Where is that computer guy from the hotel? Is he still down here?"

"Wayne? No, he was dismissed and went home yesterday. He'll help you, and if he's not on duty tonight, he'll tell you who is." She gave him Wayne Cattrall's home and work numbers.

"Okey-dokey. Now listen, sugar, I know that you've got your knickers in a big old twist about this, but don't sweat it. I'm sure things like this happen all the time."

"Oh, sure they do—all the time. I'm at my computer looking at case law right now. I can find almost no cases in which a *prosecution* witness was impeached."

"Look at the bright side, then—you're setting a precedent. Now, you know I'm just kidding—they haven't impeached him yet, have they? And they might not after all. I say go get yourself a big strong drink."

"Not tonight, I'm afraid. But when this is over, I may

start drinking and never stop. You travel safely now, and say 'hey' to Wayne for me."

Randy Travers, unsurprisingly, was less sympathetic than Kenny. "Damn!" he shouted. "I knew that hookup between Jim Stanley and DuPree couldn't be a coincidence."

"What do you think happened?"

"It's a plain as the nose on your face—DuPree wanted to help his girlfriend come into a little money, and he got the bright idea to use a guy he knew with the same name as James Stanley to set him up for his wife's murder."

"I don't know—does Jesse DuPree strike you as that smart?"

"No. But Lynette Connell does."

"I still don't see what she has to gain."

"Guardianship of those kids, and all the money that comes with them."

"I still don't buy it. Have you seen the farm where they live? She's got everything she wants with a cherry on it out there, Randy."

"But it's not *hers*—it's the old man's. Maybe she wants some little ponies of her own. Maybe she has debts that we don't know about. We stopped looking at her when you found Jim Stanley. Maybe we should have dug a little deeper."

Laura flushed. "*We* stopped looking at *everyone* else when we found Jim. Speaking of which, I have to find that piece of . . . work now, and get him in here so Meredith can go over him. You want to be there?"

"You bet your sweet ass I do. I'll send Carlton after DuPree, and I'll be at your office in half an hour."

Laura's next task, and her most daunting one, was to find Jim Stanley. She called his hotel room and got no answer. She shrugged on her jacket and headed to look for him. *I'll make a hard-target search of every fern bar, dive bar, karaoke bar, and strip bar in Atlanta,* she thought as she hopped in a taxi. Luckily, though, Jim was a creature of habit. She knew that he had taken up temporary barfly status at a pub in Underground Atlanta which was in walking distance of his hotel. He was there, perched on a stool, eyes glued to the TV, which was broadcasting the run-up to a baseball playoff game. "Come on, Jim," she said, tossing a couple of bills on the bar to cover his tab. "We've got work to do."

"Aww, c'mon—didn't the judge say we had until Monday?"

"You have until about thirty seconds from now before I call a cop and have you taken to the station in handcuffs."

"Jesus, don't have a cow! Lemme just see this interview with Nolan Ryan . . ."

"No dice. Get moving, Jim, or so help me God, I'll see that you spend the night in jail."

"I have immunity," he whined, sliding from his stool, still watching the screen.

"Not from what I'm going to charge you with," Laura said as menacingly as she could. People in the bar were starting to look at them in the expectation of fireworks. To them, she and Jim looked like a battling couple, and she could almost hear them muttering, *Aww, lady, let the man watch his ball game.* She took his arm and tugged him firmly toward the door. He tensed, and for a moment she thought he was going to hit her, but then he acquiesced.

"Okay, okay, don't pull on me," he said sulkily. "I'm starving—can we get something to eat?"

"We're getting a pizza later. Right now, though, Meredith and Randy Travers want to talk to you." She found another taxi, which almost qualified as a miracle in Atlanta, although it was a rump-sprung and smelly carriage, to be sure. They rode bumpily, in silence, for the six blocks back to the district attorney's offices. The offices were now officially closed, and the autumn twilight was settling over the deserted streets. A small breeze sent some trash skittering around their feet as they crossed to the building. Jim seemed inclined to sulk, and Laura didn't care. She didn't dare ask him the questions that were pounding in her brain. *Did you do it, Jim? Did you pull the trigger?* It had to have been him. After all, James had an alibi now. That was the paradox: Jim's slipup about the beds had exploded his own cover story and given James back his alibi. Now, he was the only player whose whereabouts were *not* accounted for.

When they arrived upstairs, Randy Travers was waiting for them outside the locked doors of the office. Laura used her card-key and let them in. She led them back to the conference room and flipped on the lights. Jim looked at Randy and scowled. "I want a lawyer."

"You don't need a lawyer," Travers said. "You're not under arrest."

"I want my lawyer," Jim insisted. "And I'm not answering any questions until he's here."

"Listen to me and listen to me good," Randy said, emphasizing his points with stabs of his forefinger to Jim's chest. "Your lawyer isn't here, but I am, and my legal advice to you is to answer any and all questions we ask you, or I will pound the snot out of you. Got it, sport?"

Laura warmed with pride at Randy's handling of Jim. *Just to think,* she marveled, *that a few weeks ago I was all het up because some cops were violating a suspect's civil rights. How quaint.* She was halfway hoping that Jim would mouth off to Randy, and that the big cop would make good on his threat, but Jim backed down. He turned to Laura. "I want immunity," he said querulously.

"Immunity? From what? Perjury charges? No can do," she said breezily. "What do you like on your pizza, Randy? I'll go ahead and order—Meredith will be along in a minute or two."

"Mushrooms, green peppers, and pepperoni," Travers replied.

"I hate mushrooms," Jim said.

"Double mushrooms," Travers amended.

Meredith arrived while Laura was on the phone with the pizza parlor. She greeted Randy, and looked Jim up and down coldly. "I've asked for a lawyer," he told her. "And I'm not talking unless I get immunity."

"Let him call his lawyer," Meredith said.

Laura brought Jim Stanley a phone and left him alone to call Charlie Hoyt. She, Meredith, and Randy went to Meredith's office and chatted about anything but the trial while they waited for Jim to finish his consultation. In about fifteen minutes, Laura heard Jim hollering her name. "I better go see what he wants," she said gloomily.

"Charlie wants to talk to you," Jim said, and from the smug expression on his face, Laura knew that she was not going to enjoy this conversation. She took the phone and spoke gruffly into it. "This is Laura Chastain."

"Hello, Miss Chastain," Hoyt said, smooth as ever. "Jim's been bringing me up to date. I wish I could fly down there, but I think we can handle this over the phone. I've instructed Jim that he need not talk to you or answer additional questions."

"Mr. Hoyt, your client perjured himself and is about to be impeached."

"Be that as it may, he has not abrogated his Fifth Amendment right not to incriminate himself."

"We're going to charge him with perjury," Laura warned.

"If you think that's in your best interests, by all means do so."

"Let's cut to the chase, Mr. Hoyt. What are you insinuating?"

"My client has valuable information that he would be willing to share with you under the right conditions."

"We'd be happy to discuss a plea bargain."

"I think you know that won't suffice, Miss Chastain. In brief, we want your affirmation that the grant of immunity still stands, as well as an agreement that the perjury charge will not be pursued."

"What?" Laura practically shrieked. "Mr. Hoyt, your client has proved a most unreliable witness. We are not inclined to grant him *any* concessions, let alone immunity."

"As a point of law, Miss Chastain, you may have no choice. I take it you're familiar with *Corson* v. *Hames*?"

Corson v. *Hames*? Laura racked her brain. She had run across the decision in her review of Georgia case law only recently. She didn't want this Carolina lawyer getting the best of her. *Think, think . . . it has something to do with immunity.* She grabbed a reference book from a nearby shelf and flipped through it. There it was: the Supreme Court of Georgia had ruled that witness immunity could not be conditioned on "full and truthful" testimony. It seemed illogical—why would an immune witness *need* to lie?—but there it was in black and white. Laura clutched at a straw. "*Corson* v. *Hames* addresses grand jury testimony only. The Court is silent on trial testimony."

"Oh, come on, Miss Chastain, that's parsing. You and I both know that as a practical matter the venue doesn't matter. But there is really no reason to cite case law at all; the Fifth Amendment is quite sufficient to protect my client. He cannot be compelled to incriminate himself. Now, my client is willing to revise his testimony and give a full and truthful account of the conspiracy to kill Christine Stanley . . ."

"How will we know he's not lying this time?" Laura asked.

"You won't. But if you can prove your case by any means other than my client's testimony, you are certainly free to do so."

He had her; there was no other way to get at the facts on short notice without dealing with the devil they knew all too well. Still, Laura struggled against the inevitable. "We have independent evidence that your client owned the gun that killed Christine Stanley. We can indict him for conspiracy on that basis."

"You could, if you had evidence that he owned the gun other than the testimony of another interested party. I believe you're referring to Jesse DuPree's claim that he sold the gun to my client?"

"Yes."

"You'll find that Mr. DuPree is unable to back up with any hard evidence his contention that my client purchased the gun from him."

"But we have your client's own statement that he bought the gun!"

"Which you cannot use against him, as he admitted it only under a grant of immunity. It's tainted fruit, Miss Chastain," Hoyt said.

"I need to talk to my boss. We'll call you back."

"I look forward to it," Hoyt said cordially.

Laura staggered to Meredith's office, where Randy was growing impatient. "We need to talk," she said. She told them about her conversation with Hoyt. "Bottom line, we either let go of the case, or we dance with Jim on his own terms."

"How the hell can that be?" Travers said. "The sonofabitch has been lying all along."

"Hoyt has done his homework. He cited *Corson* v. *Hames*. Immunity cannot be conditioned upon the witness's truthful testimony."

"Does it apply here?" Meredith said.

"Well, as Hoyt said, as a practical matter it's irrelevant—the Fifth Amendment holds sway."

"Would you ladies mind clueing me in?" Randy demanded. "Are you saying that this jackass can get up on the stand and lie and you can't do anything about it?"

"Not exactly," Meredith said. "He's still good for a perjury charge, but we're talking about our ability to revoke Jim Stanley's immunity. I don't think we can, even though his testimony was false."

"Why, for the love of Mike?" Travers thundered. "I've had it up to *here* with the law—thank God I'm retiring at the end of the year."

Meredith patted the detective's arm soothingly. "I know, it sounds ridiculous, but it all has to do with the Constitutional protection against self-incrimination. Jim was induced to testify about his role in Christine Stanley's death by a promise from the State that nothing he said could be used against him. Now his own testimony seems to have incriminated him, but we can't use his statements to bring conspiracy charges against him."

Travers shook his head. "Unbelievable. You realize, of course, that if there *was* a conspiracy, either between Jim and James Stanley, or among Jim Stanley, Jesse DuPree, and Lynette Connell, *Jim had to be the shooter*. The others all have alibis. So now the little weasel is going to get away with murder?"

"Not necessarily, but in order to charge him, we have to prove the conspiracy *without* using Jim's own testimony,"

Laura said. "Like tying the gun to Jim, which we can't do because Jesse didn't keep a record of the sale."

"So what do we do?" Travers asked.

Meredith shrugged. "We let Jim rat out his co-conspirators, whoever they are, under his existing immunity deal."

"And he gets off?"

"Yes."

Laura put her face in her hands. "That stupid transactional immunity! Fannin was right; Jim Stanley knew *exactly* what he was doing when he asked for immunity. He's covered even if he did pull the trigger. I am such an idiot—he used me all the way!"

"There's no time for that now," Travers said, patting Laura on the shoulder awkwardly. "We are where we are, and we have to do what we have to do."

Laura was touched by the detective's sympathy, but not comforted. A murderer was about to go free, and she was responsible. "We might as well go tell Jim the good news," she said. They trooped back to the conference room, where they found Jim lobbing wads of paper at the wastebasket. "Okay, Jim, we've talked to your lawyer. We'll forget the perjury charge, and you're still covered by your immunity deal. Do you have something to tell us?"

Jim quickly replaced his victorious smile with an appropriately solemn look. "It was Jesse DuPree—him and Lynette Connell. They planned the whole thing."

CHAPTER 29

Laura and Meredith cleared away the litter of pizza boxes and drink cans while Randy set up the video camera. It was too late to get a stenographer, so they were going to videotape the statement they had wrested from Jim over the past two hours. Jim rocked back in his chair, looking very pleased with himself. Laura's feelings for him had moved over the course of the evening from dislike and discomfort to outright loathing. She really wished that he had given Randy an excuse to smack him around a little, but, as always, Jim had landed sunny side up.

"I think I have this damn thing right. Check it for me, Laura—I'm no good with technology," Randy said impatiently.

"I'm not much better," Laura said, approaching the tripod on which the camera was perched.

Jim jumped to his feet. "Here, let me. I've got one of these." He squinted through the eyepiece and fiddled with the focus. "Is it important that the date and time be correct?" he asked.

"Yes, of course it is," Laura said, exasperated.

"Well, it's not. What time do you have?"

"Eight-fifty," she replied. "October 9."

"Okay, that does it. Now, let me sit down, and you can make sure it's pointed right at me." Jim sat in his chair, ready for his close-up. "Am I in focus?" he asked.

Randy snorted contemptuously. "Can we get rolling? I got a wife at home waiting for me."

"Right," said Meredith. "I'll ask the questions. Ready, Laura? Roll camera, I guess."

Laura hit the Record button and returned to her seat as Meredith began. "This is a statement made by James T. Stanley of Winston-Salem, North Carolina, on Thursday October 9, 1999. Present in the room are Mr. Stanley, Meredith Gaffney, and Laura Chastain of the Fulton County district attorney's office, and Detective Randy Travers of the Atlanta Police Department. Mr. Stanley, please state your name and address."

Jim did, and after a few set-up questions, he rolled out a narrative with few interruptions. "I would like," he said, "to give all the details of my involvement in a conspiracy to frame James A. Stanley of Atlanta, Georgia, for the murder of his wife. I would also like to say that I deeply regret my part in this horrible plan. I hope that by telling the truth I can help to see justice done." Laura bit her tongue to keep from hollering *"Bullshit"* and ruining the tape.

"Where should I start?" he asked.

"Just begin with what you told us about Jesse DuPree," Meredith said.

"Okay. Jesse DuPree is a guy I grew up with in Georgia.

I see him from time to time when I'm down this way, and we've done a little business in the past."

"What kind of business?"

"Jesse sells guns—mostly hunting pieces. I've brought him a few sales, and he pays me a commission on them. Anyway, I was down in Georgia last year—it was early in the summer—and I hooked up with Jesse for an evening. He was all bent out of shape about a girl he was dating."

"Who was this girl?"

"Her name was Lynette Connell. He said she was good-looking and rich, or at least her daddy was rich. Jesse likes good-looking women, and he *really* likes the rich ones. But there were some problems with the relationship."

"What, specifically, were those problems?"

"Apparently this gal is a bit of a wild hair. She'd gotten herself into trouble a time or two along the way. She was about thirty when Jesse hooked up with her, but she didn't have any money of her own. It seems that her father had put it all in a trust where she couldn't get at it. She was stuck living at home with the old man, and she wasn't real happy about it. But she wasn't the type to go out and get a job and support herself, either; she liked living in a big house with servants and all that. She also liked to ride horses, and if you know anything about *that,* you know it takes bags of money to do it right. So she wanted to get away from the old man, but she couldn't give up the money. She was real jealous of her sister, too, apparently—that was Christine Stanley."

"Why was she jealous of Christine Stanley?"

"Well—this is all according to Jesse, remember—Christine had control of her money and also control of a bunch of money that old Mr. Connell had given to her two kids. They were his only grandchildren. Jesse said Lynette used to fume about her sister and her husband living in a big house in town, and having all that money to spend. She didn't like her brother-in-law, and I guess she and Christine Stanley used to get into it pretty regularly about James Stanley."

"James Stanley being Christine Stanley's husband, and Lynette Connell's brother-in-law, correct?"

"Yes."

"What do you mean by saying that Lynette Connell 'got into it' with her sister?"

"According to Jesse, Lynette was always after Christine to divorce James and get him taken off the children's trusts."

"Why was that—according to Jesse?"

"Mostly because Lynette was a trustee, too, and she didn't like the way James's firm managed the kids' money, or the way James and his wife spent the kids' income. See, the way I understood it, if Christine divorced James, he wouldn't be a trustee anymore, and he wouldn't manage the trust funds, either. But Lynette, because she would still be a trustee, would have a crack at all that dough."

"But surely Mrs. Stanley would have control of her children's incomes, even if she divorced Mr. Stanley."

"Well, yeah, but not if Christine Stanley was to die."

"I see. And who brought up the possibility of Mrs. Stanley's death?"

"I expect it was Jesse. At least he told me that they talked about what would happen if Lynette was to become guardian of her sister's children."

Laura scribbled a furious note to Meredith: *Hearsay, hearsay, hearsay!!!!* Meredith nodded, and moved smoothly onto the next topic. "Mr. Stanley, so far, all we've heard is a recital of conversations you may or may not have had with Jesse DuPree about Lynette Connell and her sister, and her sister's husband. Did Mr. DuPree ever specifically ask *you* for your assistance?"

"Yes, he did."

"When was this?"

"Like I said, early last summer I came down to Georgia for a week or two. I saw Jesse several times. We were out having a couple of drinks one night, and Jesse says to me, 'What's your full name, Jim?' I said 'James Thomas Stanley,' and I asked him why he wanted to know. Well, he says, it's just occurred to him that I have the same name—almost the same name—as Lynette Connell's brother-in-law. 'I ought to be able to do something with that,' he says. We didn't talk about it anymore that night, and I went on home to North Carolina. A few weeks later, though, he called me up. 'I got a proposition for you, Jimmy,' he says. 'Lynette and I have been talking, and we think that we can use this name thing to our advantage.' He told me that James Stanley came to North Carolina all the time on business, and he asked me if I thought I could sort of pretend to be him for a night. Sure, I said, but what's in it for me?"

"Did DuPree offer to pay you?"

"He said he had to check with Lynette, because Jesse never has any money of his own. I told him to get back to me, and if the price was right, I would help them out."

"Did Jesse DuPree tell you that he and Miss Connell were planning to kill Christine Stanley?"

"God, no! I never would have gone along—you have to believe that. I thought that they were trying to lay a little trap for James Stanley to convince his wife that he was tom-catting around so she'd divorce him. It seemed pretty harmless, and they offered me five thousand dollars."

"Did they offer you that sum of money, or did you ask for it?"

"We gee-hawed a little, if you know what I mean."

"Actually, I don't. Could you tell me what 'gee-haw' means?"

"You know—horse-trading. Dickering."

"Thank you. Please continue, Mr. Stanley."

"Well, like I was saying, they agreed to pay me when they needed me."

"And when was that?"

"It was a long time later—several months. I had forgotten all about it, to tell the truth. But one day Jesse called up and said that James Stanley was coming to North Carolina, to Charlotte. He told me where he was going to be staying, and that he wanted me to check in under the name 'James Stanley.' He made a real big deal about the time I was to check in—he had James Stanley's flight reservations, and he said that *I had to make it look as if James Stanley was lying about the time he checked in*. In other words, I was to check in at a time when James Stanley couldn't have."

"And how did you arrange to do that?"

"I drove down to Charlotte, to the Marriott, where James Stanley had a reservation. I waited in the lobby, and I called the airline several times. I was supposed to check in about the time his plane landed, but there was a delay in the flight—he was coming through Greenville, and he got stuck there, I guess. Anyway, I went ahead and checked in even though I knew that the plane hadn't landed in Charlotte yet. I had to get back to Winston-Salem, and I was getting antsy. So I ended up checking in way early, but I didn't see the harm in that. Jesse was pissed off when I called him, though, because he said James might notice the discrepancy. I guess he didn't, though."

"What else did you do?"

"That's all, that night. Then I was supposed to wait until the Atlanta cops came after me. 'How do you know they're going to?' I asked Jesse. 'Oh, don't worry—they will. Lynette's going to take care of that.'" Laura's stomach churned as she listened to Jim recount how Jesse and Lynette had played her—and Carlton and Randy, but mostly her.

"Did Jesse DuPree give you instructions about what you were to do when the police arrived to question you?"

"Yes. He gave me a story. I was supposed to say that James Stanley and I had planned on my giving him an alibi for the night of May 8. I was to say that I had checked in and gone up to the room, ordered dinner, and made two phones calls to James Stanley's home number. They even gave me the times the phone calls were made."

"When was it that Jesse DuPree gave you this story?"

"It was a few days after I checked into the hotel— probably around the twelfth or thirteenth of May."

"Mr. Stanley, do you have any record of these communications with Jesse DuPree?"

"No, I don't think so."

"Would your phone records show any calls to him?"

"No, he always called me—from pay phones, I think."

"What about Miss Connell—did you have any contact with her?"

"No, I never met her. I saw her in the courtroom, that's all. She's really something, though. I can understand why Jesse wanted to get with her so badly."

"Moving on, Mr. Stanley, I assume that you're changing your story about the gun as well."

"Well, yes, Jesse wanted me to say that I'd bought the gun from him a few years ago. But I didn't; it was Jesse's gun. He brought it up to North Carolina after the murder and told me to hang on to it. He said he didn't think the cops could trace it, on account of its being so old, and not the kind of gun they see a whole lot of. If they *did* come to me looking for the gun, I was supposed to say that he sold it to me a few years back, sort of under the table so that I wouldn't have to produce a record of the sale."

"What about the story that you lent the gun to James Stanley?"

"Oh, that—I forgot that. You know, it all got real complicated. Yes, I had a story for that—Jesse called it a 'back story.' I was supposed to just say that I lent the gun to James Stanley. I came up with that bit about James wanting to sell the gun to his father-in-law. I didn't think it was believable that I would just *lend* a gun to someone." Jim frowned to communicate his sagaciousness. Laura's fingers curled as she indulged in a fantasy of putting them around Jim's neck and choking the truth out of him—the real truth, not this Greek myth that he was spinning for them. He was the most shameless liar Laura had ever met—but she couldn't prove it.

"Let's go back to the money for a moment, Mr. Stanley," Meredith said, circling back to something that was clearly bothering her. "You say that Jesse DuPree offered you five thousand dollars to participate in this plan of his. Correct?"

"Yes, that was the figure."

"Early in our investigation, Mr. Stanley, you were kind enough to provide us with your bank records showing the transfer of that amount to your account."

"Yep. That I did."

"Please explain something for me, then. Your bank records, and the financial records of James Stanley, both clearly show that the payment was made to you by James

Stanley—not Lynette Connell, and not Jesse DuPree. How do you explain that?"

God Bless Meredith! Laura's heart leapt with hope. *Why didn't I think of that?* she chastised herself. *It's a big screaming discrepancy. Unless, of course, Jim has an answer for it.*

He did.

"Yes, I thought that was weird, too," Jim said, leaning forward confidentially. "But Jesse said that Lynette Connell had access to some trust funds that were set up for James's kids, and that Lynette was a trustee, too. She somehow finagled it so it would look as if James made the payment, and not her."

"Oh? How did she manage that?"

"Beats me. Something to do with payments the trusts made to James—you know the payment was just made to 'James Stanley,' and not James *T.* Stanley. You'll have to ask her, I guess. She must have had the power to move money around anyway, because I damn sure got paid."

"Yes, you did. Let me clarify another point, Mr. Stanley. Are you willing to swear under oath that you have never met James Alan Stanley?"

Jim nodded, and the corners of his mouth turned down in what Laura recognized as his "regretful" look. "No, I never saw him until I came into court. And I know what you're thinking: How could I get on the stand and tell all those lies about a man I'd never met? I must seem like the worst person on the face of the earth, and maybe I am. But by the time I realized exactly what Jesse was asking me to do—put an innocent man in the electric chair!—it was too late to back out. And you don't know Jesse. He would have killed me if I told what he had done. I didn't think it could go as far as it did, until I found myself in that courtroom. I think that's why I broke down the way I did. And you know what else? I think I made that mistake about the bed in the hotel room sort of accidentally on purpose. Like one of those Freudian slips, you know?" he added, mispronouncing "Freudian."

"That's very interesting, Mr. Stanley. Is there anything else you'd care to share with us now?"

"No, just how sorry and ashamed I am to have been involved in this thing. But I'm glad I finally have the chance to set the record straight. I'm glad I can give James Stanley his life back, so he can get back to taking care of his children," he concluded piously.

"That's all I have," Meredith said, cutting off further sermonizing. "Laura, Randy, do you want to ask anything?"

"I do," Laura said. "Who pulled the trigger, Jim?"

"The trigger? How should I know? I wasn't there."

"Jesse DuPree and Lynette Connell both have alibis that were corroborated by third parties. We know neither one of them could have been in the Stanley house when Christine was killed. But *you* don't have an alibi for any time after eight P.M. on May 8, do you? You had plenty of time to drive to Atlanta and to kill Christine, didn't you?"

"I do have an alibi! I . . . I already told you that I went back to Winston-Salem. I had to meet somebody. And I can't have been in Winston-Salem and in Atlanta," he said triumphantly.

"Oh? Can you corroborate your whereabouts?" Laura asked, pressing him.

"Yes. I had . . . a date. With my secretary, Candi. She'll tell you that I came to her house about ten-thirty that night."

"In that case, we'll get in touch with Candi right away. Randy, can you hit the Pause button on the camera while I make the call? Thanks." Then, to Jim, she added casually, "Our investigator is in Charlotte; it won't be a bit of trouble for him to go to Winston-Salem. Could you give me Candi's full name and address?''

It might have been only Laura's wistful imagination, but Jim seemed to hesitate before he gave her the information.

Laura pulled out her cellular phone and dialed Kenny's mobile phone number, focusing her gaze on Jim all the time. Ken picked up after a couple of rings. ''Yell-oh. Newton here.''

''Hi, Ken. This is Laura. Where are you?''

''At the Marriott. Wayne says 'hey.' ''

''Back at him. What does he know?''

''Nothing good, I'm afraid. The bed is king-size. He's checking to see if anyone's monkeyed with the records, but it looks like your man Jim was lying about being in the room.''

''Among other things. Listen, Kenny, as long as you're up there, would you mind a side trip to Winston-Salem?'' She explained what they needed him to do, and gave him Candi's address and phone number.

''Will do,'' Kenny said. ''You know what she's going to say, though, don't you? Jim didn't just fall off the rutabaga wagon.''

''I know. Try anyway.''

''Is he in the room with you?''

''Yep.''

''I see. Well, I'll shake this Candi up a little and see if I can't get something out of her. In the meantime, keep Jim-boy away from the telephone. Is he under arrest?''

''Nope.''

''Why don't you have Randy clap him in irons for a while? A night in jail would do Jim Stanley a power of good. But that's not up to me, is it? I'll just butt out and run along. I'll be back in Atlanta tomorrow.''

''Thanks, Kenny. We'll talk more then.'' She clicked

her phone closed, and looked at Jim. "He's going to see Candi tonight."

Jim smirked. "I wish you'd let me talk to him—I'd have told him to say 'hi' to her."

Laura turned to Randy and Meredith. "Do either of you have any more questions?" Both shook their heads. "Let's switch this thing off, then," Laura said, making for the video camera and removing the tape.

"Can I see you ladies in the hall?" Randy asked. Laura and Meredith joined him after Laura had assured herself that there were no telephones left in the room with Jim. They closed the door and talked in low voices.

"I don't believe him," Randy said bluntly.

"That makes two of us," Meredith said.

"Me three," Laura added.

Randy nodded thoughtfully. "We haven't heard from Carlton, yet, of course—DuPree may have been able to tell him something to contradict Jim's story. If he could prove that he sold the gun to Jim Stanley . . ."

I don't think he'll be able to," Laura said, although she hated to be pessimistic. "The conspiracy theory is the fall-back plan, and at this point I've begun to realize that Jim doesn't leave anything to chance. He has a brilliant legal mind."

"What makes you say that?" Randy asked.

"He's played the system like a harmonica. Look at where we are: Craig Fannin is angling for a directed verdict of acquittal for James Stanley. If he gets it, jeopardy is invoked and James is scot-free. And so is Jim, because of the immunity."

"Can't you stop Fannin for a while?" Randy asked. "If we have another week or two, we might be able to find an inconsistency in their stories. I'm thinking about that fiber evidence—if Jim Stanley *was* the shooter, those fibers had to come from his clothes. And he might not have known that he left fibers, or that there were microscopic blood-stains on his clothes, so he might not have been smart enough to get rid of them. Can we get a search warrant and look for clothes that match the fibers in Jim's closet?"

"Now, that's the best idea anybody's had all night," Meredith said. "Laura, help Randy swear out an affidavit for a search warrant, and get someone in the district attorney's office in Winston-Salem on the horn first thing in the morning. Randy, can you hightail it up there and execute a warrant tomorrow?"

"You bet your ass I can," he replied. "But can't we ask for a little more time? Even if I find something, the crime lab is going to need a least a couple of days to analyze it."

Meredith shook her head. "Afraid not," she said. "The judge isn't going to sit on her hands if there's exculpatory evidence. The prosecution only gets one bite at the apple, and we've had ours."

Laura nodded grimly. They had very few chances left. Once a trial began, a good judge would be loath to interrupt it for any reason, let alone because the prosecution was unprepared. There was one shameful alternative that Laura didn't even want to bring up: a nolle prosequi. If Judge Penfield granted a 'nol pros,' they could stop the trial and resume prosecution later, or even reindict James Stanley using new evidence. *But if I were in Craig Fannin's shoes,* Laura thought, *I would yell like hell before I would let the judge enter a nol pros when I was so close to winning it all.*

"Let me go with Randy," she said aloud, abruptly.

"I need you here," Meredith said.

"For what? We don't have to be in court tomorrow, and there's nothing I can do down here but wait. If I go to Winston-Salem I can help draft the search warrant, at least, and if any problems come up, I'll be on the spot."

"I'd like to have her," Travers said.

Meredith looked from one of them to the other. "Okay. Go as early as you can tomorrow, and get back as quickly as you can. No matter what you find up there, we have to be ready to face the music Monday morning. And I hate the tune that's playing."

CHAPTER 30

Randy Travers was a surprisingly congenial traveling companion, Laura discovered. He had a stoic's attitude toward airport traffic and garbled boarding announcements. He didn't even seem to mind when they were delayed on the taxi-way at Winston-Salem for half an hour with no explanation. While Laura fretted and fumed, he simply folded his hands over his chest, tipped his head back, and dozed off with the practiced air of a man who had spent many nights on stakeouts.

Laura was even gladder of his company when they reached the headquarters of the Winston-Salem Police Department. She was still tentative in her dealings with the Atlanta Police Department, let alone cops in other cities. She hadn't the least idea whom she should approach to get a search warrant issued in Winston-Salem. Randy did, though. He flashed his badge to an officer at the desk, and explained in a sort of cop-pidgin what they were after.

Laura didn't understand how so few syllables could have communicated the complexity of the proposition, but evidently they did, because in less than five minutes they were seated in the office of a lieutenant who headed a squad of detectives. Lieutenant Barber insisted that they accept a cup of coffee, and he and Randy swapped stories while they waited for it to arrive. Laura was beginning to realize that all cops liked to play a sort of "Six Degrees of Law Enforcement" when they met. Working through their memory banks to find some case that connected them, Randy and Barber were able to identify a bank robbery suspect who, fleeing Atlanta, had been captured by Barber when he was a young sheriff's deputy in Forsyth County, North Carolina. A line from a poem by John Donne popped into Laura's head: '. . . *and yet we see Formalities retarding thee.*' But just as she was deciding to interrupt the formalities the policemen got down to cases.

"So you need a local search warrant?" Barber asked.

"Yep. We've got a suspect down in Atlanta in a murder case. We're looking for the clothing he might have worn on the night of the crime. Here's an affidavit." Randy handed over the paper he and Laura had prepared the night before, which laid out the specifics.

Barber nodded. "Got his address, I see. What's this second address?"

"His wife threw him out. He's living in an apartment," Laura explained.

"But you want both locations searched?"

"Affirmative," Randy replied. "The suit could be in either place."

"Okay, then. Let's get this typed onto one of our forms, and I'll head over to City Hall with you. You want us to help you execute this?"

"Could you spare a patrol car?" Randy asked.

"Sure. I always say better safe than sorry."

City Hall was just a few steps away from the police headquarters, and it was a tribute to the relaxed pace of life in a city smaller than Atlanta that they were able to get before a magistrate almost without delay. Laura had learned one thing during her tenure as an assistant district attorney, and that, when appearing before any judge with a request, *less detail is better.* She and Randy answered the magistrate's questions as succinctly as possible; there was no need to embark upon the whole story even if there was time. Still, Laura couldn't help but wonder what the judge would say if he knew that they were seeking a warrant to search the personal goods and chattels of a prosecution witness. Thankfully, he didn't inquire, and they were back outside in less than ten minutes. A squad car was waiting for them, manned by two young officers.

"Here's your ride," Barber said. "I'll leave you to it. Give a shout if you have any problems."

"Thanks. It's been a pleasure," Randy said, wringing Barber's meaty hand. Laura submitted to a bone-crushing handshake, and Barber ambled back to his office. Randy took charge of the two uniforms. "You know where these addresses are?" he asked, displaying the warrant.

"Brightleaf Circle, yes, sir. That's right near here," one replied. He wore a badge that announced his name as DeLorio. The other one was called Butler. "You know this other place, Andy?" DeLorio asked his partner.

"Uh, yeah, I think that's one of them apartments out by the expressway."

"Guess we should go to Brightleaf first, then," Randy said.

"Y'all want to ride in the patrol car, or do you have your own car?" DeLorio asked.

"We'll take our own. It's parked in that lot," Randy

said, pointing across the street. Laura was disappointed; she wanted to ride in the patrol car. It is always a good thing to make an entrance. But she went with Randy, who pulled the rented car out into traffic behind the patrol car. They followed it through a couple of turns, and they were soon in a residential area, a neighborhood of attractive houses with well-groomed lawns. The cop car drew up before number 1341, Jim Stanley's house—or his former house, at any rate. There was an SUV parked in the driveway. "Good—someone's home," Laura said. "Must be the wife."

"Yep," Randy said. "You can bet she won't be too happy to see us."

"Why? She's already been questioned, and she's talked to the press."

"They don't like cop cars in neighborhoods like this," he replied. DeLorio and Butler were out of their car, waiting for Randy's instructions. "Let's roll," he said.

Laura scrambled from the car and straightened her jacket, eyeing the house. "I don't have great expectations. Do you? If he's living in an apartment, he's probably taken his clothes."

"He might have left some here, and it's always interesting to talk to an angry wife. No telling what we might find out. Okay, you men just hang back," he said to the patrol officers. "I don't anticipate that we'll meet resistance." They headed down the front walkway, Randy and Laura preceding the officers. Randy rang the doorbell, and the door swung open almost instantly. She must have seen the cars.

Mrs. James T. Stanley was a very attractive woman, tall and blonde, well dressed in simple slacks and a cashmere turtleneck. She was, however, wreathed in cigarette smoke, and frowning, two factors which tended in Laura's mind to diminish her good looks. "He's not here," Mrs. Stanley snapped as Randy displayed his badge.

"We know that, ma'am," Randy said patiently. "We're from Atlanta. We left your husband down there. We're here with a search warrant."

"Search warrant? What the hell for? Let me see it." She looked it over quickly, and snorted. "Well, you're shit out of luck today. I don't have any of his clothes."

"He took them when he moved out?" Randy inquired.

"A, he did not move out—he was *thrown* out, and B, no, he didn't take his clothes, not all of them. But I gave the stuff he *did* leave here to Goodwill. I burned all his papers, and I sold his precious goddamn record collection. The only things I have left are his girlie magazines and his porn videos, just because I'm too embarrassed to put them out on the curb. You're welcome to take those. In fact, I wish you would."

"No, thank you, Mrs. Stanley. Did you give the clothing to Goodwill recently, ma'am?"

"No. It was months ago. God knows where they are now," she said, with a satisfied look on her face.

Laura decided it was time for her to speak. "Do you recall if you gave away his gray suit?"

"Which one?"

"He had more than one?"

"He had two. One I gave away. The other I think he must have taken with him. Why don't you check over at that little whore's apartment? That's where he's staying now."

"You mean he's, ah, living *with* someone?" Laura asked. Jim had failed to mention that.

"You didn't know? He's shacked up with that fat little secretary of his—*Candi.*" She put the name in contemptuous italics as she said it. "And she's more than welcome to him, after I'm through divorcing him. He won't be worth much to her then—I can promise you that," she added with a grim smile. "That should teach her to try sleeping her way up."

There didn't seem to be much they could gain by staying here. Laura glanced at Randy, and he nodded. "Thank you, Mrs. Stanley," he said. "We do appreciate the time. May I ask one more question?"

"Why not? The whole neighborhood has already seen you."

"I'm sorry. You told the investigators that your husband was not with you on the night of May 8. Did you know if he was with Miss . . . Candi?"

"No, he was not."

"Are you sure of that?"

"Of course I am. He didn't take up with her until after I tossed him out. He didn't have anywhere to go, and she always had a crush on him, so he sweet-talked her into letting him move in. She thought he was going to make all her dreams come true. Bet she's having nightmares now," Mrs. Stanley added with a dark chuckle.

"Any idea where he actually was that night?"

"Not the foggiest. But don't believe him if he says he was with her—he never looked twice at her until I tossed him out. The only reason he's there is to keep a roof over his sorry head."

"Well, thanks for the information," Randy said, pocketing the warrant. "If you think of anything else, I sure would appreciate a phone call." He offered her a card.

"What's this all about anyway? I thought Jim was just a witness in that thing down in Atlanta. Y'all are acting like he's a suspect."

"Just routine, ma'am," Randy said.

Mrs. Stanley watched them as they returned to their

cars. Aware of her scrutiny, Laura remained silent until the doors closed. *"That* was interesting," she said.

"I thought it might be," Randy said. "No telling what an angry woman will tell you. I'm right eager to talk to this Candi—what's her last name?"

"Shane."

"Candi Shane? You've got to be kidding." Randy was actually chuckling as they followed the patrol car across town.

Winston-Salem wasn't a big city and it took only a few minutes for them to reach their destination, the Twelve Oaks Apartments. There were no oaks, however, visible anywhere in the complex of two-story barracklike buildings. With the uniformed officers once again trailing behind them, Laura and Randy mounted an outside stairway and traveled down a covered walkway to the door of Candi's apartment. There was no way of telling if she was at home. Randy knocked firmly on the door. A moment or two later, the door, chain lock still in place, opened slightly. "Yes?" a little voice said.

"Miss Shane?"

"Who are you?"

"I'm Detective Randy Travers of the Atlanta Police Department, and this is Miss Laura Chastain. I believe you've met her."

"I don't want to talk to you."

"I'm real sorry, miss, but I'm afraid you have to. I have a search warrant here. We need to take a look around your place."

"You can't come in! I . . . I'm not dressed!"

"We'll give you a minute to put on some clothes, miss, but I am going to have to insist that you let us in." Randy gestured to Officer DeLorio, who stepped into a position visible to Candi.

"Miss? I'm with the Winston-Salem police. Please open the door, and we'll get this over with as quickly as we can," DeLorio said authoritatively.

"No!" Candi screamed, very loud. "I can't . . . I won't! I'm going to call Jim's . . . I'm going to call my lawyer."

"Oh, crap," Randy muttered as the door slammed in his face.

"What do we do?" Laura asked, concerned.

"Well, I'm not going to beat the door down—that's for sure. I guess we wait for this lawyer."

With a great sense of foreboding, Laura realized that the lawyer in question was probably Charlie Hoyt. She was not eager to meet him again, especially in these circumstances. "Can't we try again? Let me talk to her."

Randy shrugged and stood back from the door. "All yours," he said.

Laura rapped on the door, softly at first, and then, when she got no response, more assertively. "Candi? Please come out here and talk to us. I want to explain to you what we're looking for. I promise that we won't get you involved." There was no answer. Laura turned to Randy. "I don't want to break the poor girl's door in. You don't think she's in there destroying evidence, do you?"

Randy raised his hands in exasperation. "How could she get rid of a man's suit? She can't flush it, and I don't see chimneys, so she can't burn it. Worst she could do is cut it into ribbons—if she even knows that's what we're after. She didn't give us much of a chance to explain why we were here."

"And yet she seemed prepared for us. But I guess we have to wait for Hoyt to get here."

Randy snorted. "That guy again? Great."

"I know. He's beginning to get on my nerves, too. The

only comfort I take is in knowing that his bill is going to be *huge*."

"Let's go wait in the car. No point in standing around out here. Boys, I'm afraid we're going to be keeping you tied up for a while."

"No problem," DeLorio said. "I'll radio in. Y'all want me to go get you some coffee? There's a place down the street that has good coffee. Sandwiches, too."

"I'll pass on the sandwich, but I'll take a cup of coffee," Randy said. "How about you, Laura?"

"One for me, too. Lots of cream."

Laura's coffee was still too hot to drink when a black Mercedes pulled into the parking lot and stopped alongside the rental car. "Here we go," she said. "I'll handle this guy."

Charlie Hoyt was looking fresh as a daisy, and as dapper as ever. "Hello, Mr. Hoyt," Laura said. "This is Detective Randy Travers of the Atlanta Police Department. I suppose Candi told you why we're here."

"Hello, Miss Chastain. Detective. Candi was a bit upset when we spoke on the phone. I understand you have a search warrant for her premises—may I see it?"

"Of course," Laura said, and Randy produced the document.

Hoyt glanced through the paper quickly, and then returned it to Randy. He reached into his jacket pocket and extracted another paper. "This is a stay, Miss Chastain. It prevents you from executing your search warrant until my motion to quash the warrant is heard."

"What the . . . ? How did you get this so quickly?"

"The county courthouse was on the way. I just popped in and saw Judge Sidney."

"I see. And on what grounds are you moving to quash?"

"On the very logical grounds that, as my client has immunity, anything you find will be inadmissible."

"*I know* your client has immunity, Mr. Hoyt, but his clothes don't. The existence of that suit is critical to our case against *James* Stanley." Laura was not being entirely candid with Hoyt when she said that. In truth, it would be of little help in the case against James Stanley. She was hoping to use the suit to threaten Jim's immunity deal and get him talking again.

"You certainly will have the opportunity to convince the judge of your point of view," Hoyt said genially. "He's expecting us right about now. I'll meet you in his chambers." With that, Hoyt returned to his car and drove off.

"Does he have a chance?" Randy asked.

"Of course not! It's completely illogical," Laura fumed. "He knows very well that if I find independent evidence that Jim was involved in the murder—*more* involved in the murder—I can introduce it, even if I can't touch Jim. Jim's immunity doesn't go away, not even if I find independent corrobation that he pulled the trigger, so I can't understand why Hoyt is taking this aggressive stance." She shook her head. "Anyway, we better get going."

Randy explained the state of affairs to the patrolmen, and dismissed them. "When we get the warrant confirmed, we can request another patrol car," Laura said optimistically.

Too optimistically, as it turned out. From the moment Laura was ushered into Judge Melvin Sidney's chambers, where she found Hoyt lounging in a comfy chair and talking football with the judge, she knew she had lost. Hoyt proceeded to tie logic up in knots, first arguing that the transactional immunity made any new evidence of Jim's involvement in the murder moot. When Laura challenged him aggressively, he fell back on a flimsy argument that his client had only perjured himself at Laura's urging. Indignant at the implication that she had suborned perjury, Laura lost her temper. "You're one to talk!" she cried. "The only mistake I made was trusting that *you* had verified your lying client's story. How was I to know you were shielding a murderer?"

"Now, that's enough, Miss Chastain," Judge Sidney intoned. "We'd needn't stoop to ad hominem attacks."

You were perfectly happy with ad hominem attacks when your pal Hoyt was making them, Laura wanted to say.

The judge continued in a calm, friendly tone. "This matter seems perfectly plain to me, Miss Chastain. You may regret having given the witness a grant of transactional immunity, but I'm afraid that it limits your ability to seek evidence against him. That is, even if you were to find evidence of his guilt, you could not use it. The search therefore would be nothing more than a nuisance to the witness and his roommate. The motion to quash is granted."

Slack-jawed and reeling, Laura rejoined Randy in the hall outside the judge's chambers. She didn't need to tell what had happened; he read her face. "No go, huh?" he said gruffly. "Cheer up, kid—you just ran into a little hometown officiating. Any chance of an appeal?"

She shook her head. "It's an error, but it would take too long to reverse it."

He threw an avuncular arm around her shoulders and led her down the hall. "Well, can't be helped now. Let's go home and have us a weekend. We'll think of something before Monday. I don't know about you, but I've always done my best work when my back was against the wall."

CHAPTER 31

Randy Travers might have relished the challenge of fighting with his back against a wall, but Laura was too battle-weary even to contemplate her next move. She called Meredith as soon as she reached her house. Her report was bleak. "The best—the *best*—I think we can do is get a nolle prosequi and buy some time. But you know what the odds are against Judge Penfield entering a nol pros at this stage."

"I wouldn't count it out," Meredith said soothingly. "But what I really think you should do is turn loose of it. Leave the whole thing to me, Laura, and get some rest this weekend."

"But this whole . . . *train wreck* is my fault, from start to finish!"

"Laura," Meredith said with admirable patience, "I was with you every step of the way. I agreed to everything we did. There was no way either of us could have seen this coming. Now, what are your plans this weekend?"

"I have none."

"Well, get some. I don't want you to come into the office until Monday morning. I'll meet you there at seven—I'll bring breakfast. We'll draft a motion for a nol pros. It's all going to come out right in the end, you'll see. I've stared at worse disasters than this."

Laura doubted that, but she hung up the phone with the intention of at least attempting to relax and forget things for a few hours. She called Amos. It was almost eight, but he was at home. "Hey. I'm back," she said.

"You don't sound too happy," he remarked.

She told him what had happened, and he listened without comment. "Sounds like you need a drink. Why don't I come over there?"

"Have you eaten?"

"No. I went to the gym, and had a beer with a guy I met there. I was just going to order a pizza."

"I've got some leftover lasagna in my freezer. There's plenty for two of us," she said.

"Okay. I'll bring a bottle of wine."

"Thanks. Could you pick up some ice cream on the way?"

"What kind?"

"Surprise me," she said, too weary to decide even that matter. "But don't get any of that low-fat junk, and no frozen yogurt, either. I want the kind of ice cream that comes with a warning label from the surgeon general."

"Got it. See you in about half an hour."

Laura shucked off her work clothes and put on her most comfortable jeans and a black turtleneck. She had already opened a bottle of Cabernet when Amos arrived. "I started without you," she said. Amos was adept at reading

Laura's moods, and he made no attempt to bring up the subject of the trial. He adroitly maintained the flow of conversation on more benign topics, and kept Laura's glass full, leaving her pleasantly muddled by the time they finished the ice cream.

"Oof!" she said as she cleared the dishes. "I feel like I just gained ten pounds. Let's take a walk—it's a nice night. And if I sit around here, I'm going to open that second bottle of wine, which I know I would regret in the morning."

"Let's walk, then."

It was a cool night, so Laura slipped on her good old barn jacket and inhaled its comforting horsy smells of leather and sweat and hay. They left the house and walked down to the dead end of her street, then turned right. Laura tipped her head back to look at the sky. "Pretty night," she said.

"Yep," Amos replied.

"Do you know anything about astronomy?"

"Nope. I couldn't find the North Star with the Hubble telescope."

"Me neither." They returned to silent contemplation of the universe. Laura thrust her hands into the pockets of her jacket. "It's getting chilly," she said.

"Chilly? You Southerners are such wimps. This is warm." He wasn't wearing a jacket, just a long-sleeved denim shirt.

"You Yankees! You talk a good game, but I haven't noticed a lot of y'all lining up to move back to Chicago."

He laughed. "True. They couldn't get me back there unless they made me the King of Illinois. And even then they'd have to promise to get a full-time lackey to shovel my driveway for me."

"Do you really like Atlanta?" she asked, fumbling with something she felt in her pocket.

"Not really. I sometimes think about moving to a smaller city. This place is such a mess—the traffic, the politics. Sometimes I get fed up."

"I know," she sighed. "I sometimes wonder if I shouldn't just go back to Nashville." She pulled her right hand from her pocket and looked at the object in her hand. "What's this? I must have left a credit card in here."

"No, it looks like one of those electronic hotel room keys," Amos observed.

"Oh. I wonder where that came from." Laura shrugged. "Anyway, I'm getting a little tired of Atlanta, too. I'd hate to quit my job after such a short time, but I haven't exactly been an asset to Meredith."

"Don't sell yourself short. Meredith wouldn't have hired you if she didn't think you were the best."

"She may have thought so at the time, but she must rue the day now."

"Stop it. Let's head back. You're tired, and I have an early squash game tomorrow."

"Okay." They walked back to her house in silence. They said good night in the driveway. Laura stood and watched as Amos's truck pulled away, and then she went inside. As she hung her jacket on the peg in the laundry room that was its home, she remembered the hotel key in the pocket. She took it out and looked at it. She couldn't recall having taken this ratty jacket on any trips recently. She knew that she hadn't taken it to Brevard, which was the last place she had traveled. Then she remembered: She had been given two keys when she checked Jim Stanley into his hotel room. She thought that she had given him both keys, but one must have slipped from its little folder and remained in her pocket.

She twiddled the key thoughtfully in her hand as she headed for her bedroom. Jim Stanley's hotel room—why hadn't she thought of it? He might very easily have brought the gray suit with him to Atlanta, not realizing that it was evidence against him. She could get a search warrant for his room easily, and have it executed before Charlie Hoyt could interfere. Hoyt could try to suppress any evidence they found, of course, but without his home-field advantage Laura doubted that his ridiculous arguments would hold water. Of course, they might find nothing in the room, and the search warrant would be a wasted effort. More than a wasted effort, really, because if Craig Fannin got wind of what they were up to, he would have a great argument for a mistrial, or even an acquittal. She had been pondering Jim Stanley and Charlie Hoyt to the exclusion of Fannin in the past few days, and that was not good. One slip, and Fannin would make sure that James Stanley would be a free man forever.

Laura sat on the edge of her bed and puzzled over the key a while longer. Finally, she gave it up. Her head was buzzing with exhaustion and wine, and there was nothing she could do at eleven o'clock on Friday night anyway. She put the key on her bedside table and started getting ready for bed. She was sleeping soundly fifteen minutes later, the key forgotten.

Saturday morning Laura awoke well rested for the first time since the trial had begun. In fact, for the first time in weeks, she didn't wake up thinking about the trial at all. It was only the presence of the key, glowing white against the dark cherry surface of her night table, that reminded her that there was a trial at all. As soon as she spotted the key, however, she formed a resolution. *I'm going to break into Jim's hotel room.*

There. It had seemed absurd last night when she had the same notion, but now it made perfect sense. If the suit was there among Jim's things, she could get a search warrant and discover it legitimately—and quickly, before Hoyt could interfere, and before Fannin got a whiff of what they were up to. If there was nothing in the room, she could continue to pursue other tactics against Jim— that is, if she could come up with any.

Having formed the resolution, Laura tested it. Even though she had a key, and even though she planned to take nothing from the room, it would be breaking and entering, a felony. On the other hand, if anyone at the hotel questioned her, she would have a good cover story. She could simply claim that Jim had given her the key and asked him to meet her in his room. The only other risk was that Jim himself might interrupt her. She could manage that problem to some degree, however. She could call before she left home to his room to make certain he wasn't in, and she would call again from the lobby to make sure he hadn't returned. She figured that she would need no more than ten minutes to nip up to the room, get in, look around, and nip back out. Ten minutes was an acceptable window of risk.

Laura pulled herself up short. *What am I thinking?* she asked herself, amazed. It was easy enough to rationalize away the practical and legal risks, but not the moral and ethical ones. Laura prided herself on her honesty. She was the kind of person who returned to the grocery store to tell the clerk she had been undercharged for an item. And now she was thinking about cheating the system just because things hadn't gone her way. *But why haven't they gone my way?* she asked herself. *Because I'm up against the biggest liar I've ever met and his slicker-than-goose-grease lawyer, that's why.*

That decided it. She was surfing on a wave of indignation now, angry at the way the system had been manipulated. *Jim Stanley is hiding behind that poor stupid little secretary of his,* she stormed as she got up and headed for the bathroom. *And Charlie Hoyt is shielding him,* she added as she turned on the shower.

By the time she dried her hair, all doubt had been vanquished. If she thought she would run a risk of discovery, she might not have been so sanguine—the shame she would feel when Meredith, or Amos, or her parents learned that she had been dishonest would be too much to bear. But they weren't going to find out; no one was. She hastily dressed in casual, comfortable clothes, grabbed her purse and keys and headed for the door. She snagged the barn jacket off the hook and replaced the hotel key in the pocket where she had found it, where it would be handy.

She had one foot out the door when she remembered that she had intended to call the hotel. She half turned, starting back toward the telephone on the kitchen wall, but then thought better of it. A real professional wouldn't make a call that could be traced. She decided to stop for a cup of coffee at the Starbucks on Piedmont and use the pay phone there.

There was no answer at Jim's hotel room, so Laura got back into her car and headed down Piedmont toward downtown. Stopped at a red light, she thought through her strategy. It was a bit of luck that she had actually been inside the room on the day Jim had arrived in Atlanta. She would be able to cross into the bedroom and locate the closet without hesitating. She tried to visualize herself making the trek on silent feet, putting her hand on the closet door . . .

Fingerprints! She couldn't run the risk of leaving fingerprints. She was just passing the shopping center at Pied-

mont and Lindbergh, so she pulled in and found a
drugstore. They had only large boxes of latex gloves, so
Laura bought what amounted to a lifetime supply. Now
completely prepared for her mission, she continued downtown in her car.

The hotel had no parking, so Laura found a lot nearby.
Downtown was, as usual, nearly deserted on a Saturday
morning. A few tourists and some conventioneers were
wandering toward Underground, but most of the store-
fronts Laura passed on her way to the hotel were sporting
Closed signs. She would have preferred more of a crowd,
in which she could be less conspicuous, but she knew she
could rely on her unassuming appearance to shield her
from notice. There were times when it was good to be
average-looking.

When she reached the door of the hotel, she took a
moment to gather her resolve. Then she marched into the
lobby. As she expected, it was sparsely inhabited; the few
people staying over the weekend would have headed out
into the sparkling fall sunshine. She hoped that Jim had
made the same decision. She crossed to the house telephones and picked up a receiver. It was then that she
realized she wasn't sure of the room number. She tugged
the card key from her pocket. No, just as she remembered,
it did not have a number imprinted on it. She stood for
a moment, straining her memory. She didn't want to draw
attention to herself by trying to weasel the number out of
the desk clerk. She doubted she would succeed in any case.
Think, Laura.

It was on the third floor; that much she was sure of.
And they had turned *right* off the elevator to get to it.
Laura was fairly sure that she'd recognize the door when
she came to it; she navigated by landmarks, whether on
foot on in her car. She'd find the door that *felt* like the

correct one, and if the key didn't open it, well, since she knew that the door lay to the right of the elevators, she would have to try, at most, half the rooms on the third floor before she found the right one.

Proud of that bit of logic, she returned her attention to the phone. She hit the O button and was connected to the hotel switchboard. "Jim Stanley's room, please," she said lightly. There was a slight click, and the phone began to ring. And ring, and ring. Finally, the operator came back on the line. "There's no answer, miss," she said. "May I take a message?"

"No, thank you," Laura said. She hung up and looked around. *Now or never,* she thought, and she stepped away from the phone and back into the lobby. She strode toward the elevators trying to look as if she belonged there. No one challenged her, or even gave her a second glance. An elevator was waiting, doors open, and she stepped quickly aboard, pressing the Close Door button so she wouldn't have to share the car with anyone. She jabbed at the button marked 3, and the elevator started with a slight jerk. She pulled out the latex gloves she had stored in her left pocket. She would put them on only when she got inside the room, she decided. A woman, however innocuous-looking, might attract attention if she wore latex gloves in a hotel corridor. She would have to remember to wipe the outside handle of the door as she left.

The elevator doors slid open on the third floor, and Laura stepped out. She looked quickly to the left and right. *Damn!* The housekeeper's cart was stopped outside a room to the right, very close to the one she thought was Jim's. She forced herself to walk casually past the open door. She passed room 345, then the open door where the vacuum cleaner was running. The next door, room 349, was Jim's; she felt sure of it. The only question remaining was whether it had been cleaned. Would the housekeeper discover her in the room if she went in? On the other hand, if she waited until the room was cleaned, she would waste precious time. Jim might even return. She decided to risk it.

Breathlessly, she inserted the flat plastic card into the slot in the lock, hardly daring to look at the row of lights that ran across the top of the mechanism. Red would mean that she had the wrong room; green that she had guessed correctly. She withdrew the card, and looked down. The light was flashing green. She looked at it in disbelief, and it stopped blinking. When she tried the handle, the door would not open. Once again, she inserted the key, and this time she did not hesitate. She turned the handle and opened the door, slipping through the narrowest opening she could manage.

The room was dark, the curtains drawn. Laura could tell even before her eyes adjusted to the dimness that the room had not been cleaned. The remains of a pizza, still in the box, were spread across the coffee table, and the air smelled of stale beer. Laura hurriedly pulled on the latex gloves and passed through the living room and into the bedroom. The closet was to the right, on the inside wall of the room, with the bathroom beyond it. She quickly approached the mirrored closet door and slid it open.

Jim had brought few clothes to Atlanta with him. There was the blue suit he had worn every day in court, a few shirts, a pair of tan slacks, and a leather jacket. That was it. No gray suit. Laura swallowed her disappointment. The chances of finding the suit had never been very good; it was probably in some Goodwill bin, if not hanging in Candi's closet.

Laura turned from the closet, disappointed but relieved that she could at least get out of the room. As she did, her eye fell on the dresser. *I've come all this way*, she thought.

Might as well snoop a little. She took a few steps and stood in front of the dresser. She didn't expect to find anything but the Gideon Bible in the drawers, but she pulled them open just the same. One contained Jim's underwear; she shut it quickly. The next one held the phone books and the expected Bible, but in the third drawer she saw something that aroused her curiosity.

It was a bulky padded envelope, marked "Tapes." *What tapes?* Laura wondered. She pulled the envelope out and peered down into it. There were several cassette tapes in plastic boxes, held together with a fat rubber band. She pulled out the bundle. The top tape was labeled, in a neat hand, "February 1–28." She pulled off the rubber band and sorted through the rest of the stack. Each one was labeled with the month and date, but there was no other information on them. Laura wished she had her Walkman with her so she could listen to them.

But there was something still inside the envelope, a thick sheaf of paper. She tugged it out of the envelope and read the top page. It was a letter, typed on the letterhead of Jim Stanley's firm and addressed to Charlie Hoyt at his law firm's offices.

Dear Charlie:

Here are the transcripts of the conversations I have on tape. I am also enclosing the original note in Stanley's handwriting. As we discussed, you will hold these until it becomes necessary to produce them, if that day ever comes. I appreciate your assistance in this matter.

Laura flipped through the pages in disbelief, astonished at what she was reading. They were transcripts of conversations between Jim and James Stanley. Some of the passages were trivial, ranging from the weather to sports, but some paragraphs and sentences leapt out at Laura:

> *My plane is due to arrive at seven-thirty . . . You should check into the hotel sometime after eight, because it'll take me a while to get to the hotel. Go ahead and check in, though, because if you start too late for Atlanta she'll be upstairs, and I don't want it to happen there . . . I'll send you the alarm code later. We change it every month or so . . .*

Right here, in her hand, Laura held the record of the conspiracy between Jim and James Stanley. It was just as she had speculated; Jim was actually the gunman. Her hands trembled with excitement and anger. It wasn't only Jim and James who were involved—Hoyt had knowledge of the crime. When Laura had accused him of shielding a murderer she had no idea how close to the truth she had come. She read as much of the document as she could, as quickly as she could. The very last page in the sheaf was a photocopy of a handwritten note. It was unsigned, and Laura didn't recognize the handwriting, but she knew who had written it:

> *Jim—the code for the burglar alarm is 7-4-3-6. Punch in the numbers and hit Enter and the system turns off. Good luck.*

Laura's stomach churned—in her worst imaginings she hadn't supposed that James was capable of wishing his wife's killer "good luck."

She was holding dynamite in her hands, pure, hundred-proof *inadmissible* dynamite. This was evidence that would never see the light of day. For one thing, taping conversations without the consent of all parties was illegal in most states; Laura presumed that it was illegal in North Carolina, as well. But for another, and more important, thing, there was no way that Laura could divulge the existence of these tapes and transcripts without revealing that she had entered Jim's hotel room illegally. Her mind raced, trying to solve the puzzle that confronted her. There had to be some way to get this in front of the court. Wild ideas popped into her mind, only to be dismissed immediately. *Take the papers, have them copied, and return them before Jim missed them?* She could then mail them to herself anonymously. No, too risky, and anonymously submitted papers wouldn't be admissible without someone to corroborate that they were not forgeries. *Get a search warrant for the hotel room?* That was more promising, but there was the problem of swearing out the affidavit. Who could have informed the investigators of the existence of the transcripts?

Laura turned to the last page of the transcript. There, at the bottom of the page, was a typist's notation: *JTS/cs.* Laura almost laughed aloud. Good old Candi—conscientious to a fault. She began to form a plan. She returned the pages to the envelope, careful to place them behind the tapes, as she had found them. She replaced the envelope in the drawer, closed it without making a sound, and made tracks for the hall.

She opened the door cautiously and looked from right to left before she stepped out. The housekeeping cart was still in the same place it had been when she entered Jim's room. *How long was I in there?* she wondered. It couldn't have been more than five minutes. She stripped the gloves from her hands, stuffed them into her pocket and gave the door handle a quick rub with the sleeve of her jacket. She then made for the elevators with all deliberate speed. As the doors closed, she sagged against the back wall of the car with relief. She had done it. Not only that, she had the germ of an idea, which, if she could make it work, would take all the tricks. There was a lot of work she needed to do; it would mean all afternoon in the office, but it would be worth it. *If* she could convince Meredith. *If* she had the case law on her side.

She was so preoccupied when she exited the elevator that she didn't notice, standing right in front of her, Jim Stanley. She pulled up short, and she could only hope that she didn't look as horrified as she felt. "What are you doing here?" he asked, his eyes narrow with suspicion.

Laura's brain, limber from the exercise she had been giving it, quickly suggested a solution. "Looking for you, that's what I'm doing! Where the hell have you been?" She managed to sound genuinely indignant. "I've just been up knocking on your door!"

Jim looked taken aback, but only for a moment. "What were you trying to do? Serve a search warrant on me?" Naturally, he would have spoken to either Candi or Hoyt; either one could have told him about yesterday's failed gambit in Winston-Salem.

"No," she said. "I wanted to talk to you about what's going to happen on Monday."

"Oh," Jim said. "Why didn't you call me?"

"I *tried* to call you, but since I was coming downtown to the office anyway, I decided to stop in at the hotel."

"Well, you've got me now. Tell you what, I'll buy you lunch and you can bend my ear as long as you want to."

Laura considered declining, but she realized it would seem suspicious to be so eager to see him one minute, and to refuse his invitation the next. And so she ended up having lunch with the man whose room she had just burgled, unable to erase from her mind what she had seen, hoping that she wouldn't say or do anything to betray herself. She was painfully conscious of the gloves in her pocket; her hand went to them continually to ensure they wouldn't protrude and give her away. She gulped down a salad and left as quickly as she could, leaving Jim to wonder, no doubt, what had made her so nervous.

CHAPTER 32

On Monday morning, Meredith Gaffney arrived in her office promptly at seven A.M., but Laura had been there for two hours already. She had arranged a group of papers on the boss's desk, knowing that they would surprise, possibly even shock, Meredith. Then she retreated to her cubicle to read the paper and await Meredith's summons.

Meredith came to the door of the cubicle in person, wearing a puzzled expression and carrying the stack of papers. "Laura? What *is* all this?"

Laura grinned. "It's a new tack," she replied.

"That much I can see. What I want to know is why, and what you're up to."

"Let's go into the conference room and I'll lay it out for you."

"Okay. I brought breakfast, just like I promised. You haven't eaten already, have you?"

"I'm starving," Laura said sincerely.

In the conference room, Laura took the papers from Meredith and put them in front of a place at the table, arranging them in the order she had planned. Meredith unloaded scones and coffee from a bag, handed a cup to Laura, and took the seat Laura indicated. Laura took the chair on the opposite side of the table and pulled copies of everything from her briefcase. "Okay, what do you want to know?" she asked Meredith, a smile pulling at the corner of her mouth.

"Start from the beginning. What is this—a motion to dismiss the charges against James Stanley?"

"Yep."

"Why?"

"Because we're going to lose. And if we let the trial get to the jury phase, or if Judge Penfield directs a verdict, jeopardy is invoked and we'll never get another crack at him."

"But I thought we had agreed to ask for a nolle prosequi today. And now you say you want to drop the charges?"

Dropping the murder charge was perhaps the boldest part of Laura's strategy, and the one she anticipated having the most difficulty selling to Meredith. A nol pros would allow them to resume prosecution under the existing indictment, but if the charges were dropped, the indictment was voided. That would mean reindicting James Stanley, and there was always some risk involved in going before the grand jury. Laura explained her thinking to Meredith. "Last week, we thought a nol pros was the best we could do. But now I think we can do a lot better; I think we can get an indictment and a conviction using a new set of facts. Besides, the nol pros isn't a sure thing—at this stage of the trial, Judge Penfield might say no. And then we'd really be in trouble. We'd have to finish out the trial, and I'm afraid that James would be acquitted."

"Understood. But to drop the charges at this stage . . . won't Fannin object?"

"Of course he will. But we have a very good reason: It's because the indictment was invalid—which is absolutely true. There's been an error at the heart of this trial from the get-go. Look at the next document."

Meredith obediently turned over the next page. "It's a grand jury memorandum, calling for a panel to assemble to investigate the murder of Christine Stanley. I assume you're going for a reindictment of James Stanley?"

"Correct. And maybe an indictment of Jim Stanley, too."

"What about his immunity?"

"I'm going to try to void it. I'm going to argue that we would have inevitably discovered his role in the crime without his testimony."

"How would we have done that?"

"We are going to challenge his alibi, for one thing. For another, we are going to have some hitherto undisclosed evidence to deal with."

"I see. And how are we to accomplish this feat?"

"Read on, McDuff."

Meredith pulled out the next document. "A grand jury subpoena for Candi Shane. Who is Candi Shane?"

"Jim's secretary."

"Is that her real name?"

"So she says."

"And why are we subpoenaing her?"

"We believe that she has guilty knowledge of a crime committed by Jim Stanley."

"And what is our basis for this belief?"

"Information from a confidential informant," Laura

said, poker-faced. "And she is Jim's alibi witness for the night of May 8," she added, not wanting to seem too mysterious. The fact that Candi might break Jim's alibi was almost as important as the physical evidence she could testify existed.

Meredith looked closely at Laura. "Gosh, and I thought that the blueberry scone was going to be the big surprise this morning. What's next in this little trick deck of yours?" Meredith turned over the next document. "Another subpoena—a subpoena duces tecum, for Charles Hoyt. Hoyt! Good grief, Laura, isn't he Jim's attorney?"

"He sure is."

Meredith sat back in her chair. "Child, have you never heard of privilege? You can't call Stanley's attorney to appear in front of a grand jury."

"I can if I can show that he has in his possession physical evidence which is *not* privileged. That's why it's a subpoena duces tecum—I just want Hoyt to produce the evidence. I don't care if he testifies or not. A defendant can't confer privilege on evidence simply by putting it in his lawyer's custody; I can subpoena papers and other materials that are evidence of a crime. It doesn't matter if Jim's attorney has them; I don't care if the *Pope* has them. They're *not* privileged, and all the lawyers in the world can't make 'em so."

"I know that—but what evidence do *you* have that Charlie Hoyt has this evidence?"

"I have Candi Shane's testimony."

"Whoa, Nellie. Aren't we going in circles?"

"A little bit. I'll stop playing games with you now, Meredith. This is what I want to do: After we drop the charges against James, I want to go *immediately* to the grand jury. My chief witness is going to be Candi Shane, Jim's secretary."

"She knows about the murder conspiracy?"

"Yes and no. She doesn't have direct knowledge—not that I know of anyway—but she does have knowledge of the *evidence* that the conspiracy exists."

"And what evidence would that be?"

Laura took a deep breath. "I'm not at liberty to say just yet."

"I see. This is the information you got from your 'confidential informant'?"

"It is," Laura said.

Meredith gave Laura a long, searching look, but Laura made sure that her face showed nothing. At length, Meredith turned her attention to the last item in the pile before her. "And what's this? A brief, I see."

"That's right. A brief citing all the case law I could find for voiding attorney-client privilege. Only a couple of cases deal with actual concealment of evidence, but there are quite a few regarding attorneys who have guilty knowledge of a crime. Hoyt will fight back, but I'm ready for him. We've got plenty of law on our side."

Meredith shook her head. "This is a very, very long shot."

"Not as long as it looks, Meredith," Laura demurred. "Think about it: If I can get Candi Shane to tell the grand jury that she knows that Hoyt has certain evidence, I've got my nose under the tent. I think I know how Hoyt's mind works, and I think he's going to be looking for a way out as soon as that subpoena hits his desk, because he *knows* I can break privilege if I get Candi's testimony. It's virtually inevitable. He'll try to have the subpoena quashed, but if I know Hoyt, he'll also open a back-channel negotiation so that he has an avenue for escape. And I think we can negotiate—we can agree not to force him to testify, and we can certainly agree not to charge him as an accessory. We're not interested in putting *him* in jail."

"I see. Let me clarify one thing: You're planning to call Hoyt only *after* Candi Shane testifies, right? Because the subpoena refers to the evidence you believe Hoyt has, but only Candi Shane can attest that he does indeed have it. And you can't call Hoyt unless you have probable cause to believe that he has material evidence. Right?"

"Right. We don't issue the subpoena for Hoyt until Shane has appeared before the grand jury. That will also preserve the element of surprise to some degree. And you're right—as of now, we have no cause to call Hoyt."

Meredith pushed the papers away from her. "Laura, is there anything else I ought to know?"

"No. This is the strategy I worked out over the weekend. You don't have to do anything with it, but I believe it's our best—our *only*—shot at getting a conviction in Christine Stanley's murder."

"Can you at least give me a hint of what evidence Hoyt may be holding?"

Laura thought for a second. "It may consist of communications between James Stanley and Jim Stanley. It *may* include a note in James Stanley's handwriting."

"I see," Meredith said, eyebrows lifted. She looked at her watch. "You haven't given me a lot of time to make a decision," she grumbled.

"I know. I'm sorry; I worked on it all weekend, and I was in here at five o'clock this morning. I only finished the brief about an hour ago, and I wasn't sure this would work until I had really combed through the case law. I had to make sure that we were standing on solid ground."

Meredith nodded. "Understood. But I don't have time to review the brief now; we're due in court in twenty minutes. And if we really are going to go into that courtroom and drop the charges, I have to let Marshall know. This could be a public relations nightmare, and he wouldn't take kindly to being surprised by it."

"Does that mean you'll do it?"

Meredith paused for a moment, then stood up. "Yes. I'm going to do it. I'll find Marshall right now." She picked up the papers and started to leave the room. "And, Laura—whatever you did, don't ever do it again."

Thirty minutes later, Judge Penfield gaveled the courtroom to order. Meredith immediately rose and requested permission to approach the bench. Laura and Craig Fannin joined her there. Fannin looked puzzled; Laura just hoped that her face didn't betray her anxiety. She held her hands behind her back and twisted them compulsively. "Your Honor," Meredith began, "the State moves at this time to dismiss the charges against Mr. Stanley."

"What!" Fannin ejaculated.

"Quiet, Mr. Fannin. Mrs. Gaffney, would you be so kind as to tell the Court why, at this late hour, you have come to this decision?"

"Yes, Your Honor. We have information that indicates that the original indictment of the defendant was based on errors of fact."

"On perjured testimony, she means, Your Honor," Fannin said, barely bothering to hide his anger.

Judge Penfield looked stern. "Mr. Fannin, I expect no more outbursts from you. You will have a chance to speak when I am satisfied that I understand this matter. Mrs. Gaffney, if I may say so, this move smacks of desperation. I note that when we adjourned last week, Mr. Fannin was on the point of impeaching your key witness."

"Exactly, Your Honor. Our investigation also indicates that the witness, Mr. Jim Stanley, has been . . . less than truthful about his involvement in this matter. That is why we wish to withdraw the charges against the defendant at this time. While we continue to maintain that the defendant was involved—deeply involved—in the murder of his wife, we do not believe that the original indictment was based on the true facts in the case.''

"I see," the judge answered dryly. "I suppose that the Court should be grateful that the error has been discovered now. You seem to be intent on saving the Appeals Court some tedious work.''

"That is not my motive, Your Honor," Meredith said. Laura cringed; it was she who had subjected Meredith to this withering sarcasm. Meredith was taking it like a good soldier, though.

Judge Penfield turned to Fannin. "Now, Mr. Fannin, you may speak. I'd be interested to know what's on your mind.''

"Your Honor, the defense moves that a directed verdict of 'not guilty' be entered. We also wish to continue with our impeachment of the witness. We believe that when Your Honor understands the extent of the perjury committed in this courtroom by Mr. Jim Stanley, you will see that the only possible outcome is a verdict of 'not guilty.' ''

Meredith respectfully rebutted Fannin's argument. "Your Honor, the State disagrees. We will stipulate to the perjury, but not to Mr. Fannin's logic. The fact that Mr. *Jim* Stanley perjured himself does not prove that Mr. *James* Stanley is not guilty of taking some part in the murder of his wife. In fact, Your Honor, we hope to produce evidence very soon that James Stanley *was* in fact the originator of the conspiracy to kill Christine Stanley. Directing a verdict, as Your Honor knows, would invoke jeopardy, and in this case, that would allow a murderer to go free. The State merely wishes an opportunity to correct the underlying error in the original indictment.''

"The State merely wishes a second bite at the apple, Your Honor," Fannin remarked bitterly.

Judge Penfield sighed. "This is a difficult decision, and, I'm afraid, one fraught with peril for the Bench. I am prepared, however, to render a decision. Counsel may return to their chairs."

Laura, Meredith, and Fannin did as instructed and returned to their chairs. Judge Penfield rapped the gavel to quiet the buzz that had broken out during the conference. "There are two motions before the Court at this time, one to direct a verdict of 'not guilty,' and the other to dismiss the charges against the defendant. There are strong arguments to be made for and against both motions. Defense counsel argues that the State has put his client in jeopardy, and that a directed verdict is the only outcome that can be satisfactory in the circumstances. While I see the rationality of his argument, I do not necessarily agree with it in its entirety. The State, on the other hand, wishes to dismiss the charges against the defendant. If I were in the same position, I might do the same—the defense has shown that it can effectively impeach the prosecution's chief witness, which would virtually destroy the State's case. The question is whether the State deserves a chance to rectify what appears to have been an honest error, that of accepting the false testimony of a witness as true. There is no indication that the prosecution suborned the perjury; in fact, the prosecutors seem to have been the chief victims of the false testimony of the witness. Therefore, the State's motion to dismiss the charges of murder and conspiracy against the defendant is granted. Mr. Stanley, you are free to go. Ladies and gentlemen of the jury, the Court thanks you for your service. The Court is adjourned."

There was a moment of stunned silence in the courtroom, which then erupted into clamor. "That should keep the reporters busy," Meredith remarked.

"Are you going to make a statement?" Laura asked.

Meredith nodded. "Marshall doesn't want to be involved unless he has to be."

"I'm going to try to get away then without talking to the press. I'll meet you back at the office."

With Meredith as a sop to the reporters, Laura was able to leave the courtroom unnoticed—or almost unnoticed. As she headed for the stairs, she heard someone calling her name. She turned and saw Lynette Connell hurrying after her. "Wait! I need to talk to you!" she said. Laura stopped and waited for her. "What is happening? Why did you drop the charges?" Lynette asked.

"We couldn't have won. Craig Fannin had us penned up, and he could have gotten a not guilty verdict, either from the judge or from the jury. And I—we—have reason to believe that we've been working under the wrong set of assumptions all along, anyway. Our whole case was predicated on James returning to the house and killing Christine himself."

"And that's not the way it happened?"

"No. It was Jim Stanley who did it—with a lot of help from James."

"So, you're going to charge Jim Stanley?"

"Not exactly. He still has immunity, and it's going to be tough to get around that. But we are going after some additional evidence that will incriminate James. Look, I really have to get back to the office. I'll explain everything later."

"But what am I supposed to say to my father?" Lynette said, beginning to look angry. "I left him back in that courtroom almost in a state of shock. He can't take much more of this yanking around. Neither can I, for that matter.

This thing has been hanging over us for six months, and now you tell me that you're going to drag it out even longer. I don't think any of us can take it anymore. Why couldn't you have figured all this out from the beginning?''

Lynette's anger might have been justified, but Laura, short on sleep and battling anxiety herself, was in no mood to take it lying down. "I'll try to forget you said that," she replied. "But I don't think your father would have liked hearing what Jim's new story was, either. If I hadn't stopped Fannin, he was going to put Jim up there and have him give a new version of the murder conspiracy—one that involved you and Jesse DuPree. I think you'll find this outcome preferable to being accused of your sister's murder in open court."

Lynette looked as if she had been struck. "That's impossible—I have an alibi! And Jesse does, too! No one would believe that I . . . that we . . ."

"Wouldn't they? No one would have ever been able to prove that you did it, but they wouldn't have been able to prove that you *didn't*, either. You would have lived under a cloud of suspicion for the rest of your life."

Lynette shook her head. "That can't be. Jim Stanley can't just get on the stand and say whatever he wants to!"

"Yes, he could, until we stopped him. This is why there are safeguards against taking co-conspirator testimony, Lynette. There are people out there—and Jim is one of them—who would say or do anything to save their own skins. Now, if you'll excuse me, I really do have a lot of work to do. You can tell your father that James has only been reprieved temporarily. Tell him that I'm sorry for the strain, but we're doing the best we can. We've had interference every step of the way, but we're finally close to getting this thing sorted out."

Lynette nodded. "I'll tell him. But please promise to call me and keep me posted."

"I'll try, but this is going to be a hell of a week for me. I do promise, though, you won't read it first in the papers. I'll call as soon as I know anything for sure."

"Thank you," Lynette said, and she turned back toward the courtroom. Laura ran down the steps as quickly as her pumps could carry her. *It's time,* she thought, *to fight the real enemy.*

CHAPTER 33

Once Meredith committed to Laura's plan, the real work began. A great deal had to happen in a very short time. Laura lived in fear that Jim or Hoyt would destroy the tapes and the note, especially once they learned that Candi would be appearing before the grand jury. There could only be two reasons for Candi to appear: as Jim's alibi witness, or as a witness to the existence of incriminating evidence. Laura wanted there to be very little room between cup and lip, so to speak, so she urged Meredith to schedule the grand jury hearing as soon as possible—within the week, if it could be done.

It could be. Getting the grand jury hearing set up was a snap with the district attorney, Marshall Oliver himself, clearing the decks for action. Marshall was taking all the heat, just as Meredith had feared he would, for the abrupt ending of the Stanley trial. If he could have explained the prosecution's new strategy to the reporters, he might have had an easier time of it, but he couldn't reveal the strategy without crushing any chance it had of success. Instead, he had to keep peddling the same story over and over: New facts had come to light during the trial. It would be necessary to examine all the facts and possibly to seek a new indictment. What new facts? When will James Stanley be reindicted? They wanted to know, but they couldn't be told. The sooner the grand jury could return a bill of indictment, the better it would be for the district attorney's office.

"It will all come to a head soon," Laura assured Meredith. "Once we get Candi Shane down here and in front of the jury, I am almost positive that things are going to happen." She kept her fingers crossed when she said it, though.

The grand jury was scheduled to begin hearing evidence in the case on the Thursday following the end of the aborted trial, which gave the prosecution only two full days to subpoena Candi and get her to Atlanta.

"We need to delay serving the subpoena until the last possible moment," Laura told Meredith. They were having a war council over cartons of Chinese food in the office Monday night, with Randy Travers and Carlton Hemingway in attendance. "We don't want Candi turning to Jim or, God forbid, Hoyt for advice. We just need to convince her that there's no harm in coming down here to answer a few questions."

"But we don't want to deny her the right to counsel, do we?" Meredith said.

"Of course not! But I think it would be helpful if someone pointed out to her that she's *not* a suspect. Someone needs to get it through her air head, too, that Charlie Hoyt does not have her best interests at heart."

"And who's going to do that?" Meredith asked.

"I thought," Laura said, sneaking a glance at Carlton, who was abstracting a shrimp from one of the containers, "that Carlton would be the best person to go."

"Me?" he said. "I'm no lawyer."

"That's just the point. She knows me, and I don't think she trusts me. Trying to serve that search warrant on her may have been a mistake, in hindsight. But she's only met you once, that day we were in Jim's office. She'll be more likely to trust you. Besides, a cop is an authority figure. No one respects a lawyer, but you can work miracles with that badge of yours. Not to mention your personal charm."

Carlton objected strenuously, but in the end they agreed that he would go to Winston-Salem on Wednesday morning, with subpoena in hand, to fetch Candi personally. "If she seems reluctant," Laura instructed him, "just remind her what the penalty for contempt of the grand jury is."

"What is the penalty for contempt of the grand jury?" Carlton asked.

"Twenty days," Meredith answered. "She'd also be liable for obstruction charges, which could get her a year. And that's a felony, which carries an onus of its own."

"You wouldn't really lock up that poor kid, would you?" Carlton asked.

Meredith shrugged. "Everyone's equal under the law, lying scumbags and poor kids alike."

"But I think she'll come right along when you lay out the picture for her," Laura added hastily.

"What do I do if she says she wants a lawyer?" Carlton asked, still seeming reluctant to take on the assignment.

"First, point out that Hoyt has a conflict. He can't ethically represent her. She needs someone down here anyway. She's not entitled to a public defender, but there's a legal aid co-op that all the associates from the big firms participate in. I used to be on the board. They can help her. I'll give you their number, but specify that no one who knows me can take the case."

"Okay, but what if she calls Jim?" Randy asked.

"Oh, she *will* call Jim—you can bet on it. He can't talk her out of coming, because once we serve that subpoena, she's got a date with the grand jury, come hell or high water. But he can tell her what to say. Just stick close to her. He'll try to get her to take the Fifth, or some nonsense. But the only way he can stop her from testifying—or going to jail—is to marry her," Laura said with a smile.

"Or kill her," Randy said dryly.

"Don't even joke about that!" Laura exclaimed.

"Why don't we offer her immunity?" Meredith suggested. Laura blanched. *"Limited* immunity," Meredith amended. "I think I've done my last transactional immunity deal for a while. Hook her up with some eager young lawyer, Carlton, and tell him we'll cut a deal for his new client."

"I think that's a good idea. It should convince her even if nothing else does," Laura said. She hadn't dared suggest immunity herself, but she was relieved that Meredith had.

"Okay, then," Randy said, looking at his watch. "Sounds like we're all set. And I hope this is the last trip to North Carolina I'm going to have to explain to the bean-counters."

As Tuesday and Wednesday rolled slowly by, Laura found that she had planned everything so well that she had almost nothing to do—nothing related to the Christine Stanley murder, at least. She dug out some overdue reports and tried to work diligently, but she spent all day Wednesday with one eye on the phone, afraid to go to the restroom in case Carlton should call. Finally, at about one o'clock, her phone rang. "It's me," Carlton said. "I've got her."

"Where are you?"

"I'm in my car, with Candi, outside Stanley's office. I came here first, and waited for him to leave for lunch. She was a little reluctant to come with me." Laura could hear muffled sobbing in the background. "I thought you could talk to her." There was a note of desperation in his voice.

"Give her to me," Laura said. "Candi? This is Laura Chastain. We've met before. Do you remember me?"

"Yes," a tear-soaked voice replied.

"Do you understand the paper Detective Hemingway has given you?"

"I think so," Candi snuffled.

"You don't have a choice in this matter, Candi. You have to come back to Atlanta with Detective Hemingway. We'll pay all your expenses and put you in a nice hotel. But you have to come."

"I want to talk to Jimmy first."

"Nothing Jim says can change the fact that you have to come," Laura replied sternly.

"But he'll call Mr. Hoyt . . ." Candi objected.

"Candi, let me explain something. *You* have been called in front of the grand jury, not Jim. You have a legal problem that is entirely separate from his. Mr. Hoyt cannot ethically help you, because he has to take care of Jim's interests— which are *not* the same as yours. But if you come down here, we'll hook you up with a good Georgia lawyer who won't charge you a dime. He'll only have you and *your* interests to worry about, and he'll give you the best advice in the world. I wouldn't *dream* of questioning you without a lawyer, Candi. How does that sound?"

"Okay, I guess," the little voice conceded.

"Then why don't you and the detective go on to the airport and come down here? We can meet as soon as you get here."

"I have to tell Jimmy . . ."

"Run in and leave a note for him," Laura suggested, anxious to get Candi away from the office before Jim returned. "Now let me speak to the detective again."

"Yes?" Carlton said.

"It's a done deal. Get her out of there quickly. Did you line up a lawyer for her?"

"Yes. Some guy named Michael Barrett. He's agreed to meet us at your office at five."

Laura's conscience was somewhat assuaged by the offer of an impartial attorney. She just hoped that the unknown Michael Barrett wouldn't be an eager-beaver, Atticus-Finch-wannabe type who would give her a lot of trouble. She knew, though, as soon as she saw him, that she could handle him. He was tall and gawky, with Coke-bottle glasses and idealism written all over his face. He was no match for a lawyer trained by Tom Bailey. Laura played gracious hostess for about two minutes, then went into full attack-lawyer mode. She made Candi cry; Barrett held up a little better, but in the end, they agreed that Candi would appear in front of the grand jury the following morning and tell everything she knew about Jim's communications with James Stanley.

Laura had arranged for a typist to stay late and take down Candi's statement, which she delivered haltingly, looking to Laura and Barrett for approval as she spoke.

My name is Candi Shane. I live in Winston-Salem, North Carolina. I work as a secretary at First Statewide Mortgage. My boss is Jim Stanley—James Thomas Stanley. I have worked for Mr. Stanley for about two years. I do all kinds of work for Jim—Mr. Stanley. I type and file and do the bills. I also answer the phone and make his travel reservations and all that. Mr. Stanley has an answering system on the office phone that also works kind of like a tape recorder. I know that he records some calls, because every once in a while he asked me to get new tapes. One day about I guess four or five months ago he asked me to transcribe some conversations he had recorded. I think it was in June. There were about four tapes, all full. It was about twenty pages all typed up. They were all conversations with this one man whose name was also James Stanley, but he called himself James, not Jim. At first, when I was typing, I didn't know what they were talking about. It was all about going to some hotel, and Jim going to Atlanta to do something. It was very confusing. Then Jim started talking about a gun, and they started talking about money. I knew then that they were planning something bad. I knew that some police from Atlanta had come up to Winston-Salem, and this James Stanley lived in Atlanta, so I knew that they had done something in Atlanta. Anyway, I can't remember all the specific details, but it was something like Jim was supposed to go to this hotel and pretend to be James Stanley, but he was really going to Atlanta. James was going to pay him five thousand dollars, so I knew they must be talking about something real bad. I didn't tell anybody, though, because Jim and I . . . we were living together by this time.

Candi was crying again as she reached this stage of her narrative; they had to stop several times to let her recover her composure.

He was getting divorced and he was going to marry me. Jim is a really wonderful person; you just have to know him. I know he had a lot of trouble with money, and his wife never understood him. He said she was obsessed with status, and Jim just isn't that kind of guy. He's real down to earth. Anyway, I typed all these things, but I knew that

Jim never could have killed anybody. I asked him what he wanted me to do with them, and he said to send them to Charlie Hoyt, who is Jim's lawyer. So I did. And I also sent a note that Jim gave me. It didn't have a signature on it, but it was something about a burglar alarm. I sent it all to Mr. Hoyt. Jim told me later, when he had to come to Atlanta to testify in the trial, that James Stanley had killed his wife and that he had tried to get Jim to help him. Jim said that he didn't do anything wrong, but his conscience bothered him so much that he had to turn James in and testify against him. He said that he had sent all that stuff to Mr. Hoyt as a safeguard, like if James Stanley accused him or something. I didn't think the tapes were important, because Jim said he had told the police everything he knew. Jim told me to tell anybody who asked that we had spent the night together on May 8, which we did not because he was still living with his wife then. That's really all I know about it.

When the statement was sworn and signed, Laura could revert to being a well-mannered Southern girl once again. "Thank you, Candi," she said sincerely. "You've been a great help to us. I'm sure you're tired and hungry after all that talking. We've made a reservation for you at a nice hotel near here. There are a lot of nice restaurants, too. Detective Hemingway and I would be happy to take you and Mr. Barrett out to dinner."

Candi's eyes lit up. "They have a Hard Rock down here, don't they?"

Laura's heart sank, and Carlton rolled his eyes. Even Barrett looked appalled. "Of course we do! Atlanta has *everything!* And I'd just love to go to the Hard Rock," she lied. She prayed that the line would be short on this chilly weekday evening. Laura could handle all sorts of challenges, but the thought of being spotted by anyone she knew while standing in line to get into the Hard Rock Cafe made her toes curl. One of Tom Bailey's time-tested maxims, however, was *do whatever it takes,* so they set out for the hotel to check Candi in, and thence to the restaurant.

Maybe it was because victory was in sight, or maybe Laura was just goofy with exhaustion, but she really enjoyed dinner. Candi was a sweet kid, and Michael Barrett was bright and funny when he relaxed. Even Carlton unbent and had a good time, or at least he seemed to. Laura hated to break up the party by reminding Candi that she needed to be at the courthouse at eight the next morning. "I have a couple of witnesses to present ahead of her," Laura assured Barrett, "but it won't take long. She'll be on a plane home by tomorrow afternoon."

By skillfully presenting all of the background testimony through Randy Travers alone, and skipping motive witnesses, Laura was able to keep her promise to let Candi go home Thursday afternoon. In fact, Candi finished testifying before the grand jury requested a lunch break. There was only one hitch: Although she testified to the existence of the tapes, the transcript, and the handwritten note, and to the fact that Hoyt knew about them, Candi adamantly and tearfully insisted that Jim could not have committed the murder. When Laura gently reminded her that he had asked Candi to provide him with an alibi for the night of Christine's murder, Candi broke down and cried. "I . . . I *was* with him! I just said I wasn't because I didn't want his wife to find out that we were in love before he left her. She'll use that against Jim in the divorce." Laura couldn't budge her, and she didn't think it worthwhile to threaten the poor thing with the penalty for perjury. She had what she needed.

After Candi had been packed off to the airport, Laura dropped a dime and set the process-server she had hired in Winston-Salem into action. He was instructed to serve the subpoena duces tecum on Charlie Hoyt at Hoyt's offices if possible. Laura expected a fight, so she notified the grand jury clerk that she would not be able to present her next witness for a few days. Then she settled in to wait for the storm to break.

She didn't have to wait long. At five o'clock, as she was getting ready to go home, Cheryl buzzed through to announce that there was a man in the lobby asking for her. Laura didn't need to ask what his name was.

"Mr. Hoyt!" she said in delighted tones as she approached him, hand outstretched in a welcoming gesture. "You certainly got here quickly!"

Hoyt ignored her greeting. "What kind of a game are you playing, Miss Chastain? I'm going to have you up on charges for harassment."

"I hope not, Mr. Hoyt. Shall we continue our discussion in the conference room?"

Hoyt followed her into the small room, still glowering. He angrily refused Laura's offer of a Coke or a cup of coffee. "I'm not here to socialize with you. What is the meaning of this subpoena?" he asked, producing the paper from his briefcase. "Where did you go to law school, Miss Chastain?"

"University of Virginia."

"Didn't they teach you about privilege there?"

"Of course they did, but they also taught me about obstruction of justice. Mr. Hoyt, I'll cut right to the chase: I have testimony that you are in possession of certain documents given to you by Jim Stanley that are evidence in the murder of Christine Stanley. I want those documents. If you turn them over to me—as you *should* have done months ago—you needn't appear before the grand jury. If you don't, however, I will pursue the maximum civil and criminal penalties against you."

"Never threaten a man who knows your gun is unloaded, Miss Chastain. Jim Stanley has an immunity deal that you cannot circumvent. Any evidence against him is utterly useless to you, and you know it."

"I'm not after Jim—or I should say, I'm not *only* after Jim."

"Regardless, your tactics smack of desperation. I can have this subpoena quashed before noon tomorrow."

"Will you? I don't think so. Here's a brief I've written on the topic of attorney-client privilege in the great State of Georgia. Pay particular attention to the Court's comments in *Johnson* v. *State*. I think you'll find that the situation here is very similar. Defense attorneys cannot extend privilege to evidence that is not inherently privileged. I also draw your attention to *Shelton* v. *State,* which establishes that a lawyer is expected to withdraw if he knows that his client is lying."

Hoyt tossed the brief back across the table at her. "I have no interest in your attempts to impress me, Miss Chastain. Your action is illegitimate at its heart. My communications with Jim Stanley are protected by the highest form of privilege our system recognizes."

"Okay, then, if you insist in going down with the ship, I'll indict *you*," Laura said, "for obstruction of justice, contempt of court, and anything else I can think of. As a matter of fact, I believe that your actions *define* accessory after the fact in the murder of Christine Stanley. You have been shielding a murderer, Mr. Hoyt, and *I will not have it.*" Laura rose from her seat as she spoke and leaned on her hands across the table.

"What's your evidence? The testimony of Stanley's secretary? That's hearsay."

"That's *eyewitness* testimony, Mr. Hoyt. Candi Shane *heard* those tapes, and typed transcripts of them. *And* she's testified that a note in James Stanley's handwriting exists, containing details of the murder plot."

Hoyt snorted. "The tapes and the transcripts of them are inadmissible. Jim Stanley did not have James Stanley's permission to record their conversations. As for any note, Miss Shane doesn't know James Stanley's handwriting. She doesn't know who wrote the note, or why—if such a note even exists."

"She does know who wrote it, and why. And if that note no longer exists, I will see that you serve the maximum sentence for obstruction of justice and tampering with evidence, which is a felony in Georgia even if you North Carolina lawyers don't take it seriously. You can give me the documents I'm seeking, Mr. Hoyt, or I *will* have a search warrant executed on your business premises. I will have the cops go through every phone message, memo, birthday card, and used tissue in your office. Is that what you want?"

"I've quashed one of your search warrants, Miss Chastain, and I believe I have it in me to quash many more. This is all sound and fury and, I might add, a waste of my time. I have already drafted a motion to suppress this ludicrous subpoena, which I will present to the Superior Court first thing in the morning."

"If you want to fight, I'm game," Laura said. "I'll offer you an easy way out one last time: Simply hand over the transcripts, the tapes, and the notes, and you'll be on your way."

"My answer is no, Miss Chastain. I'll see you in the morning." Hoyt rose, nodded curtly at her, and left.

Laura sank back into her chair, heart pounding and mouth dry. Charlie Hoyt was a damn fortress of a lawyer.

If she hadn't been so angry about his shenanigans she would have admired his style. She picked up the phone and buzzed Meredith's office. "Boss?" she said. "Hoyt was just here. It's war."

"Better go home and get a good night's rest, then. I'll meet you here at seven."

"Right-o." Laura packed up her things with a familiar sense of exhilaration that she hadn't felt in a long, long time, not since she and Tom were fighting side by side in a courtroom. *Oh, God, I wish he could see me now,* she thought. *I think he'd be proud.*

CHAPTER 34

Laura and Charlie Hoyt met again in Judge Byron Copeland's chambers Friday morning. Meredith declined to attend. "I think you can handle it," she said, and in so doing she gave Laura all the confidence she needed to go against a dozen Hoyts. They observed all the proprieties in the meeting, of course—their sentences were grammatical, their arguments were erudite, and they were scrupulously, if edgily, polite at all times. Below the surface, though, the dynamics of the meeting were similar to a sandbox brawl between two determined four-year-olds.

Judge Copeland was a patient man, and one of few words. He set the ball rolling and then sat back and listened as the two lawyers thrashed it out in front of him. Once the basic facts were on the table, the real arguing began with Laura. "Your Honor, Mr. Hoyt cites privilege with respect to his communications with his client as sufficient reason for quashing this subpoena. I am not challenging that privilege, as my subpoena clearly indicates. I am seeking only documents, tapes, and other evidence of communications between Mr. Hoyt's client and James Stanley. Communications between Mr. Hoyt and his client will remain a closed book.''

"Your Honor," Hoyt rejoined, "it is a shame Miss Chastain forgot to put on her hip waders this morning, because she is surely on a fishing expedition.'' Laura noticed and deplored Hoyt's tendency to get a little folksy when he was in front of a judge. He'd probably sound like Goober Pyle in front of a jury. "My correspondence with my clients— all my correspondence—is privileged. This subpoena is a poorly disguised attempt to probe for evidence in an area clearly off-limits to the prosecution. In fact, she has only her own wishful thinking as a basis for asserting that this so-called 'evidence' exists.''

"That's right," Laura said sarcastically. "I have no basis for this subpoena at all, except for a *sworn statement* from his client's secretary, Your Honor. She *saw* the documents referred to in the subpoena. She testified that it was she who sent them to Mr. Hoyt, in fact.''

"Miss Shane acted merely as a conduit for communication between my client and me. It's like subpoenaing the postman to get access to a letter he delivered, Your Honor.''

"It is nothing like that. Miss Shane didn't just lick a stamp—she typed transcripts of conversation between his client and a suspect in the murder of Christine Stanley, conversations that contained details of a murder plot. Mr. Hoyt is blatantly disregarding the rules.''

"Miss Chastain raises an interesting point, Your Honor: part of the evidence she seeks consists of transcripts of telephone conversations that my client made without the consent of James Stanley, the other party. I can't think of any circumstances under which those tapes, or transcripts of them, would be admissible."

"That may be, Your Honor, but the transcripts are not the only evidence we are seeking," Laura countered. "There is also a note in the handwriting of our chief suspect, James Stanley, which contains incriminating details of the murder plot. That *is* admissible, and it can't be privileged, because it's not a communication between Mr. Hoyt and his client."

"*All* communications between me and my client are privileged," Hoyt maintained.

"If he mailed you the murder weapon, would you argue *that* was privileged?" Laura asked in frustration.

"Certainly not," Hoyt said. "I would readily turn over any actual evidence of a crime, if I possessed any. I can assure the Court that I do not."

"Is there a note, Mr. Hoyt?" Judge Copeland asked wearily.

"There is a scrap of paper which I wouldn't call a note. I have no idea who wrote it," Hoyt said smugly.

"Candi Shane knows who wrote it—she can identify it," Laura argued. "I'm not relying on Mr. Hoyt's expertise as a handwriting analyst. I'd be happy to have the note examined by forensic experts."

"Candi Shane's testimony is irrelevant, Your Honor, and it should be stricken from the record."

"Are you so moving, Mr. Hoyt?" the judge asked.

"I am, Your Honor."

"On what basis?"

"That which I stated earlier—that Miss Shane merely prepared communications from my client to me. Her presence in the chain of custody cannot be used to break privilege."

"Your Honor, that is outrageous. His client was indiscreet

enough to rely on his secretary to keep silent about a crime. By no stretch of the imagination is her knowledge covered by attorney-client privilege, and the last time I looked there was no secretary-client privilege. She was fair game, Your Honor."

"Perhaps if Miss Shane had been allowed to seek legal counsel, Miss Chastain would not be in a position to make that argument to you, Your Honor," Hoyt said.

"Miss Shane was given access to counsel, and it was on his advice that she made her statement."

"Legal counsel handpicked by the prosecution, Your Honor," Hoyt interjected.

"Your Honor, I had nothing to do with the selection of counsel, beyond referring Miss Shane to a legal aid co-operative."

"A co-operative on whose board Miss Chastain serves."

"Your Honor, I resent Mr. Hoyt's implication. I resigned from that board when I accepted a job with the district attorney's office because it was a conflict. I have had nothing to do with the organization for nearly a year!"

At this point Judge Copeland had heard enough. He rapped his knuckles on his desk. "Enough! This isn't the *Jerry Springer Show*. I have briefs from both of you, and I think I've heard enough of your oral arguments. I'll take some time to review the briefs, and I'll render my decision later today. Please be back in my chambers at four o'clock."

"Thank you, Your Honor," both lawyers said in chorus as the tension in the room dissipated. They left the room together. In the hall, Hoyt looked frowningly at his watch. It was only eleven o'clock, and somehow he would have to fill the next five hours with activity away from his office. Laura felt in the mood to make a gracious, sportsmanlike gesture. "Can I buy you lunch, Mr. Hoyt?" she asked.

He looked surprised, as she expected he would. "No,"

he replied abruptly. "I have phone calls to make." His tone implied that lunch was a frivolous distraction for those weak enough to get hungry in the middle of a workday.

"Suit yourself," Laura said. She was growing accustomed to Hoyt's machinelike composure. He wasn't really rude; he was just . . . not quite human. He gave Laura a curt nod and turned away from her. "Mr. Hoyt!" Laura called after him. It never occurred to her to call him Charlie. He turned and looked at her suspiciously, possibly afraid that she was going to suggest some other foolish waste of time, like a cup of coffee. "Where are you staying? If the judge reaches his decision early, I'll need to get in touch with you."

"Oh," he said, relieved. "I'm at the Hyatt at Peachtree Center."

"Thank you," Laura said, and this time she managed to turn away first. *What an odd man,* she reflected as she reached the street outside the courthouse. She had noticed that he didn't wear a wedding ring. *He's the type they always say is "married to the law." Well, at least the law can't divorce him and take half his property.*

Laura sought Meredith as soon as she reached the office, and gave her a blow-by-blow description of the meeting in chambers. "No decision yet," she concluded, "but I feel pretty good about it. Hoyt was really stretching, and he's not on his home turf this time."

"Keep me posted," Meredith said. She looked at her watch. "I'm hungry. Do you have plans for lunch?"

"I was just going to run downstairs and get a sandwich. I didn't want to be away from my desk if Judge Copeland's clerk calls."

"Forward your calls to your cell phone, and let's go eat."

It was one of the last really nice fall days, with just a

hint of winter in the air, so they decided to take their sandwiches outside for what might be the last time for months. They were just finishing when Laura's phone rang. It was Randy Travers. "Bad news, kid," he said. "Candi Shane is dead."

Laura reeled. "How? When . . . ? Oh, my God," she said, picturing a plane crash, a car accident.

"It looks like murder," Randy said.

"Oh, no," Laura moaned.

"What is it?" Meredith asked. Laura told her hastily, not wanting to miss anything Randy was saying, and yet not wanting to hear it, either.

"She was battered and strangled," he was saying. "Strangulation was probably the cause of death. I got a call from Lieutenant Barber up there in Winston-Salem. A neighbor found her dead this morning. It must have happened late last night—the neighbors on both sides heard people arguing around eleven, a man and a woman. They said it sounded like he was thumping on her pretty good, but of course no one thought to call the police. Anyway, the girl who lives two apartments down noticed that Candi's door was open this morning as she passed. She checked it out, and found her. She's the one who reported it."

"Where is Jim?" Laura asked.

"Gone. They put out an APB on him right away, and they found his car in the parking lot at the Raleigh-Durham airport. They're trying to figure out if he really got on a plane or if he just ditched the car to throw them off."

"What do you think?"

"I think he probably took a flight, probably to someplace with connections to Miami, or Texas, even California. There aren't a whole lot of flights out of Raleigh to check, but if he went to Atlanta or some other big hub, it could take a while to trace him. That's assuming he's traveling under his own name, of course. If he's not, it will take even longer, and in all likelihood he'll slip through."

"He couldn't have faked an ID that quickly, could he?"

"He could at least have gotten a fake driver's license, if he knew the right people. Remember, he's done some jail time, so he knows a bit about the seamy side of town. They're checking his bank accounts to see if he withdrew a large sum of money. He could hide his tracks for a while, maybe long enough to get out of the country, if he's smart enough."

"He's smart enough," Laura said grimly. "But why kill Candi? He had to know he'd be the only suspect!"

"He wasn't divorced yet. Otherwise, I think he would have done just what you said—married her to keep her from testifying. As it was, this must have seemed like his only option."

Laura remembered with some pain the joke she had made just a few nights earlier. She hadn't been serious, and neither had Randy when he suggested that Jim could kill Candi. Neither of them thought that he was capable of *that*. Laura had never intended to put Candi in harm's way; if she thought for one minute that she had been, she would have taken precautions—kept her in Atlanta, sent her anywhere but back to Winston-Salem, back to Jim. But Laura was foolish to have forgotten Jim's history of violence—his abuse of his wife, and especially his cold-blooded willingness to kill Christine Stanley for a few thousand dollars. That made him by definition a psychopath— remorseless, without a conscience. She should have known, she should have known.

Meredith was asking questions, and Randy said he needed to go, so Laura hung up and told Meredith as best she could what had happened. "It was Jim. I have no doubt about that. He's fled, and there's a national alert for him, but Randy thinks he may already have made it out of the country."

"It's not your fault, Laura," Meredith said, anticipating her assistant's reaction to the news.

"I should have kept her down here," Laura said. "It would have been so easy to do!"

"And Jim would have found her and killed her down here."

"She didn't want to testify against him," Laura said.

"She had to. And it was she who should have been more careful," Meredith added remorselessly. "For God's sake, Laura, we're talking about a girl who typed up transcripts of a murder plot and never breathed a word about it to anyone. She could have quit her job—a person with a normal sense of conscience and duty would have gone to the police. She should have realized long before it came to this that Jim was trouble for her. But she let him move in with her, knowing what she did! You can't take responsibility for people who take foolish risks."

Laura nodded. On the surface, she could appreciate what Meredith was saying. But Meredith didn't have a mental picture, as Laura did, of a happy Candi running amok with her credit card in the Hard Rock Cafe boutique.

CHAPTER 35

I should call Hoyt, Laura thought. She was still numb with shock, but she knew that Hoyt ought to be told. She didn't feel any sense of triumph or vindication at the prospect of proving to Hoyt once and for all that he had a violent and conscienceless criminal for a client. Instead, Laura felt a little sorry for Hoyt. Even an aggressive defense attorney likes to keep the respect of the community, and there was little chance that Hoyt would escape public censure when all the facts were known.

He was staying at the Hyatt; she found a phone book and looked up the number. She asked for his room, but there was no answer. "Would you care to leave a message?" the operator asked. "Yes," Laura said. Then she thought better of it. This was not the kind of message that could be left on voice mail. "No, thank you," she said, and she hung up.

Maybe he had gone out for lunch after all. If so, he

would probably be in or near the hotel. Laura knew that, with Candi on her mind, there was little chance of her doing any substantial work, so she made a quick and possibly illogical decision. *I'll go to the hotel and look for him. He should hear this in person.* She tidied her desk, packed her briefcase, and headed for Meredith's office. "I'm going to find Charlie Hoyt before time for our meeting with the judge," she announced. "I think he should be in full possession of the facts before he goes into the meeting."

"Do what you think is best," Meredith said. "Just keep me informed."

"I will. But I probably won't be back in today." She grabbed her coat and left the building.

Peachtree Center lay just to the north of the heart of downtown Atlanta, a cluster of dull-beige office towers spiked with hulking hotels. Laura didn't like the Hyatt, one of those atrium hotels that tried to create an "experience" indoors with no reference to the city outside it. And it had a ghastly blue glass dome on the roof that contained a revolving restaurant. Laura had never voluntarily set foot in the place. She *did* like the Peachtree Center MARTA station, however. It was an engineering marvel, a manmade cave blasted out of the deep gray granite that was the bedrock on which Georgia lay, more wildly beautiful than any station that the Paris Métro had to offer. The temptation of walking through its mountain-king vastness convinced Laura to leave her car downtown and take the train. Fifteen minutes later, after ascending to the street on one of the longest escalators in the world, she entered the Hyatt.

Her first step was to find a house phone and call Hoyt's room again. He easily could have returned in the time it had taken her to get there. But she got the same repeated ringing, and the same offer to take a message. She declined once again and set off walking through the echoing lobby with the intention of looking into all the public bars and restaurants in the hotel. There were a variety of choices, so she started with the coffee shop. Hoyt seemed like a coffee-shop guy. She certainly didn't expect to find him in the revolving restaurant, and she didn't think there was much chance that he was seated on a barstool enjoying a midday tipple, either.

He wasn't in the coffee shop, and he wasn't in either of the fancier restaurants the hotel boasted. The bars were virtually deserted, so she quickly eliminated them. She was on the point of returning and trying the phone again when she thought of the gym. Hoyt *might* be the type to take advantage of a day away from the office to sweat off a few calories. It was worth a try anyway. She approached the concierge's desk and started to ask where the gym was located. Then, out of the corner of her eye, she saw a man who resembled Hoyt, far across the huge lobby. He was in his shirtsleeves. Laura was surprised that he would appear in public with his clothes less than perfectly ordered, but there was something in the man's bearing that convinced her it was indeed Hoyt. "Never mind," she started to say to the concierge, when she noticed that there was someone with Hoyt, standing close alongside him—unnaturally close. The two men were crossing the lobby, and as they turned to avoid a huge planter, she caught a glimpse of their faces. She froze in shock for just a split second before turning back to the baffled concierge. "Call 911, *now!* Tell them there's a kidnapping in progress. Then call the Atlanta Police Department and ask for Homicide. Ask for Randy Travers, and tell them it's an emergency. Give him this message: *Jim has Charlie Hoyt.* Got it?"

The concierge nodded and proved that he was good for more than getting tickets to *Miss Saigon.* "Call 911," he repeated. "Kidnapping in progress. Call Atlanta Police Department Homicide and tell Randy Travers that Jim has Charlie Hoyt."

"Great. Now one more thing. See those two men?" She indicated Jim and Hoyt, now approaching an escalator.

He nodded again.

"Where are they heading?" Laura asked.

"That's the escalator that leads down to the parking garage," he said.

"Tell the cops that, too," she said as she hurried away across the lobby.

By the time she reached the head of the escalator, Jim and Hoyt had disappeared. She ran unhesitatingly down the moving stairs. At the bottom she took a moment to look around. Signs pointed to various meeting rooms along a corridor directly in front of her, but another sign pointed to the garage, behind her and to the left. She chose that direction. *He must be trying to take him away,* she thought. But why? She knew only one thing for sure: Charlie was not accompanying Jim willingly. There had been only a brief moment in which she had seen his face, but she could tell, even at a distance, that he was frightened. Hoyt was a hostage. *Dear God, that must be it. He's going to try to get away using Hoyt as a shield.* She reached the glass door that led to the parking deck, and looked through it before she pushed it open. At first she saw no sign of the two men. Then she saw two pairs of legs ascending a ramp on the far side of the garage. She plunged through the door, across the sidewalk, and almost ran into an oncoming car, but she didn't stop.

Laura was following Jim and Hoyt on instinct. There was nothing she could do to overpower Jim, her common sense told her—she had no weapon, and she didn't know if he was armed or not. Still, she didn't want them to get out of sight. She was keeping the two sets of legs in sight from a safe distance as they walked up the ramps of the parking garage. They were walking fast, though, and she was hampered by her skirt, a narrow midcalf thing. Her modestly heeled pumps weren't helping things, either. She couldn't do anything about the skirt, but she slipped off the shoes and left them. She could at least make quieter progress without them.

Up and up they went, in silence. Laura strained to hear Jim or Hoyt's voice, and she strained to hear sirens. She heard nothing. The awful possibility crossed her mind that the concierge had thought she was a nut, and that he had been humoring her. Maybe he hadn't called the police at all. No, no—of course the police were on the way, and Randy would get her message and understand it. But in the meantime, they were running out of garage.

Jim and Hoyt had stopped walking now. They were on the top level of the parking deck. Laura hid herself behind a concrete pillar and cautiously peered around it to see what was happening. They were on the far side of the flat-top deck, in the bright fall sunshine, about five stories from the ground. There was a light breeze blowing. Jim appeared to be talking to Hoyt, but they were too far away from Laura to hear what was being said. He was gesticulating frantically, and every so often he would shove Hoyt, not hard enough to hurt him, but as if he was trying to emphasize a point. Laura still couldn't tell if Jim was armed; his right hand was hidden from her view, and he was keeping it tucked in close to his body. *He could have a gun,* she thought. That would explain why Hoyt had left the hotel with him without any apparent struggle.

They were moving again now; Jim was forcing Hoyt backward to the rail of the deck. Jim turned and Laura saw that he did have a gun, a small, snub-nosed thing.

Suddenly, with Hoyt's back against the deck rail, Jim swung the gun at him. Laura couldn't hear the impact, but Hoyt's head snapped back and his hands flew to his face. He staggered forward blindly, obviously in pain, and Laura's heart leapt with fear for him. *Where are the cops, dammit?*

Jim was pushing Hoyt, who was still bent double, back against the rail. He gestured with the gun, instructing Hoyt to do something. Hoyt slowly raised his head and shook it. Jim cocked back his arm and hit him again, hard, with the pistol. This time, Hoyt fell to the ground.

"Stop! Stop it!" she screamed, unable to bear it any longer. She ran across the concrete deck as Jim spun around and saw her. He pointed the gun at her, and she pulled up about twenty feet from him. "The police have been called, Jim. This will do you no good. Let Charlie go—let him walk to me, and we'll leave you. You'll have a chance to get away."

"Shut up and get over here with him," Jim ordered.

Laura assessed her position. She had no way of knowing if Jim was a good shot, but she didn't care to find out the hard way. There were few cars parked on this level of the deck, but there was one to her right. Would it be worth the risk of making a dash for it?

Yes, she decided. As Jim leveled the gun in her direction, she saw that Hoyt was crawling toward him. If she could distract Jim, and get him a little off balance, Charlie might be able to tackle him. She hoped that Charlie was thinking along the same lines as she took a deep breath and lunged to her right, seeking the shelter of a minivan.

She heard the gun go off and a second later the air was filled with screaming sirens and squealing tires. A patrol car screeched to a halt to Laura's left and two armed cops leapt out. "Get down! Get down!" they shouted to her.

"Help him!" she screamed, frantic with fear for Charlie. She ignored the officer's orders and ran to the front of the van where she could see. Jim had dragged Charlie, whose face was covered with blood, to his feet and was holding the gun to his head. The cops were trying to talk to him, but Jim was screaming incoherently. Hoyt was stoically calm and perfectly still in Jim's grasp, but it was clear that neither of the policemen was going to be able to get off a shot at Jim without hurting Charlie. Then Laura saw the sharpshooters taking their places at the windows of a neighboring building. She prayed that Jim hadn't noticed them; he was screaming and cursing, threatening to kill Hoyt. Laura drew a deep breath.

"Jim!" she shouted.

"Shut up, lady!" one of the cops growled.

"No! Let me talk to him! Jim, you don't have to do this! Let Charlie go. I can make a deal for you—I can get you safe passage out of the country."

"I don't want to listen to you!" Jim screamed. "You bitch! You bitch! Look what you've done to me! Look at what you've done! You stupid bitch, you ruined everything. I should kill *you!*"

"Do it, then," Laura said, stepping into full view of him. "Go ahead and shoot. You won't live long enough to enjoy it. Just let Hoyt go and you can have me."

"Shut up and get behind the goddam car!" the cop ordered.

"No," Laura said. "Let me talk to him. Jim, I can help you. We can work this out." Laura took a cautious step toward Jim, and watched Hoyt. As she moved, Jim relaxed his grip on Charlie. Did he notice? Laura was taking account of Jim's position relative to Charlie; Charlie was bigger than Jim, and Jim's grip on his hostage was awkward.

If Jim allowed a little room to open between them, Hoyt would have sufficient leverage to throw him off-balance again. *Watch me, Charlie,* she said to herself, concentrating as hard as she could. *Watch me and make your move when I do.* She could only pray that he would do it.

She took another step, and as she did, Charlie spun out of Jim's grasp. A shot, then two, then a dozen cracked the air, and then there was silence. Jim lay on the concrete deck, blood seeping into a pool beneath him. Hoyt had staggered back to the rail, where he stood panting, bleeding—but alive. Laura sank to her knees; her legs were suddenly unable to support her weight.

A firm hand pulled her back to her feet, and a familiar voice was saying her name. "That was the stupidest thing I have ever seen anybody do," it said, and the harassed tone was very comforting. "Leave it to two lawyers to do everything completely wrong and still come out smelling like roses."

"Thanks, Randy. I'm glad you appreciated it," she said, smiling weakly at Travers as she slumped against him. "Aren't you glad you're retiring next month?"

There were more sirens, and ambulances were arriving. Laura tugged herself out of Randy's grasp and stumbled toward the ambulance where they were treating Hoyt. "Is he going to be okay?" she said, anxious.

"Yes, ma'am," the burly EMT said.

"Can I see him?"

"Just for a minute, but he can't talk."

Laura climbed into the ambulance. Hoyt was pale; there was blood soaking a bandage on his head. "Charlie?" Laura said. He opened his eyes. "Are you okay?"

He nodded. "Is Stanley dead?"

"Yes, he is. I'm sorry." And she was, sorry for Jim and sorry for Charlie.

Charlie weakly raised his wrist and looked at his watch. "Miss Chastain, I'm afraid I'm going to miss the meeting in Judge Copeland's chambers this afternoon."

"I'm sure he'll understand. I'll call his clerk right away."

"Please tell him that I'm sorry, and ask if he could deliver a ruling without my being present."

"Don't worry about any of that now, Charlie. I'll tell him what happened. He'll delay the ruling."

"I don't think the ruling *should* be delayed. I'd like this matter cleared up."

"Are you saying that you'll release the transcripts and the note?"

"Certainly not. Privilege survives the death of a client, Miss Chastain."

"For crying out loud! I can't believe you're still arguing a motion on behalf of a man who just tried his damnedest to kill you! You are truly a piece of work."

The EMT plucked at Laura's sleeve. "Don't be getting him all riled up, miss."

"Nothing riles this guy," she said, exasperated. "I have to go now, Charlie. I'll let you know what happens with your motion."

"If the ruling goes against me, my secretary has the items you subpoenaed. She'll send them right along," he said, his voice growing weak. "I don't expect that will be necessary, though."

"But I expect it *will* be necessary, Mr. Hoyt. I expect the ruling to go in my favor."

Hoyt tried to lift his head from the stretcher to reply, but the attendant pushed him back down. "Please, miss," he said. "Don't upset him."

Laura stepped down from the back of the ambulance. Randy was waiting there, having listened to her conversation with Hoyt. He shook his head in bemusement. "Lawyers," he said. "If that don't beat all."

Epilogue

Laura plunged the knife into the top of the pumpkin and sawed a circular opening. "You look like you're enjoying that just a little too much," Amos said. They were on the front porch of his house on a warm golden afternoon. Only a week had passed since Jim's attack on Charlie Hoyt, but it seemed like the events of that day belonged to some remote past. All Laura wanted now was to bask in this beautiful day and revert to her childhood, when her biggest challenge had been choosing a Halloween costume.

"I love Halloween," she replied, thrusting her hand inside the pumpkin and fetching forth a handful of goo. "Got something I can put this in? No, not the garbage can—I want to toast the seeds. That's the best part. Now, what kind of face do you want? Scary or goofy?"

"Scary, definitely."

"Coming up. Hand me that marker, will you?" She was

soon intent on drawing a snarling face on the gourd while Amos sat in the porch swing with a beer. "Well?" he said after a few minutes.

"That's a deep subject," she replied, borrowing one of her mother's more annoying ripostes.

"You know what I mean. Or do I have to read about your exploits in the newspaper like the rest of the rabble?"

"What do you want to know? Hand me that little knife, please. We finally got the note that Hoyt was holding for Jim, the one that gave Jim the burglar alarm codes. I can't believe that guy—he lost the motion, his client was dead, but he appealed it anyway. He's lost half the battle, though—the Appeals Court gave us the ruling on the note, and he handed it over. *Now* he's trying to fight the subpoena for the transcripts of the tapes."

"Why?"

"He says they're inadmissible."

"What are you and Meredith doing about it?"

Laura shrugged. "Nothing, really. What Hoyt doesn't know is that the Winston-Salem Police found the original tapes in Candi's apartment. They sent copies to us. Hoyt's right—Jim made the tapes illegally, so they probably are inadmissible, but they're incriminating beyond anything even I had imagined. I mean, I just got a glimpse of the transcripts; I had no idea how detailed the tapes would be."

"Where did you see the transcripts? That's one thing I still don't understand."

"I, umm, had an anonymous source."

"Really? Who could that have been?"

Laura looked at Amos sharply, but his face was a blank. "Just a concerned citizen. Thank God they still exist. The important thing anyway is not *how* we knew about the tapes, but what's on them. God, Amos, I wish you could hear them. No, maybe I don't want you to. They're depraved; there's just no other word for it."

"In what sense?"

"The way they talk about killing Christine is horrible. They're so *casual* about it—like they're planning a fishing trip."

"Whose idea was it to kill her?"

"It's hard to say; the taped conversations began after they first hatched the plan, so it's never explicitly stated. But it's clear that it was James who initially got in touch with Jim, after he learned about his existence from poor old Jesse DuPree. The tapes completely exonerate Jesse, by the way."

"And Lynette?"

"Her, too. It all points to James. We sent copies of the tapes to Craig Fannin. Even though we can't use them, we thought it would be helpful for him to know that his client is a monster."

"What have you heard from him?"

"He's trying to buy time, but I think he's ready to deal. We're prepared to take the death penalty off the table if he opens negotiations. But James is now insisting that he only wanted Jim to help him in a little fancy financial footwork, using the coincidence of their names. He says he was just going to swipe a little money from the trusts, and that it was Jim who came up with the murder plot."

"Could James be telling the truth?"

"Who knows? There are places in the tapes where it *does* seem as if Jim was trying to talk James into the killing. And James probably never would have done it on his own. James actually tried to back out a couple of times, but Jim always revved him up again. I think Jim had waited all his life for a chance to kill another human being. He was a psychopath waiting to happen. The really amazing thing is to hear Jim talking about how he can get an immunity deal and virtually get away with the murder. He really understood the law. I had assumed that Hoyt advised him, but Jim had picked up enough from his own experience to plan out the whole thing. It was brilliant, in a way—especially convincing James that he would have to stand trial. There's no question who the mastermind was. But it doesn't matter, legally—James ultimately went along with the plan, and that makes him just as guilty as Jim."

"What's going to happen next?"

"We'll use the note to get an indictment of James Stanley for murder. That should bring Fannin to the table to negotiate a plea—he won't let it come to trial again, I hope. Lester Connell—Christine's father—has asked us to be as lenient as we can be."

"How lenient is that?"

Laura sighed. "It's hard to say. He *should* get life in prison. There's no way Fannin will let him get the death penalty. The Connells want us to drop down to voluntary manslaughter, which would give the Court some wiggle room in the sentencing—the maximum for manslaughter is twenty years. But I don't know if Marshall can do that politically. We *can* offer to get him committed to a minimum-security facility, though. Mr. Connell owns some property out in Green County, and he wants to take the children there, away from Atlanta. There's a minimum-security facility out there, so we could arrange for James to be near his children, at least."

"It sounds like you feel sorry for James."

"In a way, I do. But it's really old Mr. Connell I feel for. He lost the most."

"What about Lynette?" Amos asked.

"She'll be okay. She's selling her horses and quitting

the show circuit to take care of Christine's children. She'll move wherever her father wants."

"I'm glad it all turned out right, Laura, but you never should have followed Jim and Hoyt like you did."

"What was I supposed to do? Let him kill someone else? I already had Candi on my conscience. Anyway, I was the one who messed everything up. It was up to me to fix it."

Amos shook his head. "You were very, very lucky. If things had gone the other way, you might not be so cocky. You might not even *be* here."

"But I am here, so you don't have to lecture me. I promise I'll never, never face an armed gunman again, okay? There," she said, surveying the pumpkin, satisfied with her work. "He's terrifying." She turned him around so that Amos could see. "What do you think?"

"I think you and your pumpkin are both masterpieces."

BOOK YOUR PLACE ON OUR WEBSITE AND MAKE THE READING CONNECTION!

We've created a customized website just for our very special readers, where you can get the inside scoop on everything that's going on with Zebra, Pinnacle and Kensington books.

When you come online, you'll have the exciting opportunity to:

- View covers of upcoming books
- Read sample chapters
- Learn about our future publishing schedule (listed by publication month *and author*)
- Find out when your favorite authors will be visiting a city near you
- Search for and order backlist books from our online catalog
- Check out author bios and background information
- Send e-mail to your favorite authors
- Meet the Kensington staff online
- Join us in weekly chats with authors, readers and other guests
- Get writing guidelines
- AND MUCH MORE!

**Visit our website at
http://www.pinnaclebooks.com**

"Book 'em!"
Legal Thrillers from Kensington